THE THIRD BOOK ABOUT ACHIM

UWE JOHNSON

THE THIRD BOOK
ABOUT ACHIM

A HELEN AND KURT WOLFF BOOK

HARCOURT, BRACE & WORLD, INC.

New York

THE THIRD BOOK ABOUT ACHIM

so I thought I'd start out simply, soberly, something like: she telephoned him, period, then I'd add: across the border, casually, as though it were the most natural thing in the world, to catch you off guard, to make you think you understand. It discourages me (not that I like to appear tentative at this early stage) to have to add that in the Germany of the fifties there existed a territorial frontier; you see how awkward the second sentence looks after the first one. Still, I'd be tempted to describe that border as long and beginning three miles off the coast with leaping patrol boats, young men keep it in the focus of their field glasses, loaded guns can reach all the way to the barbed-wire fence that runs down to the pleasant beach of the Baltic Sea, from some of the isolated villages on one side you can see the church towers of Lübeck on the other, a ten-yard-wide plowed control strip pushes into the forest that has been cleared for just that purpose, sunken overgrown wagon trails and footpaths, perhaps I should festoon them with a few flowering bramble vines to give you the idea. Then I would have described for you the border crossings—on the street on the rails in the air:

what to say at the control points (and what they say to you) first on one and then on the other side, how different the barracks look, how differently the guards salute, and the startling sensation of being in a foreign State that befell Karsch as he drove across the strip of no man's land, and Karsch was used to traveling in foreign countries and not knowing their languages besides. But Karsch, the way he looks, the reason for his trip, are far less important at this point than the absolutely natural suddenness with which streets break off in front of earthworks or in ditches or before walls; I admit: I'm at a loss for precision. I don't mean the width of eleven yards, perhaps it was only eight, under the last snow or in the first rays of sunshine that is drawing a green down of useless sprouts from the plowed-up earth, I mean: the earth has to be loose over a stretch wide enough for footprints to show and be tracked and stopped in time. Now don't expect me to tell you the name and vital statistics of a breathless scampering silhouette in the cold morning fog with small wet lumps of earth flying at each step, the quiet edge of the forest once more ripped open by leaping figures, eager stupid barking of dogs, official commands, panting, a shot, someone suddenly falls, I wanted that no more than the man who fired the shot will want to answer for it on his deathbed; all I had in mind was a telephone call that was not to end with the voice of the West German long-distance operator, a girl's, asking the caller to hang up and wait while she calls Central and says: Hamburg. Give me Hamburg . . . and after some time she is able to plug in one of the lines, I've watched myself how it's done, they also show it in the movies, somewhere, at some point, the wires are connected between East Germany and West Germany, that's where they cross the border; not really surprising. But I'm reluctant to add that there are disproportionately few lines, consequently it would not be hard to listen in: somebody might get the idea of wire tapping and think I'm spiteful; I merely wanted to mention it and give a hint that one has to be prepared for a long wait on any evening of the week and even late at night if one insists on such a call, and that she couldn't be sure the long-distance operator would say: yes certainly or: you can't be serious. Incredible then after the wait the voice saying: Hamburg on the line. Go ahead. And that's not all. Fortunately Karsch was still awake, he had been drinking, he recognized her voice immediately and said yes without asking why. Yes: he said and hung up, after this actually inconceivable impossible telephone conversation, since he was on the other side of the line of demarcation: after our misunderstanding with the fleeing figure and the shots at dawn you'll see what I mean by precision: I mean the border: the distance: the difference.

Karsch lived in the outskirts of Hamburg; however, he could be reached in town at regular hours between the post office, dinner and the café; he left word every time he went on a trip. He is said to have lived with an actress in Berlin, after the war, she was from the East; and when they separated they very likely said to each other: I won't forget you. If anything goes wrong . . . or something to that effect. Because, when she telephoned and asked him to come, he left right away. Without leaving word as to where he was going or when he'd be back, his entry permit did not cover more than two weeks. He was merely out of reach, and the rumor had not yet spread.

He is said to have packed up and disappeared from one moment to the next, even as his friends still confidently reached for their telephones and dialed his number, still as certain at the first ring that Karsch would take his left hand from the keyboard, mechanically reach for the receiver, hold it to his ear, with his eyes on what he had just typed (as they had often seen him do): Hello. Only when their anticipation of this unsurprised and accustomed answering coincided with the second ring and petered out at the third, the recollection of his apartment (where he used to sit at the table, take his hands off the keys, reach unseeingly for the phone) collapsed completely, as though his voice had been forgotten from the beginning. That's what you people said when he had not returned the second week and the unexpected disappointment of your calls was remembered only as the foreknown confirmation of all the warnings you had never been able to give him.

How was it?

The East German border police informed him with trained forbearance that he was to head straight for his destination (I want to see a former girl friend again); without detours and once he got there, he was to restrict himself to a certain area around the city, except for the drive back. They wished him a pleasant trip: he wished them a pleasant day's service. He understood their thin man-to-man smiles. He knew their uniforms only from the movies.

Somewhat morose in the afternoon dust and smell of grass he continued his drive on the East German part of the superhighway
and wondered why she had asked him to come. They had

5

not seen each other for years. She'd send him programs and photos; he never forgot to send her his books. Only lately did she seem to have grown accustomed to his patient readiness, three hundred and seventy miles away, to tell her about his daily life and talk about the friends they had in common from the days of a furnished room in a quiet tree-lined West Berlin street: as though they were living in the same city and used the same words for comparable things. Her invitation had sounded casual, not particularly friendly, without any explanation. He parked in the heavy twilight among unfamiliar cars as though he did this every day, and got out. Spacious sidewalks paved with small cobblestones between rain-dark grooves, high old trees with half-open buds. The weighty smoke-colored stucco of the houses would have looked less dark if he had come earlier. The short clicking of his car door was still familiar, then came the high solid marble stairs with their clean torn runners.

She pushed the window open and watched him get out; his car looked long and elegant from up there, and when he bent down to lock it he seemed to be saying good-by. She was disappointed to see him stop after a step or two with suspicion and tap his pockets for the papers that permitted his presence here. But he did not look around, he walked toward the house with quick, even steps. He stood among the worn-out furniture, and turned around. She decided to move to another room more in keeping with his arrival. Recognition took hold of them as though they had forgotten each other.

Her room was crowded with furniture that had been rented to thirty years of tenants. She had been lying on the bed close to the scratched flat varnish, smoking. The two windows facing the street stood half open. Again he turned. She was leaning against the door frame, pulled the door shut behind her with both hands. He held the outlines of her face against his memory. Not the eyes, but what surrounds them, brows, skin, muscle movement, forms the expression. When she half turned and he saw the nape of her neck with the pins stuck violently impatiently in the harsh black hair, the resemblance seized him. They dissolved their quick spontaneous embrace in the same unchanged breath.

6

—How are you: she said: what would you like to drink.

It happened on the day when it rained very hard around noon. It is true that Karsch had come for the memory of a large dark room in a narrow tree-lined street with chestnut blossoms and summer evenings on a rusty balcony quite some years before; perhaps he also recalled the impossible casual promise to help in an emergency which at the time, in the waiting line at the bus, had been said only to make their good-by less final. Which was not at all the point. She had told Achim about Karsch. Why don't you invite him: said Achim.

At the end of the third week Karsch wrote the friends he had left behind, asking them to look after his apartment and to use it from time to time to keep it from being disconnected: as though he wanted to find telephone gas electricity ready for him and be himself expected; he might have said: that's what I tried to tell you. His tone was relaxed, the signature, there could be no doubt, was Karsch's. But after a while he seemed so incomprehensibly distant, they didn't even feel like speaking of him any more.

Now he was here, could be seen in all public places (in the street at the theater at sports events) between her and Achim, the public grew accustomed to the appearance he gave of belonging and knew him like that. Relaxed, interested, West German he'd walk between them in animated conversation, he had come to visit, wanted to stay a whole week. Let him touch her arm cautiously, happily, welcome her in the morning with a surprised smile, forget they had said good-by. He was not at all the point. Ask me something else.

Who is this Achim?

Since Karsch had never met Achim, she took him to a bicycle meet. She did not want him to park the car in front of the hall but in a side street, but then she walked under the high broad light, unconcerned, straight through clusters of sports fans who had come too late to get in; at one point she reached behind her and pulled Karsch by one arm until he was half sideways next to her. Her eyes warned him to watch out for the turnstiles and made him nod to doormen who touched their caps murmuring Karin's name. He did not see her show tickets to get in. They sat in a box near the finish line. There were two vacant chairs, but the usher immediately roped them off and made a beeline toward anyone who hesitated behind them. The track was empty just then. In the enormous empty space the wide arched rows of seats hung suspended from steel frames which the floodlights fanned out in multiplied shadows across the dappled rising curves of faces and exposed back seats; the lower ranks of spectators sat in full light around the oval loop formed by the banked wooden track and its white barrier which tall black letters covered from top to bottom. Karsch had pushed back his chair as he sat down, but after the dense ball lightning of the photographers crumbled away from the racers' pit and they advanced as distinguishable individuals on the slanting incline toward the finish line, Karin reached once more across his arm with a forward movement of her flat outstretched hand, making him half rise and push his seat up front. At their level, some of the reporters swung their cameras off their shoulders, made them describe a circle, at the apex a flash shot into the box, they hardly stopped, walked on rewinding their lowered cameras. —Hi there, Karin, some of them said. She had turned her face to Karsch. He couldn't hear what she was saying, an incredible noise was coming out of the loudspeakers, he answered the polite (smiling) movements of her face recalling his cautious slow ascent of the unfamiliar empty stairs. Suddenly he could hear her, distinguish her voice from the thudding of brass, she was using her whole mouth for speaking now, he leaned forward, moved his lips; that's how they could be seen later in the papers, from various angles: the actress S. in intimate conversation with a gentleman who was not Achim, surely we'll find out more about it. The band music swelled with repetition. Bicycles were being pushed onto the track from the racers' pit toward the finish line when a young man around thirty in a gray business suit appeared in the umpire's box. The announcer was just calling another race; softly in the background of his highly amplified speech the

8

microphone caught the sound of a high lazy voice as an indistinct murmur. Restlessness arose around the umpire's box, spread to larger and larger groups, until finally the loud-speakers poured the voice of the man in the gray suit as an undertone over the rows. An unimaginable shout went up. From the vaulted ceiling the magnified sum total of all the sounds of surprise and happy release echoed inhuman into the void. The next sound was shared by everybody, in the throat, far back, they formed the first syllable of Achim's name, exhausted from the ascent the second syllable dropped low, the syllables succeeded each other faster and faster, the second heterodyning with the first, the first encased in the second, legs climbed over the tall black letters, arms exploded from the rows of chairs, the echo made the voices sound like a stampede.

The man in the business suit had taken a step forward, he spread both arms, raised them over his head, brought them down decisively before his chest, stood motionless. Silence set in like a pain: the brass music returned, festive and alone, to the loud-speakers, preparing a gentler background for the announcer now welcoming the new arrival in an unsteady high-pitched voice. Doubled-over newspaper photographers climbed the slippery incline. Karsch looked back over one shoulder, breathless talk had begun next to Karin, someone was sitting there huddled over a microphone, long hair falling to the upper rim of elegant sunglasses, the torso quivering in rhythm with the microphone in his hand, the voice grew louder, the free hand pointed toward the hall. Karsch discerned intimacy in the voice. An unprecedented honor, it said, was about to be bestowed upon Achim on his thirtieth birthday; jubilation, it said, would fill the hall, the speaker's sentences broke off, he leaped to his feet, he yelled, Karsch looked away. Now the umpire's box was blocked by black suits, through a gap he saw Achim's chin bent over a groping hand that was fastening something on his lapel, white-bloused children with flowers overtook the black suits, behind mass singing dawned the sound of the brass band. From the shore of the highest level of the pointed track where it makes its sharp turn a word leaped from many throats spontaneously across the rows of seats, somersaulted, multiplied, broke into thundering rhythms, it can best be described graphically. At this point the man with the microphone sat perched on the armrests between Karsch and Karin, one propped arm pushing the microphone high into the louder regions, meanwhile exchanging brief casual answers with Karin. Achim had climbed over the umpire's table down on the track, a cyclist in a multicolored sweat shirt came running with a bicycle on his shoulder, set it down, put one arm around Achim, laughed, said something. One could not make out what, from the five-yard distance; Achim encircled by the "Go Achim, go, go" of kneeling photographers, the man with the mike bounded out of the box in an incredible leap, the cable trailing wildly behind him, Achim swayed on his bicycle under the onslaught, the reporter threw his arms around Achim, he pushed the microphone up high, he yelled, his voice broke, cameras flashed from below, while the roof floodlights slowly shifted large circles of light in and out of each other over the groups. Achim said a few grave composed words into the raised hand, looked the sunglasses in the eye, pensively lowered his head, the circle around him vibrated like the tiny tinkle of broken china under the huge dome of noise. Reluctantly they released him. Achim turned sideways to the boxes, spotted Karin, smiled. (It seemed a friendly interruption in his bony face.) He lifted his shoulders, lowered them, pushed his lips out, looked disconcerted, turned away. With such gaiety he took hold of the grips, slipped his feet into the stirrups, let himself be pushed off, and began riding the gigantic track in his gray suit and tie, with light brown walking shoes. Again and again he held up the flowers in his right hand in answer to the happy shouts that rode along with him around the oval, he laughed, showed the teeth in the face of the famous bicycle champion that he was. At Karin's level he tossed the flowers into the box almost without looking, glanced in passing at Karsch, lifted his hand slightly, nodded. Karsch nodded. Then he rode on. They left very fast. The applause grew loud once more when Karin had caught the carnations.

How come?

Karin was quite well known. People saw her in the street, because they had seen her on stage; she was visibly active at so many official events that she could be considered part of the city, and people would mention her name when they compared the landmarks of their city with those of others. But mainly she was a remembered image from her films, almost an example of how a girl might be, stubborn and awkwardly endearing, in wide skirts, not understanding what went on in the world, refusing to have it explained to her, and yet suddenly, inadvertently, trapped by a single gesture of kindness, because everything was so completely other. A girl who could cry so truthfully, nothing could console her, certainly not individual human beings, only some large-scale festive event in lots of sunshine, because so many people were taking part in it; with her long loose hair, sandals country style and swinging skirts she had a way of making her face break into almost convincing expressions of joy: "boy she really glows," it was something one could dream about; but most of her fan mail dated from after her last film where she had played a lady in tight skirts, lean and mean, the subversive wife of a corruptible scientist, she demonstrating how wicked man can be and how a stubborn upper-class mind closes itself to the patient reasoning of men of good will who know better: however, the screenplay allowed for a four-year-old son with whom she played in motherly fashion sitting in green sunny grass, she could be sophisticated but had to be ready to help, so that at the end— despite so much stubbornness—there would be the surprising yet not unexpected deep glow that made her appear as a woman who knows life for what it is, still young enough to understand you, who will help you, no need to feel ashamed, why don't you write her a letter. (That's what Karsch was told. He never saw these films. She said to him right away: Don't you go. Don't you dare to see that!) People would stop her in the street, ask her to give Achim their greetings, or inquire why the knowing wife ends up by dissuading her husband from leaving the country, does one have to be convinced, after all, and each time, does one really? And Karsch would stand be-

11

side her while she explained to excited girls in a shoeshop how to go about pinning up your hair if you absolutely had to wear it the way she did. Later in a tearoom two old women entangled her in a lengthy conversation as though she were a next-door neighbor: on the subject of butter, about Karin's clear skin, about West Germany and pet dogs small enough to be carried in one's arms; one constantly cut off the other, she would have liked to ask for a small gift of all that money. Karin was popular, "it didn't go to her head, she's a real person," she was quite well known.

But Achim was famous. You couldn't ask him for anything, what was there left that you could approach him for, he had bigger things to do. His life was less in the public eye. Karsch generally heard people say about the training of a bicycle champion: that it never stopped, that it was incomparably hard. So it was incredible that Achim had stayed a full half hour for the bicycle anniversary celebration, he had sacrificed his birthday for it, without any advantage to himself. His fame appeared unselfish since his victories did not belong to him; unimaginable was the effort that had made them possible, "how that guy worked at it over ten years, I could never do that"; his private personality became just as impressive and remote when it stood up to praise the State or returned, victorious, from the foreign West, so that he set the actual example: it was impossible to challenge him.

What was Karsch doing here then?

In the cold midday light Karsch stood somewhat ill-humored at one corner of a wide, empty square, watching the traffic patterns of the main intersection. The colors of the lights did not change automatically but were under the command of a white-capped policeman in a small wooden booth above the sidewalk. Karsch watched him switch for a while with nothing to object to; when the policeman called an old woman who had been trying to cross against the light back over the loud-speaker,

Karsch listened to what he had to say to her from his perch, between switching and looking, he found it sensible, he would have said just that himself, except that he would not have liked being stopped that way. —The young woman in the gray suit! called the policeman. The woman in the gray suit took two startled steps back onto the opposite sidewalk. The policeman smiled amused. Skinny and wide-eyed she crossed the street, walked up to Karsch, shook hands with him, walked on beside him. Suddenly she spun around, looked at Karsch as though she were surprised to see him, hit him forcefully on the back of the neck with the edge of her hand. —I was just tired: she said, and Karsch preferred to discuss the surroundings of this type of square, comparing the disproportionately high office buildings on the one side with the low graceful façade of the art gallery dating from earlier centuries on the other, with trees taller than its roof and delicate burned-out windows, which seemed to frame the empty surface of the square much more securely; he often felt this kind of strangeness during the first few days, he had a hard time fitting himself into the language of the country. She looked up, casually scanned the crumbling blackened façade, and nodded. The farther they walked away diagonally across the weathered asphalt field the more they looked as though they belonged together: he leaping over cracks and holes full of water, she with bowed head and hands behind her back, all the more the farther the noise of the loud-speaker at the traffic light and the heavily thundering streetcars that crossed the square in four directions and the sales cries of flower women and the pedestrians waiting at crossings and stops receded beneath the vast color of the sky.

From the balcony they could see through the still sparse leafless park to the movements of the opposite street and cranes doubled over scaffolding at one end, and outside the park the wide deserted street along a row of flower beds and lawns with the squares of floodlights staring obliquely from the thin shimmer of grass at the slightly curved contiguous front of houses, which were illuminated at night and with their red sandstone gables and obese bay windows sat in the light like a prematurely aged monument. She had taken Karsch up one of the squat stair wells to an apartment with her name on a scrap of paper on the entrance door; she slipped the key into the lock turned her head and saw Karsch grumble, he didn't understand, she didn't feel like explaining everything to him, the morning had tired her. The apartment looked more lived in than the room in which he had first found her. Two large light rooms, furnished almost alike. The apartment belonged to Achim who was, however, at this moment attending a lecture on medicine and sports, after lunch he'd go to training, and every time the phone rang Karin did not move. Karsch leaned against the kitchen door, and watched her cook.

—Do you live here? he asked.

She was walking back and forth between the cupboards with quick steps, knelt before the icebox, turned over the meat in the pan. Walked up to him, asked him to tie her apron strings with her face cool, polite over one shoulder.

—Sometimes: she said.

She did not make him believe that he had been invited to ask her questions. The first couple of days Achim did not come into town, they did not see much of Karsch and seemed content to let him roam by himself and form an opinion about the city as well as about Karin's several apartments, an opinion for which nobody but he himself would have to answer.

*Did Karsch react differently than
on his other trips?*

Karsch took up with this city the same way he had taken up with all the cities of his world that he had visited after the war. At breakfast he sat huddled over a map, retracing the history of this ramified settlement as it appeared from the main streets that once, as causeways, had drawn the villages toward the distinctly structured small nucleus and in a wide lateral sweep either razed the one-story farmhouses or added to their height with magnificent Italian ornaments that already looked outmoded in the period after the last successful German war, decades of chimney soot had coarsened their claim to dignity, the shabby rear buildings looking through bomb breaches punched holes in it. Karsch knew that much. Besides, he took pictures only of what he liked, at random; he did like the two sixteenth-century houses that stood weathered alien alone amidst the desolation to which their neighborhood had been flattened; he also tried to capture the contrast between wooden hot-dog stands in the market square and the town-hall tower set in the center of the wide façade of galleries and arcades, in the golden section of a past age of architecture; accentuated by the listing of Electoral Privileges that encircled the building in authentic antique lettering, a delicate concert of chimes, coarsely amplified, boomed from the tower, as coaxing introduction to the voice that exhorted the visitor not to miss the exhibition of socialist reconstruction: because it concerned him; Karsch did not miss it; comprehended in a glimpse through the heavy window embrasures the high integrated circumference of the market square which the war had knocked out; from the gallery he looked down upon the dense stream of late-day pedestrians and felt sure that comparisons would get him nowhere (since you asked me about the differences): this was a thing in itself and could be understood only on its own terms; which he did not know. Hence he dismissed the idea of turning this trip into a book as he had his other trips. He felt as if on a visit, he thought: not tomorrow but one of these days I'll go back.

Can one give a precise, intelligible description
of the differences between the two Germanys
as he encountered them in the street?

Achim might have asked him the same question when they met outside the theater in the evening to pick up Karin; relaxed and tired he lay with his legs stretched across the back seat and asked Karsch very casually: how he liked it here. Karsch, too, was tired and in this becalmed state of waiting they discussed lazily and in detail the story that Karsch told in lieu of a reply: the first time he had gone to Norway he didn't speak Nor-

wegian; he needed to wash his shirts; and since he saw everywhere, on billboards, on houses, the name of a detergent he
knew from back home, he went into a store and unconcernedly
pronounced the name of the product in a way that he thought
sounded Norwegian and they sold it to him and he didn't
have to drag the saleswoman out in the street with him and
show her the house with the ad on it. Achim laughed softly
to himself, he was sitting quietly puffing air through his nose,
snorting with amusement. They thought they understood each
other. Actually Karsch had meant the likeness of all the cities of
his world, of their exterior aspect: billboards, window displays,
shapes of cars, the behavior of waiters, all these were so similar
that he soon began to disregard these resemblances and to look
for other means of comparison: whereas here, at the corner of
this very street crowded with theatergoers in groups and
couples dispersing toward the streetcar stop and taverns and
the muffled sound of people talking in their open windows in
the narrow side street: apparently here people ate and drank
different things, used different detergents, drove cars of different design and quantity, and only occasionally, said Karsch,
when I come across a little private shop in a suburb with the
window framed in plates of black glass on the side and at the
top, and old-fashioned script in gold dulled by the trickle of
rain . . . Achim thought a moment, asked Karsch in which direction that suburb was. It turned out that Achim knew the
shopwindow. . . . Only occasionally, said Karsch, did he feel
reminded of the past history both Germanys had in common.
Because at first he had judged from the appearance of the
streets and come to the brief, crisp conclusion: it was more
monotonous here, they had laughed at him; since then he had
given up making comparisons and tried to distinguish how
the different economic systems manifested themselves in the
look of the streets: on the one side countless initiatives com-
peting in many colors promising higher quality longer wear
fatter comfort on billboards along the superhighway or else
eagerly concerned salesmen in a well-stocked shop, here on the
other hand one had an impression of over-all planning without
the color of advertised differences, of course I'll have to read
up on that: he said. —And that's how you want to explain why

16

we . . . : asked Karin who had joined them, they sat quietly in the car looking at each other forgetting to drive off. —Is that all you have to worry about? . . . : she said and Karsch thought her violent tone sounded familiar, so he anticipated her abrupt turning to Achim, but Achim calmly said: He has enough to worry about. Karsch saw that she understood. She let herself sink back, said nothing. She couldn't have done that years ago. Karsch gave it another try. This language which he knew, which helped him to make himself understood throughout the day, still gave him frequently the illusion of belonging, again he thought that the two countries were comparable, wanted simply to add them up in his mind, since a forgotten sign over a shop, the language, the familiar aspect of public buildings called to mind its counterpart on either side of the border; but then the resemblances did not merge: the last package of cigarettes still advertised in gold and black had been sold here fifteen years ago, a different law was administered in the public buildings, the wording of this law determined the look of the streets, and not the words of the people who were walking about in them, who were looking down from their windows into the cool quiet evening, propped on pillows, chatting: Karsch did not understand the language of the official newspapers. Achim was quite disconcerted. —Oh: he said disappointed. Then they drove off.

Why are you so vague about that detergent:
who cares about the brand name

you don't, nobody does. With all that indifference it ought to have been specified to add precision and help the imagination. However, the publisher who is supposed to sell this book tells me that the manufacturers of other detergents might consider my mentioning this brand as discrimination or promotion, in a place where neither has a place, from which they are excluded by good taste and tacit understanding. People pay only for the story in which the detergent belongs, or whatever: not for that.

17

Did Karsch feel that he was being watched?

He thought he ought to feel watched. Because when the correct soldiers at the border handed back his pass, after copying it, and informed him just how far he might stray in the increasing light of the season, clear but still chilly, the image of fat crafty men rose before him against whom books films newspapers had warned him at home; so he was often tempted to withhold his trust from the most trustworthy pedestrians beside him merely because they had been walking in the same direction for a noticeable time. And he thought of all the filing cards that might come into being every time a car crossing the border was checked, that might be sent God knows where, handwriting changing to typewriting; besides he had not promised anybody to stay within an area around the city, he had merely been asked to do so, did the officials wish to appear trusting? He playfully elaborated before Karin what the shapes of the filing cabinets in the alien registration bureau might be, he amused himself with the invention of a reading machine part steel part teak sitting irritable and demure on a chair in the cellar of the town hall, trying to memorize his name. Karin turned on him, wild and vehement. —Don't be so conceited! she said: Don't be so jumpy!

How is she?

If Karsch had gone back after the first week he would have told his friends: You know what she's like. He had no answer that would have been short enough, the question reaches into all the conditions and aspects of a person's life: how is she, what makes her tick, does she like it there? Karsch saw her crouch in Achim's kitchen in front of all the open cupboard doors, nodding as if learning something, moving her lips, turning away with a frown to send Karsch out with a long shopping list. (To teach you how the other half lives.) When he returned she had vacuum-cleaned the apartment and sat happily on the clean carpet her legs crossed around the telephone, negligently she put the receiver down, sneaked up on Karsch, ready to bite, her upper lip between her teeth, and pulled bag after bag from his shopping net. —Can you guess who I am? she asked, although Karsch could not possibly guess since she had been the tiger cub that rubs inquisitively against the bars of the city zoo. Shortly after its birth this dangerous kitten had been given Achim's name, countless people had demanded it in letters to the city papers; she sat on her heels trying to paw through imaginary bars, laughing with surprise when the gesture succeeded. She indicated how impatiently the little tiger had sprawled in Achim's arms during the public ceremony, stretching its paws playfully toward Achim's solemn face. —You're not supposed to laugh at me: she said: you're supposed to laugh at him, her hand was still lifted, groping tigerlike for a face, suddenly it froze into a softly rounded paw. She stooped, put the phone back in its place, picked up the groceries and carried them off in her arms. There was disappointment in her voice. He saw her iron Achim's shirts, she sorted his mail, kept the kitchen clean, stood at the windows with her hands on her hips muttering at the rain streaks on the glass, she was twenty-eight and probably a great help to Achim in his life. Karsch knew no more than what he noticed.

How did he get along with Achim?

Achim invited Karsch to watch him at his training and got him a seat on one of the motorcycles that accompanied the eight-man team. For almost an hour the eight men stormed through the dusty scent of a quiet rural highway at the exact speed of nineteen miles an hour preceded by the car of the trainer upon whose hand signal they all went up to twenty-two miles an hour, after ten minutes changed back to nineteen, pushed up to twenty-five. Their sweat blackened the dust in their faces, the tires swished on the polished pavement, a light breeze pushed through the trees. They rode in a formation that slanted off to the left each man behind the other, each using the lee side of the man in front of him, with the leader serving as a wedge for them all. Their direction was south between the wind and the sun, the formation dropping off toward the sun: whoever was leader would signal his neighbor with eyes and nods when his time was up, pull over to the right and drop back until, with a sudden tread of the pedals, he could circumvent the back wheel of the last man, become himself the last on the extreme left. After a while the line of backs began to fidget, two men had to force themselves, but couldn't help falling behind. Achim was riding in third position just then. The rider of Karsch's motorcycle turned his head and pointed to Achim with his chin. Achim had swept to the side in one large leap, slowly pedaling he waited for the two laggards to catch up and immediately drew them along behind him at top speed. Karsch saw the trainer's car stop, with the trainer leaning heavily across the bulk of the rolled-back top, calling something loud, laughing. Achim slowly looked up, his face grave and dirty, he did not laugh, he passed. Soon after the exercise was over. While the bicycles were carried to the truck, Achim came over to Karsch and asked him what he thought of it. Not that he cared what Karsch thought, he merely showed the courtesy everybody praised him for. In this case the courtesy of the host. Karsch asked to have the relay technique explained to him. That pleased Achim a lot.

Did Achim trust such questions?

Karsch was half a head shorter than Achim, that's how they stood side by side. Achim's hard sweaty skin looked thirtyish, his eyes were directed amiably at the ground next to Karsch, they might have separated at that point. Achim raised his arms from the elbows, lifted his flat right hand, thumb up, and said: There's also relay toward the front. His left hand swept forward energetically past the right elbow until it came into position beside the right hand like a second front wheel beside a

20

first rear wheel, described small retreating circles moving outward, to indicate the other riders, his left hand was the last
man who was now pushing forward in a wide sideway sweep,
passed the right hand, crossed over to the right, was at a level
with it (at this point the hands were crossed), the right hand
lying across the left, slowly it moved back, the left one was
leading. —When the wind blows like today: Achim said, he
lowered his hands, looked up, said with a smile: Get it? Karsch
nodded. The dirty hands moving in the braking glove had
clearly become several interdependent relays with the wind
coming from the side, he had understood. He had not wanted
to play up to Achim. Karin later told him that Achim had liked
his question, he was not used to outsiders asking it, Karsch was
an outsider. They sat side by side in the trainer's car on the way
back to the camp. Karsch recalls Achim's high-pitched inflexible
voice during the conversation, slanting sunrays glistening in
the sweaty wrinkles of his forehead and in the blond hair waving above the dust-black face. —Would you care to drive back
into town with me? Karsch asked, anybody would have been
happy to drive Achim, Achim was surprised. —Very nice of
you: he said.

I bet he's conceited

The next morning at breakfast with a view of the park and the
crane Karin asked: if Karsch wouldn't mind taking them all on a
ride. He didn't know whether she was trying to be sarcastic.
She looked sleepy for a long time in the morning, only gradually collected her face, became sure of her gestures; she was sitting across from him, three fingers pressed lightly to her open
lips, her eyes were half closed, her smile off guard. In the morning she did not look like the person she would appear to be
later.
Karsch agreed. Her question surprised him. They made an appointment for a certain evening when a soccer game would at-
tract many cars from all around the city and send them back

onto the superhighway, they met outside the theater, discussed the differences in the street scenes of the two Germanys, drove off. The night was gray and cool. From the bridge entering into the highway they could see an almost infinite chain of red tail-lights in one lane, a huge noise advanced between the dark walls of the surrounding forest, constantly renewing itself. They plunged in. For a while Karsch stayed in the left lane, passing countless noisy vehicles, spraying their backs with his lights, taking their lights along with him through his rear window; the motor noise rushed to meet them, hit sharply at the moment of passing, dropped off abruptly. The days were already so long that the drivers could see each other's faces as long as they were side by side. Achim was in the back seat, bent over, his arms leaning on Karin's seat, his head on her shoulder as though he were asleep. In the mirror Karsch could see his stern gaze hypnotically focused on the thin whirl of dust and light that swept across the light concrete slabs in front of them. At a sign on the road Karsch reduced his speed to the required twenty-five miles an hour. The car shook a little, Karin sighed regretfully. —No: said Achim with conviction, then he added: Good! like a teacher giving a mark. Karsch had not thought of it that way (it wasn't that he trusted the law, rather he wished to obey it out of distrust), a side glance did not reach Achim who was staring straight ahead, nodding every now and then. From then on Karsch pulled back over to the right each time he passed a car and answered Achim's excited: Why? with: bumpy pavement. To show him he pulled over, they were shaken up a little, he pulled back. —Sure, said Achim: tanks. —Now there's a good driver: he'd say from his hard throat when an average type car passed them and at once pulled back over to the right; he particularly seemed to admire the immediate voluntary pulling back over: That one knows exactly how fast he can go, doesn't try for more. Passes, pulls over. He knows he can't lead, consequently: said Achim. Karsch tried to see Karin's face when an outside light flooded their car. She was sitting all to one side, only one shoulder leaning next to Achim's head, looking past Karsch into the blurred darkness above the embankment, illuminated in constant repetition. —How sensible: said Achim highly interested as a car ahead of them blinked a light to announce its intention to turn off, but Karsch—all the way on the left—blinked also, and the car ahead of them dropped back and let them pass; concentrated and like an umpire Achim watched the pursuers, shook his head, nodded his approval. —He's trailing us, he expects us to open a way for him: he said, and about another car that might have accepted the challenge of a race but refrained: What a shame. Karsch seldom drove for the sake of driving, he couldn't understand Achim's eagerness and enthusiasm, until he realized that Achim was completely immersed in the situation of constant riding among others and that he wanted to explain to Karin what was sensible and what was foolish in the way of reacting: that he loved his profession. From that moment on Karsch tried to please Achim with his driving. The fast unhampered return flight in the deserted opposite direction seemed to put Achim in a state of dry violent intoxication, back in the city Karsch held himself closely to the limit of the prohibited speed, was a few seconds faster at the traffic lights than the more relaxed drivers next to them, his decisions at crossings and turns grew faster and faster, incomprehensible for anyone unfamiliar with a car and traffic regulations, in one leap they stopped in front of Achim's house and Achim laughed with delight, shook Karin's shoulder, slapped Karsch on the back, all in rapid movement. —What did I tell you what kind of a driver he is! he cried beside himself. —A decisive driver, that's what he is!

She had asked Karsch for this ride not because she wanted it, because Achim wanted it.

Wasn't all that pretty hard to take for Karsch?

He was six or seven years older than she, the difference had not grown more in his favor in the meantime, he was slower now, he realized all that, she did not let him forget it. They ate breakfast and lunch without Achim; occasionally they'd mention a balcony of years ago in West Berlin, which seemed to amuse her. In the theater cafeteria she'd introduce him as an

23

unsuccessful cellist with a strange-sounding name and add: my uncle, with modestly raised eyes; by evening they had composed a ramified family for themselves and explained the intricacies and inheritance expectations of mythical aunts and great-nieces to Achim. Who looked on, detached but good-humored. He did not ask how they had come to know each other. Karsch did not feel ill at ease between them. They didn't quarrel, consequently he had not been invited to act as umpire (they did not show him that they quarreled). Apparently she had wished to see him again. Sometimes he inclined to believe that. He had certain notions about how she should be handled, he was watching out, Achim's prudence pleased him. Achim wore dark glasses on his walks through the city; if people recognized him anyway and asked for his autograph or his opinion on something or other, he had a decisive almost ruthless way of breaking through the circle that mainly teen-agers would form around him, —friends: he'd say: I've got work to do just like the rest of you; don't make me late. (He was on his way to buy shirts with Karsch.) But with Karin he was friendly and timid like a dog. Whenever possible, Karsch kept in the background, as a result he remembers impressions like this one of the first days: Both of them standing in a turmoil of racers cars policemen loudspeakers spectators behind ropes. Standing side by side, she with a threatening expression, admonishing him sternly, her anger stressed with slit eyes and lips brutally pushed out, her body twisted, shaking bitter fists under his chin; suddenly she smiles, relaxed, convincingly, as though that was what she had been telling him from the beginning. And Achim beside her, with sagging arms and hanging head, not looking at her, listening to her voice, clumsily trying to look guilty, guffawing suddenly, then still again before her sternness, something moving in his throat. He grabs her by the shoulders, pushes her to one side, still not looking at her, walks off. They see him once more later, far away, now Karsch is standing beside her. Achim's smile is so spontaneous among the dense concentration on the start, it slides over onto Karsch's face, becomes almost a nod. Karsch was perfectly satisfied with it all. I have already told you, Karsch was not the point.

24

Was she changed?

She was changeable. She had left Karsch eight years ago, she
was older, she had trained herself and her body. (—I could
look like that, too: Karsch once heard a woman say about her
in the street: if I could dance ten hours a week and didn't have
to carry any loads, swimming, horseback riding, calisthenics,
dieting! And the money! The woman who said this was Karin's
age, pretty Karsch thought, she didn't look as though she went
to work. She noticed Karsch noticing her, turned to her husband and said it would also be too much trouble.—Take a close
look at the skin around her eyes . . .) I would say that her
eyes had grown cooler and no longer betrayed anything, but
that is compared to the past and may not have any significance for you. Her face was still as bony as ever, dark skin
stretching tightly over cheeks and jaw, a deep, sometimes a
steep hollow (her main characteristic for anyone who tried to
remember her face) occasionally it looked hard and dry in the
morning, as did her forehead. If one thought she had been crying, one might also think she was very tired. I think it is useless to describe her face to you, a face is the easiest thing to forget about a person; words compare and are altogether open.
And Achim had a different face in mind. Besides, if one wanted
to judge a person's looks by the pleasantness of the face, hers
was stern: occasionally nondescript. Karsch still recognized
what he had loved about her: that she had control of her face at
all times and knew how to use it for any number of reactions a
human being is capable of, or to be more precise: she loved to
express herself without words. Which is not more precise after
all. She had adopted habits that were unfamiliar to Karsch.
She enjoyed retrieving people out of her past with gestures and
figures of speech, but since she never told him who it was she
was quoting or miming with constant twitching of her lips or
the arching of one eyebrow for astonishment, Karsch finally
thought that she was still (as always) standing away from herself, as it were, watching herself, checking her authenticity.
Since her separation from Karsch, she had apparently tried to
live without any outside help.

And that is why you stayed? Why Karsch stayed?

Not earlier, but after he had been there for ten days, he asked the desk clerk to prepare his bill for the next morning. (He is packing, with her watching, leaning against the wardrobe; he takes his ties out of her hands, never mind I'll do that myself. And here is my good-by present for you, I hope you'll have a pleasant drive back, nice to have seen you again. In that case he could have left sooner.) The pudgy young man, whose round head always lolled self-assertingly above the desk and who'd start to nod from the neck down only in conversations with foreign guests, sat intimately bent over the center spread of a tabloid, he smiled up at Karsch's words as though perplexed. Karsch did not understand his smile. He repeated his request for the bill. The clerk did not get up, with his eyes on Karsch he folded the newspaper and handed it to him. —Did the gentleman wish a newspaper? he said.

—You go on with it: said Karsch.

That evening he was to dine at the station hotel with his hosts, in the new white-painted brightly furnished restaurant, in the cellar, faithful to city tradition, with a narrow slightly spiraling stairway, all the same hung all the way down with posters dealing with domestic politics. He usually ate his dinners here, always within the serving range of the same waiter who bowed with dignity and impressive folds of fat and refrained from familiarity as though vulnerable; bade a low crisp good evening, pushed a small flower vase beside a tower of felt beer coasters, opened the menu, stood with hands behind his back looking into a distance where once, long ago, well-mannered guests in appropriately distinguished clothes may have honored him with their patronage. A pile of newspapers was lying at the narrow end of the table, he carried it away, very erect, hands stretched out before him. A self-righteous nod was his answer to Karsch's request for a newspaper after he ordered. In passing, he pushed all the illustrated weeklies onto the tablecloth, intimating that he had his thoughts, though he did not speak them.

Karsch looked at the center spreads. The second one he opened showed photos of the start of the bicycle racing season. At which he had made Achim's acquaintance. There were pictures of the racers' camp, faces looking up from behind or beside glistening wheel spokes, of the stadium director during his speech, of slanted bodies in steep curves, of Achim waving flowers during the honors lap. The accompanying text praised the development of bicycle riding since the war and commented on the prospects of this year's big race to the neighboring Eastern countries and back for which Achim had been listed. In the margin, framed, was an earlier photo of Achim placed next to an interview. It first discussed the training results. The last and longest question dealt with Achim's birthday, banteringly it seemed. Well, when are you going to get married, Achim? Achim replied: First you've got to find the right girl; there were protests that someone so famous should have this difficulty. Achim explained that each public appearance surrounded him with requests for autographs and opinions and souvenirs. Even if I want to buy a pound of apples, I can hardly move. You can't go looking around that way. Behind the photo in profile the onlooker could guess a frugally furnished room. And all those marriage proposals in Achim's mail? The brief answer: I can't go on that many dates. A bicycle racer doesn't have much free time. Question: Are you perhaps too demanding? And Achim, detached, a trifle fed up: like everybody else. Someday I'll probably find the girl in my life. And you bet, then I'll get married.

A reference to the summer races in bold type face: That is still far away! That was how the editor saw it. Immediately below, without a separating rule, a photo of cheering spectators along the track. The lower edge was the box front, with Karin behind it, engaged in animated conversation with a certain Karsch who is leaning toward her, eagerly talking. She is listening, her mouth already open in reply. The onlooker takes them for a well-adjusted, assertive couple.

Karsch ate alone. Drawn into the affair he understood it less than ever. The same afternoon Karin had been obliged to drive to the country for the shooting of a scene. The hotel sent him a note. She would have liked to see him once more before he left: her message said. She had not known whether he was thinking of leaving.

The next morning Karsch found the pudgy young clerk sleepily hunched behind his desk, his tired head propped between two fists, the night had muffled him. He did not look up at Karsch's good morning, his face swayed helplessly above his register, he had not taken Karsch's departure seriously. Now he understood, was baffled, slowly got up, suddenly he was dashing upstairs thinking he'd better ask. Karsch waited in his car outside the hotel. When he was handed the bill through the car window, he slipped the young man a headache pill together with the money. —Take it with some water: he said.

—I'm sorry: answered the confused clerk, Karsch glanced at what now looked like a very rural face and detected a sudden mirth that made him curious about this country and the way one could live here. He decided to stay. For a while: he thought.

What did he want to ask?

Karsch pulled up outside the agency that rented rooms in private houses. He found one not far from the center of town in the apartment of a post-office employee's widow, her name was Mrs. Liebenreuth, she rented rooms to overnight guests because she wanted to save her government pension for something. She ushered him into her deceased husband's study and after a few days she was proud of a tenant who appreciated a massive desk and spent his whole day assiduously covering it with written-on paper. The intimidated fussy woman grew accustomed to her tenant and began organizing her day according to the hours he was at home, she served his breakfasts in a special white apron that was not worn for any other purpose, she ended their conversations with brief little bows sideways, one shoulder pushed forward. It was not long, a week, before the other tenants began exchanging friendly hellos with Karsch on the stairs.

Karsch maintained his mood of almost amused expectation (the prospect of unexpected disclosures) with which he had entered the reddish sun haze of the empty narrow street the first morning he moved in; for a week he sat, contented, amidst the heavy uncomfortable furniture, the wind blew warmer through the curtains, lifting the noise of playing children and conversations at the vegetable stand up to his window. In the afternoon, the windows from the house across the street reflected sunshine into his long dark room and made it bright. On such an afternoon, Mrs. Liebenreuth knocked softly, hastily at his door, pulled it open with one large step backward, pressed her open palm to her body in an old-fashioned gesture of introduction and announced: A lady. A gentleman. She was flustered. Karin rushed in, pulling Achim after her by the hand, caught herself just in time and bowed to the timidly smiling woman. Karsch looked up as though he had forgotten her existence.

She walked up to him with an abstracted expression, greeted him as always, reminding him, gave him a slanting look from below. Karsch knew that this was to express stubborn contrition, Achim stood beside her, watching. All three met in a smile and the feeling: they had known each other for quite some time.

—What are you doing: she asked. They had cautiously lowered themselves on the artfully embroidered cushions next to the desk. Achim sat stiffly, embarrassed, remote in the other corner of the sofa, studying the magnificent oils of hunting scenes on the walls. Karin had mentioned plans of filming in the snow. She had a suntan, she had improved her skiing. And what was Karsch doing?

He hadn't asked her anything. He gathered up his pages and straightened them by thumping them on the desk. —I'm writing a book about a bicycle racer: he said politely.

How come?

Karsch hadn't even thought of it, when it was suggested to him. One day at lunch in town a gentleman had come to his table and explained that it was possible. He was a lanky bony chap (you know), he bowed angularly and with rapid words and glances at the car outside the window found out that Karsch was Karsch, said that was why he had come, why he had the pleasure of joining him at his table. His pallor seemed absolutely unchangeable. He was wearing medium-strong glasses that made one think of the days when one could not buy any other; Karsch found out later: that this was on purpose, as was Mr. Fleisg's much-worn suit, crude and baggy it stated the same conviction that such things had to wait till later. He had joined the staff of the city newspaper, after college. —Fleisg, he said, but this was not his only reason for approaching Karsch with his request. One immediately forgot how the man looked, he was so determined.
—You've already been here for over a week: he said.
—What are your impressions?
—All I see is what shows in the streets: said Karsch and went on eating. —I don't think one week is enough: he said.
Mr. Fleisg, leaning back, watched him, now he shot forward, twisted nervously, tilted his long nose. —Of course: he agreed. He sounded enthusiastic. —You should be able to lift the façade. The most important things happen behind it.
—Yes: said Karsch: that's just it.
—And even what you see in the streets tells you something, if you think of what it used to be! said Mr. Fleisg.
Karsch agreed. Now as later he had the impression that Mr. Fleisg sanctioned and inspired himself with his own words, he needed no answers, in mute excitement, marking time, his eyes looked inward.
His purpose pulled him back. He breathed as though he were waking up, forced himself against the back of the chair, focused once more on Karsch.
The city and county newspaper whose editorial staff he represented: said Mr. Fleisg: had the interests of the ruling party no less at heart than those of the entire population. At this mo-

ment a guest from the Western brother country was showing his good will by coming to visit. In cordial intimate conversations the common points of the German nation emerge. As their conversation about the street scenes had just proved. Would a mere interview not be miserly under such circumstances? It was no secret whom Karsch had come to visit, and especially after the most recent photo coverage (he placed the illustrated weekly on the table, but did not open it, Karsch looked up with curiosity), Mr. Karsch would surely understand the people's as well as the ruling party's heartfelt interest in Achim. Who was a symbol of the force and potential of the country. While West German journalism had come face to face with this symbol in the person of Mr. Karsch.

—Really: said Achim when Karsch arrived at this point. He was frowning, irritated. But Karin put down her glass, leaned upon her folded arms and rocked with amusement. She pushed back against the cushions, waiting. —What a story: she laughed. It's true. I know the guy. He's exactly like that.

Whether Mr. Fleisg was actually exactly as Karsch described him or whether he was merely the pretext for a good story, a meeting of this kind did allow one to expect—in the editor's opinion—a meaningful piece of writing, he was making brief brusque gestures as he talked, so absorbed by his idea that he rumpled the paper. "My Meeting with Achim" on the Sunday page for art and literature would demonstrate that Achim stood for all of Germany wouldn't it. Again his speech dropped off, into the void so to speak, since Karsch had not uttered a sound. Almost surprised his eyes met Karsch's focused on

—I see: said Achim

him, attentive and alive. Would Mr. Karsch think it over? Karsch said it was certainly worth thinking over. Because several times during his explanations Mr. Fleisg had placed one hand vertically on the tabletop and the other hand in the same position at a right angle, changing angles as he further illustrated his idea, constructing it with his hands, filling it with such tangible reality that one could indeed talk about it. And could Mr. Karsch still be reached at the same hotel? —Yes: said Karsch. He had moved two days before.

31

Why this lie?

Karsch did want to give his meeting with Achim some thought. But he didn't know if he'd get any ideas about it. He had nothing for or against Mr. Fleisg, who did not resemble the devious, sly fat men against whom they had cautioned him at home. I've already told you how the dour, pale, bony face behind the old-fashioned glasses would light up with eagerness when his idea took hold of him, if only one understood him, Karsch had not understood him. The more Karsch forgot the man's radiant trenchancy the more his suggestion seemed possible, two days later Karsch had described how he had met Achim. Virtually the same text that you read in answer to the question "And who is this Achim"; the first paragraph is new, Karin wasn't even mentioned, the birthday described in greater detail. The voluminous tightly corseted manager of the typing agency breathed deeply with surprise as she read the manuscript. —And you wish to have this copied? she inquired: You need a permit. She was leaning against the railing, heavily, sideways, only at the end of her question did she look up and search her client's face for an understanding for which he had no background, he wasn't from here.

—What's more: she said, started a long hesitation, extended the silence with one raised eyebrow, tilted her head. Karsch cleared his throat, not knowing what to say. He merely wanted the thing typed up while he waited. Only once did her eyes look out from under doubting eyebrows when he gave the address of the official city newspaper. Then she sat in her voluminous dignity, with almost motionless arms and short fat fingers she hammered away, handed him the pages to check and conducted herself altogether as though he had admonished her to be reserved. She accompanied him stiffly, formally to the door. She bowed, handle in one hand, recalling Karsch's first impression of kindness. —You can also rent a typewriter from me: she said. —Then you need no permit, nothing.

Karsch gave Mrs. Liebenreuth's address on the envelope. You see. He could not have anticipated that. Hardly ever had he felt so unsure in a foreign country: here he could not fall back on anything from his habitual way of life which was fading, becoming practically useless. He ought to have used it here.

What gave Karsch the idea of writing
a book about Achim?

The almost intimate noise of the crush of a countless mass of men (pressed out of individual faces) around the exit that cut through the rows of seats like a shaft, with bodies boiling crawling over the railings; his title: Cross-country champion. The panting onslaught of young girls shoving their way toward Achim, pressing thighs and breasts and skin against him, his carefully bent head amidst scented arms held high, eyes raised with the glow of adoration; their entranced sighs as they turned away, in possession of the thin sharp line of his capital A, turned back for another comparison with Achim's reliable face that did not show the nervousness of his slow script formation. Achim's celebrated virtues: courtesy, modesty, helpfulness (his eyes almost always cast down). The open twisted mouth: to be seen on a photo of last year's race: for ten years now. Imagine ten years. Anyone who bore his name shared in the glow of precious emotions: his name was pronounced with greater tenderness. In the streetcars in the morning, during trips to the places of Achim's youth, Karsch captured the movement which prepared the newspapers for reading: one practiced twist of the hand would fold the title page with news, exhortation and editorial comment back together with pages three and four, clipped between two fingers at top and bottom, stretch the paper between two thumbs: sports page five. Achim was living a public life, paid for by the State Institute for Physical Culture. The State loved him, he loved the State: he had said so himself. Where would it all end? As though explained by the high black lettering on white ground, shouting bodies jiggled along the edge of the track, as though nourished by the line: SPORT IS A MEANS TO A SOCIALIST EDUCATION. The fibry edge of the newspapers, their stilted language. One should be able to

33

get behind that. The early photo said: first you've got to find the right girl. Achim's disarmed look at Karin's hard hairy neck each time he said good-by. The unfamiliar tone in her voice, expressing something Karsch did not yet understand: you're not supposed to laugh at me, but at him. And where was it all to end? He sat bent diligently over manuals, studying to become a sports instructor, what is the structure of the human spine, radiated happiness after passing an examination. The irritable young cat in the zoo pushed against the bars, tore and devoured fresh bloody meat, pawed the feedbox, trailed the guard with its eyes, yawned distractedly. It would grow large, be respected because of its intelligent brothers that had learned to leap through flaming hoops and to stroke with harmless caressing paws their trainers' courageous heads, the valiant danger of it all attracting spectators; and might as well have been left behind bars; why should a tiger be called Achim? We shall do our best: he replied gravely, with a reliable confident smile, to the interviewer's first question. All this and more gave Karsch the idea you asked about, and gathered importance from the unexpectedly cool look with which Achim studied him.

—About me? said Achim. I have two books already. (He meant: about him, two books that he had made possible.)
—Do you think yours will be better? he said.

How did Karsch try to start out?

The book in which a visitor named Karsch wanted to describe how Achim became famous and how he lived with his fame was to end with Achim's election to his country's parliament: the collaboration of sports and the power group combined in one person; as such, to the visitor, it seems a self-contained story. The beginning would be directed toward this conclusion, fully aware of its goal. He wanted to start in a way you'd all approve of; he didn't know what all of you would approve of, he thought about it a great deal. Where did he start?

34

At first he thought the central railroad station would provide him with the means for a satisfactory exposition; he had in mind a morning in the year Achim was born, there would be a casual group of people whose conversations, destinations, newspapers and clothes would portray the condition of human coexistence at that time, which brought us to where we are now, where Achim's thirty-first year was made possible. The station sat so squatly in the empty square (in whose center a chain of hotels used to welcome the traveler in former days) that it elbowed out its official name, then as now streetcar lines converged from virtually all directions on the Station Square and not on that named for the Republic or for the defeated general who had presided over the German State thirty years ago. Separate lanes on its borders channeled the incoming and outgoing traffic and sluiced it toward all sides. This made the station the natural meeting place for residents of widely separated sections, it became the city's center offering for twenty-four hours meals, or goods, or entertainment. (That is why Karsch wondered whether he would not find more fertile material in a nocturnal setting.) The imposing gray building advanced into the square from East and West with soaring halls and spilled over into the street, before the recessed connecting front cabs and trucks kept coming and going. Outside, the brick façade had been covered with a heroically rugged sand mix (a procedure known as rustication), inside, the high ceilings had classic casemented vaults on sturdy columns that did not show the steel actually supporting the whole structure. Only a small fraction of the useless height was occupied by booths for flowers food tickets souvenirs cigarettes, the tunnel leading to the twin hall was just as diminutive; if one climbed the flat steps to the platforms one could see the wooden ticket booths crouching low in the vastness and the dust on their roofs. Then one stepped out onto the spacious transverse platform with its heavy glass roof on steel arches at the height of the sky, and was faced with the barred entrances of thirty tracks—not to be taken in in one glance. Subdivided into six halls, the smoke-blackened roof arched onto the platform columns; locomotives came to a stop close underneath, blowing their smoke over booths and newspaper stands and baggage

35

elevators, they could be seen from the upper stories of restaurants, stair wells, offices which filled the tall, more gently rusticated façade fronting the hall where the trains arrived and departed. Under these vaults, upstairs, downstairs, crowds of people milled and streamed all day and far into the night, only some of them leaving or arriving or meeting visitors. Until far into the night one could spend one's time here, in restaurants or at the hairdresser's, in the shops, have appointments, stroll about among faces and gestures which constantly changed and merged into other faces and gestures, even the expected turned into surprise, was exciting, symbolized distant places, the night beyond agglomerations of houses, the thundering speed of engines, a face suddenly recognized (a stranger's, a friend's, one's own): all of life's movements condensed and more than met the eye.

Achim was inconceivable outside this city that met here, met itself and the world around it. Why then shouldn't Karsch put six people into the harsh October evening air of years ago under softly hissing lamps, in the way of honking baggage carts, beside clanging beer glasses and let them, amidst all kinds of noises and shouting, also discuss the events of those days that prepared Achim's ascent to one of the highest civic honors: or led toward it: or, at least, preceded it in time? The collapse of the North American economy reached Europe and Germany in short pounding tidal waves that swept many employees out of jobs, metaphorically speaking, sucked the rewards of life up to ever higher crests, washed all confidence in tomorrow out of the sense of existence, spared and lapped politely only about the rusticated walls that housed money in unfair massive quantity, living and growing on the energy of those who, in spite of all, produced the wherewithal of life in daily work shifts of eight hours? Communists and Social Democrats marched through the streets, promising different solutions on pennants and posters, provided that the exploited join forces and put an end to capitalist rule and without delay; while the National Socialist association brawled with them and promised specific tangible improvements and the maintenance of order rather than one great joyous revolution, provided that Jewish capital be transferred into Aryan hands and the people recall their origins and that all the disenchanted join forces, also at once without delay? But capital extended a hand to the latter and did not withdraw it and the deceived bribed government let them go ahead? Mixed with the sports news of the time. Thus condensed, the events of those years were to grow and merge out of the meeting of six or seven travelers on a commuter train and be differentiated by means of the number and quality of their suitcases, their various moods and behavior, from the shouts of newspapermen with their carts, from the relative price of six or seven tickets, the conditions of the tracks and the walls and compartments: from an over-all view of the station, from bits of conversation between strangers. But already at this point Karsch had misgivings.

In the sequel, the events of the intervening years: the government taken over by the association that had rooted for small improvements, economic equality and modest prosperity due to rearmament, annihilation of the enemies within in preparation for annihilation of the enemies without, five years of war, the German State overrun, defeated by the united world, its land and men and cattle divided into the newly born Eastern half of the globe and the Western half, one tightly bound together in dedication to the capitalist system while the other, equally tightly bound, existed on the overthrow of this system, with the borderline running smack through the center of the vestiges of the German Reich, is that how things are, can one describe them that way? Karsch was not particularly happy about the intervening years, he was not sure how to get a grip on them.

Fifteen years after the lost war Achim was celebrated in East Germany for speedy riding on a two-wheel contraption propelled by circular treading movements on pedals which were transmitted to the rear wheel by means of sprockets and chain, at that time he had just been unanimously elected people's representative in his country, with the following obligations: to know the people and not to look down on them, to uphold their rights, to decide on their fate at all times according to their own will and to the best of their advantage. And it happened that this position had been bestowed upon him by the newly founded party for socialism and communism which the vic-

torious Soviet occupation forces were instructing in the demo-
lition of private ownership and in the construction of a new order in which everything was to belong to the people, was to be
managed in the name of the people by a correctly elected government to the sole benefit of the people. Karsch knew that all this
would have to go in first, otherwise only isolated happenings
would stand out for explanation and there could be no spontaneous development of an encompassing view; yet he had his
doubts whether life could be found under the labels usual in
the trade.

But he was still satisfied with the ramified possibilities and the
vastness of the central station. Now trains were (comparatively)
infrequent on the thirty tracks, the country maintained little
communication with the Western areas; also the speed was more
limping than thirty years ago, consequently the arrival of engines coming to a halt brought less pride and power into the
halls. For eight years the halls had lain naked under the skeletal
roof beams, by and by the horizontals had been covered with
wood and the verticals with chicken-wire glass, the rain was no
longer waiting for the trains together with the passengers, but
the hall was darker than before. During the last year of the war
bombs had plowed up the transverse platform as far down as the
basement storage rooms, concrete slabs had been put in even
before the surrender and new floors, but as late as a few months
ago the lamps had still illuminated the dark sky, we'd stand and
talk in the open air with the wind rushing in at the top, the light
coming in directly from the sky would make us think that evening was outside the station, or early afternoon: Karin said; he
got that from her. But now the columns between the lateral and
the transverse hall had also been repaired, alone and uncon-
nected they loomed along one half of the station, while on the
other side, behind screening walls, a giant crane on wide tracks
lowered the prefabricated new roof onto the columns and the
cornice of the façade; several windows still stood empty and
ragged, open against the sky, but across tirelessly shining neon
rods white-smocked masons were crawling on scaffolds rebuild-
ing the façade up to the cornice of the future roof. The crowds
today were if anything denser, because the two lower large halls
were alternately blocked off by ladders and scaffolding from

38

which casements and columns were being scrubbed and repaired; under ladders along winding fences opposing streams of
people rubbed against each other, outside the kiosks the lines
grew more and more crooked with each additional customer,
people squeezed through narrow tunnels and bulged more
amply in the narrow open hall on their way to the platforms.
Baggage carts bypassed the blocked elevators, crossing the over-
crowded pathway step by step as though they were going at the
pace of pedestrians, blue-smocked women with yard-wide
brooms reached for dust and refuse between the legs of indifferent people, announcements roared from the no longer visible
loud-speakers, two drunkards were fighting it out but ten yards
farther on one could only guess that they were the nucleus of a
milling circle, at the platform exits people stood pressed
to arches, craning their necks, in the tiny window shops sales-
women worked three at a time with silent rapid motions, the
restaurants were filled to bursting, thick clusters besieged the
nonstop movie, outside the ticket windows, half of which were
closed, jetties of people and luggage grew incessantly against
the stream of arriving or departing travelers all of whom were
swept past an artificial stone plaque beside the swinging door
informing them that the west hall had been reduced to rubble
one midday in July by American terror bombers and had been
reconstructed with the assistance of the victorious Soviet Union
which, at that period, evidently had not yet been able to build
or purchase sufficient terror bombers for its flights over Germany, in which case the travelers would be reading something
else. That day in July may have been very much like those on
which Karsch walked around the station, looking for the six or
seven random travelers who could exemplify and explain
Achim's present situation.

It is of course awkward to put purely imaginary people in places
where they did not stand and make them say things they would
not say; this was the next obstacle; neither their expressions nor
their destinations would shape into the pattern of the changed
conditions from which an athlete and son of modest parents grew
to be a symbol (as Mr. Fleisg put it) and the representative of
the people before the People's party (a phrase that becomes
blurred the moment it is formed). Just as six or seven travelers

39

of thirty years ago did not unanimously blame the Jews or the capitalists for all that was happening: since death neither in prison nor in war nor under a collapsing house obliged them at that time to arrive at such an unequivocal, almost scientific concept, mind you, so seven people, uninjured, spared, or too young, would not feel like explaining their situation on the crowded platform of the central station with assertions that thirty years ago were already neither expected nor welcomed. Optically striking but of no use was the information to be gleaned from the headlines of the papers they were reading; they might be happy or unhappy for reasons of their own; the most luxurious leather suitcase may merely be a hand-me-down. Moreover, it went against Karsch's grain to dispense insidiously and hiddenly, by dint of hints, imaginary conversations and descriptions of the platform pavement, an opinion about the antecedents of the German differences (especially this particular one) which you'd better form yourself on the basis of what is there, and what is there? and how did it come to be? Which was what he wanted to describe as mentioned earlier, but it did not come to that. And finally this method might not offer the attraction and suspense one may rightfully expect from the life of a German bicycle champion; and besides, the more recent German history would distract from Achim's person to an almost unfair degree, even though it had decided what he would be, before he had his first look at the world. Karsch resigned himself: he would have to distribute such comments throughout the book. He made several new starts, each from a different viewpoint and setting, increasingly disappointed he gave up the idea. But he hated to lose the central station: the bursting whirlpool of Achim's city, with Achim sucked into it as though he were present.

And the four pages for Mr. Fleisg?
Those at the beginning, everybody knows at once

Does it also make you think of the rich old man in the warmth
and quiet of his house that was built for him and him alone, as
a boy he used to sell shoelaces on windy street corners, now he
has made it? Karsch could not escape the comparison each time
he tried it from that angle (because, of course, he tried); and
had Achim really everything a man could wish for? Karsch preferred to piece his earthly belongings together one by one; his
unsuspecting eye of the first evening had not encompassed them
all: because all of Karsch's perfectly well-meant questions again
and again dropped off into the void, found no foothold. It
dawned on him once when he saw Achim alone in his splendid
much-envied apartment, whistling softly, hands on his hips, he
was inspecting his furniture and the large sunny window and
did not go near anything, behaved like a stranger; he was in no
way prepared for what Karsch wanted to see in him. This is just
an approximate impression. But I didn't want to hit you over
the head with the need for this book just by showing you five
thousand shouting people, you don't have to leap over hurdles
and race down the slanting track to lift Achim on your shoulders, four people are already carrying him, four are enough, also,
the track had to be cleared for the next lap. Although it would
have pleased him to see his four pages in the paper, impressions of a visitor. They did not get there.
They didn't please Mr. Fleisg enough for his column, he said,
regretfully, leaning forward, hastily and negligently leafing
through the stapled pages. He had asked Karsch to come into his
other office, a room in the attic of a villa on the western edge of
the city. The flatly arched window overlooked a shadowy tennis
court between gabled roofs and tall bare poplars. The streets
were quiet. For some hundred years the house had belonged to
the family of a doctor who had recently slipped across the border; the State Publishing House for New Writing had taken it
over. Mr. Fleisg was one of their advisers. The clatter of typewriters on the ground floor climbed the wide stairs to the former maid's room, lively banter rose from the foyer. Mr. Fleisg

was listening to his thoughts with a worried look and nodded to himself, then looked up, bare-faced and enthusiastic, began a halting explanation: He had not taken the easy way out. His thoughts kept racing ahead of his words, a laboriously prepared sentence was stopped short by hasty (just sighted) interpolation: could he give it to his friends to read? Karsch indicated agreement. Mr. Fleisg had already discussed it with the foreman of the composing room, a small assembly had formed during the reading, even the apprentices had come up and asked if they might see it too. After an animated debate the foreman had said: that's how a book about Achim should be written! —Hum: said Karsch. Mainly to shorten Mr. Fleisg's listening pause with a contribution of his own. He yawned. Why is he telling me this?

But there are already two books about Achim!

—About the athlete: said Mr. Fleisg raising a hand as a stop signal. A very thin wrist with an excessively heavy watch emerged from the tightly buttoned cuff. Mr. Fleisg wore colored shirts with the collar out. He crooked his fingers as though he were discarding the following: descriptions of every bicycle race since the war and anecdotes from Achim's childhood and training (Sure! he said: those books fulfill their purpose!) did not reveal the whole man. Because the whole man consisted of the arrival of the Soviet army and the building up of a new economy and the new satisfaction in life plus all the cheering fans along the tracks! The foreman's wish then (you'll meet him) was that Achim be described thoroughly from the outside without any preconceived sentiments as in the other books: the book he had in mind was something well rounded, complete.
—Oh: said Karsch. That was the foreman's suggestion.
—You must bear in mind: continued Mr. Fleisg. Karsch cannot think of him except seated; in a big place like the composing room for instance he'd fill too small a space with his vehement gestures, with his intense though not loud voice. Here, under the low ceiling, at the wide table facing the wall, his leaning

42

backward, smiling, leaning forward with outstretched hands seemed to be in proper proportion to a fitting environment.
—That there are: he said, hesitated, searched for the word, was overwhelmed by it: traits: he said, it may look as though? as though the enthusiastic crowds were hysterical, shouldn't the author be more open to . . . ? But it would be better to apply all these minor improvements within a larger framework. Hum.
—Where will you ever find another opportunity like this: asked Mr. Fleisg and his hand dropped languidly, as though this question required no laborious support.
—I'm a journalist: said Karsch.
Would Mr. Fleisg like to go out for a beer? Mr. Fleisg didn't have time for a beer, his table was piled high with folders, Karsch's manuscript was placed in a fresh one on top. He scooped up an armful of books that the house had published and gave them to Karsch, here, you might study these. Karsch threw the lot into the back of his open car and left them there when he got out to have a beer in the rebuilt outskirts of the city. He sat down at a window to see if anybody would steal a book. Karsch certainly would have helped himself. The people who passed didn't.
The next day Karin was back. For a long time Mr. Fleisg was for Karsch nothing but a stranger's conspicuous gesture at a great distance, whose words the wind tears incomprehensibly from the mouth. And they hadn't talked at all about beginnings.

Which was to be different, more original than
the midwife who appears at the door with
a screaming strange-looking bundle of flesh and
names it something, if I see what you mean

It was a problem of differentiation: Karsch looked for the differences, so far he had nothing to make comparisons with. There had been no special need for Achim. His present role did not begin with the midwife, or in the delivery rooms of the city hospital (Achim had been born in this big city in which he con-

43

tinued to grow), he wasn't really expected, the world might possibly have got along without him. Karsch's outline began to wobble, he was happy now just to discover a few details. How did Achim grow up?

Usually he'd telephone Karin at the apartment before the evening performances. She'd have just come back from town with Karsch, she'd be running back and forth dressing, but never far from the telephone, she'd answer at the first ring. She'd sprawl on the carpet in her bathrobe, push tumbling hair out of her face and say: yes, or: no into the receiver, name a day, an hour, reshuffle them slightly according to Achim's inaudible answers, the conversation sounded coded. That was during a training period, when Achim could not come back into the city in the evening, regularity and abstinence guarantee the athlete's success, after the workout he'd rush to the transportation ward (that year the camp was taken care of by armed police), still in his soaking sweat shirt and bespattered he'd sit so close to the telephone operator, it looked as though he were speaking to him, squeezed what he had in mind into a certain clock time and was so in tune with her that she could answer a sudden, extremely colloquial exclamation with an equally colloquial one, grew through long silences to a precisely contoured reality of teasing, remembering, stretching; in the end the onlooker had a better idea of their conversation than the listener to whom it seemed to convey very little. If she'd wink at Karsch, Achim had just asked about him and she'd answer Achim's subsequent question with a pitying almost tender smile that was translated into an affirmative throaty grunt which gave Karsch to understand each time that they were speaking of his work, but he didn't know how. They'd say good-by until tomorrow without to do. Karin stretched her hand toward the phone to break the connection the instant she took the receiver from her ear. This moment was still theirs together, and perhaps the pale wet evening sky below which she'd comb her hair while Achim would walk back to the barrack over the new grass, slow enough now to notice it.

But one day Karsch reached for the phone. Karsch: he said after she was through, and then he asked the question he had prepared during the day: In nineteen-forty . . . you were ten at the time . . .

Not angry, sullen rather, Achim's voice at the other end: Why don't you read my books. They'll tell you more than the truth. Okay: Karsch retorted just as promptly and hung up.

The next minute the phone rang again. Karsch reached for it automatically, although Karin would not have answered this time. Achim's voice sounded worried. —I'm tired: he said: he hadn't meant to be so curt, Karsch said he understood, but Achim thought he had offended him until they saw each other again a week later. (He had been referring to the books about his career. He knew Karsch had read them.)

At the theater Karin got out, but turned again, leaned halfway back into the car and asked: You know don't you that his family lived somewhere else for some time, when he was five to eleven? Karsch knew. She looked into the distance, pondered something, straightened up, slowly stepped onto the sidewalk. They arranged to meet after the performance.

Where was: somewhere else?

A small town at the edge of Thuringia. Karsch had gone to look at it, it was still inside his "limits." It was built around a castle in gray sandstone on the north side of which the business streets of the inner city ran in semicircles toward the wide driveway that petered out into a park at the end of a gentle slope. Narrow streets kept channeling the view diagonally up toward the domineering round tower. The town hall stood away from the streets, singled out by distance rather than height; through many small-paned windows the squat cube-shaped building looked out at old-fashioned patrician houses that huddled and crouched around the empty space under their steep blue slate roofs, with rows of windows running all the way up to the peak. The square was almost always empty, except for a strip of rebuilt driveway in front of the town-hall stairs for the administrative cars. The drivers were standing around outside, leaning against the graceful banisters, coloring the thin sunlight with cigarette smoke. They watched Karsch take photographs in relaxed silence; afterward they called over to him, telling him that it was

45

forbidden. Karsch asked why, he would have liked to talk to them. But the drivers didn't feel like talking. The cobbled paving rolled in slanting waves down to the town hall, the evening light disclosed large live shadows and made it look like the furry back of a sleeping beast. Steep steps led down to the Ratskeller, the thresholds of the houses on the upper side lay considerably below the level of the sidewalk. The whole square was scarcely younger than the squint-eyed round castle whose walls sweated water and saltpeter in wide fibrous streaks. On its south side, the street broke off abruptly at the wall and directed the eye toward the vast plain across a belt of narrow fenced-in vegetable gardens. Farther away groups of trees stood about the small stream that came from the south between flat meadow banks. On the other side of the town, beyond the park lawns, was a factory workers' housing development, put there for the industry which had expanded before the war. A population of forty thousand. Here: in the lower floor of a one-story ribbon building Achim had spent five years of his life, the five years his father had been assigned to war work; from the age of five to eleven. The existing books about Achim's career mentioned average marks and good conduct in school during this period, the distance of the town from air-raid areas, stacks of tires in the vulcanizing plant across the street (on which Achim used to climb: a child at play), once he had climbed too high up into a young tree and come down with the splitting top (a child's pranks), and all in all this period had been: for his family as for all decent people: a tough time.

He might have asked somebody

Achim wanted to keep his father out of this. He didn't know any more than one could read in the books: he said. Karin had known Achim only for two years. Anyway Karsch didn't feel like asking her.

The evening of her return from the snow they had to leave in the middle of Karsch's story. A short cut led from Mrs. Lieben-

46

reuth's house through newly planted trees, construction areas and ruined streets to the streetcar stop. Lightly, caressingly spring rain hit their eyes, thickened the sand underfoot from which puffs of dust had risen around noontime. The night sky pressed down, vast and colorless, on the roofs. Karin walked under Achim's arm; he grasped her not around her shoulders but, strangely, around her long high neck. She was gulping the quick wet air.

—Let go: she said suddenly. Achim let go of her, singly she led the way across the boards along the building fences, Achim was now walking ahead of Karsch. He started each step from the heel, rolling the foot forward over sole and toes, with swinging arms. He was remotely silent as he often was in their company, their earlier acquaintance didn't concern him. His attention seemed completely absorbed by his body: how to advance efficiently without unnecessary effort; he was always in training. Back on the paved street Achim said good-by to Karsch with a slap on the back and turned away. Karin looked on, met Karsch's eye and shook her head in imperceptible negation. He'd better leave it be.

Later she asked more about Mr. Fleisg. Karsch had not seen him again. —Are you staying here just for the fun of it? she said. But she began stealing writing paper for him; what he needed wasn't to be had in the city.

As he waited for her, at the beginning of his visits, he had to think by which dress or color he'd recognize her. But for some time now he began sensing her presence again before he actually saw her, as though she filled an open, only temporarily covered spot in his attention with the long-expected reality of footsteps and echo and long-limbed motion; I mean: he'd recognize her from the way eyes followed her, like a furrow, as she walked from the door to the counter. Karsch had suggested this place because, a couple of days ago, through the door, he had spotted the high stools along the bar which he liked at home, here they were unusual. In the bar area sat the regular customers and people who'd stop by, they'd call out their order to the proprietor, in the back room through the wide open doors one could see dancers under colored paper lanterns, couples and groups with drinks at the tables along the walls, waiters running back and forth. Occasionally joint singing to the orchestra spilled through the door to the front, during the pauses the sound of heavy steps and voices stood out more strongly. It was late and people thinned out, every half hour two policemen in blue uniforms walked in side by side, nodded to the proprietor and went up to the door of the dance hall, just standing there and watching. Together they turned about, tipped their caps to the proprietor who held up a bottle in their direction, they shook their heads, not unamiably, and made their way through the young men who stood talking and smoking about the entrance. Karsch sat in the corner between bar and wide window; the light from the small table lamps, the wind-ridden light from the street lamps and the gray radiance of night merged across his notebook. While he sat waiting for Karin he jotted down what he remembered from his drive to Achim's former town. She climbed onto the stool next to his and aligned her hand with his.

You may assume that he climbed trees in spring: she said, clutching the edge of the bar, settling into position on the spare saddle of the wooden structure: as though she had just stepped out of Achim's childhood. She was thinking of this time of the year after the heavy rains when the air suddenly smells alive. When Achim ran outside it was the thick sweet young grass that would draw him and his playmates into the woods. Where the young leaves would make one feel that everything was growing. At no other time were they so eager to dig hide-outs in the wet black earth or play cops and robbers in the thicket, or gangster and detective (where the best was allowed to win), or climb high up among the fragrant leaves, forgetting themselves for hours in the wild swaying treetops. —And would you want that in a gracefully swaying style: a happy childhood scene! said Karsch irritated: as though they hadn't been sent to the woods to collect medicinal herbs for the greater strength of the German nation: the blossoms of linden and white nettle, milfoil and coltsfoot, and they had to present sufficient receipts to their teachers if they didn't want to be reprimanded or punished! She nodded, her head lying against one propped-up arm. Her face was as remote as though asleep. —Yes: she said. —And then we mustn't forget the girl from the one-family house at the corner. Remember there is a road with only a few houses that leads from the town to the development, at the time only a few houses were built along it, and at the end, just before the gas station, was a house with a wide stoop, they'd always sit on it (he has forgotten all their names. One might have been called Eckehard) and wait for the girl who didn't belong. She'd usually look out a window on the second floor and shake her head between the parted curtains when they'd whistle or call; but sometimes she'd sit with them, on the highest step, the one closest to the door, and listen to them show off, comparing pocketknives, mimicking their teachers, or they'd fight: to show off their strength in front of her, but she'd keep her eyes cast down and her hands clasped around her knees. Her eyes looked as though she were unendingly terrified by something: he said, he still remembers that much. There was a lighter rectangle on the wall beside the door with deep holes at the corners, as though a heavy enamel plaque had been torn off. Her father was a fat timid man who'd stand at the street corners in town all day, or they'd see him in the station meeting all the trains, politely, almost cowering, he'd stand outside the gates, but nobody ever seemed to arrive for him. He never spoke to the boys who sat around his daughter on the stoop, he'd smile lamely and say something to her alone, too low for them to hear, and stretch out his hand behind him while he unlocked the door and she'd go in after him without turning her head. They couldn't leave then, they'd go on sitting on the stoop a little longer as though something were holding them there, finally they'd walk off, separately, one after the other: as though they had lost their reason for being together. It never occurred to them to compare her to the girls at the development with whom they played soccer or tag on the unpaved streets, she didn't know about such games. She seemed as remote to them as the grownups who'd march festively through the city on Sundays in uniform behind an army band: for that you had to be older. Achim remembers just once: when she went with him to the woods and let him show her his favorite dugout under a heavy sod of grass that kept growing back, a hole paneled with narrow planks against the wet earth, containing an iridescent glass ball, a strand of flexible wire, and a nail four inches long; intently, awkward, she knelt

49

beside him and let him show her everything, but he could not explain to her their why and wherefore. No, of course not: she wouldn't tell anybody. They had met there, but when they returned to the street, she ran away, looked back over her shoulder as she ran, called out something he couldn't understand. Once she also let him persuade her to go on a Sunday walk with him and his parents, there is a photo, that's how I know what she was like. On the grass in the park. Achim is standing slightly away from his parents, holding her by the shoulders, he is laughing with all his teeth, she looking gravely into the camera, trying to hold his hands in place. His protectiveness dates from that time. And the word "slim" by which he describes certain girls, and an unmistakable look when he meets one now with such hard thin limbs, her face is alien and vulnerable, and she had thick black braids and was good to hold by the arms and to protect. He can't understand it: he has forgotten her name.

Karin looked up, into the quiet attention of the proprietor who had been standing before them for quite some time, wiping glasses. She straightened up, took the glass out of his hand and set it down. The proprietor bent forward, poured what Karsch had, she said: I look like her, I looked like her at the time.

(When Achim had met her.)

She lifted her glass and swirled the brownish liquid, watching. —Then she disappeared. With no one to protect her. He came home from school and saw a furniture truck outside her house, new tenants were carrying their belongings inside, a woman with a bird cage, a grandfather clock swaying aslant into the foyer. They probably didn't have much to carry into the house. And next to it a heap of broken furniture and glass from picture frames and torn books, he still remembers that: his mother didn't know the people. They had moved there only recently. His mother's headshake made her seem all the the more irretrievable, gone forever as though she had never existed, and she didn't exist any more.

She set her glass down in front of Karsch, not having touched her drink, stuck two fingers into his closed notebook and opened it. She was about to go on talking, but was interrupted by a young man from the group at the door who was finally following up on his preparatory staring. He was very tall and lanky and operating with that impression, all of a sudden the eyes in the longish, oval-shaped head winked at Karsch. He pulled Karin toward the dance floor, and meanwhile delighted impatiently kept rubbing the thick, short carpet of hair that covered him from forehead to neck. Karin turned at the door, her nose wrinkled in amusement, her partner's hand waved very high. And when her jacket came flying through the door and the proprietor presented it to Karsch in his corner across sink and bar, he, too, stood up and walked over to the door and stood between the two policemen who had come back for another check. From here one could see the band at the front wall. Which was now playing, tough and intent on visible twitchings, one number from the permitted quota of West German dance music; its hard beat stood out in contrast to the more gentle and melodious dance tunes of the past; it was not singable. Karin was now dancing at the side of her lanky, nimble partner, linked to him by the hands, they were jumping faster and faster across the rigorous syncopated steps, their whole bodies twisted, in step with the accelerated beat, the small head of the boy on top of the long body had lost its rigidity, soft and relaxed his face was participating in the dance, absently his hand slipped to his throat under the tight knot of his tie and let it trail triumphantly through the hall. Karin grabbed the end, their hands worked their way toward each other along the strip of cloth while their steps went farther and farther apart from each other on the floor, the sharp steps set her skirt swinging in hard folds about her hips. The policemen nudged each other, neither wanted to be the first to interfere. But when they noticed the attentiveness around them, the younger one (who had, up to then, been smiling to himself) stalked in his hard boots across the dance floor toward the two and said something to them that nobody could hear, he spread out his legs and fastened his arms by the thumbs in his wide shiny belt. Something seemed to bother him. From the spectators milling around the other policeman, Karsch could not make out what was going on, until a girl's voice somewhere in the back piped up: The police—your friend, your helper? Everybody laughed. It did not convey tension to Karsch. The encircled guardian of the peace tried to turn his neck and peer between the heads that were all turned away

from him, but the question was not addressed to him, and was it a question? Karsch knew the slogan from posters. In the meantime Karin had promptly and deliberately misunderstood the younger policeman's call to order and was hanging around his neck as the band, with brisk, severe gestures, returned to the discreet sounds of a homemade song about the sun setting over the Baltic Sea contemplated collectively from the terrace of a State vacation home, the younger policeman posed a hesitant hand on Karin's long taut back, tried to remove her hand from his chest, was already dancing with her, the nervous ragged circle of dancers from before froze to a tight ring of spectators, people laughed and clapped, because Karin was clinging closer and closer to her partner, tenderly stroked the leather strap across his uniformed back, she forced him to bend down over her head and at least to look the way she looked: with a lost look, visible to all but him, she pressed her face against his stiffly angled arm, broke the sweetness with a sudden frown, like spun thread longing grew from the saxophone, each time she touched his gun holster her body quivered in pained ecstasy, setting off sharper clapping from the spectators, somewhat too loudly they joined in the reconciling refrain: You and me . . . and we, we all! rushing it through to the end, the musicians packed away their instruments, the band leader turned his back. The policeman felt the weight of Karin's arms slide from him, with a sigh of relief he bowed to her, bowed once more into the void, walked back to the door, alone and deep in thought, while a large empty space grew behind averted backs that were shaking with giggling. With a radiant smile Karin's ·initial partner led her back to Karsch, shook his hand with an excess of gratification, reluctantly returned to his friends who were calling to him something about a speedy boat; in passing he had asked Karsch: Say, are you from the West too?
—When they come back, we'll buy them a drink: she said, looking relaxed about her, but the policemen were gone. Very erect she sat beside Karsch on the bar stool, slenderly rising from the sturdy seat, exhausted, blowing small loose hairs off her forehead. Suddenly bitter she said: Don't tell Achim!
(Karsch thought she sounded bitter.) Then she asked Karsch to take her away. Her face completely closed, barely responding to

the calls with a tight smile, she walked through the barroom, sat rapt in thought during the ride, asked to be dropped at the station and took a cab into the night, to God knows where. Later Karsch passed the illuminated gray semicircular house and saw the light on in all four of Achim's windows. A shadow moving in the foreground might be or it might not be hers.

That he couldn't possibly put into the book!

They didn't give him much to put into the book. If it had been for money, Karsch would have turned down the job: write it yourself. But he had started on his own. And Achim's relation to his country (the country, Achim himself) was incomprehensible to him, and that was what he was supposed to write about. True, he was familiar with the State Administrator's modulating tone, from public speeches in newsreels and over the radio, but he would have liked to know why the trusting slogan about the police was mimicked with such brio and practice by the same people who also filled the huge gray vaults of the stadiums with unmimicked applause (or, more precisely: what attached her to Achim, why he didn't let her go, since the strange girl at the street corner of times past wouldn't come back to life in her, nor did he want to marry her and live with her for another couple of years as in the two last). Well then, how did Achim grow up?
—It's so long ago: said Achim. —More or less like everybody else . . .
—Tell me something about your father: asked Karsch. —What was he like, twenty years ago?
—Oh . . . he was never one to say much.
His father never said much. His face was inscrutably silent, he'd indicate his wishes and opinions with an occasional word that would seem spat out, only his lips would move; sometimes the son would be caught, suddenly, by a gray narrow glance, approving perhaps, watchful. That didn't happen very often, he'd remain at a puzzling distance, to this day the sight of him

53

caught you at the throat. The mother counteracted with chatter, always poised to turn her face aside and fall silent. With the neighbors she'd be more relaxed, words streaming easily away, she liked to laugh, as though taken by surprise. With a lot of friendly talk and fuss she held the State's women's organization together in the development, with deep satisfaction she'd place bags of collected food on the pulled-out serving tray of the sideboard in the living room and count them over and finally add the biggest one herself: she wanted a people united against its enemies. That was what she had been told. During Hitler's hour-long excited speeches that would surge from every kitchen into the empty streets on Sunday mornings, she'd sit resignedly darning socks, occasionally shaking her head while his father would lean his forehead on his arm propped against the table corner out of view. When the ultimatum to Poland startled her into speech and she modestly argued that such behavior was unreasonable and couldn't possibly lead to a good end, his father said nothing and didn't even look up, as though he had not heard her (perhaps he was just in his grouchy mood that day), and she'd drop her voice as though apologizing and stop talking after a quick glance at the boy whose head felt befogged under the loud-speaker. Still, she had to explain school to him, and all that one saw of the government and the world. One didn't speak to the father unless the father spoke first. And one's answers had to be concise and prompt, very much like the order that started in the workshop in the basement and penetrated, wordless and precise, into their apartment. He was not afraid of his father. Only once did Achim see his mother lean against him with her arms around him and her face on his shoulder. Slowly he disengaged himself under the boy's eyes, walked up to him with an almost open smile, leading the mother toward the boy by the arms. Achim had been a wanted child. On Christmas and birthdays his gifts arrived without lists and letters to Santa Claus, but were chosen with care: not the platoon of soldiers to play with, the papier-mâché trenches, command posts and cannon which Achim would stare at when the family went for walks in town (that's what I want. All of it!), but a paper model of the fighter plane which his father helped assemble during the day. Achim liked that even better, once he'd glued the cutouts together correctly, if a little lopsided, he was given plywood and saws and glue to build a larger model, and permission to use the workshop in the basement. Achim knew they didn't have much money but what really impressed upon him the need for economy was the attention with which his father watched when he unpacked and used his presents. He seemed to worry. He never saw his mother's Christmas presents. For her birthdays, however, she received novels which she was not allowed to have around the rest of the year, since father didn't approve of reading for pleasure. Small and wiry he'd stand at the kitchen sink after work and wash himself from head to toe, read his home-town paper during dinner and then disappear into the basement to work and reflect on the construction of a radio set according to a special diagram. He wanted to become a technician, he thought he'd have a better job working with engineers rather than performing the same repetitive motions in the subterranean factory. Now something about bicycles! In the afternoons Achim would wait along the highway. It ran past the settlement in a steep climb to where the closed-down copper mine was, its boundaries marked off by a high wire fence, and the hangars spotted with the colors of the forest. Every day at the same hour the head of a multisectioned worm would appear at the top and start to creep downhill, uniformly thick with countless identical motions. Where the road turned off to the settlement dense packs of cyclists would break away from the column, over the small blue cobbles of the highway, still the wheels would flash by without gaps past the crouching boy, racing downhill with a crashing swing, muffled blasts torn from the air, the sticky black chips in the roadway ground smooth with a powerful swish. Bent, propped on its arms, figure after similar figure rushed identically from behind the bark and the new shoots of the last tree, came tearing down toward Achim above a purring spinning-top of legs, and was past him without looking up before he could have made out the face. He'd recognize his father a few paces away, by the veering of the bicycle and braking of the tires. When the bicycle stopped beside him, he'd still be scrambling to his feet.

—Can I have a bike too?

—What for.

—Everybody has one.
—Everybody who?
—Eckhart, and Dieter Ohnesorge too.
—Everybody, huh.

As always, his father let him push the bike across the street and ride a few steps ahead of him standing on one pedal, without any further comments. Weeks later, again coming home, outside their garden gate, he held the bicycle by the saddle, looked at it darkly and said: It's got to be your own, huh?

Achim had not been thinking about his wish just then; it almost seemed to him as though he had forgotten it. He felt ashamed.
—Oh no!

His father shoved the bicycle toward him, he just about caught it. After he was through washing, Achim saw him come back out into the street, the bike in hand. He didn't look grouchy. He came up to him.
—Let's go. I'll show you.

Something like that. Approximately. Or else Achim might correct Karsch's guesswork later. At this point Karsch recklessly filled in what he knew of those days, what he thought probable for Achim. Forbidden bathing in the shallow though rapid river outside the town, how they'd climb around in the young trees, naked, shouting with joy; boys lying in the grass, their noses in a manual of German and foreign airplanes, trying to guess from the shape and the speed which type plane was making that noise in the glistening blue-white summer sky overhead, I'd like to be a pilot, no: I'd just like to fly like that: fine, then I'll be the pilot! So many things they wanted to be in the war game they were playing, because Hitler had promised them a war, but nobody wanted to be a Hitler: that was too awesome and holy, the way he'd appear, modest and unassuming among the mighty rustling flag clouds, and happily sobbing women and the vigorous men who'd stand straighter in their uniforms with visible lumps in their throats at the sight of the German savior, because that's what they called him. The shudder down the lean suntanned boy's spine, a first inkling of one's powerlessness before the authority of the State; would you like to visit him? Oh no! but I would like to see him from very close without him noticing. And his photograph behind the teacher's desk, and what will the

Führer think if you can't do fractions, and the classroom odor of old dust warmed by the sun and the chalk-soaked sponge; the endless road, for a boy of nine, from his seat to the blackboard: All your classmates collected more bones and rags than you. Don't you want Germany to be strong? Paper: Iron: Bones: and rags: Broken teeth we put in bags . . . Everything we find we gather! for our—: the melody had no room left for what, and to change the ending like that, one had to be mad or else one lost one's grip on the world, a grip that held animal bones covered with rotting flesh (stolen) from the knacker's yard together with the greatness of a historical personality, that's what they called him. Arithmetic, spelling, reading: good, religion: dash, conduct: satisfactory, except once. Winter vacations in the grandparents' house in Thuringia, the unsuspected force of his own body pulled him down the slope across bluish sparkling snow, one inattentive breath and it got ahead of him, threw him over. How did this happen? A goat is an animal with curved horns and a thin straggly beard (just as in the picture books), it climbs on a slant much more nimbly than a human being, it gives milk and knows those who feed it by their step, may I feed her today? For the first time the feeling of happy exhaustion when he came back in the evening from the snow, two more days and I've got to go back to school. A new way of foiling the other teams at soccer or Völkerball (to get the girls to play too), Germany against America, I don't want to be an American, they're sure to lose. Some girls would hardly come out any more; they're offended suddenly, for no reason, they're becoming unpredictable. One can't really play with girls! There is an underground passage from the castle to the river, all we have to do is dig straight through the forest. They're showing a film in town, Frederick the Great and the cavalry general, they are all wearing wigs but boy, can they shoot, let me tell you! Are you coming? I'm sick of wearing long stockings, I'm no girl, I don't want her to pat my head all the time, I'm too old for that kind of thing. Do I get ten pfennigs if I go to the store? Sometimes the father lets him have the bike, after work. There is a winding road along the development with very high poplars next to a muddy ditch, it leads to the vegetable gardens, first you must learn to keep your balance, balance, what's that? The father is

57

holding the bike by the (lowered) saddle, Achim reaches for the handle bars, tries to steer, the front wheel sways, it's easier when you go fast. Just in time he falls against the father's protecting arm. Know something? Dieter Ohnesorge's uncle says there'll be a war.
—Nonsense.

What had Karsch wanted to ask about 1940?

Achim was ten years old in 1940. But neither of his books told whether or not he had joined the premilitary children's organization, Hitler Youth, like every ten-year-old in those days, tough days for decent people, according to the books, that was all they said. Karsch thought he had probably joined. Although: when he came across the father's previous connection with the (since then forbidden) Social Democratic Party, he began toying with the gap between this fact and the other probability, it allowed certain conjectures: if Achim won't tell him now, he'll have to set it straight later. His own fault.
—Tomorrow we'll be almost one thousand on the fairgrounds, I've already got my uniform: said Eckhart. —Are you coming? He looks away, nods. —Nine o'clock then, at the corner. —See you at nine. That evening his father is reading the paper, doesn't say a word, but it's the paper from the big city, not the local one. Perhaps the announcement isn't in it. Achim goes into the bedroom, gropes around the sewing machine in the dark, can't feel the rough fabric of the brown shirt anywhere. (And he'd also need black pants, belt, shoulder strap, black kerchief through its brown leather holder.) Things you need aren't gifts. They wouldn't be hidden away. —What are you doing in there by the sewing machine? —Oh—nothing. Outside, the chips on the road glisten under the lamp. —Can I go out again? It is windy, a warm drizzle on mouth and forehead. The high gate of the vulcanizing plant is closed, is something moving in there among the stacks? Nothing. He goes back into the house, listens to the brash pounding music from upstairs, no one calls

him. He gropes his way down the dark stairs into the basement, a light shines out from under the door of his father's workshop. An unfamiliar voice is speaking, unfriendly, informative, endless, as though the speaker were talking to himself with nobody sitting opposite. Achim hesitates, his foot pushes a small stone out of the loose concrete of the last step, it hits the floor, rolls bouncing down to the laundry room. The door swings soundlessly open, a light falls on Achim, reveals the fuzzy shape of his father. —Come in. But there isn't anybody in the workshop. On the workbench, screw drivers and pliers lie neatly side by side. They look unused. A thick tube is gleaming in the open radio, with a tiny head on top which glows. What is humming like that? The transformer. —Did you want anything? A hesitant headshake. The father leans forward, switches the silenced radio off. He leads the boy by the shoulders to the stairs and locks the door. —Time for bed.

The next morning Achim doesn't get up from the breakfast table. —Does school start later today? A cranky grunt. But he is wide awake (what did I say, yes or no?). His mother hastily starts soaking the laundry, checks the gas, unties her wet apron. With a sigh and a smiling headshake she pulls him from the wall along which he was trying to sneak out. Her wet hand holds him by one arm, pushes a strand of hair off his forehead, this time he is not embarrassed. —You'll be just like your father. She is startled by her thought, looks at the floor, wants to say something else but doesn't, runs downstairs to the laundry. From the stairs her voice sends him to the store. He dawdles on the way, forgets the ration stamps almost on purpose, has to go back. The grocer's wife hands him his change between candy jars, says: It's not your turn yet on the fairgrounds this year, is it? He is spared the answer, a woman steps ahead of him, he giggles soundlessly about something. He hesitates on the stairs. The air is thick and white with haze, with the sunlight filtering through on all sides, stinging hot. He takes the long way around the development, the asphalt is black with humidity. The ditch is steaming. He stops, swings the full milk can in a complete circle, flexes his knees in response to the obedient tilting of the ground. He enjoys not thinking of anything. Silently he appears to his mother in the haze of the laundry room. She is bent over

59

the drain wringing out sheets. —Here, give me a hand. And now it's time to go.

It is half past nine on the kitchen clock. Eckhart is not at the corner. Achim seats himself on the long stone that protects the edge of a garden fence and waits for Eckhart. (At nine.) Groups of boys his age pass him on their way from the city, they're talking about the meeting which the fairgrounds will be too small to hold. He knows some of them, they're from his school.

—Hi, Achim!

—Hi.

—Aren't you coming?

—I'm waiting for Eckhart.

—Aw, come along.

—No no.

—Leave him be—he's waiting.

The street gets emptier, now it is completely deserted. It is too early for the housewives to go shopping. The haze grows brighter and hotter, and throws his shadow between his feet. No school today. No one to play with. A truck pulls up beside him. Two men in blue overalls begin rolling large tires over the edge, they bounce once, hard and high, hop clumsily forward, finally topple heavily to one side, lie flat. He would have liked to ask if he might help, but the men had looked at him with such astonishment. Limply he gets up off the stone and walks, stiffly at first, then skipping toward the town. There is always something going on at the station.

—How did it go? his father asks that evening. Achim refuses to understand, although his father means the roll call on the fairgrounds. He'd known about it already last night.

—I didn't go.

—Why not?

—(Because you didn't say anything about it.) Uh . . .

His father makes him explain how he waited for Eckhart, precisely at what time and when he got there, repeats some of his answers with a mocking grunt. Achim realizes that he didn't wait for his friend.

—Shall we say that you forgot, or for reasons of illness my son was unable to: says his father. His eyelids are quivering gently, he is greatly amused.

60

—Sick! And tomorrow too, or they won't believe it.

That way Karsch managed to work in another day without school. Since nobody was paying attention to him anyway. He took another one of the sheets that Karin mysteriously found for him and made some drafts on it: where to place Achim's second day off: at the station, in the woods, in town; he remembered a certain cobblestone street outside the school, a ten-year-old boy could still sneak along the wall without his hair showing above the sills of the open windows and listen to the others inside endlessly reciting the same poem, as a reading exercise, about Chancellor Bismarck: Eckhart read haltingly, and then continued in rapid singsong; the street was dry and hot and smelled like vacation. During the main recess Achim stood against the fence of the girls' school and watched the girls stroll across the courtyard arm in arm in long rows, bite gracefully into their sandwiches with the wrapper still half on, stick their heads together, the teacher shooed them away like chickens; they were much older than the boy at the fence and paid no attention to him. Three tanks came driving across the market square, rattled heavily over the castle driveway; a policeman leaped into the street and with outstretched arms stopped the only car coming from the opposite direction, raised his hand briefly to his star-studded shako, the tank commanders waved back gaily. Bareheaded and bare-armed they were leaning out of their turrets, looked with amused contempt at the pedestrians below them in the street and had complete power over all that steel. At the city wall Achim let them go on alone. The steep mound bore a thick growth of many-colored weeds. This is a gallnut. They make ink out of that. Doesn't smell like ink.

And what if it was all completely different?

Probably Achim had avoided the roll call differently or not at all, but Karsch thought: he could always use that day out of school. Surely Achim had played hooky at least once: although perhaps in a different building with a different smell. On the whole it was too bad about the futile wait for Eckhart, but all that could just as well be used by Karsch for a different purpose. For some other day, for other circumstances.

These were merely preparatory drafts Karsch was trying out on Achim's former residence; brief annotations mainly, with many question marks, the way I record them for you more or less at random. (Achim kept the manuscript.) As a matter of fact his turn came only a year later, because he was three months younger than his friend Eckhart (who might just as well have had a different name, or spelled it differently), and he was just as glad: he didn't enjoy standing around the streets by himself, watching the young marchers return to town, tired and scratched up, he wanted more than just being told about what they called duty.

—Boy, did they make us crawl around today!

Later, the family moved back to the big city where Achim was born; his father had been promoted to technician. That was during the second year of the war on the Russian front, there was a need for new airplanes. Achim postponed re-enrolling for quite a while (unintentionally) and roamed about the city rediscovering it for a couple of months. But afterward he stayed in the youth organization until the end of the war. (I didn't offer you this story just because it had been written. Achim said: It could very well have been that way. I didn't want to join at all, at first, and my father wouldn't give me a penny for the uniform. Later he did pay for it anyway. But he is supposed to have called it: That monkey suit.)

So Achim was discussing this with Karsch after all?

Not then: later he told Karsch as much as he remembered of his family's return to the city. (He admitted Karsch couldn't know about that. He worried about what that guy might do to his life. —How many pages up to 1944: he asked. —Thirty, maybe forty: Karsch thought. Achim's frowns too should not be mentioned ahead of their time, or else that time'll run over into his childhood. Let us tell first what he told Karsch: later, when he told it.) Consequently there were fewer question marks on the following pages.

According to these pages the city seemed much more compressed at first and confused than his memory had predicted. The slow entry into the city in the moving van on the wide avenue struck him as strange; he had forgotten the streetcars, which after coming modestly out of narrow side streets usurped with their wheels the entire center lane of the avenue as huge rail cars between hedges and fences; in addition, the countless turns right and left all looked alike and recalled again and again the narrow high tunnel between rough-surfaced converging house fronts, each announcing the street on which they had lived before they moved away, startling trees at the estuary or a thick stream of traffic would disappoint his expectations again. Long before midtown they turned east, from a seemingly endless overpass Achim could see rail systems and factory yards with chimneys and gas storage tanks vanish entangled into the distance, toward the hazy thin church spires in the heart of the city; how did this all hang together? —You're so quiet? asked his mother who was telling the movers where to put the furniture, dull and docile he went back and forth between the house and the moving van. He was becoming aware of the lost small-town intimacy of the place they had left. He would have to forget his friends, here they could do nothing for him. The woods and the river, and the familiarity of each paving stone: lost.

After a six-month trial period his father was promoted to a position in an office run by the air force where blueprints of new planes and bomber models were graphically translated into the most efficient construction diagrams; now he designed the prototypes and variants of the parts that he used to build. The housing authority allotted him a one-family house in the southeast suburbs of the city. At that time approximately ten identical houses had been built around an unpaved square, with a dolmen in the center to commemorate the dead of the first German world war, though not yet those of the second. Each house had a lateral glassed-in stairway, a grayish-brown saddle roof, windows in identical formation, and sheds in the large back yards. (Today the square has become a side street without a monument and is part of the suburb from which the former development had been separated by a mile of fields.) His father's face lost its gray touch, he shaved every day instead of once a week, he wore white shirts which he kept buttoned and a tie, he returned from work bathed as for a holiday, he no longer spent his evenings in the basement but bent over large sheets of paper at his desk, he seemed more readily amused. During the day at work he now stood at a drawing board in a huge glass hall, in a white smock (that was much easier to wash and nicer to look at than torn dirty overalls), they ate breakfast together, they no longer listened to Hitler's Sunday speeches. Before visits of new colleagues, his mother would sit at her new dresser, nervous and flushed, putting powder on her face, and creams and rouge; Achim would stand and watch until she'd catch his eye in the mirror and ask him if she'd put on enough and he'd nod and feel embarrassed. She was much tenderer with him and he felt old enough for it again now.

For a long while he did not make new friends in school, but exchanged fewer and fewer letters with the ones he had left behind. Almost shy he sat at a desk by himself and tried to learn big-city manners, but he was too intent to feel secure. As a result he exaggerated his zeal in classwork and his assignments so that he moved close up to the seat of the head of the class; three classmates ambushed him one afternoon in the deserted street and beat him up, a sharp stone thrown after him tore a wide gash in his temple, that's the scar beside the left eye. (—Is all that really so important? said Achim.) The next day, a radiant bandage around his forehead, he knocked two of them down, first one and then the other, with the quick well-aimed uppercut (which his rage made him remember, he practiced it thoroughly with Eckhart during their scouting practice); then, freshly bandaged and sewn up he went back to his classroom at noon and the third boy (who had run away) sat at his desk alone and Achim was invited to sit in the center of the class, at last he fitted the image of the ideal German boy; tough as leather, hard as Krupp steel and swift as a greyhound. He joined the youth organization. He advanced to command over one hundred youths.

64

—It was what I had wanted: said Achim. —If a kid didn't feel like walking the beam across a ditch filled with stinking water, I'd let him have it. He who showed that he could be finished would be finished off for good. And then there was . . . there was one in my group, you know what I mean . . . with delicate bones, always close to tears, skin like a girl's. (Our skin was that way too, but on him it showed.) His mind would wander while we were standing in line, suddenly he'd wake up, wouldn't know where he was, it made the others sore, they were serious about being on the shooting range. They got him so scared, he'd volunteer for all the things he couldn't do: like man-to-man combat, they'd pick the toughest guy as his opponent, what can you do with a kid like that? Let him have it right away. But they'd do it slowly. It soon became a habit, they'd get him so upset every time, he couldn't do any of the things he had practiced at home, he'd practice like crazy. Attention! To the rear, march! and he'd drop his hand grenade or throw it at somebody's head. Once I saw him walk from school to the streetcar, head down, changing step, intent solely on his feet, because they had tricked him with that once. At the next exercise the question: who knows how to change step. He raises his hand: he knows. Not raising his hand would have been just as wrong. He is called out of the ranks. Three commanders with whistles between their lips take turns over a twenty-yard stretch and cure him of step-changing, he no longer knows anything, lanky, ridiculous, he keeps trying the little hop, easy as child's play, they keep changing commands, one couldn't even feel sorry for him any more. But then he had a way of flinging himself into the mud with such disgust, he'd always find the time to say shit, at snake-crawl they'd tell him to keep his feet down and he'd ask a modest: why? When he knew why: so that the enemy doesn't shoot up your ankle. Then they'd flatten his ankles with their heavy boots and he'd say: aha, I see. That I liked. I began helping him after a while. After I was made platoon leader, they left him alone. His name was Siegfried. We never became friends, incidentally, he didn't like me, I was too tough for him.

—And there's something else: said Achim. —After a while it stopped mattering to me that the guy in front of all the others

65

(in front of the assembled ranks) can send them crawling in the mud, back and forth for hours in the wet grass, forward march! The only thing that mattered was: they could no longer do it to me, not to me.

—And that you were able to look on from above? Karin asked.

—To know, you understand, that their mouths go dry as they hoist the flag or during parade, they're swimming in faith with all their defenses down. But the guy in front gives the order for it all to start, to hoist the flag, he makes them all feel holy—except himself: since he's the one to do it. He can also give the command to stop it.

Achim hesitated. —I don't think so. After all, I was pretty much indoctrinated: he said, and: we were only kids, don't forget.

When he was not on "duty" after school and didn't have to watch his baby sister (because yes: for three years he had a sister), he'd roam about the city. (—At no other time of my life did I feel so greedy for a city.) On his father's bicycle. His first Christmas present after they moved back, because a gray-green bus stopped outside the development every morning, it picked up the employees from all over the city and brought them back to their houses at night, if their house was still there.

—My father taught me as much as he knew about bicycle riding: said Achim. Remembered in silence, continued gropingly, hesitating, as though it could not be explained after all: you've got to ride alone to get the feel of a bike, of the way it moves, I mean: you get control over your bike as though it were part of your body—you can tell within inches at what speed and when to put on the brake before a garden fence, not that you think about it, it's automatic, you just do it! your body surprises you: only much later I noticed that I'd applied the brakes on the straightaway before a curve, that I'd press the upper part of my body toward the inside of the curve and flex my leg in an internal angle (had I thought about it, the opposite would have seemed more logical, except that you'd fall off), my leg would adjust to the curve before I gave it an order: long before I learned about centrifugal force that must be counterpoised by a shift in inclination; I'd still be in a slant, but I'd start pedaling again: just as unconsciously as I had stopped before the curve. And

66

then there is the difference between wide curves and narrow curves: he said, he placed his arm in a loose arc on the table: This is the kind you can straighten out a bit by cutting in from the outside, provided you see where it ends. Try this one: he said, holding out a sharply bent hand and driving into it with the other one, bent just as sharply; the impact crushed it to a fist.

Was his city bombed?

About the air raids of the united world Achim said: You know all that as well as I do. He rediscovered his city only after it was disintegrating under the bombings. One afternoon, shortly after their return, he stopped his gardening, suddenly overcome by the memory of their first apartment in the dry hot sun; he had been four years old, leaning far out the window, staring down into the canyon of the street. Half of it lay in deep shadow that accentuated the moldy smell of the shop on the ground floor and the cool stones in the hall and the gray light on the stairs, all of it huddled in the shadow, and on the other side a maid pushing a baby carriage on the gleaming pavement of the treeless sidewalk, he heard singing. The heavy silence was made heavier by yelling roller-skating children who drew lines of chalk after them at the curves, a giant face grew out of the heat, it knew him. At the last moment his mother had snatched him back in and closed the window. He wanted to see all that again. He asked his mother how one got there, he took the streetcar to the other side of the city. People looked startled when he asked them the way, hesitated before they told him how to get there. The day was as warm as the one he remembered. For a long time he walked down a street parallel to the one on which they had lived, he wanted to turn the corner where the pharmacy was and go straight up to the house. It all came back to him: the transformer cubicle in the bushes at the crossing, the shrubs had been less high before, the door of the pharmacy was open as always, when he used to run in and ask for a twist of licorice, the houses were gone. The open sky threw him back half a step. Before him lay a long mound of debris all the way up to the edge of the street, the houses on the other side were nothing but hollow walls. —There must have been a fire: he thought quickly, in vain, he knew it had been the bombs. Never would he have thought that five stories (with all that furniture! and there had been ceilings, inside walls! and the people?) could be flattened like that. The wind was blowing dust from the mounds onto the splintered path, tiny whorls that rose from under his feet and danced, like flags, over the crest of the rubble wall. It was very quiet. One high wall was still covered with tiles, and above it, on an intact wall space, a clean ceramic picture plate in a blue and white pattern. That must have been a kitchen. A man in a gray uniform was digging, a young woman watched him, leaning against what was left of a chimney. He stooped, and from between his feet pulled up a small colorful kerchief. It looked intact. He threw it to the woman. They laughed about something. The soldier took off his jacket, folded it neatly, laid it down beside him. Whistling, he went on digging. Achim ran off.

He kept waiting for the great event, the attack that the frantically hurrying people promised him with fear-ridden faces after the sirens began to howl. He had just heard talk about it. The first pinpoint bombing came one afternoon in early summer, the whole family was sitting in the laundry room in the basement, through the open door they saw white friendly clouds in the sky. The wind carried wavelets of airplane sounds and then smothered them with silence. The ground shook a little. Achim burst out laughing, he was shaking with giggles. His father jumped up and hit him across the face. Beyond the green ridge of weeds outside the basement stairs, white delicately shaped clouds were rising in the distance. They screened out the other clouds. They turned gray. Achim was writhing with laughter. They were still alive. They hadn't died.

How did this tally with his war games?

He claims that it did. Because he did not recognize what made
him shake: a German Boy knows no fear. Consequently he tried
to forget about it. His memory was more insistent. He started to
climb about the ruins, he wanted to fight the overpowering pressure on his chest. He collected bomb fragments. He picked up a
cuckoo clock that his foot had dislodged from among the rubble.
After a step or two he sat down to see if it was still running. It
was. It seemed undamaged. He looked at it for a while until he
realized that it had died. His arm reached back all by itself and
threw the clock all the way up on top of a jagged wall, much
higher than he'd ever been able to throw a hand grenade on
purpose. Then he wanted to make himself climb up after it: a
German Boy knows no fear. He sat motionless in the sweetish-
smelling silence and tried to force himself. Hesitantly he stood
up and climbed the footspikes of a chimney in pursuit of the
clock. Which now lay on the front edge of an apartment floor;
behind it, between three walls, under the polished sky, a middle-class living room with puddles of rain in its shadowy corners;
a sofa, a floor lamp, and a chess table hovered immobile and
dust-covered above the desert that spread below the lonely
boy: charred wood, mashed stones and decay in the buried base-
ments. He jumped down: he simply let himself drop, didn't look
where he would land. Limping and bleeding he dragged himself home (this time without stopping to wash at one of the old
pumps at the street corners of the old section of the city) and
showed himself to his father that way and had him forbid climbing about the ruins and was once more able to believe that the
world was destroying German cities out of sheer wickedness.
That's how he made things tally. The way his father, too, seemed
able to make tally fear of the howling sirens and the planes he
helped to build.

How come Achim had a sister:
only for three years?

His mother disappeared with his sister in her arms, that was the
last he saw of them. He knew perfectly well that the corpses were
not recovered intact from under the houses, and he had seen the
enormous trenches in the graveyards and the countless rectan-
gular boxes lined up in front with legs and heads thrown in
helter-skelter, the way they found them, don't you think so,
Achim? —Sure. Achim imagined death being with the small
cluster of black-clad persons inside a circle of brown uniforms,
one caught a glimpse of them through a further line of brown
leather-strapped backs, hills of flowers covered the hurriedly dug-
up earth and the sticky odor that seeped from the direction of
the boxes; death was also one of the older guards who'd turn
around and say with friendly roughness: Get out of here, kids,
and later repeat, a trifle contemptuously: That is an order. But
his mother was not in those coffins. She had disappeared. She
had taken the streetcar into town in the morning. She wanted
to buy the father a watch for his birthday. Later she'd meet the
father at the central station for a cup of coffee (because she
hadn't been able to get used to the higher-class cafés in the
city). That's where the air raid must have caught her. Apparently
she had not been crushed under the west wing nor was
she sucked into the basement beneath the main platform. Because they did not find her there. It was very late at night when
his father came home. He had been helping to fight the fire and
rescue people all over the burning neighborhood. He had found
a doll like the one the sister had been carrying, but it was charred
and could just as well have belonged to some other child. It was
a very ordinary toy. His father did not weep. Gray-faced and
singed he sat in the kitchen and questioned his son until morning. Achim did not tell him that she had gone to buy him
a birthday present: he didn't want to spoil the surprise for her.
Was Achim sure, had she really taken the streetcar to the city?
Had she really mentioned the central station? Had the sister not
been left with the family next door? Hadn't his mother come
home hours ago and hidden somewhere, as a joke? What would
Achim like in exchange for the truth? For a long time he sat on

the chair in the kitchen, leaning over the back, thinking. With a start the sleeping boy woke up under the stare of wide eyes wiped by a blackened hand, wiping off half an eyebrow as though it were dust: had Achim walked her to the streetcar? When did she intend to be back? Had he seen that streetcar with his own eyes? She was not dead. She hadn't come home, that was all. She had left in her blue Sunday dress with the white polka dots, she had waved from behind the windowpane with the sister on her lap clutching the doll to her chest, looking pleasantly at the big brother who couldn't wait for the streetcar to start. Shortly before the sister had cried, because she had had her hair washed, two short black braids stood stiffly away from her head. His mother's mouth had moved as he waved, but he couldn't hear what she was saying. They had left in one of the heavy streetcars with a sunken platform in the center and leather benches in the compartments, as they're still running on that line today.

Soon after the police came and searched the house. Three men who locked the father into the kitchen while they questioned the boy. At first they threatened to thrash him, but when they saw his books about the war heroes and the heroes of the State Association, they drew up chairs and became friendly the way teachers were.

—Why is Germany at war?
—Because we don't have enough space to live in, and the others are no good anyway.
—If somebody tries to harm the Führer, you understand, what should be done to somebody like that?
—The Führer will destroy and annihilate every one of them.
—Who comes to see you?

They pulled his mother's clothes out of the closet. One of the men is said to have stepped on them, accidentally. They tore out the dresser mirror at which his mother used to sit. They tore his sister's toys apart. They broke up the desk, board by board. When they wrecked the picture of the disintegrating war leader, the boy—who had been watching them in silence, hands behind his back—said: I'll report that.

When they were alone again, the father locked every room in the house. He left everything the way the three agents had left it.

71

They lived in the kitchen. When the glass-covered hall where the designers worked was destroyed, he went on working in the kitchen. He left the house only when the factory bus stopped at the garden gate. He saw to it that the boy got fed, but he let him run wherever he pleased. Achim once asked him why they had searched the house. Because an error had been slipped into one of the blueprints for remote-control missiles.

—It was okayed, signed and built: said his father.

—It was built, but it doesn't work. Now it'll take six months longer before they become operational.

—I see: said Achim. Secretly he apologized to the three agents for his fit of fury.

But had his father slipped in the error?

Achim doesn't dare think so. When his father explained the consequences of the sabotage to him in such detail, he had merely seemed astonished: that anybody could do such a thing, could bring himself to do a thing like that, what sort of thoughts must have preceded such a decision: and that it had not occurred to him. Perhaps he only wanted to explain to Achim, the boy was fifteen, one should be able to talk to him.

But Achim said something about how despicable such an act was and also other things that he had been taught. His father gripped the edge of the table, regardless of the paper he was crumpling, a pencil seems to have rolled to the floor.

—And who started this war! he said vehemently. His face was again as it used to be three years ago when he came home from work. His colored shirt was crumpled, the collar tucked in, he had grown a dark-gray beard, his eyes stared. Achim noticed the blood vessels at the corners.

—The Jews: said Achim.

His father's hand reached back halfway, abruptly he looked away. He sank back, continued his own thoughts with averted face. —He didn't even feel like beating me any more: said Achim. I think I disgusted him. (And there used to be quite a lot of beatings in our house. I'd tear my clothes, or my new shoes would split open after three weeks from all that crawling about. And after he'd tell me three times without results, he'd beat me for fifteen minutes: we didn't have much money, later there never was enough on the ration cards, that's what he taught me. But he'd always explain why he was beating me. Now he didn't feel like explaining anything to me any more.) He also realized that he himself had let it come to this. Since he wouldn't talk to me. He may of course have thought I'd understand him without words, and for that reason Karsch should leave his account of his joining the youth organization as he had it; if I happened to hit on the truth, he'd think: he had given me the hint. Perhaps that kind of understanding exists between other children and their parents, perhaps I was too dull. I disappointed him again and again, finally he gave me up.

—If only he had once talked to me! but he abandoned me completely to this school and that Hitler crap.

—I must have lived (as I remember it now) in those days as though I had no feelings. Has that happened to you? I must have seen everything: the small flags with which we followed the movements on the various fronts on the map in class were moving westward toward the German borders. There was a pocket in the north where the red forces had encircled half a German army, the papers said: from here Germany's fortunes of war will turn, I'd run whenever I heard the trumpets signaling a special bulletin on the radio, I was waiting for us to get out of that pocket, for weeks I lived in that expectation; as I think about it today, I no longer remember anything about that pocket, I guess I never really imagined it. In the newsreels they'd show us German tanks plowing through Ukrainian farmhouses and all I could think was: how large they are. There was a tobacco store on the market square, they'd sometimes put a little something aside for my father and didn't ask for coupons, one day I arrived before an empty vault in place of the shopwindow, the basement had caved in, water had risen to where the floor had been, the city kept disappearing that way, when there was not a soul left in whole sections, I'd just forget about that neighborhood, I'd stop thinking about it. Low-flying planes would come across the road to the settlement in broad daylight and aim at the streetcars, at bicycles, at trucks marked with Red Crosses: I'd have no thoughts beyond the regulations about taking shelter. All of a sudden we'd get beaten up in certain parts of town when we were in uniform or entered a shop raising one arm in a Hitler salute; so what? I'd think. We'd dig tank traps a yard wide all around the city, whole days we'd be digging, I don't know what thoughts I had in those days. They'd also use war prisoners for that crazy work, they were always hungry, they'd fight over a piece of bread you'd throw away, I'd just look on, I didn't know what it all meant. I lived as though I were speechless, how would you put it? If my father had only explained to me what it all meant. I might have been able to grieve over my mother's death in a sensible way.

—But he had let me wander so far afield, he had to be afraid of me: said Achim. —And he was even right: I would have reported him. We were ordered to. If I was at home in the evening he'd often send me across the street to get some beer at the bar (you know?), so he could turn the radio knob to the forbidden wave length without risking his life. The risk was I. One afternoon a man came into our garden and asked vaguely for my father, calling him by his first name, had trouble inventing one of his own. I sent him away, I told him to come back in the evening. When my father heard this, he said nothing, he got up and took the bike and rode into town. A relative from Berlin, supposedly. We have no relatives in Berlin. If only he had let me come along! You know: I never once heard the London radio station identification, that meant something in those days; nor once the: gavarit Moskva. Now I read about it in books, I see movies of how it was during those days, but of course I can't realize it. Perhaps that was the right way to live, in those days. Nobody told me.

Is that exactly the way Achim told it?

Karsch wrote it down from memory. Achim's sentences were more in the past imperfect, some of the words he would not intentionally use. But when he checked it later, he said that's how he would have liked to have said it. On one of the spring mornings that already have the dry light of the season to come, Karsch met him and Karin in a garden restaurant south of the city. They sat at the rim of a widespread assemblage of empty tables under high chestnut trees with their buds already sticky; at the other end, a waitress went back and forth with a pile of tablecloths, threw them over the tables, clipped them to the edges. Sometimes Achim was moody after training, but here he seemed quite happy: in the bright warm silence and the festive forenoon air, here he knew only whom he wanted to know, he had removed his sunglasses and sat, relaxed, in front of a glass of tea. Although he supposedly was apprehensive of the many questions that were approaching across the gravel. Karsch's car was the first on the spacious parking lot. From the gate he saw Karin leaning across the table, talking to Achim. Achim nodded, waited, showed agreement, disagreement, finally he reached across the table and caught her hands. They were laughing when they waved to Karsch to come over, across the mote-streaked square. To the observer they looked like a trusting and intimate couple.

During these hours before noon Achim suddenly began to talk. What did you really want to know the other day? he said, broke off at once and apologized to Karsch. He was almost embarrassed. Karin watched him with curiosity. He stared at the tablecloth, crossed and uncrossed his fingers and tried to explain to Karsch in a low voice that, in certain moods, one couldn't avoid giving curt answers. Karsch was at a loss, until Karin nodded to him with half-turned face to hide her smile, a hint of it showed in imperceptibly raised eyebrows. —Don't worry about it: said Karsch. But Achim said that nobody should be held up in his work. Well then, what had Mr. Karsch wanted to know? Karsch had difficulty imagining his childhood home. Had his father been opposing the liquidated government? What had been the local name for the popular road in the development?

Achim answered rapidly, almost without thinking. He began in formal German, weighing his words, but since Karsch was not pursuing him notebook in hand, his enunciation began to soften, he skipped into dialect, used colloquialisms, from time to time he had a sideways glance, amused as though after all it had been fun to live the things he was telling. In his explanations of the last years of the war he addressed Karin; they were eating their lunch then, Achim kept putting down his knife and fork to shape with his hands what he was saying. Karin kept her head leaning against her folded hands, she was listening, occasionally a swift glance would assure her of the famous head that was speaking at her side: not disguised behind black glasses, eager to be seen the way Achim saw Achim. Only once did she stop him with a question, she did not communicate with nodding, her face was a blank. —See what I mean: Achim was saying, but before he took time to enlarge on the topic, he was carried away again. In the end he stopped as though disappointed. Karsch had no longer interrupted with questions. To him it seemed like a conversation between only the two of them about another and moot subject, with himself an accidental listener. That's how it seemed to him. He recollects that Achim laid a hand very casually against Karin's propped-up arm, at times he thought he understood him.

Why had Achim decided to co-operate?

Yes. Why did Achim sacrifice an entire morning, during training, when he was not even permitted to drive back to the camp in Karsch's car but had to work his way all around the city on his bicycle, in order to remain aware all the time what motions went into the riding of a bicycle?
—Are you satisfied? asked Karin on the way back to town in Karsch's car. Ahead of them Achim's back in the light windbreaker glided from the vibrating noon sun of the road into the dark coolness between the trees; doubled over whirling pedals he disappeared. Softly, mockingly, she laughed after him, stood

up behind the windshield, her clothes fluttering, trying to distinguish Achim in the overgrown forest path under the wide bounding sweeps of the power lines. Slow down to about thirty: she asked. Leaning into the wind, she let the reduced speed polish her skin. That was a bicycle racer's average speed on cross-country runs. She fell back on her seat, shouting against the wind: But we want to get somewhere!

Karsch stepped on the accelerator. The belt of the woods stopped on a wide, sloping pasture, villas appeared, surrounded by gardens, they were back at the main highway in the closely knitted skein of streetcars and trucks. People waiting at the streetcar stops watched indifferently as the open car came toward them and followed it with their eyes; in the rearview mirror the street receded into busy brightness, the red letters of slogans popped off walls and banners suspended across the road, next to the fresh green leaves.

Karin threw her coat over her shoulders, tied a scarf over her hair. —I'm quite satisfied: she said seriously, tying the knot.

—About something else: Karsch answered with a grin. She found his eyes in the rearview mirror, studied them thoughtfully. —Yes; she said: you're so ready with your trust.

And why was Achim so co-operative all of a sudden? What had made him change his mind?

Didn't Karsch have any idea? she asked. No, no idea. What did he think: had Achim changed his mind all by himself, or in conjunction with others? All by himself: thought Karsch. The truth was just the opposite: in conjunction with others. Who were they?

They were the party for communism. No kidding! I thought they were busy ruling the country? Of course they are, but would you hold a country together from one angle only? So, you see.

The row of columns of the former entrance to the university was blocked off with stones retrieved from the ruins, the stream of pedestrians was using the flat steps as part of the sidewalk. A recruiting poster for the State Youth Organization hung slanted above the heads of the allegorical figures (who knows Pallas Athene by sight?). It was round like a clock, they called it the progress compass. A red arrow pointed to decimals and digits of one of the years ahead, showing in which direction progress was to

77

be made; if the arrow had been movable, it might have pointed to other goals, such as reconstruction aid or foreign exchange students or reserve duty during summer vacation, whereas it was pointing to the year in which the country was supposed to have caught up with the economic rehabilitation of capitalist West Germany.

Therefore, the ruling club concentrates naturally on all potential danger spots and the areas where it might envision success; only the man among them who has the confidence of everybody is given the rank and power of administrator, although every man must administer to the best of his ability from wherever he is placed. But did Achim belong to those things that you can afford to look at with indifference, that you can let pass, that don't endure, that don't suffice? No, Karsch wouldn't exactly say that. But what I don't understand . . .

Right in the middle of town, next to the daylight-diluted neon of a twenty-four-hour bar, a truck had pulled up loaded with fruit from Jerusalem and Egypt. Its shiny snout was sniffing the sandy, empty window of a vegetable store, its back opened into a large marketing stand from which two women were handing out the fruit in paper funnels rolled from the local newspaper, to the steadily lengthening queue which swelled with passers-by. A man was pushing the crates toward the women, after each crate he'd disappear a little farther into the tarpaulin-covered darkness. Astonished shoppers craned their necks at the rapidly vanishing glowing fruit and the growing stacks of empty crates and snapped at those who pushed. The driver had remained in his seat, relaxed and engrossed in the business at hand, he was cutting the skin of an orange into sections, finally the naked fruit lay as though enwreathed by white and pink petals. Tossed carelessly onto the sidewalk where it glowed in the sun, the hollow blossom drew the unsuspecting to the other side of the truck, made them grope for their wallets and join the winding wriggling crooked serpent of waiting people.

Who was Achim? A bicycle racer, since he rode a bicycle with a team of others, trying to be faster than they were. But didn't he have friends? he did have friends. Wasn't his job drafting? he helped construct the State. Was he going to found a family? he would add to the community of the people. Didn't he exhibit his citizenship to the world, together with his bicycle? What was there to watch that might be useful to the club of the administrator: everything, don't leave out a thing. Could one pick out this rather than that, omit one thing in favor of another? How are you, Achim? How are you all shaping up for the summer races, tell us? And

They stopped the car and walked past an already half-blocked square at the intersection of two business streets where a foundation was being excavated in the basement of a ruin. The rubble had been cleared only as far as the street level and then covered with topsoil, thick healthy grass had provided a friendly mantle for the vast area. The adjoining party walls had been plastered and bore neon advertisements for all the typewriter plants in the country, one under another, they all belonged to the State, not one tried to lure a buyer away from the others, they were there, that was all. Withered tufts of grass hung over the edges of a large cavity that the dredgers were noisily deepening, dump trucks were lined up obliquely behind them, trembling softly each time a load of rubble was dropped into the hopper. A narrow strip of earth had been left along the plastered walls, mounted on the perilous ledge slender scaffolding clung to the wall, men on it took down the fraternal signs at a leisurely pace. People stood crowded against the red and white fence watching the dredgers' teeth bite into the ground, scoop up the rubble with a crunching noise and balance it high above the vibrating trucks. As they dug down, the basement arches and supports of the former merchant house emerged, sixteen years ago its solid generous structure had concealed the dignity of the market square from this street. —Do you think they'll build on top of that? It's still good, was already too solid then. —It'll be ripped out: the onlookers told each other.

It should be like a conversation among friends, all interested in each other's welfare, and if Karsch could trust Karin's changed tone then the real Achim was the high harsh dialect with the pensive pauses, whereas the other one with his spurts of joviality was a big man who held his chin on his chest, who has looked deeply into life and was more at home with the class struggle:

—What's he doing, your visitor from West Germany?

—Looking at everything. Now he also wants to write a book about me.

—He does. Congratulations.

79

—I'm against it.

—Why? Is he against us? Doesn't he understand you?

—No. He didn't know much about socialism before. Except in theory, if you see what I mean.

—Can't one talk to him?

—Oh sure. He writes down whatever you explain to him.

—Achim! Give it a try.

—Another book about me. What for? I'm one of a team. If they were less good than I am, they couldn't have tried for the title. Why not a book about all eight of us? I'm a bicycle racer like the rest of them, I'm tired of having my life described.

—You're not a racer like the rest of them.

The government sporting goods store under the arcades had no merchandise in its window, the entire width was taken up by an exhibit heralding the forthcoming race through the neighboring countries. In the background an enlarged photo showing a bird's-eye view of dusty country road with thick clusters of riders in muddy sweat shirts growing smaller in the distance, a banner with the word "peace" written on it in the various languages of the guest countries, a helicopter hanging over treetops, its tail raised. Under the trees along the road a dense waving leaping yelling crowd had been paralyzed by the camera, in the front row the mouths were larger than life size. All alone out front Achim's silhouette came racing flower-waving at top speed toward the onlooker. To one side against this backdrop the bike on which Achim had won the championship, and beside it, between glass panes, the rainbow-colored sweat shirt with stretched-out empty sleeves, a photo of Achim in the center of his team, all jumping and hugging with joy, also a row of awards, ribbons, laurel wreaths, trophies spanning the years of his rise to fame up to the present day, the eyes of children at the store window were taking a step-by-step inventory, until they'd come to rest on the enlarged portrait of Achim from the photographer's studio. Here it was framed by a poster from last year's elections for the people's representative, clean-cut above a clean collar Achim looked at one as though explained by the text underneath. I want to stand as an example not only for athletics. Less eager than the children, adults were drawn to the window, casually they'd stand side by side, comparing his bike to ordinary bikes, reread the familiar poster, since it appeared all by itself here, out of the context of the election campaigns when it had been smiling at you from everywhere, dominating the streets, but too numerous to be read, and also because it recalled the newsreels about the people's representatives with the friendly affable face of a young man who is politely trying to understand what you are saying to him: who is there for you: who will take care of your needs: will take your side against the government and the world.

—Why don't you ask him along, Achim. Let him get a good look. Explain it all to him. That shouldn't be too much bother.

—If you think so.

This is trying to answer the question: and not more than Karsch understood that afternoon. He understood that some branch of the government had talked to Achim; he remembers where it was explained to him. Karin was leaning against the store window in front of the high stack of envelopes that had reached Achim's address during the past year. On a number of them he recognized the date of their arrival marked in her handwriting; she had committed herself, this was exhibited behind glass. Actually Karsch had not really started working. It made her laugh, she pulled the owl-eyed glasses off her nose and looked at him as though she really didn't know him after all.

—Just for once, make up your mind: she said.

Karsch wanted to go and buy a typewriter.

But he had a typewriter back home!

If he had crossed the border (to go and get it) he would have lost his permit to stay here. He doesn't know any more why he wanted to stay a little longer; perhaps he didn't want to give up the state of beginning with information coming at him from all sides and so suddenly that the simplest insights (a racing bicycle is called a machine. There is an impenetrable frontier in Germany) appeared like the first clues to a puzzle that he wanted to go on solving, which could not be solved from a distance. Also: his preoccupations might have detained him. All he did was write the friends he had left behind to keep an eye on his apartment, and promptly forgot about the letter.

Program: to buy a typewriter.

Late one afternoon, on one of those spring days when the air is balmy, people keep wandering about the streets after work, aimlessly, a lady accompanied by a gentleman entered a store for office equipment, a smallish shop in one of the main streets that offered prospective customers the view of a stylized human body bent over a stylized typewriter in glowing sunset colors; or else the modern office furniture, adjustable chairs and glass desks may have lured one or the other nearer. The lady might have been married and walked very straight without exhibiting the origins of her movements. However, her footsteps were of such determination that the skin under her eyes shook; she walked as though performing a task. As to the gentleman, there is nothing to say but that he entered the store sluggishly as though dragged along. This is, after a brief reflection, the complete impression the salesman has retained of the two customers, while the picture of himself that he left with them contains a pleasantly neat shirt collar and a fumbling eagerness to be of service to the couple, whom he called lady and gentleman because a few changes in the society had not changed the etiquette. This is a local detail.

A short exchange of words between the two informed the salesman of the outlines of their expectations, embodying a device for writing that would be long in life span, light in weight. The lady employed the expression "heirloom," but looked the salesman so straight in the eye that he couldn't make up his mind what exactly she was trying to depreciate. With a practiced gesture he indicated four tables along the wall where four of the most popular typewriters of the desired weight were standing in a row. Since there could be no question as to their quality, he began to explain their differences in terms of color and technical details while the couple stood in silence, looking at him. He enlarged, for instance, on the delicacy of charcoal gray. Finally the lady, who had acted as the purchaser anyway, decided to slip between one swivel chair and table, placed her fingers on the keys and looked with undefinable expectation first at her companion and then at the salesman, her head slightly turned over one shoulder. Of course this can be said more simply. Certain basic performances may be expected from a device of this kind: actuation of the type bars by means of key levers, printing through an inked ribbon, imprinting of type on paper by trigger action, line spacing and carriage release, fast and smooth turning action of platen, this is common knowledge.

After any doubt about these basic capabilities has been eliminated, the examination concentrates on the touch, tries out a few letters, at random, inquires about inessentials, then the appearance of the typewriter is compared to that of the other typewriters and according to the customer's disposition and prejudices of taste, the final choice is made even on the basis of this last criterion. A survey of the keyboard disclosed that the variety and number of characters sufficed for the preparation of most European type matter, the numerals at hand offered themselves for seclusion within brackets, also the signs of exclamation of astonishment of disbelief of the sharpest disapprobation of joyful approval of strong affirmation of straightforward question could be reached at easily discernible points above the punctuation marks. While the gentleman on one side of the table and the salesman on the other, both with slightly bowed heads, watched the lady's fingers (which, darting down from level hands alternately leaped toward each other on the keyboard and in the same rhythm strove for the farthest reaches: lengthening this sentence and, moreover, printing the image of these movements clearly and regularly on the horizontally as well as vertically moving paper)—they all were irritated by an interruption in the sales transaction. The door had opened and loud talk in Saxon dialect entered with a draft of cooler air.

With his hand on the half-closed door, an elderly man had come to a halt on the threshold, the collective attention of those present so disconcerted him he had to make several attempts before he managed to close the door; he was distracted by his desire to say first good evening, he first wanted to inquire before taking the time of these people. The salesman, who anticipated dealing quickly with this new client, left the other two customers. And he addressed him as Sir.

—I wonder if you can help me: the man began. Hesitant speech and broad dialect confirmed the salesman's impression of awkwardness in unfamiliar surroundings. With a benign nod he made it clear that he was used to all kinds of people: that, nevertheless, he was always at the disposal of customers.

—That mimeograph machine you have in the window, the Czech one, five hundred sheets an hour: said the man; is it for sale?

Several possible answers made the salesman stammer, he managed a breathless sound of affirmation, recovered his composure, named a very high price in a tone that invited careful consideration and declined from the start any responsibility should the client's budget be impaired.

—That would be okay with me: said the man: I just wondered . . . He seemed a goodhearted, obliging person who was so artlessly out of control of his face that he scarcely noticed the expressions around him because of the effort to be more harmless than his inquiry.

—Well, you just wondered: the salesman tried to speed him up. He still shows no impatience. You should try that in a grocery. There's that grocery next door, you've heard that kind of talk a minute ago, when the door opened.

—I just wondered . . . would you have to take the number of my identity card, if . . . : continued the man. He was twisting a cap in his hands, the type usually worn by masons on their way to and from work: but also by the administrator when meeting with larger groups of the population.

—So that everybody would know . . . : The man tried to explain. He cast his eyes down in embarrassment and the salesman prepared to exchange a contemptuous smile with the couple near the wall. But the lady was so intent on typing the last paragraph on the machine she was trying out that the smile bounced off her neck into the void and could not be retrieved under her companion's steadfast concentration.

The disconcerted salesman began to explain that the identity card number was required only for the purchase of typewriters and adding machines to be transmitted to the police who watched out for offenses against civil rights. The man thanked him again, and stepping backward, he bade everybody a good evening, he did not move quickly, yet, after only a step or two he had disappeared into the many-bodied stream flowing by the shopwindow. Perhaps a young man would soon come in his place, wearing an undistinguishable leather jacket, with a frequently seen haircut, inspect all the models on display and quickly, firmly, express himself in favor of the Czech mimeograph machine and a few weeks later astonished householders would receive mimeographed texts in unaddressed envelopes with an appeal: to do their shopping during the day and not to crowd the stores in the evening, as a courtesy to the working population; of course, that is only a hypothesis, who would associate the coincidental appearance and disappearance of a simple man in cement-powdered clothes with the mimeographed text establishing a relationship between the scarcity of food and certain government measures, on the wall of a building, implying cause or effect, according to commitment or conviction? Karsch saw him come in and liked him at once, because of his obliging awkwardness, but he saw him go out again, merging into the city's eight hundred thousand inhabitants (who were not in the shop), and that was all he ever knew about the man.

In the meantime the couple, ready for a purchase a minute ago, behaved in an unusual fashion: the lady tapped her escort's chest, withdrew a foreign identity paper from the jacket of her undisturbed companion, showed it to him and to the salesman, explaining to all concerned: that the purchase was impossible. With several timid shrugs the salesman intimated that the number and pattern of that identity card could not possibly fit into the indigenous archives, an error, of course, might always happen, and now the conversation assumed an intimacy that made the lady ask: whether the type faces of all machines of the same manufacture were indiscernibly the same.

Not at all. During the casting of the type faces differences arise which can be detected through a simple microscope and which, after comparison with the type sample on file, allow the identification of the serial number and purchaser of the typewriter with which he, for instance, had prepared the stencil for his mimeograph machine.

—Oh: said the lady in a tone of anticipated satisfaction, and so the information was complete.

—A strange guy: added the salesman, and since the couple

85

could conceive of such an opinion, among many other opinions, they parted in complete agreement. I have refrained from giving a more detailed description of the participants in this superfluous incident, since it could have happened to anyone.

But Karsch could no longer afford such a typewriter. He sat for another couple of days at the late Mr. Liebenreuth's polished desk, transforming the first sixteen years of Achim's life into a sequence of longer narrations, but the lengthening balmy breezy afternoons also made him want to drive back to the border with what remained of his changed currency, back to a country where his money would be legal tender once more and he would be supported by everything and could forget about this project.

Then why are there so many more pages?

Achim told him to go to his apartment, to a narrow cabinet beside the balcony door. It stood against the light-colored wall all by itself, one hardly noticed it with the baskets brimful of mail on top. A rather intricate key opened the sliding door, the sides folded back, to the kneeling observer appeared, on unpainted wooden shelves, quiet and dustless, the expensive instruments one can buy to fight the passage of time: Achim never used his camera, he had merely let himself be photographed holding it at the gates of the zoo, he dictated his letters to the secretary of the sports academy instead of writing them on the efficient typewriter that stood there; he was fond of lengthy aimless conversations, but he did not record them on the reels of the tape recorder in his cabinet; Achim rode against time. Silently the apartment overlooked the efficient gestures of the crane on the construction site and the unused park that was slowly growing impenetrable at the edges. Karsch might stay here until the end of summer if he liked. But he simply borrowed the typewriter and returned the apartment key to Achim, because, on certain evenings, he had seen the small-paned windows lighted and a shadow moving all alone presumably making sounds behind the

86

gray illuminated house front. Mrs. Liebenreuth didn't object to typing at night. —Actually I rather like it: she said. So I know that someone is always there at night. Now he could read what he wrote.

After a week all the still missing permits converged on Karsch like gifts since he had not applied for anything: he was allowed to stay longer, to leave the city, to attend the big bicycle races in May, to go wherever he pleased (but why should I bore you with the description of the two houses? On the suburban street that slopes down toward the bridge. Two different families had built them semidetached, long ago, four stories separated by a continuous wall, with entrances at the outside corners, away from each other; after the air raids, government and administrative offices shared them, built a plywood cubicle for a doorman into each lightless foyer and finally cut through the middle wall for official purposes: so that swarms of advice-seeking people were now drifting, unadvised, from a crowded hallway on the left into a quiet lateral ground-floor room from which an unidentified door hole was supposed to lead to the continuation of the hallway in the other half of the united house, to more doors with more door plates and arrows and a strange-looking stairway down to the other doorman who refused to recognize or accept the pass issued by the first doorman, which meant another search for the exit back up into the house through the truncated hallway down the old-fashioned circular stairs to the paneled foyer of the first house where the first doorman would scrutinize the signature on one's pass that was valid for no one but him and his stairway. Why mention the invitation received by a certain Mr. Karsch to come to the Alien Registration Office where he was processed like everybody else through the confusion of intricate hallways, around diagonally placed walls, upstairs, straight ahead, until he finally reached the noiseless morning room that overlooked the greenery of small vegetable gardens between innumerable houses from its prosperously clear bay window, reminding one of the well-to-do families who had built this lookout and lived in it, amidst muted dark wallpaper and furniture that had been moved out before the municipal offices moved in; and what would you gain from the view of a zealously scribbling gentleman who rose, ready to help, as

Karsch appeared, and walked up to the railing that served as the borderline on the rhomboid parquet floor that had turned gray from so many feet: for wouldn't you want to infer a lucky turn of events from his colloquialisms and his politely bent arm while he stamped and filled in Karsch's residence permit, a happy coincidence that grew fairy-tale-like out of the comfortable atmosphere and the individual helpfulness of an underling who found Karsch's wishes to his liking and therefore made them come true, he's all right, let's see what he can do? who had no private thoughts and wished him good luck for the weeks ahead and reached for his lunch parcel with a distracted hand. It did not begin in this house, Karsch was merely given a hint as to which house, and even if we followed the wires underground and came up in front of a telephone and a man seated at his desk: somebody has said something, but what is he saying and what good does it do us and what's it got to do with bicycle racing? nothing), he received a certain amount in local currency with the promise of more to come, everything was permitted him, except the things that were also forbidden to the citizens of this country. In exchange he signed a contract, and mailed it back to the State Publishing House for New Writing: for a mutually trusting collaboration on the life story of a German bicycle champion.

Well, had he been able to have a beer with Mr. Fleisg in the meantime, did he understand him now?

No. In the bar where Karin had danced with the power of the State he had something like a standing appointment with the regulars who'd wander in thoughtfully out of the clear evening into the talkative atmosphere of the bar and began the night, come what may. (Dancing only twice a week.) Almost every night two masons would come in and sit beside him, toast their friendship, quarrel fiercely, make up and exhilarated by the length of time they'd spent together they'd slap Karsch on the

88

back as they left and call him their old pal, you're so quiet tonight, anything wrong, do you want a girl? Young army officers would sit in pairs, over a furtive beer, answer questions about their insignia with suspicion, leave the table when intimate company joined them, would turn for a last look at the breathless distance, the scent, face, voice of a girl at another table; they had come the wrong day. Boys would arrive on motorcycles, be rude and loud with the policemen, sit apart in lumpy conversations brazen against chair backs, would quarrel for the fun of it, show each other off without conviction, dutifully pinch the waitress, all this could probably be described in a much more exciting manner, but what for. Occasionally they'd ask Karsch to come on over for a game of cards. Hand me a butt. What are you always sitting around here for in this old dump, what the hell do you do all day? And you, aren't you sitting around here too? Karsch was writing a book about Achim.
—What the hell for? Nobody reads that stuff any more.
—Nonsense, everybody'll read it. A book about his technique?
—He still racing?
—Maybe we'll read it.
—He isn't with the actress any more, is he, the one from the films. You know him in person?
—How can you want to write a book about a guy like that. Forget him!
—No no. You try to do what he does.
—As if we didn't work all week.
—Nice pile of dough he's making.
—You ride free on the trains, if you're a member of Parliament.
—You put that in the book too?
—Free streetcars too. They get some kind of pass or something. And an elderly gentleman whose suit and tie sat strangely alone amidst overalls and leather jackets and sweaters asked during a long-awaited moment if Karsch couldn't get him the stamps on Achim's foreign mail, there weren't many from France though, were there? Mr. Fleisg didn't come there, he didn't see him. Anyway he wouldn't have heeded warning headshakes and frowns, he was too busy watching the clicking of meters he could hardly keep up with: in the gas stations. In the bakeries he had begun to notice the price of bread.

*But doesn't one get acquainted with the people
before one starts to do business with them?*

No. Picture a little old woman in a tailored jacket and slacks in
what was once the spacious living room of a middle-class home;
her gray hair is cut short at the neck; stubby and inquisitive she
is leaning against the table across from her visitor's chair and
shows concern with his living conditions. Was Mr. Karsch satisfied with his quarters? Was there anything he might need?
Only writing paper.
He had been afraid of offending her, the way he knew Mr.
Fleisg. With imperturbable kindness she promised him all the
paper he needed from the stock in the house. The lower part of
her face looked scarred with age, thin and loose her lips shiv-
ered between the wrinkles, above the dark, deep-set eyes the
forehead trembled, controlled by arching muscles. And what,
pray, were Mr. Karsch's impressions of the way things were
done in this country?
He could only comment on the street scene; the people looked
much older to him: far fewer young people, compared to the
people at home.
Surely Mr. Karsch couldn't prove that statement! He would
hardly want to be so statistical about reality: would he? He
hadn't expected such hoarse voices to be so flexible, asking:
would he? She walked down the long side of the bare conference table, lifted her leather-colored old-woman's face toward
the scent that came drifting in from the garden through the
open terrace door; with drooping shoulders, energetic, she strode
up to Karsch, again stepped back; the sound of her words floated
toward him, lazily, from a distance, flooded gradually over him
from all directions. For a long time she stood in front of him,
not moving, leisurely balancing herself on firmly planted hands,
she craned her neck toward him, sideways, in an undertone she
warned him against the conditions of their contract. He would
not be speaking to her, to her as an individual: but to the people, through her, and the government of her country which
were intensely interested in a useful book about Achim. Did Mr.
Karsch agree to write it?
He could always give it a try.

She stared past him with narrowed worried eyes, fixed him with an expression of concern, recommended with a sigh that he take care, almost wanted to protect him. Explained to him, dry and brittle, that he was, perhaps, not the ideal author the publishing house had in mind. Her name was Mrs. Ammann.

What sort of author would she have preferred?

The person male or female whom Mrs. Ammann might have trusted implicitly to write the life story of a German bicycle champion had in common with Karsch precisely what did not count: he or she was nondescript. Sad or gay, casual or cautious, eager or hesitant, apt or clumsy, lyrical or down to earth: after a certain age these aptitudes and attitudes toward writing were unalterably part of a person, she granted that, provided that they did not interfere with the final result. Because the expected result went beyond the limits of the private person, as he was present here, in arrested motion. But motion should not be arrested. The writer (male or female) had to appear worthy of the confidence individuals and larger groups placed in him, and no matter what his personality he had to encourage everyone to talk, report and debate about pleasant as well as unpleasant aspects; quite particularly he should be able to communicate spontaneously effortlessly with the worker: even if he kept him from dinner or from enjoying his spare time or disturbed him at his work, even if he risked irritating him with indiscreet questions; a writer should not only be able to communicate with him, but should know all about him: his grievances, his habits, the significance of rude throat clearing and flippant retorts. And so forth. Mrs. Ammann spoke of the workers as though they all did the same things, as though they were a single being. She mentioned the teasing grin of anticipated friendship, recognition manifested by shoulder slapping, phone numbers known by heart, genuine concern communicated in the tone of voice and the wrinkles around the eyes, and other gestures exchanged between worker and writer, less from worker to writer,

91

more from writer to worker, they should live in the one thought of united progress toward an unquestioned goal. For what made this surprising intimacy possible? Right: as it was the task of the worker to produce the food and implements of daily life eight hours a day so that someday he himself could partake of these things in adequate proportion (in a friendly world with equal rights and progress for all, etc.), so it was the task of the writer to contribute his share toward the strengthening and widening of the chosen road toward the goal. This was a simile. Because, as each new building block toward a better future rose squarely from a foaming crest in the apparently unchanged vortex of everyday life, the growing honesty of the worker computing his output against the wages he received from the State, the individual's collaboration within the team for the purpose of increasing the manufacture of implements for housing, transportation, food and armed defense, the spontaneous effort beyond all expectation for the welfare of the community rather than the individual: this was what the writer had to recognize and snatch forcefully from the aforementioned vortex of everyday life, which was another simile. Instead of laziness and selfishness and irresponsibility, this should be held up to the workers: See! That is how it's done, if you want to do it differently, then it must be even more profitable to the State which is the first of its type in the history of mankind. She said. She described the sense of responsibility in the writer as he sets his words, words that may change the thinking and conduct of an unpredictable number of people in a negative direction while they ought to change it positively, as it had been laid down in the scriptures; she held out the sensation of pride and joy experienced in such work, the enthusiastic response of the reader to such encouragement (of the reader who reads this); the tangible improvement of the general conditions of life that would result and in which the writer participated, no longer excluded from the community the way he used to be, and as he still was in the West. That she was sure of. Karsch couldn't help imagining the presence of a tall broad-shouldered man in his thirties, sitting with a group of workers over a beer around a scrubbed table, talking with them about the reduced production of cars, speaking up about what they are trying to keep secret: dissension in the family, and sooner or later he turns it all into readily readable stories with an easy style and the useful moral: the State needs another car, stop dawdling; or: your wife isn't growing unattractive to spite you, but because she's worked hard and long for the common good, consequently, from now on, start treating her better. The writer's heartiness might be due to hard knocks or lucky breaks, he may be talking theory or experience, his brotherhood with the workers may be shrewd speculation or passionate conviction: the way he sat unflinchingly at that table, surrounded by trusting talking people, showing his sympathy with nods or earnest advice about things he knew more about: Karsch did not recognize himself in this likeness, nor did he think he could learn to be that way. But that was expected of him.

In that case he was out!

It wasn't quite that clear. After this and several other similar conversations with the purchasers of the manuscript, Karsch went to see Karin in Achim's apartment. Once and for all, let me give you a description of Achim's two rooms: they grew brighter in the thick-leaved early-evening light coming in through the windows that overlooked the skimpy park, waiting for him she had fallen asleep after her day's work, beside the silent telephone at the other end of which nobody would be asking for her, not Karsch either. He looked to see if the slip of paper with her name on it was still tacked to the door frame, let himself in and went to sit at the window until she woke up. Later they talked. All those afternoons have fused into one, in his memory, they'd invariably talk about Achim's life and whether it could be described after all. No reason to offer you each time meaningfully hesitant cigarettes, to emphasize certain expressions, with teacups moving in front of mute mouths: what would you gain if I told you how she breathed, about her pouts, about her much-photographed long lips (what does that mean. And even tears can have more than one meaning), will you

93

get more out of the glasslike brittleness of her voice when she is teasing, if I imitate it more than once; and each time the same colorful Slovakian blanket with fringes, and you know about her legs; softly breathing she'd lie as the hostess of the bright clean vacuum in which no one lived, that belonged to anyone who came in. Later they'd talk. She with her eyes closed for a while longer, motionless, still clutching her sleep.

—Did you sign: she said.

Karsch had signed.

—You could have sold me your car: she said.

—You'd have lent me money: he said.

—You didn't sign because of the monthly check you signed because you were curious about this also?

—Yes: said Karsch.

—Such a sweet old lady.

—Yes.

—I am not speaking with you as an individual, you are speaking with a representative of the State and its interest in new and useful writing.

—Precisely.

—And she has a very curt way of saying: No. No.

—Maybe.

—You needn't wriggle out of it.

—Why? She asks you: how are you? You know . . . (He tried to express what had struck him: the unselfishness of her old age. The admitted puzzlement over the change of one who could watch all this. His curiosity was aroused by the tougher lineaments of the girlish face that suddenly, startlingly, would remember itself, in the midst of the dissolving bulges of age, take on almost angular contours in the small plane between eyes and lips, the delicately tattered thin skin across cheeks and forehead moved in contrasting expressions. Where did it come from, the unshakable: No. I have to contradict you here.)

—Not this sweet old lady: said Karin.

—I know: repeated Karsch.

—Is it really true about the wine?

—Yes. She keeps a squat stemless glass between her folders and sips a bit at the end of her sentences, it adds to the weight of what she has said, she studies you across slow little gulps. This

94

stubby woman with her hands in her trouser pockets, the way she strides around her visitor, fixes him suddenly with radiant wrinkle eyes . . . I must say.

—With pouches under the eyes, wiser: because she is sixty?

—Of course. The unevenly gray hair.

—What's she holding against you?

—That my Achim is the same that he was in his childhood.

—I see.

—You understand that?

—I see what she means. Didn't I tell you . . . . : she said. Her sleepy skin lay on her face like a mask, soft tiny hairs sneaking toward the temples, he hadn't seen her for eight years, he didn't know her.

—He never planned to be a bicycle champion. (Then what did he want to be?)

—You surprise me: she said.

Until she stopped looking at her watch and got up with the blanket tucked around her, holding it up with one arm, and stumbled out of the room stepping on the trailing folds, rubbing her eyes, turning at the door with a soft laugh to catch the look of her spectator. Then he'd drive her back into town.

*Is this going to be after all the story of a
lady and two gentlemen?*

The gaps in these conversations are not meant to create pleasant suspense; they are due to the story. Because: if a man visits this country and understands nothing, everything must be considered separately, comparisons are impossible, he speaks the language but fails to communicate, the currency is different, and so is the government: and he is supposed to reunify himself with that one of these days; what does the visitor do? He asks questions, he says more than is written here. This has been selected because that was why he stayed, and he might have realized from the blanks even then what he didn't perceive: that he ought to try the unification.

95

Moreover, this is not a story.

Besides, Achim wasn't away, although his working year had started: although he had taken the mudguards off his bike and rode, doubled over the naked wheels, and got the wet mud of his country in his face, the racing teams of the city, the workers, the army crossed the laboring country from border to border, rushed more and more wildly around and across a mountain that dated from the planet's middle ages, from the peak they'd overlook the wide sweep of the sloping valley and human settlements huddling among trees and railroad crossings and chimney smoke rising from radiant roofs at noon and the serpentine road they'd be going to ride, with people clustered like grapes at the curves in the valley, and spanning it all the drifting cloud shadows predicting rain, but the next ascent led them all the way up to the highest turning point with the sheer cliff dropping off on one side, pitching with the violent cradling treading above swaying bikes they trampled up to the clouds themselves, that burst white and blue out of the entertaining sky of the low-pressure systems on their spring migration, the wind grew stronger and colder and pressed the less powerful riders back down the slope, as a reward the peak sent the mottled hunchbacks hurtling on their way down with the increasing weight of their accelerating descent, thin ribbons of rain anointed the tires, squished them along faster and faster and fanned up like flags, spraying with the increased torque of centrifugal force into the tauter, more distorted faces; finally they'd get back to the starting point, proving that one of them was first. Achim never got lost, not for a moment, the radio cars stayed on his track, transformed him into a report, an exciting image they fed into houses all over the country and with Achim the enthusiastic sound of the crowds who stood in the windy drizzle deputizing for you and me, waiting for those who had left to return, and screamed and yelled when they arrived, which made conversation on the stairs of this particular house and all over the city (and so forth), came out no different from those on the grandstands at the level of the wet slapping cloth panel with the word FINISH.

—Would you have thought of him being fourth?

—But mountains aren't Achim's specialty.

—Wait till he gets into shape, they're only just getting into shape.

—He doesn't always have to be first; I bet he's been helping others again.

—Sure, he's got to look out for his team.

—Yeah, field work, that's what it's called.

—How about a drink on that

and the next morning every newspaper would be flipped over to the Sunday sports page, hey did you see that, while the front pages would be staring at the floor and dropped together with the latest reports about the West German State plotting against theirs and further measures taken by the administrator in defense of their State's accomplishments, we'll get that soon enough, first let's see what he had to say, what did Achim say? He was never forgotten, he was remembered even in the emptiness of his high-rent apartment that was as public and interchangeable as a station platform or a lobby in a movie house or any place where people do not live, but meet and talk about all kinds of things, you know.

Well, all right. And what were Mrs. Ammann's objections to Karsch's Draft?

Yawning gracefully and leaning back with dignity into the fatigue of the early morning, she listened to how Karsch had failed to understand her.—And you didn't get any new ideas in the last three days? she asked.

Karsch had not followed what she had in mind.

Without another word she bent over the tape recorder on the table and, poking about blindly, tried to distribute the plugs among the appropriate inlets; finally, behind closed eyes, her head sinking between pensive elbows found the entrance to the loud-speaker and sent the left hand to the switch while the right one slowly climbed to her temple which it supported in an oblique pose of listening. Her radiant beckoning eyes

—the year the war ended for our country, you understand: she had switched on the tape of last week's conversation: constituted a turning point, a return. All that was beginning to take shape then must have had earlier origins, all those who have worked for our socialist cause since then must have been ready for it and capable, change is always possible but not exchange, whoever is with us must have been with us for many years, must have defended the socialist order already in the criminal days, and he was

for the brittle tough voice of a different life.

—Where were you up to nineteen forty-five: the tape was asking in Karsch's voice, recalling the other morning in the polished living room with the light filtering in through low fruit trees outside the window, the quiet between the widely separated houses, the wind knocking against the aristocratic French doors that opened into the garden with its preserved emptiness, the blank tape continued to grind thinly

and once again Mrs. Ammann's hand, reaching for her glass, stopped the co-operation of the muscles and twisted the movement into visible fear for the duration of one brief look out of the corner of one eye, although Karsch may have imagined it, he knows only what appeared to him, he thought he did not understand what she meant, but how she had arrived at whatever she meant; Achim was one of those. One of those tough-mouthed kids in uniform who would gang up and ambush single prisoners of war, beating them with clubs and rocks, with the enthusiasm of hunters they'd stalk the freight stations and drag the escapees they caught, and bound neatly according to the book, to the armed guard; earnest, fascinated, they'd crowd around the piece of lawn at the south end of the old city, the section in which he was now living, at that time he had watched a man being hanged, he has forgotten what the man had done, sold food on the black market maybe, or hung out a white flag, since the tanks were already driving through the streets, they hanged him, the tree still has its sturdy horizontal branch slightly above the height of a man, somebody climbed up, the noose had to be tied rather close to the branch, somebody ran to get a stool from the dairy store nearby, and people crowding all around, the soldiers who were bringing him had a hard time getting through, they had only ripped off his tie, he didn't understand what was going on, from somewhere far in back his wife kept screaming very high crazy screams, he was unable to climb up on the stool, they helped him up, young soldiers looking helpful, they always have such open faces, he slipped his head through the noose all by himself, when he tried to say something they hit him in the face with their fists rather than with their rifle butts, it looked actually tender the way they were hitting him with their fists, they pushed the stool out from under him and well yes he died, didn't take long to die, he kept growing longer and longer after the jerk, his feet pointed downward, his face was all colors, after he hung motionless he started to spin and they felt his pants to see if he had a hard on and spun him around some more, probably didn't have a hard on they weren't experts after all

One of those eager-to-learn but unable-to-learn kids who watched the hanging with their young, unmarked faces, future henchmen standing beside adults who accepted the execution in meek silence, like a spectacle, and at night stole the dead man's false teeth that had fallen out from underneath his feet, and the next night his black boots, his jacket was ripped, from trying to pull it off maybe, and all these potential and actual henchmen live among us today, lend you their newspaper with a friendly wink or offer you a light or their seat in the streetcar and are modest and courteous which is truly surprising from such a famous bicycle champion. They are famous and touch your arm with a smile when they overtake you in the street on a Sunday stroll and work at your side for the good of the respective State and sleep with you and are your friends and you can depend on all of them if you can depend on one, so let's make the assumption.

—You mean then: said Karsch: that a man who leads a different life today and proves himself useful to a new government should have preferably already at that point

fought a queasy feeling in the stomach, say, Günter

—Yes yes I can see just fine. Do you think they'll tie a sign between his hands as in the Hermann Löns book?

—Say, Günter.

All around the small square, rubble fields were dustily waving leaves and first blossoms over the spectators' heads. At a distance, behind a line of soldiers, five men with pneumatic drills were working on the second floor of a caved-in air-raid shelter; when they take the cover off, a colorless smell, thick and sweet with anguish, will inundate the square, that's the decomposition, I know all about it. The soldiers were looking over, curious about the people crowding the entrance of the park where the monument was.

—Achim, where you going! what's the matter!

I don't take orders from that guy. If Eckhart were here at least; this one's only an acquaintance. Everything around here is dead anyway, what are they hanging him for, we've seen all that in the movies.

—Got to go home.

What if he says coward now. He'll tell them at school.

—I'm going over to the other side. You see better from there. And ran off across the square, which the bombs had cleared, his briefcase slapping against his leg, his heart in his throat: what if he says coward now, yellow, can't even watch them hang a guy: a German boy knows no No. I can't picture it quite that way. He told me that differently.

—Let's take a different example: said Mrs. Ammann patiently. She was nodding under crankily raised eyebrows, that was not what she had meant; Karsch thought he was taking up her time. Blinded by unfamiliar considerations she groped for her glasses, didn't find them, busied herself. The house surrounded her with soft never-ending sounds of people at work. She leafed through files, leaned over, pulled out two of Karsch's pages, held them very close to her eyes reading with effort, tapped the paper with the back of her hand, it sounded hollow, she sent it sailing across the table. More amiably she asked: What about the sabotage?

But that is impossible!

No, wait a minute. Let's give it a try.

Because she was amenable, the suggestions came from her, she was prepared for a constructive two-hour conversation, Karsch hadn't said anything but No and I don't understand. What was it she was up to?

—What you tell us about Achim's life toward the end of the war: she said: is not enough. It's not instructive. Think of all the people who'll read this book and believe it and change their lives to model them after Achim's.

—All right then: said Karsch. It had not occurred to him (was he supposed to rectify other people's memories). So what about the searching of the house?

This like everything else was as Achim saw, remembered, told it. Who was Achim in those days, how much did he know, how much could he understand? Didn't that still make him one of those?

—I see: said Karsch: you mean Achim's father could have learned some lesson and that a potential reader might share it with him

neat rows of corpses in the summery park outside the smoking central station, feet quiet or twisted lined up at equal distance from the street in the healthy grass, some faces recognizable. The wife is not among them. She did sleep like that, softly curved on one side, but she did not have a dress like that. Doesn't have, perhaps she was late, Oh no she wasn't late, we wanted to meet the boy here after school, lunch, stroll, birthday, the smell of it all, I hope she died right away, but I'm not even sure she's dead, here, give me a hand. If we hadn't moved back to the city, if I hadn't wanted to better my position. No. This was my right. To blame is

don't know. They couldn't have done it without planes. They couldn't have done it without war.

I don't know.

After which one has to mention one hand sliding off the drawing board, a mindless stare out at the blocked yard with the guards, trying to remember forgotten explanations with absent eyes. The sudden shock of being alone among softly grating

drawing machines and unrecognizably bent backs and endlessly
moving arms. What is a face, can one depend on its expression.
What do they want, what do I want. What does it mean to be
talkative, is one talkative so as not to take sides, what fills or
should fill a pause between two sentences. He had lost touch
with his comrades, he had wanted to lose touch, in this place he
didn't know anybody. They would have advised against it. He
had to do it by himself. Hesitation, doubt: he doesn't know
enough, he hasn't been to the technological institute. He knows
how to draw an air hole by himself or a lock, will he know where
to hide a mistake. I don't want them to catch me. Got to make
a man out of that boy. Can't implicate anybody, this is my business, just wait. If I could talk to someone. Does one launching
less make any difference? Do six months make a difference?
—Do you have a garden plot too, comes in handy on the side?
—No.
The meticulous stitches make the old rip stand out on the sleeve
of the smock. They say the whole north section was laid flat
last night, not a house left standing. How would she have looked
as a corpse.
Until he succeeds in curbing his fear. Changing a blueprint
from identical to similar is a technical problem for a draftsman.
Who is the next man to get the sheet, who is going to check it,
who will sign it? When are the sheets collected. An error of one
cubic millimeter has got to be intentional, who'd think that of
me.
He becomes sociable again, lets himself be drawn into conversations. Say what you please. You can't tell me. After the concealed mistake has been stamped and sent out, he puts his house
in order. He is able to touch his wife's clothes without shock. A
whole closet full of clothes. The white one with the blue flowers is missing.
Of course the technical part of the sabotage must be told with
more detail, I'll ask someone who knows.
—Yes. This way it's still too private: said Mrs. Ammann. Hands
in her trouser pockets she let herself slide off the chair into
standing position, doubled over with eagerness she marched
along the shelves filled with the books she had nursed up to now.
She stopped, turned her head over an immobile back, contem-

plated Karsch crankily. She stepped swiftly behind her desk, with pensive unseeing eyes placed a glass in front of Karsch and poured him some wine, turned away, walked some more, while Karsch wondered about the looks of her private room in which she conceived her public thoughts, he imagined a dark glossy wooden floor and old brown furniture with the sun slanting in through the window, her past preserved in this room, he wondered what sort of people came to see her, what kind of pictures she hung on her walls, how did she arrive at her opinions? Accidentally she bumped into the back of Karsch's chair, grabbed at it as though she were unsteady; leaned over him and confirmed almost tonelessly, helplessly: Too private. Too private; strict and delicate her ambiguous head was held together by the trust she represented

What are you trying to say by too private?

(her hoarse articulate voice chafing in the overworked throat. And still less explicable the cool forenoon that she'd never be able to improve no matter how long she lived, was the truth about a bicycle champion a purpose of her life); yes. She meant: that was still no more than Achim's father's truth: seen through the father's eyes, which didn't see enough. That was still not enough.
She had the other truth in mind, and Karsch's voice on the tape that was running again, we don't have it, I'm repeating approximately from memory. First the crackling of the overloaded switch and then Karsch with inquiries: what you are trying to say is:
the association for the deterioration of life in Germany
—why don't you call them: the German fascists who, in the pay and service of capitalism
it (they: take your pick) demanded enthusiastic approval of their acts and got it readily enough; one should remember the ardent clusters of German women in the stations of small Saxon towns during the arrested noon hour when the pyroma-

niac came passing through on his special train; Achim's mother standing among the sobbing or quietly ecstatic women, like them she had come to see the demented leader, remote as on the screen he was leaning at a window, over imperceptibly gliding wheels, as slowly and earnestly as they he raised his hand to the breathless assembly of childbearers; who died in communion with their sons, or in the solitude of their collapsing cellars, and couldn't foresee that they would, any more than they had known about the ovens for the cremation of victims and enemies, they didn't know, they clung to him as life grew worse and more distorted every day, and denounced anyone who damaged a machine or wrote on walls or gave a bed and breakfast to unknown persons and tried to change reality, or at least opinions about reality.

—That deserves more than a relative clause.

—And in what proportion did the venerating sobbing or grouchily approving masses stand to the others? To those who turned grenades into duds and made unused bombers vulnerable to the pull of gravity of the earth, who adopted the persecuted as relatives, right under the nose of the police, who sat huddled under blankets listening to foreign radio stations and passed the news on to people with nothing in back of them but clubs and rifles and the understanding of what Germany should eventually look like? they had a joint program, one depended on the other; but what about the others, those who lent support to the corruption, who supplied the criminals with bread and tools Made in Germany for their murdering and burning, aren't they the ones who belong in the main clause? Few were like this stocky medium-sized man, who lacked particular characteristics, who had a hard but not a noticeable face, and wore the same kind of clothes as the others and couldn't be distinguished from the others and didn't know how many there were of them and felt all alone hiding in the silence, he had lost touch after they moved back to the city, he wasn't a comrade any more, he stood alone. Achim's father arrived at the office, a taciturn capable worker, readily embarrassed at first. After a couple of months his new colleagues took a liking to him and came to see him in his house and in an emergency might have trusted his round stubborn skull and unpracticed oblique smile; but they'd speak unambiguously about summer houses in Brandenburg and ambiguously about the end of the war, and nobody mentioned emergency cases: weren't there any? or because he was not educated? No conversation stopped abruptly when he walked up to a group, but none started either. It's not because they're educated, I just can't talk to them. He remembered conversations at his old job (that had established an order: I know where I belong): on the first of May the parade moved through the streets whose grayness was not relieved by the few swastika flags in the windows but by lots of feather beds hung out for airing, you don't expect a swastika on red feather beds spread out in the windows, shining, one after the other, on the feast day, he didn't belong here, in the small development of better one-family houses one didn't put beds out to air. (Although his was the smallest of the flags, but didn't he have a reputation for thrift.) There might be a description of how he went on a quick visit to the small town on a Sunday two years later, and saw a freshly sealed-up door and his lonely fear on the ride back, sitting in the local train amid weekend travelers and engaged couples: that guy had been doing something, can a man do that kind of thing alone, was it worth it, worth one's life? It does not work out anyway. His wife had been afraid of the foreign radio station identifications, somebody got arrested for that a couple of days ago, think of the children, don't we want to live in peace. For your sake.

He is said to have disapproved of such a decision, but if he actually reached it, it must have been after his wife and daughter disappeared: I mustn't let them take everything away from me; the sabotage is possible, there is proof that they searched the house, and there is also the man who came to the garden gate and whom the boy sent away: my father has no friends here. Where do you come from?

—Snappy kid you've got. Is he just acting that way?

—Well, I thought: if I tell him. He may let something slip.

—Man, he's already fourteen.

—All right, what do you need?

—A blank travel permit.

—For yourself?

—Go on, keep on asking questions. For the party, you dope.

—Yeah sure, anybody can say that.

—You see.

—Let's go somewhere else.

It might have happened that way; some harmless street corner, two men who happen to meet over a beer. Or dropping a
complete man's suit off at the baggage claims desk in the central station, or pamphlets in coat pockets, subterranean space
suddenly beneath the daily routine, prudent digging in the garden at night. And why not an overnight visitor. Fearlessly talkative he is running back and forth in the kitchen, puts a cloth on
the table, tries to cut the bread in even slices. Puts his jacket
back on to eat. Would you like another blanket. The visitor will
leave with the memory of a grumpy host and a sense of security.
The dim friendly lamplight unites the kitchen against the
blacked-out night. The house feels lived in again.

—I've sent the boy to relatives in Thuringia. Can't I work with
you now? The Americans are already across the border.

Something like that, and only six months before the American
troops marched in, and for personal (private) reasons: to feel
decent again, to live a useful life. Something like that? Is that
what you are aiming at?

—Please understand: said Mrs. Ammann withdrawing. At this
point they were strolling about the garden beside the quiet sidewalk, Karsch felt her elbow small and fragile in her sleeve when
he helped her step over the jutting stair. Her eagerness made
her look downhearted. Her concern had the vehemence of older
relatives worrying about grandchildren who must be kept from
making the same mistakes. She had never gone to watch a bicycle race. —Please understand: she said: In your final draft you
must not accuse him of behaving like a Social Democrat at a
time the Communist Party was already selecting the future mayors; he is still alive. His mistakes are not important, only the
things that link him to our new era.

—But that's not at all what I intended: said Karsch. Don't you
like the Social Democrats?

And so forth.

Any comments from Achim's father?

Karin says she took the streetcar out one afternoon. From the stop you walk past the old firehouse across the tree-darkened playground that opens toward the semicircle of the development. Wire mesh lies rusting between the low plants in the gardens, doors hang lopsided by their hinges, quite a few houses have gangrenous spots and holes in the stucco. They are rented houses. The house of Achim's father among them, you recognize it by its lawn running right up to the pebble path, since he set the new wooden fence back along its entire length. The small square window under the roof was Achim's window once, it has no curtains. The frugality of bed and table near the window and slanting walls covered with all the trophies of Achim's early years are known from the photos that sports magazines reprint year after year, they're also in the books about Achim's rise to success, it has all been described as an example of the difficult life in the years after the war, and groups of the State youth organization as well as classes of school children come to see it. The tile just in front of the stairs is loose, you can lift it with the toe of your shoe, that's where you will find the key, because there is only one left. But Achim couldn't come here. She unlocked the door and walked through the foyer, through the kitchen out into the spacious garden behind the house hidden from the neighbors by thick bushes all along the fence. She waited in a deck chair under a blanket. The weather was hasty with wind, occasional cloud strands fluttered in the sunlight. The apple trees are twenty years old now, the leaves are almost as large as they will be until autumn. But the place where Achim's mother used to plant vegetables is now a lawn. With only a few flowers at the rear edge to conceal the shed. In which they lived after the surrender, because their house was full of refugees. Later, the city administration moved them out and offered Achim the house in appreciation, but Achim wanted his father to have it. He lives in one room with what is left of the furniture with which they had moved in at the time. In the evening he sits in the garden or at the kitchen window without much to do. He doesn't care for bicycle races: he says: They are over my head, take too much figuring.

When she woke up he was standing next to her chair; he had just put a second blanket over her, his arms were still spread out. You always sleep so much: he said with a tone of regret: Almost like Achim . . . He looks narrow in the shoulders. His face has grown more subdued, his only occupation seems to be thinking all the time, but when you ask him, his answer is slow and vague, —Oh . . . : he'll say, he wasn't thinking of anything. With an awkward smile he sat down by her feet and muttered about the wind, it'll make you catch something. He didn't look at her, leaned forward, his hands between his knees, occasionally he looked at her obliquely. He had to get used to her.

So she tells him: she knows someone who wants to write a book about Achim. You know he speaks just like Achim when he wants to make a point, the same high-pitched aloof tone. —Whatever for? he says.

She explains to him: he's a West German, reunification for two people, etc. Well, Karsch?

—Go on: said Karsch.

Achim's father was completely relaxed: Karsch. Yes, I know him. What's he want to know?

What actually happened when they searched the house.

—I see: he said, not at all disturbed.

As can be surmised their conversation was accompanied by various expressive movements and took place in a garden well into the harsher evening; I might say something about her chair. A deck chair, Achim's father had built it himself; the sturdy frame was adjustable, by means of a crossbar it could be raised or lowered, spreading the sailcloth either in a flat or a tight curve. He sat on the stiff footrest, raised her by lifting the sailcloth, saying: I see, but does his bending over her and busying himself indicate hesitation and an effort to divert her, or is it gratuitous after all and need not be mentioned?

He did not pause, he fitted the bar into the notches and made sure she wasn't less comfortable than before (her neck rearranged against the pillow). He looked uneasy, lifting her shoulders, reaching for her arm, letting go again, finally he made up his mind. But he didn't look unhappy. Who knows what he was thinking.

—It won't tell you anything: he said. —Everybody in the office had his house searched. The engine exploded on its first test, nobody got hurt though. All the things you have to consider. But six months' work was shot. You'll only forget it if I explain it to you, I'll jot it down for him if he can use it. The mistake had been built in secretly, but after the explosion they all knew where it could be inserted. Once, I had the idea myself. But it took two to carry it out. The second man had to have access to official channels. Besides, I didn't know enough. What's the use, if they catch you in the end. Two other men did it. I only knew one of them, he got hanged. The other one was from Berlin, went to see his wife every weekend, a tall guy with reddish-blond hair, dry face, narrow earnest eyes I mean. A college graduate. Nice guy. Of course he'd started in on this as soon as all that Hitler crap got going, I've thought about it for a long time: what goes on in a head like that, to be so sure right away. We sure were right, too; but with a guy like that I'd have started something myself. It needn't have paid off at all cost. But I was sitting there all alone, don't you see! I'd listen to the foreign stations and send money to people whose husbands had disappeared, twice I did that, and I let someone stay overnight when it was safe. The time the boy was away in Thuringia: Achim. I behaved like most people: just with good intentions. You can't count that I didn't give a damn for a while. Now it's only those others who get talked about. But that guy wasn't stuck up you know, even though I was one of the dopes. He talked to me a couple of times, promised to give me stuff to read, but then they caught him. Reported, by his brother. There are families like that, but can you understand it? They condemned him to death, but before they executed him, they kept him working in jail, we'd still get his blueprints, he'd no longer sign them, but I'd recognize his writing. For weeks I still had to transfer his writing which was condemned to death, and one day it was missing. You know. By then it was too late, the city was done for, the Americans were at the Rhine. Such an intelligent considerate handwriting. And everything had become useless. Afterward I went to where his family used to live. I wanted to see the kind of wife a man like that has, but I couldn't find her.

That's about what he said. Later that night they sat in Mrs. Liebenreuth's kitchen so as not to talk her out of her fragile sleep.

Karsch stood close to the stove, beside the moaning kettle, Karin was softly rapidly pacing up and down among the scratched-up furniture, talking bewildered into space: paying hardly any attention to Karsch, a sidelong glance, a lifting of the head, finally she asked as if indifferently: Well what did you decide.

—I'm not sure yet: said Karsch.

—Listen: she said, she was standing behind him, she pushed him under the light, he could see her. She was narrowing her eyes which he knew to be a sign of anger, she was calm.

—I'll give you the money, you return the advance, forget the whole business and drive home.

—Have I stayed long enough? asked Karsch.

—Aw come on. Make up your mind. Which version do you want to hand in!

—Sh. Don't scream at me. I don't know. You admit he'd become quite attached to that red guy with the tough skin.

—You haven't changed a bit. Your fairness, what good is it? to whom?

—Quiet.

—I'm sorry. She had come back from Achim's father around midnight, she had thrown pebbles at Karsch's window to wake him. When coffee was ready they sat facing each other across the table, their arms moved on the oilcloth, they talked the night away. The open windows shuddered. Seen from the outside: seen from outside, the light carved one narrow cell, against the countless unseeing glass eyes of the courtyard that was sleeping, withdrawn, under the wandering clouds of the night.

How come he knew Karsch?

—By sight: he said. Because, almost every night, he's been sitting in that crummy bar at the corner, questioning everybody about Achim. They don't tell him much. They all think he wants to talk politics.

That was during supper at the open kitchen window. The lamp hung low in the middle of the room so that their hands and plates were in the light, but they saw each other's faces in the hazy mixture of lamp shadow and somewhat brighter evening sky. Blackish-blue clouds were slowly drifting westward, obscuring the spot where the sun had set. An occasional motor sound in the driveway would break the soft lull of conversations at garden fences and yellow-glowing windows and the odor of new leaves all around the development. Often they'd look out the window. He tried to serve her. He'd treat her with an appearance of nagging; he talked with relish and presented a grave face if she happened to look up. Unexpectedly he said: Why don't you come more often.

—It's just because he lives alone: she said: Think of all the girls who passed through the room in the attic in those days, and he always (says Achim) showed such forced gaiety at breakfast, none of them would care to remember. He doesn't believe in daughters-in-law. He wouldn't want me. I've been a worker all my life (he says), you're not for us.

—Is the wardrobe still in the room next door? with Achim's mother's clothes.

—No. They've all been sold on the black market. The dresses first, then the wardrobe. And her dresser. The one she had wanted all her life. Now he rents the room out. Ever since the State cleared the house for him.

All this has to be seen together with his bent-over, quiet after-work pose, there are long silences, his hair is almost white, clipped close to the head, his hands are broad and short, he gives an impression of stubbornness, of tenderness occasionally, would they have elected him for mayor fifteen years ago? One can't know anyone by sight.

She had asked him about that too.—You know, he moves his mouth a lot. And gives you a fixed friendly look, with hard slow-moving lips; as though he had a joke in store for you or knew more than he was saying. That's how he looked at me, and I at him, politely: no other reaction necessary. He thought for a while how well he knew me, knew what I'd say and later do.

—Don't tell anybody: he said with a smile. He got up, pulled the lamp by a string knotted to the cord over the kitchen table, hooked the noose into one of the window latches and began searching through the papers he kept in one of the sideboard

111

drawers. He peered closely at each piece, rubbed his eyebrows, stood for a long while with one hand to the back of his head kneading the grayish-white cropped hair with his hard fingers. His sideboard and stove stood about him as though they didn't belong to him.

—That's how I know him: he said and pushed a batch of type-written sheets toward her with the edge of his hand after he'd once more sat down across from her. Hunched on his elbows he watched her, moved his lips with satisfaction, drank from the beer bottle without taking his eyes off his visitor. He laughed soundlessly with a jerking of the throat, the mouth formed angular pleats at her question: Where did you get that!

—What was it? asked Karsch.

—What was supposed to be in the paper. Your Meeting With Achim.

But not the old-fashioned type face of the copy bureau on the hard fibrous paper that Karsch had put into the mailbox of the city daily for the people and the party. Karin remembered a typing error at the end of a line that had been corrected in this copy in the middle of a line and in more modern type, on nice solid onionskin, the kind Karsch would have liked to buy and couldn't get here.

—Do you realize that it has been copied? she asked; she says she explained it to the old man with nodding head and emphatic voice, but he only swallowed amusedly that his surprise had come off, and growling out of the corner of his mouth he confirmed: Possibly.

And Karsch repeated with equal satisfaction: Possibly.

She very nearly raised her hands but couldn't help laughing: Don't you fall for that!

But she didn't answer his question until Karsch decided to write a new version of Achim's life before the war; if he had decided to leave she would have deprived him of the information that the student (who had rented the room from Achim's father) had brought this crumpled copy home two days ago: I had told them where I lived, the other day, so they gave me this, would you care to read it?

And Karsch did fall for the interest that several, though not clearly perceptible, persons were taking in a still unwritten book about Achim; he imagined the typewriter on which his text

112

had been copied before a hand put it back into Mr. Fleisg's mail basket; he thought about the pens and pencils with which equally unknown persons had collaborated on his description of Achim's life: inviting him in the margin and between the lines to bring out the hysteria of mass gatherings a little more clearly, they reproached him for neglecting the link between sports and politics, and accused his style of being too roundabout, no need for all that sophistication, he should be more down to earth: how many among the city's eight hundred thousand inhabitants had been reading this, possibly a (or several) student of mathematics, hands on the keys of a typewriter, shouting sports fans maybe, stampeding the stadiums, potential readers from different professions who suggested that he give it another try although their comments had only very accidentally fallen into his hands and he had no idea with what intentions all these persons, who were unknown to him, passed such inconsequential texts on to each other and although the annotations had been carefully erased until halfway down the second page and then left: as though some interruption or change of mind had occured at that point.

—And next?

Next we went to the bar at the streetcar stop and had drinks until eleven. He was in excellent spirits. Told me all sorts of stories. No need to tell Achim. Then I left finally, he stood chewing his lips, closed the door for me, thought some more and when the streetcar pulled out he looked up and said with those stiff lines around the mouth (I can't imitate it for you, I'd have to know what it expresses to imitate it): Why don't you bring him along.

Is this your idea of suspense?

There was no suspense. Although there might have been the exciting sight of a clean fingertip with a clean round nail pressing Mrs. Liebenreuth's bell thus closing the open electric circuit and causing a small hammer on the other side to hit an isolated suspended bell at regular intervals: the well-known racket rings through the dark corridor, empty as yet between closed doors, and stops as decisively as it began. In the intensified silence one hears the turning of doorknobs and hinges, light shuffling steps become distinct, the bolt of the front door window grinds, Mrs. Liebenreuth's sleepy face appears behind the artfully wrought iron grille. It is afternoon, she likes to take a nap after lunch. She is tiny, she has to raise her arm very high to unlatch the window, her delicately shrunken head appears at the bottom edge of the hatch. Meeting the eyes of two gentlemen of medium age who keep their hands in their pockets and who ask for Mr. Karsch without explanation or conciliatory airs. They show urgency, she doesn't know them. Mr. Karsch's name isn't on the door. He didn't tell her he was expecting visitors, he isn't expecting anybody. The two gentlemen peer through the grille over her head, to them she is only in charge of opening doors.

—I'll see if he is in: she replies curtly, she is an old woman, she has been disturbed in her nap. She pushes the window so hard that it slams and bolts it. With unexpected (unseen) nimbleness she hastens to the end of the corridor, knocks inaudibly at her tenant's door, soundlessly turns the knob, enters hurriedly. Mr. Karsch is lying in his chair with his feet on the sill of the open window, and in this position is reading the fat book about bicycle racing that she had noticed yesterday as she was dusting his room. She knows what he is busy with, he's asked her what she thinks about promoting sports with the unsuspecting taxpayers' money, he wants to write it down, she does not think well of it. He does not hear her come in.

—Mr. Karsch! she says therefore. —Mr. Karsch!

Before he can turn around she surprises him with the whispered explanation: that the moment had come. Now they're here. Two strange gentlemen at the door, she'll tell them he isn't in, meanwhile he can go to her room and keep quiet. It was the same way when they came for the student next door. I knew it was going to happen, with that kind of a book.

At this point the spectacle has to be interrupted. Because some time earlier Karsch had asked his landlady: and what had he done, this student next door?

—That was a year ago, it was: said Mrs. Liebenreuth. When the breakfast ceremony turned into a conversation, she'd cradle the tray on one bent arm to have the other hand free for demonstration and emphasis; if Karsch relieved her of the tray, she'd feel dismissed. —He passed West German newspapers around and had friends come in for discussion. It was all written up in the *People's Paper*. There'll be no eggs until tomorrow.

Karsch had not passed on any West German newspapers. The administrator's emissaries couldn't come for him, what he was doing was out in the open and whatever the government did not like about it, it tried to talk him out of once every two weeks. He did not touch the life of the State, he hardly knew anybody except Achim.

On the other hand: why shouldn't Karsch invite the two visiting gentlemen in? They'll nod, a trifle disconcerted after the long wait, and follow each other down the corridor. The last one takes the door out of Mrs. Liebenreuth's hand and closes it; she is quite worried, stands outside, her hands on the doorknob and one ear close to the crack; one of the gentlemen remains standing approximately at that very spot on the other side of the door, inside the room, watching the other one.

Who cautiously sneaks up to the desk and looks searchingly about.

—Well? he says. Where is it?

Karsch stands by, hands in his pockets, he shrugs and says: Sorry. There isn't anything. The one at the door shakes his head. He is annoyed. —You must have something: he says coaxingly.

But Karsch said: No: nothing. Sometimes he really hadn't written anything new. He remembers a whole week of lying on Mrs. Liebenreuth's couch five hours a day, studiously engrossed in thought about his four different versions of Achim's life before the war; there's no way of showing that.

The one at the desk leans on the edges, crosses his arms, murmurs in disbelief: Two weeks. And nothing.

The one at the door might express his agreement with a disappointed face or perhaps regret. But to make this scene probable, the awkward-mannered one ought to have been Mr. Fleisg and the other one somebody on the editorial staff of the Publishing House for New Writing, who were on their appointed rounds to check whether their contracted authors were doing something in exchange for their advances, on which they were living, and if a discouraged author once in a while could not present the emissaries with a stack of manuscript of justifiably expected girth, they were supposed to say to him something like: Well now, dear fellow, what's wrong? Would it help you to discuss it with us? But that wasn't what it was either, because Karsch had objected to the customary clause in the contract and consequently it had been deleted. The truth is only this: one day two close-mouthed persons asked for Karsch, whereupon Mrs. Liebenreuth slammed the window shut and said her tenant was not at home just now (or almost); but even if this were the case, could we say more than that they came and nothing else? And would Mrs. Liebenreuth's nervousness make for suspense?

Also, one could give a breathtaking description of the so-called racing scene: Achim fell right at the beginning after the first few miles, because paper streamers which cheering children had thrown on the road had blocked his rear wheel and gear shift, he fell over to the right, very hard. He had no visible wounds except that the gravel chafed into his thighs, the scabbing breaks open again and again, there was no time for proper bandaging; his bones must hurt severely, since he wasn't able to pull out in front, he's let himself drift somewhere to the middle and doesn't seem to care. The radio reporters are squatting in the roof hatches of their transmitter cars, the mike at their mouths and field glasses before the eyes, and describe to their distant audience how Achim looks with words like tenacious and moral and concentration or something to that effect, the children that have been left behind stand dejected about the loud-speaker which emits reproachful sounds, again and again the high-powered lenses of the telecameras zoom to pluck Achim's lowered head from among other lowered heads, he doesn't care, the normal lenses again show the view of the dusty sun-flecked road, in the distance the vanguard is climbing the slope like insects chained to automatic clockwork, suddenly, now! the turned-up brim of a cap appears at the lower edge of the image, followed by a neck, by a hunched-over back that grows smaller and smaller as it slides to the right of the screen, the back has Achim's number on it, it is Achim, immediately the front of the pack perks up, pedals after him, keeps straining forward with determined jolts, they have almost caught up with him, are all herded next to his rear wheel, while two of Achim's team manage to squeeze through, unnoticed, on the left, Achim is closed in, only now they notice the two that got away, but they're already too far ahead to be intercepted; with his last ounce of strength Achim has duped the pursuers, he still had that much in him, now he lets himself fall back, doubled over, apathetic, he rides in the center of the track, tenacious, moral, concentrated, or something to that effect, he doesn't seem to care. But his tired knowing smile in response to the delirious calls from the accompanying cars will become legendary and send shivers down people's spines: he didn't think about himself, the others will win for him as well as for themselves, we belong together all of us. Well.

One spring he rode in twenty races with varying glory for the winner, Achim only had to be along. The incidents kept repeating themselves: Predictably someone always would be first, whoever dropped back was obliged to help the others, it was a method described in the manuals and thoroughly drilled into each beginner. Not they but Achim would remain the exemplar: that is the truth; does it make for suspense?

To depict absorbingly the day of an actress: Karin's juicy curses under the hands of the masseuse, Karin entering the beauty shop, received by three white-smocked delegates, Karin in the whirlpool of city gossip, cranky and talented on rehearsal stage, a door opens all the way in back of the dark theater, frames the silhouette of a young man who stands there for a while with his hands in his pockets, and doesn't come all the way in, stands watching what goes on on stage; but when Karin, propped on one hand, swings down from the ramp to the floor and becomes invisible among the twilit chairs next to the director, the young man pushes himself off by the shoulders, concealed now by the slamming door: Was that Achim? Was it the one with the car from the West? Or the one who keeps sending her flowers? Who walks off through the corridors of the theater, through a basement exit, across the walled-in courtyard on clicking heels? Who's seen him? Shall we go after him? The promising young actress whose career we've been following for a number of years in approving newspaper reports has just returned from shooting a film in Romania: at an informal get-together in the restaurant at the central station we inquired about her future plans. Asked for her reaction to the recent standard-setting injunctions of the administrator, she commented: that she most certainly shared the opinion of all decent people. Our best wishes accompany her, vanishing she waves from her cab. The intensity of her performance as Emilia Galotti (that left us with such an unforgettable impression) permits the assumption: that, through personal experience of the new way of life in our unique State, she has much matured since last year and become what she is now. But to get back to our subject: let us choose from the possibilities, provided they still exist, one race around an oval track with both start and finish line at the grandstand, excited spectators on rows of wooden benches under the awning or behind ropes, watching what fills their Sunday, Achim is leading, ever since the fourteenth lap Achim has been leading. As the leaders and the main pack disappear around the north bend and the honorable passage of the stragglers becomes mixed with radio reports about the bitter competition on the opposing straightaway, the crests of encouraging shouts subside, that's a simile: the calm spreads, the ocean grows placid, reduced to the regular splashing of private conversations, look, down there, to the right, next to the race managers. The one in the blue suit. That's Achim's girl. That's the one he sleeps with. Oh no, that's over, now she's with the one who's writing a book about Achim, a guy from the West. Is he her boy friend now? Some life these people lead, let me tell you! Tirelessly unified voices, toppling wave, repeated simile surge over the renewed arrival of the three leading cyclists, one obliquely behind the other they slide across retinas and running films, in alternating upsurges roaring voice masses await the field, that packed close together drifts swirls up and drives through the second-highest yelling wavecrest, only the microphones at the guardrail register the swishing of the tires over the fluted cement and hurried gasps and low calls of the breathlessly moving cyclists. Every time but especially during what is called The Struggle for Position Has Begun, as he approaches the grandstand Achim snatches a sidelong glance up at the glass cabin of the race managers and in front of it mirrored by it Karin's long serious face above a radiant blue collar, perhaps also Karsch's comradely hand-raising hammers against the pain from the combustion of lactic acid that begins to boil in the vessels of an exhausted body as its ability to absorb oxygen declines; did you see how he always looks up to where she's sitting? that's what keeps him going, he's got to keep going, it's she who ought to get that wreath around her neck. Look how pleased he is.

For Karin, bicycle racing was Achim's profession, she didn't feel like watching him work every time, she didn't visit grandstands. It held no suspense, but then you weren't promised that it would.

Granted. How did Achim grow up?

Achim didn't come back from Thuringia for another year and a half. In the meantime his father had tried to live with the widow of one of his colleagues, whom he had kept from committing suicide. They separated shortly after the armistice, because he didn't feel up to fighting the authorities for his right to live in the house and she couldn't stand the wretched life in the unheated garden shed, now that there was no longer a war on. Achim didn't know about this.

In the meantime he lived in Thuringia with his mother's parents. The village lay widely spaced out within a deeply notched valley that was surrounded by rising tiers of pines on all sides; you'd have to lean your head back to see the sky. His grandparents lived in one of the ornately gabled frame houses at the humped market place. He slept in the room under the eaves, in the morning he'd see the meager land climb up toward the snow or toward the chilly sunrise. They loved him very much because of his resemblances to their lost daughter. The grandfather was withered and stubborn, his temper would flare and he'd drink the more his fellow citizens avoided him. He had accepted the position of mayor as an honor, brooded a great deal on the mistrust which the party regulations brought on him. He was thought to be cruel since he never deviated from the printed word; a friendly hello he had no longer expected loosed tears in his voice. He was not frightened only confused when the Americans had him beaten without animosity and sent him off to a camp for State criminals; bitter, completely at a loss, he cursed and blessed the liquidated government, shouting against the motor noise of the agile truck that was speeding him away from the lovely valley. It was the first time he was leaving the vicinity of his village. He died in the camp. He hadn't understood much.

The grandmother taught Achim. Short and chubby in colorful skirts she ran through house and stable with brief rapid steps and worked for their meals in the low narrow rooms which she hadn't time to use. She had a happy disposition. The contour of her temples reminded him of his mother. At the third move Achim found no friends, at fifteen he refused to take orders and showed contempt for the boredom of village life; he was afraid that he might have to live there forever. She cured him of his stubbornness with apples on his pillow, but she could also slap and make it hurt. Still, there is nothing like the tender weight of her hand stroking his hair. If the grandfather shouted at Achim she'd watch and make an intricate face and nudge Achim in the ribs, as though she were a man. She'd listen to the grandfather's speeches with frowns and pouts and raised eyebrows, her face seemed pointed with mockery. She didn't grieve over her husband. She sent Achim with a food basket to the wife of the new mayor whom the Americans had found in the camp for enemies of the State. He had to mount the town hall steps very very slowly. He'd clutch his chest, and his face shrank. —That's no way for a mayor to look: she said, and sent him eggs and sausages. The foyer smelled of her coats with their long-lived velvet collars.

The Americans didn't stay long and kept to themselves; they'd be friendly only to children. Their military salutes were remarkably casual and the different vehicles were interesting, like all the things that could explain their victory. They'd squat on their helmets outside the elementary school, friendly as the early-summer brightness, they'd laugh about the Germans who'd walk past; I can't tell more than what Achim said. They didn't stay long enough for him to learn to distinguish between their insignia: the boys would guess at it according to the number of wrist watches some of the soldiers would be wearing all the way up to their elbows. Whatever they'd do in front of spectators they'd explain to them. How many Jews did you kill? Gesture. Jeep: a rounded finger, two fists quickly moving one against the other. They'd not always give you something in exchange for party buttons or alcohol; one guy grabbed the bottle out of Achim's hand, held it to his lips, hesitated, said invitingly: Wine.

—Wine: said Achim. Jeep. Nazis. You dirty little brat.

Later, under the Soviet occupation, abortions were permitted only when the pregnant woman predated the time of the conception to the American period.

The Red Army entered the village on horse carts. Ten, fifteen soldiers lying on top of their bulky baggage, in dirty sweaty uniforms. They even have a different alphabet. Before and behind the columns, their officers came riding in sleek jackets, stiff necks held up by high collars, they'd look straight ahead from under impeccable caps. The star of the new power in golden embroidery on bottle-green saddle cloth. Some of the soldiers would cycle alongside their tired horses, doing loops and circles around a cart or a whole formation, highly delighted with the steering potential of their conveyance and the swaying of the unpracticed riders. But before their entry into the village they climbed back up on their carts; singing and curious and trustingly they rolled in. One of them had an accordion. They had stopped in the market place and jumped from their wagons when a latecomer rode past the neat officers and German spectators on a bicycle, describing gay little circles on the cobblestones, from time to time he raised a hand and shouted something that sounded like a greeting to this friendly little village and its inhabitants and laughed excessively as the front wheel began stubbornly to sway. Maybe someone gave him a push. When Achim ran up to the group standing around the fallen bicycle, its rider still lay flat on his back, carefully feeling his elbow. He smiled at the lanky boy with the shy scared face who had been running too fast to stop, had run right through the

group of watchers, came to a halt only in front of the soldier.
—Bolit: he said very low, with a smile. He looked quite helpless.
—Bolit? said Achim. He touched his own elbow, made a grimace
of pain. The soldier nodded quietly.
—Bolit: he confirmed. It hurt. Bolniza is a hospital, dai mne
means give me a hand. He got to his feet; an arm around
Achim's shoulders he took one limping step, stopped again.
With his eyes he indicated the twisted bicycle on the ground,
then turned his head back to Achim. The bystanders reached
out almost simultaneously. They picked up the bicycle and
pushed the handle bars into Achim's free hand. Some of them
followed as far as a stopping wagon and commented worriedly
upon the foreign soldier's deep moans. He leaned back against
the tailboard of the wagon and looked at Achim with tenderly
amused eyes.
—Kapoooot? he asked.
Achim was holding the bicycle by handle bars and saddle; he
examined it from all sides. He made it bounce on both tires,
looked up at the soldier. —Nein: he said. He laughed because
he had said it in German. He shook his head.
The soldiers winked at him to come closer. Achim looked at
the German bystanders and at the Russians on the wagon who
were nodding encouragement. He took a step forward.
The soldier reached for the saddle. Achim withdrew his hand,
held on only to the handle bars. They looked at each other.
Achim felt very embarrassed. He tried not to look away. The
hand on the saddle pushed the bicycle toward him.
—Dlya tebya: said the Russian.
Achim felt ashamed. In those days he wore his hair long with
a part in it, pushed a strand off his forehead. Everybody was
talking to him in German and Russian. Achim nodded.
—Thank you: he said. Before he had been nervous, but now he
began to blush. The soldier turned away, satisfied, but the oth-
ers called to him from the wagon how to say thank you in Russian.
—Spaseebo: said Achim.
His friend shook his head. He was not much older than Achim.
He looked happy again.

—Nyet: he said, shaking his head. He didn't want to ride on it again, not any more now that it had thrown him off, the treacherous thing. He repeated: Spaseebo. Nou?

Achim was standing in the street, alone, holding the bicycle; he looked after the wagon. They were all waving to him. He wanted to shout and laugh, but he was sad. He suddenly knew how alone he was.

Perhaps this episode would not have come up, if it didn't fit in with his later career?

Is the author trying to cover up the abuses of the occupation forces with this story?

No. Nor does he want to suppress this gay soldier with the shiny eyes in his yellow skin.

Karsch was interested in Achim's experiences, not in those other people had, or could have had. Of course he wanted to avoid errors: he drove to the village to have a look. Which permitted him to add that a local train crossed the valley halfway up on the slope, which Achim had forgotten about, because later he always rode there on his bicycle. Karsch asked Achim's grandmother: What had happened in the village while Achim was there. The first time she was hospitable and suspicious, the only information she offered voluntarily was about the death of the new mayor and the contemptuous behavior of the Americans. He went back a second time and took Karin and brought greetings from Achim's father. She didn't believe that Karin belonged to Achim, she offered them the room under the eaves for their vacation, she stood with folded hands in the doorway as she watched them drive off into the twilight. —Why don't you come back someday: she said in a low voice smiling, and leaned against the door frame. She had become very small. She worried about who would bury her. Achim had not mentioned the women who'd sit in the kitchen with her almost all day long, without conversation though talking. Now Karsch was able to add: that the Russians built a plank fence flush around the elementary school and painted it green, the entrance was a blunt-angled wooden gate, on the side walls the foreign lettering alternated on a red background. She had not explained to Achim about the State criminals who were being taken to their own concentration camps, it had seemed incomprehensible to her at the time. Shortly after the arrival of the Soviet troops the town crier stomped from house to house swinging his bell, shouting: Because of the imminent arrival of the general . . . the inhabitants are requested to hang out red flags; red flags appeared in the windows with the swastika of the crushed Reich carefully removed, except for the imprint the rain had bleached into them and which was still there in soft-edged transparency; emptied red feather beds fluttered on the poles in front of the town hall and halfway up the church tower. The first-story windows of the town hall held portraits of gentlemen in collar and tie who were governing the State of the occupying army, above them hung portraits of gentlemen in uniform who had brought about the victory, from the windows under the roof gentlemen with old-fashioned beards stared into the blue hollow of the sky, they had predicted that the working classes would come to power and conquer the world; which had to be mentioned for the sake of correctness. A step-by-step description of all the reasons for the shame and the lost war and the hope for a better beginning (the unusual dull green of the fence for the foreign army and so forth), understandable and a lesson to all, but for Achim all this would always have a face that had made friends with him for the duration of a few seconds, that had given him a bicycle, that he never saw again: that was Achim's Red Army:

that's what he says, and he's the one we're talking about.

After he finished elementary school in the village, he returned to the city to his father, became a mason's apprentice and almost in a beeline an exceedingly famous East German cycling champion. At the Republic's fifth anniversary he no longer marched past the representatives of the governing administrator, he stood among them on the platform.

What does it mean: He was alone?

For a while he was alone. After the armistice the school in the neighboring village opened its doors again (not in this village then; that was an error). It was an hour's walk, but Achim rode over on the bicycle he had been given. The upper grades sat huddled together in the low run-down room whose windows looked out on the church square. They were taught two hours in succession, one group watching the other. Diagonally in front of Achim was the neck of a girl between stiff black braids. They'd jerk each time she moved her head. After some time he'd feel inexplicably startled when he saw the outlines of her face from the side against the November light with the temples in the shadow above the eyes.

Once every two weeks his father would send him a picture post-card. They showed the opera house the way it no longer looked and the market square without the rubble and the central station intact. Achim answered: We took the turnips in. I'm fine. He had no idea why they were estranged.

He enjoyed working his grandfather's fields. He liked feeling tired. He remembered where he had seen the girl who sat in front of him in class. He had passed her on his bicycle, coming back from the meadow with a pitchfork in one hand. She was herding the cows home that belonged to the farmer with whom her mother had found lodging. She had to herd the cows. The hoofs of the thin beasts with their brown and white markings were rubbing low dust clouds off the path. She was following them, barefoot in the swirling sand, the stick dangling loosely in her arm. The path sloped gently down toward the first houses, the bushes on either side were white with sand, her skirt was torn and full of spots. She looked up when he passed. He would have liked to say something. She lifted her head and looked at him, quietly, gaily. Tiny curls fell from her part onto her fore-head. After a while he turned to look back and saw her trim little figure leap over the fence around the pasture. The bushes along the path were silhouetting the slope against the sky, her surprising glance lay in the shadow of the colored evening light. All the boys his age had a girl friend.

In the winter his father stopped sending cards for some weeks, but people would come from the cities with their woolen clothes and optical instruments in knapsacks, to be exchanged for potatoes or maybe turnips. The grandmother had begun to ask Achim every time she bought or gave away something; he was sixteen now, he was the man in the house. He sat with a frozen woman close to the stove, questioning her while the grandmother filled the shabby shopping bag. She was grateful, she took him for the farmer. She told about the dead American soldiers lying face-down around the last Hitler fortress, not one of them shot in the back. The streetcars were running again every now and then. The Soviet headquarters had been installed in the town hall. The troops weren't distributing food any more, but the bakers still didn't have enough flour. The pillaging was over, but the streets were still unsafe at night. They've just cleared the rubble at the corner of the market square. Many many thanks. Do you want me to take a letter? Achim shook his head. He lived as though he couldn't feel. He saw everything, but he couldn't put it together in his mind. He hoped his uniform had burned up. Sometimes he felt like writing long letters to his mother.

After the Christmas vacation he passed the cow girl several times on the way home. She didn't always walk with the others. He rode quickly past her. He saw her worn-out shoes on the crunching path and the clouds of her breath in the icy air. Then he turned around and barred her path with his bicycle. —No need to walk: he said clumsily.

She looked up, questioningly, friendly. Her frosted shawl fluttered about her head. She hadn't understood what he said. She was a refugee.

—Do you know how to ride a bicycle? he asked. She nodded. He took his satchel from the handlebars and held the bike out to her. Let's take turns: he said. He looked after her, wobbling off on the swaying bicycle. The saddle was too high for her, she had to stand on the pedals. He was prepared to be happy. He was disappointed.

After two hundred yards she leaned the bicycle against a tree and went on walking. She had her hands in her pockets. When he passed her, she looked up with a quiet laugh. He waved to her when he got off again and left the bike for her on the path. She waved back.

For three miles they took turns that way. She had already reached the end of the little forest down the long slope close to the first houses when he saw three men in uniforms come out of a path. They barred the road, waiting for her with outspread arms, stopped her by the handle bars, made her get down and walked off with the bicycle. The confusion of small black creatures in the snow looked very graceful seen from the top of the hill. They tried to ride all three at once, one on the handle bars, one on the saddle, and one on the rack, at the bend they disappeared out of sight. Achim was already running. When he reached her, she was still standing at the same spot, hugging her satchel, in tears. She was fourteen.

—But it isn't your fault: said Achim. He tried to wipe the tears from her face, but he hurt her with his stiff frozen glove. He took it off. He felt happy touching the skin around her eyes. And when she raised her head. For a year and a half he went with her, always waiting for the pulsing in his temples to return, but it would only come as a memory or when he thought of her, not when they were together. He thought he ought to trust her now. —So your mother is dead? she said placidly, she had seen lots of people dead or dying, during her flight. He hadn't been able to say it. And he didn't like to speak about the destruction in the city and the war games in uniform. The only thing that remained from those days was his sure, hard-hitting fist that defended her and himself against the teasing and the jealousy of their classmates; that was one useful thing he had learned.

He asked his grandmother to allow her and her mother to stay in the living room. She had to work so hard in the farmer's house, and the farmer screamed at her, once he had beaten her even. But nothing came of it. One day Achim found his father sitting in the kitchen when he returned from the fields. Both of them were embarrassed, they hardly looked at each other when they shook hands. The high embarrassed tone of the question made Achim forget himself.

—Yes: he said. I'll come with you.

Then it struck him that he had forgotten her. That time they both had gone to the Soviet headquarters together and described how they had lost the bicycle. In their awkward Russian each of them had tried to explain to the lieutenant that it hadn't been a German bicycle any more. That it had been a gift. The lieutenant laughed a great deal about their way of speaking. Finally he allowed them to go out in the yard and find their bicycle among the others. When they came back, they saw him standing on the stairs, jiggling his hands in his pockets. —You've got a very pretty girl: he said to Achim in Russian.

—Yes: said Achim. Now he had a girl. Like all the other boys his age. And she was even prettier than the others. He felt sorry for her because he was leaving. Only much later did it occur to him that he could have stayed.

—I'll come to see you: he said. That was the same evening at the fence, he had called her out of the stable. She was holding on to the slats with both hands and paid no attention to the farmer who kept shouting for her. She didn't cry. She looked at him inaccessibly and said: So it's over.

—I'll really come to see you: Achim said distractedly. He wasn't sure where he actually belonged, perhaps he couldn't take her seriously.

It may seem less of an answer to you than a putting together of approximations. Karsch was able to use the following details: Achim's father: "He wanted to come right away and gladly. But he was sort of quiet at first. It started all of a sudden, on the way back, as though he'd suddenly remembered something."

The smooth footpath sloping downhill between the pines and the remoteness of little houses at the edge of the forest. The smell of hay mixed with sand dust about the winding, climbing paths between the meadows. The sight of a young woman with two buckets coming out of the farm, who leaned forward to call her children. The fence gate, high-school children walking stiffly, noisily, amidst the grade-school kids, etc. (Inspection.)

The story itself: the confiscated bicycle, taking turns riding it, the lieutenant, three high-spirited drunken soldiers, you've got a pretty girl.

128

Mrs. Liebenreuth: "Today young people aren't careful, and later they've missed it forever. My son . . ."

The grandmother: "I remember, sometimes he'd bring the girl from East Prussia home for lunch, the one at the Lehmanns'. Her mother was ill. Later they went to the West, to relatives. Old Lehmann made her work much too hard, it was a crime, she was only a kid. Well, he's dead too. She had such delicate bones. Still a child she was. Still children both of them."

Karin was very quiet. She was walking through the village, hands behind her back, every now and then she'd stop. They'd say hello when they met someone, but the older people would turn away and not answer. (Second inspection; they came just at the time the collectivization of the individual farms was in full swing.) On the way back she merely said: How confined and narrow-angled it was, and to Achim it seemed so vast and filled with memories: although (he says) he couldn't get used to living there.

"Would you say I ditched her, she was only fifteen, would you say I did. Would you?" (Achim, in conversation.)

And how did he get into racing?

Until the following spring he rode over to see her. It was a little less than four hours by bicycle. He'd get there before noon, eat lunch with his grandmother and do for her whatever chores remained to be done (the water buckets were beginning to be somewhat heavy for her and when she chopped firewood she'd often have to rest against the block). In the afternoon he'd try to see his girl. Her mother liked him; she thought him faithful for riding all that way to see her, she'd send her daughter out to him. Then it was as she had said: over.

—I came on my bike.

—Did you?

—Three and a half hours.

—And halfway down the hill the chain popped off.

—Did you see my father the day he was here?

—No.

For hours she could walk beside him and never say a word. But she didn't look angry; almost content, with her hands in her coat pockets, letting him do the talking. He couldn't get through to her. Her firm fifteen-year-old silhouette that seemed so tender in his memory grew less familiar when he saw her, more indispensable from a distance. When he shook her hand in the evening, she'd turn and run. His hand would remember the shy polite pressure of her fingers on the ride home through the night, blindly raging against himself he'd pedal faster and faster and keep seeing her from the back, sometimes behind closing eyelids.

Three and a half hours? Why not less? He was happy getting up alone on Sunday mornings, tiptoeing past his sleeping father to the door of the shed. The garden lay cool and untouched. He'd ride toward her in the very early morning, the air still moist with dew along deserted road ribbons and Sunday villages. Trade school and building lots, the strangers in their house, orders from the Soviet headquarters would form an irritating indistinguishable mixture in his head; suddenly he'd wake up and notice that he was pedaling very slowly, as though his legs were hesitating, pondering. Only when he'd concentrate all his attention on the relationship of body and bicycle (the sensation of motion) and speed up his pedaling, carefully breathing, until he'd experience a bearable and pleasant feeling of exertion, would his contentment be complete. He'd feel in tune with himself. Rushing downhill, sometimes with the wind coming from a certain angle, this feeling would soar very high.

The ride back was unhappy. He was clumsy enough to bring it up. —Can't you forget it? he said, he was already lying, he couldn't forget it either. But he could only imagine how it felt to live four weeks of disappointment. He felt obliged to feel guilty. In a fury she kept slapping his face, her lips were taut and attentive as though she were accomplishing a difficult task. She was still crying when they came back to the village, it made him feel ashamed because of the people. The next time he came, she seemed to have been waiting for him.

Four and a half (and when I told her what the foreman had said, her eyes wandered and swam a bit and then she did say that she'd had a girl friend in East Prussia wherever that is who

hadn't come along. Or perhaps that was some other time, before. What did she mean, and when I stopped talking, she
looked quite friendly in the face, still I, hell well I don't know)
hours. The roads were thick with snow, he had to keep in the
car tracks. Then he'd get onto untraveled stretches where the
narrow tires sank into the hard snow, he'd topple back and forth
over the front wheel. For ten minutes he lay in the ditch and
didn't care in the soft soaking cold. Then a truck came by and
cleared a track for him. The sky was completely dark, the forest
so very black.

He should have touched her

He couldn't. First he had to forget the barn in which the occupation troops unanimously, one after the other, had torn
the German women up between the legs. They'd lie on the
floor in the hay, but there was a small platform under the roof
where the village boys would squat and stare down at the rough
mechanism of the bodies clamped together in the nocturnal
light. Achim had gone along only once. They could climb down
only well after midnight; on the way home he'd had to half
carry the teacher's son who felt sick because he had seen his
mother, who had not screamed. Achim didn't look into the
faces of the girls when he saw them the next time in broad daylight, in the street or on their way to church, he shuddered at
the way a face dissolves in the groin. And he didn't understand
why his grandmother would spit when she saw them. He
couldn't even bring himself to kiss his girl. Except once.
Three hours and a quarter. Three hours and twenty minutes.
All of a sudden she had forgiven him. She no longer protested
when they teased her at school or in the village square about
her lover from the city; Sunday mornings she'd wait along the
road and in the evening she'd ride with him for a bit on the handle bars and wouldn't run back into the forest before he was
completely out of sight behind the bend of the road at the three
big rocks: She'd asked him never to turn around.
And yet he couldn't wait for the feeling of hard joy that came

at the fast ride into the city under the first street lamps between sporadically mushrooming house fronts: he was home
again, here he knew everything, here he was safe.

Three hours and five minutes, but that was an accidental
result: someone on a bicycle passed him during the last thirty
miles. It had never happened before, that's why he tried to
catch up with him, to show the guy, and he was surprised how
much effort it took. He saw the apparently effortless spinning
of the other guy's feet, his bicycle sounded different. For the
first time Achim noticed a slim free-wheeling clutch shining
beside three black toothy disks, wires ran along the frame, the
whole structure looked much thinner and curved differently.
That's easy. The other guy turned his head through one bent
arm and nodded encouragement. Achim flattened his back like
the other one and pedaled like mad. The other guy was wearing a sweat shirt under the puffed-out collar of his windbreaker;
he let himself drift so that Achim could catch up. He was watching him. —Too angular, the way you pedal, too angular: he said.
After a while he shook his head, regretfully. He spoke calmly
with ease, while Achim panted. Sorry, man: he said: I'm in
training. And pulled away, simply vanished (Achim said with
a laugh, wanting to express how dumb and surprised he'd been
ten years ago), quickly he was out of reach, impossible to
catch up with, pedaled away smaller and smaller, disappeared
as a dot on a straight stretch of road. A few more times Achim
tried to pedal in the same frequency of tread as during the few
minutes they had ridden side by side, but each time he'd fall
back, more and more out of breath.

Those three hours and five minutes must have stuck in his
bones until the clammy Monday mornings that fall and re-
asserted themselves as a memory; when loads of bricks and mortar tore his arms out of their sockets, when he sat behind the
frosted glass of the trade-school windows, it may have occurred
to him that everything was quite different: every idle second
could be compressed into the heightened sensation of complete
absorption, the obediently laboring bicycle would draw body
and attention into a proud speedy solitude, cut through villages
and leave them behind, rush through unknown forests, pass
horse carts, tractor convoys, bicycling peasant women, more

nimbly on the only road. Arriving meant delay, the skin around a girl's eyes tight with expectation arrested him and threw him back, finally, in the spring, the ride had become an aim in itself and expelled the image of the arrival: a child in a Sunday dress who'd appear out of the colorful grass, grave and happy she'd walk toward the clearing with demanding steps—
(although this reminded Karin of the final scene in a film of a year ago, with a love affair between two children ending in similar brightness of spring, because of the difficult political circumstances, and Achim admitted that he might have seen it)—
after twenty-two miles in one hour the stop ought to be allowed to settle undisturbed with softly clasping brakes into the comforting exhaustion and the memory of a steep curve that had swallowed him up with a roar, crushed and dismissed him.
Approximately the same distance in the opposite direction took him three hours, without stopping; he turned around at once.

Did this satisfy Achim?

Achim didn't like his life after the war the way Karsch let it happen. It bothered him on one of the rest days during the big race through the countries allied to the East German partitioned State: Achim was lying among his teammates in a gym suit, on bent elbows, in the dusty lawn of the park outside his hotel, pushed the flattened back up on arms and feet, flipped his body backward into a crouch, flung one leg forward and then the other, stretched both arms, twenty-two arms shot forward beside his, stretched in a straight line from the shoulder, described two circles, one horizontal, one vertical, fell back against the well-trained bodies, came forward once more, the men sank into a squatting position with the precious legs twirling underneath, on the sidewalk people who happened to pass and school children who had come on purpose with a second's delay conveyed

133

what they saw in similar movements of generally profitable early-morning exercise. Then breakfast with the first press conference of that day, chewing faces were flashed home to the respective editorial offices, the reporters trailed Achim to the repair shop, children with notebooks milled outside the doors of the dining room, smiling, bent over shivering spines, he'd sign his tall A over and over, before lunch he was supposed to lie down for an hour, limbering-up exercises were scheduled for the afternoon, and Karsch did not dare hope that the brisk May air of the city of Prague could be kept out of Achim's answer to the twenty pages with which he had disappeared the previous evening, immediately after the honors ceremony. Karsch didn't stand more than a few minutes at the hotel clerk's desk, Achim was still able to notice him, with his head he pointed to the right side of the street, repeated patiently the Czech word for "good" and removed his long legs cautiously from the whirling acoustics of the crowded lobby. A young man in a gray suit approached leisurely from the side street, took the sunglasses from his weathered face and pulled Karsch by one arm up flat steps into an entrance hall heavily framed by columns, where for half an hour nobody would expect him to be. He did have his pass with him and could get in on a student ticket.
—Well, you know . . . : he murmured, his eyes were unfocused, he moved his hand with the dangling sunglasses, they were surrounded by the peaceful paintings of a bygone Bohemian century, he stretched, slapped him on the shoulder, he winked as though they were accomplices, he (probably) wanted to confess that he couldn't accept having lived the way somebody else was putting it on paper: that it is impossible for one man to write the way another lives; reddish brown cows tinkling their bells along a railroad track belonged to 1946 for Achim, he had forgotten it, then why return to him something he no longer had any need for?; the surprise of a boy drilled in Prussian style at American soldiers sitting on their helmets had lost its exclamation marks in Karsch's description and immediately led up to the miserable barter deals which hadn't really got under way until a week later; and the mention of the wretched mayor's face arrogantly pushed grocer's widow and town crier and gravedigger and visiting aunt into the background, whereas

they, too, existed and sometimes more impressively under the starving sky; the fucking in the barn had stalked three-worded across the square outside the town hall, suppressing the supporting wooden beams in the building's interior, of undeniable reality; the forest, as Achim used to call the brush wood with its pathways, had reached Karsch's awareness enriched with delicately interlaced branches against a flaky snow-laden sky; Achim had no idea what Karsch associated with the words "holy curiosity" applied to a fifteen-year-old girl from East Prussia; one of the two words he never used at all, and the other he did not use in such contexts; the image of the girl Karsch had put together suppressed for him the reality of the small terrified hand trying to wriggle out of his clasping fingers that had become tangible when he told Karsch: She'd make such big serious eyes. Karsch crossed out the unsuitable word, but it didn't help much because the gap had to be filled with some other word which Achim didn't have handy nor had he had any need of it while he was living it. (Perhaps Karsch could have compared the events and contexts for which Achim used words singly or in combination with others; find out whether one of them alone equally condensed and set into perspective November sky, three-hour meeting, the sound volume of more than forty phons, chapped lips and childhood drawings, so that from their overlay he could limn Achim's approximate experience and image of a November sky, and then use no more words [and no other words]than Achim to designate a three-hour meeting; but the repetition of the same word designating a lot of noise, for instance, wouldn't yield more than the verbal skill of Achim's life, while, by the same means, in a presumed nerve cell of Achim's the trembling outline, the groping for the flowerlike moist unfolding memory of the kiss might be evolved, and if Karsch wanted to arrest in writing, with the [same] word, the clumsy drawing of a bird feather—which Achim kept for thirteen years because it was her last postcard and good-by—it is not guaranteed that everyone [who was not Achim] would respond to this thoroughly exercised verbal imitation of Achim with the same readiness to vary applications of sadness . . . which Achim had in mind when he applied this one single word to all these things.)

Karsch would welcome it that Achim brought his person and the history of his person to the meeting place that the communicating quality of language provided; he stepped into the space that had been prepared and fenced in for him with words, with little more enthusiasm than a potential reader, a stranger who'd be willing, we hope, to enter into it, remembering the time when he himself was sixteen years old—if he weren't ready to accept borrowed words. Well, if one could have stepped into the other's shoes! As it was, one could not speak of the other and mean in his place: I, although Achim was perfectly willing to believe that Karsch was thinking about him rather than about himself, he was that polite, who was that polite, Achim who else. His seconds would always stretch either longer or shorter than Karsch's sentences; and were they not standing side by side, each in his separate skin, and could Karsch ever be expected to understand even vaguely the slyly well-intentioned slap between his shoulder blades, to draw the proper inferences? Because the two gentlemen at the window that was ringing with forenoon light did actually not comment upon mutual understanding, and as to the other's interest, they may at best have had it in mind when the hesitant hand of one of them, holding a folded pair of glasses, slid from the back of his own head across to his companion's shoulder; even thoughtful museum guards, who have acquired their white-haired dignity from years of dealing with such difficult objects as paintings and gallery visitors, may not have been able to tell for sure, as they passed, whether the hesitancy in one face was producing, or had produced, an expression of unmistakable understanding on the other face. The two men at the window were concerned with a number of written pages, and before they started in on a discussion of the details one slapped the other on the back and said something confidential in German. —Well: said Achim: you know . . . perhaps as a renunciation of what he wasn't mentioning, before he conceded more decisively: But on the whole it was more or less like that.

—If you say so: said Karsch doubting, because he had not caught up.

Then they discussed the ten pages which Achim forgot irretrievably the following morning on the window sill in his hotel room and which slipped his mind completely during the following rainy hundred-and-twenty-five-mile ride: in which Achim's life after the war had not been condensed into a single episode about the Soviet army and his consequent career as a bicycle champion, the way I now answer your question. On those pages Karsch had described Achim's apprenticeship, construction sites, the early-morning rides on the streetcar, the hardening of hands and muscles and how the laborious patience with beer cases and backaches changed to a feeling of pride to be wearing the white smock and to speak in the masons' jargon. If we don't build those guys any houses, they can't run the country. But that's what they did, and made up a curriculum with bicycle rides on weekends, and black market deals behind the central station; the symbol for the new State Youth Organization was a stiff radiant half sun on a blue shield under the equally golden initials of Free and German and Youth, all the main streets were renamed, people on damaged trucks waved flags and loudly screaming requested the nationalization of all big industrial enterprises, now what do they mean by this. Is it all starting all over again. Many-headed crowds milled through the reopened department stores and gazed with amazement at carpets and pots and blocks of cheese with price tags about which there was no more haggling. Perhaps we'll make good again. When the money was exchanged at a tenth of its previous value, Achim saw a reserved elderly gentleman set fire to the wastepaper basket in the exchange office with hundred-mark bills. Rumors stated that the liquidated State power had caused the war and murdered a lot of people besides. Hey, look: a brand-new car, what do you know! A photo taken the year the East German State was founded shows Achim tall and thin next to a much smaller girl in a white Sunday dress and hair gaily hanging about her face; in the background you recognize the door of the garden shed. Actually we didn't notice at what point we stopped being hungry.

Appalled by the sound of bugles and drums that turned the corner of a side street to take the lead of the masons on their way to the meeting and later flooded the market square between speeches with their disciplined noise from the height of the red-draped podium, Achim declined to join this club. We can picture him here as a status-conscious though sociable mason's apprentice who lets his foreman speak his piece but then shakes his head.

—I don't know. I'm still fed up from the last time, you know.

—But this is different! Of course there's got to be discipline if you're marching, don't you see, but the thing you're marching for!

—I know all about discipline. I simply can't stand that kind of noise any more.

—You know, this is an offer I'm making you. I'd give it another thought if I were you.

—I want my spare time. Do I work less than the others? Go and ask them. As long as the cash's all right . . . he broke off. The confidential conversation with his foreman seemed to be a distinction, he didn't want to contradict him outright. It would have been uncivil.

But if Achim preferred these details to be replaced by a sentence said slowly, to be taken down: After initial hesitation I realized (Of course you'd have to write: he) that one must not confine oneself in one's private life, but that one must take part in society, and asked to be admitted as a member—it was up to Karsch to realize that Achim's memory of owning that button moved faster than the entire year he had spent in (initial) hesitation. And so Karsch thought that he might fill the deleted section with a rough blue cotton shirt, they wore this shirt as a uniform inside the trousers, two breast pockets with flaps for the membership pass, etc., with buttoned tabs on the shoulders for some purpose Achim had forgotten. —But by all means, Achim said. —We didn't wear it to work, only to parades and that sort of thing.

What sort of thing? Were those the black pants for which the country only later had to supply fabric and factories, the short and long-legged ones with the buttoned-down flaps over their deep pockets? Or the heavy leather shoes that would not shine? No. I meant meetings, of course. We danced too.

All right: as he had first surveyed the city in all directions on his bicycle, now he took possession of it by his profession. The smooth walls and polished floors we inhabit so thoughtlessly had been put together by him stone by stone; there were certain

138

houses that belonged to him; he understood and recognized the streets more thoroughly now that he was able to relate the appearance of a house to the various constructions of its basement and window casings and the shape of its roof, they made the outlines stand out more sharply for him. And the meetings would tell him: for this purpose yes, for that purpose no; why are we building up a State without American loans? First let's get to work, then we'll eat without debts; everything shall be our property. It is a matter of honor to go hear the administrator speak, dressed in the garb of our proud million-member association; he said: today when West Germany is once more taking the road that leads to war, why are you scratching your neck: don't you believe that it's true: he said: nobody any longer has a right to say: Count me out. That's what I understood at that time, understood it for life, and you must describe it as though you'd understood, and that passage here you'd better cross out: said Achim, pulled the first two pages out from under the clip and handed them back to Karsch.

—I see: said Karsch. On those pages he recognized the girl from East Prussia, the pretty one with the bicycle that had been given back to them, that may actually have belonged to a farm in another village.—Well, whose business is it, anyway?

—No: added Achim in a nagging, still dictating tone, disappointed he shook his head. Perhaps he could tell by the hesitation and tone of another person's answer whether he had been understood or not and didn't have to listen to the words. He was gingerly sitting on the radiator under the window, slightly swaying between anchored arms he looked up at Karsch his head raised sideways, hopefully. But Karsch hardly showed any reaction this time. He waited, and Achim waited, and finally one of them said in a tone of persuasion: Well. Well?

—The Red Army must come out: Achim said. He lifted his sunglasses to his eyes as though he were nearsighted, studied a couple of newlywed tourists who had now come to a narrow space between paintings in which two gentlemen were waving typewritten sheets, solving riddles for each other.

—The way you've described it: said Achim, but perhaps the couple didn't understand German at all, he took the glasses away from the environment of the eyes by which one recognizes a person. —The way you have them roaming around confiscating bicycles.

For that reason Achim's grandmother had told him to take the bicycle apart for the time being, while things were so bad, and to hide the parts in different places, not to have it taken away. At sixteen the future world champion had squatted in the shade of the Thuringia summer, wondering, with his rough unskilled hands, how one went about dismantling such a contraption. All he had was a pair of pliers. It took an hour to work out how the rear wheel was attached and to take it off; tenaciously he memorized where each screw had sat. The rod that supports the saddle is held in place by the mere tightening of the head of the back frame. He unscrewed the front wheel fork, and the ball bearings rolled out of the ring; on his knees he crept about the hard-trodden floor groping for the invisibly tiny balls and polished them with his shirttail. With the back of his hand he had wiped so much grease into his sweating face, the dangling ends of his hair were black. He took apart even what might have stayed together. Tires, screws, saddle, handle bars, everything was arranged around him in a complicated order. Every now and then he'd close his eyes and picture where a certain part belonged and what a mounted bicycle looked like. He groaned with excited satisfaction. In the evening his grandmother came to look for him. He had put the whole thing together again and was playing with the free-wheel brake that squeezed the swishing onrush of the rear wheel every time he pressed the pedal arm softly in the direction counter to the chain. And now a little less softly. And now in two phases, not so tight: see. Coming.

—Do you want them to take it away again? said his grandmother. Her hands on her thighs she stood before him, almost angry; he should have hoed potatoes that afternoon (that's how late they had been put into the ground that year.) That's not what she told him, she shook her head, grumpy but amused, and told him to go wash his face and hid the bicycle in the haystack outside the stable. The plunderers stabbed the vegetable garden with their swords and poked at the floor of the barn, but the hay between the stable doors, which looked as though it had been freshly stacked, escaped their attention, because the first Soviet troops in the village came from farm regions:

Karsch didn't like to give up tangibles.

—In those days, in those days! prompted Achim. He couldn't make himself comfortable on the radiator, he leaned sideways on one elbow, straightened up again, crossed his legs, uncrossed them. He'd move the minute he felt stiff. He lengthened his neck out of the restricting tie, stared upward with raised chin. —Listen! he said, conciliatory. —Karsch! he tried to persuade him. But Karsch wasn't obstinate. One of the gentlemen, the one standing up, was talking rather rapidly to the other one, slapped his forehead in a symbolic gesture, tried to pull the sitting one by the forearms into his own opinion. The sitting one countered with extremely brief questions, with pauses that he bolstered with relaxed questioning: Right?

—You can't put in everything anyway, right? he said.

—So you've got to make a choice, right, so naturally you pick the most important, right? the thing that's essential, man!

Now Karsch was supposed to ask what was essential. He tried it by nodding and Achim reacted to his reaction, said: It's more important, right? as we look at it today! that the Red Army liberated us from the fascists and helped us start a new life, right? and not that they lay down with a woman once in a while, or bicycles, or things like that.

—I see: said Karsch, because he thought that Achim wanted him to write down his opinions, and this time Achim thrust a confirming index finger in his direction: not that he wanted to conceal any girl from East Prussia. His life didn't belong to him: my riding over to see her for so long did teach me endurance, and instead of the passage we crossed out, you could lead it into my first tryout . . . his finger drew a sweeping line across the first page, flipped it over, sure of its aim the finger landed halfway down on the next page. Three years later in his life. —Listen! he said. —Karsch! he said.

First tryout was the term for an amateur race to which the bicycle sports clubs invited young men to test their ability. Idly, just curious, Achim hung around at these events and looked at the bicycles that were leaning against the low thin linden trees. It was a gray March day, with a wet wind coming in on the avenue. Achim stopped at the outskirts of a group that was talking in impressed tones around a shiny structure. The narrow profile of the tires, the efficiency of the totally chrome-plated frame filled Achim with longing. He heard the seventeen-year-old owner repeat a flattered: From my uncle. My uncle gave it to me. In West Berlin they're already making such things again.

—Quit showing off: said Achim. In talking he grew angrier.
—Who's showing off? said the bicycle owner. His hair was very blond, almost white, it reminded Achim of the blondness of girls' faces; he looked at Achim, gentle and pretty.

Achim had nothing more to say, his casual posture across his tilted bike grew stiff. The blond boy came to his rescue by drawing the heads of the group back to him with a negligent: Half a day's ride from Berlin on a bike like that. Real fun.
—What sort of gearshift is that? asked Achim.
—Three-speed: replied the other one politely. They were just about to make peace, but the group to which the other boy evidently belonged were cross at Achim. —Go ahead and try it on your coffee grinder: they said (not with complete conviction, since they were speaking to someone older than they) and turned their backs on him.

Achim found himself standing before the table of the race management so suddenly, he muttered: We'll see, into the chairman's face.

The functionary looked up without surprise and repeated that indeed they would see, then turned to the others to distribute his smile.
—Name? Occupation?

Questions like that always calmed Achim down and gave him a feeling of belonging. He was asked for, he was not forgotten, he was needed, he wasn't alone. He wanted to be friendly, to feel intimate; he managed a gesture of disdain when the chairman asked him: Let's have a look at your bike.

Achim swung his leg back over the rear wheel so that they could see the entire bike. It was his only possession of value, familiar even in his dreams as the sensation and sound of motion. It was the same as the machines on which masons from all over the city rode to work. In many places the paint had flaked off, the naked spots were rusting more and more, even though he tried to protect them with grease. The handle bars were still bent out of shape, he hadn't been able to straighten them. The gear teeth were worn down, sometimes the chain slipped. He'd been worrying about the spokes lately. The fenders were too thick in proportion to the frame; every time a spoke ripped off, the distorted felly would knock against the frame. Especially in the rear wheel they kept breaking one after the other. There was nothing he could do to improve this roadster. New ones weren't for sale. However, he promised himself that he didn't really mean his gesture of disdain.

They let him participate.

The newcomers were given a ten-minute handicap over the regular club members. Achim waited with an absent face, let himself be shoved to the start line, tried, at the first pedal stroke, to memorize the streets this twelve-mile race was to pass through. His memory came up with houses and garden fences in the northern residential section and they'd push their curbs and curves and pavement toward him, he'd calculate the shock vibrations across a stretch of rough stones before he even got to it. The precious bicycle from West Berlin had not pulled away that marvelously, he could see it. He even delayed one pedal stroke to try the blond boy's rhythm, they were pedaling approximately at the same speed, but the shift was concealed behind another rider, perhaps there was still another gear left free to go into a higher ratio. Thinking about the shift (how's that, I wonder) had slowed down his legs to daydreaming; he was almost at the tail end, straightened himself on the pedals, threw himself into it heavy and furious, pushed forward along the side of the street, enjoyed his adroit dodging, passing other bikes, his bicycle was helping him again, he was his bicycle, swaying, knees bent outward, he swung close to the panting nephew and pulled him on with a jerking of the neck, together they rode faster, the length of one bicycle ahead of the pack. Come on. Quit showing off. After a few minutes he was sure that his neighbor's chain ran on the lowest gear. But his two or three glances had made him slide back into the lee side of the cramped hunched-over body that was weaving obliquely in front of him. He was extremely surprised how much easier it suddenly was. He rested in the diminished pressure of the ripped air, talked to his aching lungs, consoled them, deceived them with the remaining nine miles and forced them finally, almost blinded, up against the batch of club members who were now overtaking the two newcomers on five-gear racing bikes. His attention grew selective. It dismissed windows and calls and perplexed spectators on the sidewalk without a glance, focused only on the distance from neighbors, tire tracks, potholes, constantly bending curbs, rushed toward them, left them behind. Inside his body his heart and lungs were howling as though they had been torn loose, he no longer talked to them, he had ceased to exist command over the feeling of what to do next, over his painfully whirling legs, had been usurped by what he'd define today as discipline, hard blind determination placed above the body's weakness and reason.

He came to, fallen against a tree behind the finish, his head was trembling against the rough crumbly bark of the tree, he thought he had his eyes open, but everything around him was blackness. He had forgotten again whether the ratio increases or decreases when the number of teeth in the rear wheel sprocket is reduced, how's that. He also felt that he had been warned. This was his second experience of indifference (in the snow. And the trees so very black. The sky completely dark); this one lasted longer.

Equality came up to talk to him. A whirl of shoulder slapping, hellos, thin rainy cold and remote conversations awakened him to eleventh. He had become eleventh. He had left sweat shirts behind. You rode like a madman. See here: your saddle is too low. Your leg should bend only slightly when you put your foot on the pedal. No. The ball of the foot. There, now try it. Sit down. See? (With this strung-together piece of junk he managed to stay in the race!)

The manager shook his hand. They invited him to the club's training runs. Told him to become a member. Did he belong to the State Youth Organization yet? Here, sign your name.

—Yes: said Achim. —Yes. Yes. No . . . not yet. Yes. (The blond boy whom he rather liked had given up. After six miles. Got sick of it. Didn't have the guts, probably.)

He saw the functionaries talking. They were speaking about him. They were saying: this still growing lanky lad who rode that kind of a race in bad weather, on a bike ready for the scrap heap, in his street shoes, with a fluttering jacket acting as a wind trap, that lad showed promise. He'll go places. His modest confused smile was the same as in the days of his coming fame. He stayed with the club members until evening. He rode to the club grounds with them, and didn't let them out of his sight, he copied the way they talked, he had discovered a proud strange world. At nightfall he rode home, deliciously slowly. He felt sad that he was no longer being talked about. The thin walls of the wooden shed were humming with wind. He saw his father's head asleep in the moonlight. He would have liked to make peace with him. Anything to be crossed out here?

Achim had told somebody else about even this place: somebody was whistling outside the windows, breath whirling across two fingers on a tongue, up into the noon air, Achim left with long strides, an old man with a white beard looked after the papers that had not been exchanged. Museums are supposed to be favorite places for exchanging things. Karsch had the eyes of the assembled visitors on his face because, toward the end, they had joined the guided tour through the exhibition, Achim's loud harsh-throated gesticulating talk had invaded the guide's explanations from the outer edge of the group and made the natives think of the Germans during the war. Left alone, Karsch looked at the paintings pointed out by a Polish hand, walked through centuries with the other visitors around him and was left to think it over on his own. He was almost sure that he should say: after initial hesitation, every time the East German Youth Organization was mentioned; however, he still had not understood what Achim was driving at with the West Berlin bicycle: had this unequal race not been symbolic of the difference in the recovery of the East and West German economies, work first eat later, now we're also building machines like the ones they had in the West as soon as the war was over, Achim representing Achim plus symbol, doubled over a machine rattling with age, and Karsch said: But the Soviets also dismantled a good many things. Achim was still patient: We've gone through that: he reminded him. In his thoughts Karsch grouped objects and events according to their chronological sequence and reciprocal effect, Achim stretched his opinion using it to tie his life into one single bundle, all Karsch wanted to know was how it had happened, in what sort of weather and in front of what witnesses, he had no opinions, opinions which Achim was willing to substitute for weather and witnesses and the tender skin around a girl's eyes. And the dismantling of the East German industry for the benefit of the damaged Soviet Union, about which they evidently were in agreement, except that Karsch didn't know how.

—Listen: he said that afternoon in Achim's hotel, because that same evening he had to leave the city into which the great race had rushed the previous day, where it was standing still today, from where it would burst forth tomorrow through splendidly decorated streets past breathless men with microphones at their larynx; Karsch could not follow it; he had come with a tourist visa in a bus crowded with travelers who would know more about the city of Prague tomorrow than Karsch knew about Achim's life. The seemingly natural growth of thoughts is to be highly recommended, but a man in a hurry must hurriedly confess that, once again, he has not caught up. —Listen: he said. Almost all the men of the East German team were still sitting around him and Achim at the table, all of them in gray suits wrapped in hip-long jackets, turning their heads toward the conversation between Achim who was their leader and the man who wanted to write a book about bicycle racing, who still had a couple of questions. Karsch knew them all by sight, he had sat at each and every one's bed and made notes on their parents schools places of work, how did you come to bicycle racing? After lunch Karsch had passed in back of their chairs, he sat down by Achim's chair, but they made room for him, they waved to him like acquaintances who recognize each other immediately and say hello. —Well: they said and Karsch smiled and said: Fine.

Achim dispersed Karsch's questioning look with a headshake, introduced him with a sweeping hand to the helpful attention of his team for whom he had no secrets. Karsch insisted: but Achim had actually told him all the things he now wanted crossed out.

—To give you the idea: Achim said; —Since you weren't here at the time: added one of the boys who was leaning across the table on his elbows. To judge by their faces, Karsch thought they all understood even the question better than he did. They were on familiar ground.

—But it is part of your life: said Karsch. (And why not mention the Czech May air in a quiet side street outside the open window, the smell of the much-washed massaged alert bodies, their sparing politeness toward the bothersome intruder: that transferred the feeling of their brotherhood to him, invited him to join them.)

—You can't know anything of my life except what I tell you: said Achim. He was relaxed, leaning back against his chair, peeling an orange, hard, pleasant wrinkles formed around his eyes. They were all watching to see if Karsch had understood what had become clear to all of them, Karsch nodded like someone who is undecided but who does know his way home. Everybody was standing up with much noise and they swarmed out into the lobby where they mingled with the teams of the other countries and Karsch had to ask the Danes what they thought of it all. There hadn't been time to ask if everything he put down about Achim's life had to fit in with Achim's opinions; whether Achim wanted to deny having said whatever did not fit in; whether it amounted perhaps to the same thing in the end. Only on the basis of the customs of his own country could he have understood which opinions Achim would not hold in a foreign country.

I have tried to answer your question: whether Achim was satisfied. They couldn't have any desire to quarrel. Achim sometimes made a great effort to address Karsch formally, he was used to terms of intimacy, because, in his world, everybody was equally close to him. (Which wasn't intimacy, but made it easier to deal with people.) From the day Karsch accepted the first advance from the Publishing House for New Writing, Achim kept a supply of liquor in his apartment although he did not drink himself, and watched with suspicion when Karin did (but she did not change). At certain of Karsch's expressions Achim answered with a smile of recognition and acceptance, —Our good old Karsch: he'd say with indulgence. When Karsch arrived in Prague in the evening, Achim introduced him to his team: This is the man. Looks as if you couldn't get across to him. But he's improving. There is a photo of this meeting: in the sports weekly, Achim and Karsch standing side by side, Achim's hand is reaching out to slap Karsch on the back, both are laughing with open mouths, one looks shy, the other boisterous, they get along great, that makes them more alike, but it's Karsch who looks more like Achim.

And is that all about Prague?

More or less. (Really now: you'd say to that and wonder about the questions people ask sometimes.) Really now all the undamaged street fronts pleasantly merging into an over-all flight of vision: were only an obstacle to Karsch behind which he went looking for Achim; he noticed fountains and monuments and buildings of the past about which he had learned in school; and people did ask him what he thought of the city in general and he'd compare it, because it could be compared, it showed prosperity. For the first time it made him remember the friends he had left behind, he sent them postcards of glass-cubicled housing projects and street scenes with women in light dresses and small dogs under low trees. He wanted to convey the special light to them, he underlined the date, he tried to amplify what he had seen by naming the cities in West Germany of which a certain street or fountain reminded him; he didn't want to leave out the difference that (A) was administering the country from within the government buildings and (B) was able to exist without banners stretched across streets, on houses and garden fences, with slogans in red and white admonishing the over-all aspect of the city to a proper conception of itself: and tore up what he had written. He thought he'd better ask once more.

—I'm not supposed to unify with that: he said, but Achim shook his head skeptically which meant: even more so, it's after all a socialist country; and Karsch said: Cut it out, cut it out, and this way he didn't learn anything about Prague. And why talk about Prague?

Why should Karsch's incidental weekend trip get more mention than Karin's long-term moving? because she had moved; she no longer sat waiting among rented furniture, but she hadn't told Achim. Achim rang Mrs. Liebenreuth's bell one midnight, stood in Karsch's room before the sleep-drugged terrified woman could refasten the chain; he seated himself on the book about bicycle sports next to which Karsch had fallen asleep, and after sitting together for a while, one awake and the other asleep, he started to shake Karsch. —Where is she! he said. —Karsch! Where did she go?

—Who? said Karsch, and Mrs. Liebenreuth appeared at the door and offered them coffee for this late hour. Achim was trying to understand something. He let go of Karsch and stood up. He went to the door, held out his hand, almost tenderly he straightened Mrs. Liebenreuth's coat over her nightgown. His smile reconciled her. —I know who you are now: she said, her wrinkled face radiated good intentions. Shy and tall he was facing her and smiled the way he had learned it. —I'm sure Mr. Karsch would love a cup of coffee: he said.

He walked back toward Karsch, smoothed the pages of the book, closed it with care; he leaned over the typewriter with a half-torn-out page still in it; he sat down on the edge of the couch and said: I'm terribly sorry.

Karsch told him the street and the number of the house.

—In this city? said Achim.

He was in his gym suit. He had returned from the cross-country race only a few hours ago and not among the last. Karsch had gone downstairs with Mrs. Liebenreuth to the restaurant to watch the race on television. It had taken her an hour to put on her Sunday best; her graying hair stood in curly confusion about her excited face when she walked into the restaurant with Karsch, the last time she had come here was probably thirty years ago with her husband. The owner came up to welcome them and sat at their table for a bit while the first shots of the stadium lit up the screen. The camera showed pleasant afternoon clouds above the edge of the crater that was fuzzy with the motions of tiny figures, a happily shouting man with a little flag

149

soundlessly filled the screen; farther away one saw a section of curved tiers of innumerable dots that were spectators; the cry of expectation pounced large and dangerous onto the cinder track, that lay empty and increasingly unbearably tenser within the crescendo of the gradually blurring screams. The entrance catapulted dots onto the track, they swung in a wide curve, seemed to align themselves arbitrarily, advanced with uneven jolts, in a panoramic view of them turned into a hard rainbow of sweat shirts above machines petrified with speed, because the slowness of the human eye simplified the breaking through the finish line and saw the riders as disheveled projectiles. The feverish conversation in the crowded restaurant ripped into shreds of calls and shouts; as if present Achim's name went from table to table until finally the loud-speaker and the acoustics in the restaurant fused as though relieved into the heavy vibration of an expanded A followed by a decisive *chim* that kept its intimate fusion in spite of repeated overlaps; Karsch could hardly hear Mrs. Liebenreuth's little voice say with helpless reverence: Yes. Yes. Yes.

—She's still in the city? Achim asked.

Achim was in the second group; the telecamera focused less often on the finish line, didn't let the Red Cross tent at the edge of the stadium out of sight. Achim had appeared, bent over the handle bars in the exemplary pose that consisted of an immobile back above extremely mobile legs; the screen showed him standing still, choking for breath, he was breathing into the microphone (that showed at the lower edge of the teakwood frame), completely bewildered he looked at the first-aid men and the coaches of his home team who were protectively standing about him. When they lifted him off his bike and started to carry him in their arms, his face at first contorted into an angry grimace. Later, at the straw barrier, he was seen waving flowers and a tired arm into the welcoming yaps, while bicycles still kept coming in behind him, too late since Achim was already there. The men who were carrying him did it out of enthusiasm. He wouldn't have been able to take a step.

His voice became softer, almost toneless. He listened to Karsch telling him that Karin had rented the upper story of a low house amid city trees, the roof had several gables, the window was semicircular. It is the house on the south side of the devastated area in the center of the city, with an almost intact wall around a tidy garden among forests of wild unkempt weeds. The street-car stops at the garden gate, it is the last house, then it continues for a long stretch of uninhabited night into the southern suburb. If there's a light on in the house, it comes from the flat oval window under the sky, then she is at home, all alone amidst her new furniture. Do you want us to drive over?

Achim shook his head.

He'd come in too far back to have to participate in honor laps and winners' speeches; abruptly he had disappeared into the entrance to the underground passage between the playing field and the hollow interior of the cement torus. He was sitting on the stretcher, his arms crossed on the seams of his sweat shirt, he tried to lift them. The gesture collapsed. His face was unrecognizable behind mud and fatigue. They undressed him and washed him and awakened his body with thick sprays of water, they kneaded him and gave him juice to drink. For two hours he rested under a blanket.

Karsch couldn't sit still when he talked. Whenever he fell silent they heard Mrs. Liebenreuth groan behind the door. She was tossing and turning before she fell asleep. Achim was leaning against the back of the couch with his legs half pulled up. He blinked into the pale lamp, trying to keep his face open. When Karsch had helped Karin he said he had said: That he knew a man with a wife and two children who'd been waiting for an apartment for years, who didn't even need generous rooms in an old house with beautifully proportioned windows and seasoned architecture surrounded by a park: and whose application had not been attended to in ten days. Karin (who remained standing at the door with her coat on, who felt ashamed in front of the movers because of her priceless slender neck and the favoritism displayed in her environment) was carefully grinding cigarette ashes into the parquet floor on which she intended to live, intent on the grinding tip of her shoe she said angrily in a low voice: Am I responsible for this State. Should I perhaps . . . and reappeared only after we had set up the furniture and were all sitting on the expensive chairs in our dirty work clothes in front of two cases of beer on the Moroccan carpet: Karsch said.

Achim forced his eyes wide open. The corners of his mouth

dipped into a stiff grimace. —Never mind, Karsch: he said: Never mind.

In a gray suit, meeting reporters. Achim apologizes: Today was a hard struggle. Photos: Achim alone against a gray background, Achim amidst his team, hanging from shoulders, end of the TV coverage. Karsch took Mrs. Liebenreuth home, but Achim added a few more words about tomorrow's program: start at ten A.M.; one hundred sixty miles, arrival same afternoon at the central stadium, reception by the administrator in person. We'll all end up with the order of merit of the Republic. If we keep it up. Our team has second place, that's not bad is it? Karin can't be distinguished in the smoke- and word-drowned background. And she doesn't appear at dinner. After which he telephones her landlady. Who says: But what's the matter, she doesn't live here any more. The team's bedtime is ten o'clock. Achim throws someone's coat over his gym suit, tiptoes down the side stairs, slips outside.

—How is she making out? said Achim. He pushed back the freshly made coffee. Tomorrow he'd be missing two hours' sleep. Coffee was completely out.

—Same as always: said Karsch, so that Achim could picture microphones and bowing from the applause-framed edge of the stage between heavy swaying curtains; he said: We see a good deal of each other. She is happy, so that Achim could think of Karsch waiting in his car outside the theater, Karin skipping sideways down the stairs, with amused patience she'd leaf through what Karsch had written and hand Achim's conceivable life back to him, without objections, but with disbelief; and Karsch said: You know how she is, so that Achim could accommodate these bits of information within his own experience of her. He did not tell Achim that she was worried. But Achim hadn't been listening.

—Was she always this way, Karsch? he said. He was drinking the hot stuff that would cost him sleep. —I mean: he said, hesitated. His eyes were nearly closing with effort.

—That nobody understands why she does what she does and yet you can't talk to her.

Karsch raised his shoulders, let them drop. He thought it quite understandable that she had moved, it was quite obvious. He didn't know what Achim's question meant.

Achim let Karsch drive him back to the hotel, but when they took leave, he grasped Karsch's elbow and said almost as an afterthought, while turning his head away: Why don't you stay here. The next morning Karsch followed the last stretch of the race in the press car. Achim had him sit at his table for breakfast; he briefed him for the race; they didn't discuss anything else. One couldn't tell the night he had had. At the start he turned and raised his hand to Karsch, whenever they met they communicated by glances about the things Achim had left unsaid, the things the underslept author of his biography, in shirt and trousers, wildly riding after flying sweat shirts talking to journalists from all countries could only imagine at best. (He hadn't felt like giving messages from Karin that she had not asked him to give. He could not imagine that a man like Achim would remain so attached.) Nobody had ever suggested that he ride along with the race.

That much about Prague. There was quite a bit that belonged or, perhaps, did not belong in the description of Achim's life.

What was Karin worried about?

That has even less to do with bicycle racing!

A friend came to see Karsch and wrote it up in the papers, she didn't deny it, so she got into trouble.

One day at noon, during the lunch hour, when the downtown streets were thickened by slowly strolling people, a thirty-year-old gentleman was walking along with idle curiosity. He had three cameras slung over his shirt, letting them alternately fall into his hand, he shot what the natives hardly considered worth shooting, he bypassed the town hall and old fountains at historical corners. He'd photograph the lateral view of a counter in a store with the saleswoman's hand dipping toward the hidden slab of butter, he'd kneel at the curb to gather store name and empty shopwindow into his memory-storing box, he'd let posters, slogans, ice-cream stands, people's faces impress his sensitive material, he was sweating, concentration pushing his tongue out between his teeth. He looked up and noticed a youngish couple dawdling along the shopwindows, their dangling arms meshing, talking hilariously in the heat of the air and the manifold odor of trees in bloom in the park and industrious chimney smoke and long-imprisoned bodies released into the brightness of this day. That's when he shouted, somewhat overwhelmed: Hey! Karsch!

And Karsch said: That's the guy I told you about, the one with the mobile nose, and he said: May I introduce you, he's a friend of mine, and Karin held out her hand and said hello and pushed her shoulders forward; both smiled. They walked on all three together.

Very West German, the other man between them spoke at the top of his voice, he'd point to things that were strange and ask questions and laugh and slap Karsch's back and take photos: all in one breath. It was true, he did have considerable control over his nose muscles: wrinkling its fleshy back all the way up while glancing sideways meant that he was delighted: that he neither offered nor expected to be offered any trust in anything: that the only thing one could be sure of was his amiability. You'd always recognize and remember him by his nose. And he loved to travel in foreign countries: not because he wanted to learn, he just liked to be on the move.

He had various newspapers with him, behind which Karsch disappeared from the conversation during lunch because ever since his arrival in this country he had been almost completely without news from home. The official city paper would report solely on West German rearmament, mention unfair court verdicts against real patriots and the daily deterioration of morals; Karsch was checking whether people were still leading a life back home: they were, but the West German papers were endlessly reporting on East German rearmament, unfair court verdicts against real patriots and the daily deterioration of morals. Karsch knew quite a few people who wrote this, he knew their offices, and certain backings and fillings and omissions in the writing met him as though he were having lunch in another city and they were all coming up to his table to shake his hand and say hello and ask him how he was. What are you doing here? Karsch's supposed to be in East Germany; what on earth can he be doing over there?

154

Karsch looked up and was drawn into the conversation between his two neighbors who were good-naturedly (as though they stood side by side and walked around each other, mutually curious, delighted with the different angles) telling and not telling each other that they would not let it come to a discussion but didn't mind just sitting there, talking and looking. Karsch noticed the sparing friendliness in Karin's eyes, her patient lips, and observed that this friend of his was treating her the way he treated her himself. He'd better leave soon.

—What are you doing over here?

He (let's call him Hans) had come over to write a report about the collectivization of individually owned farms. He had been given an entry permit on that basis; actually a farmer was supposed to have hanged himself. And what about you?

—I am visiting: Karsch said, and he also mentioned the balcony in West Berlin.

—Oh: said the reporter, withdrew his eyes politely, stiffened his neck, assumed a trustworthy pose.

—No: said Karsch, Karin pouted: perhaps they had all understood the same thing.

— . . . somebody killed himself: Karin asked stubbornly. She hadn't moved, yet she seemed to be leaning further back in her chair, stiffer, more remote.

Because of the collectivization: the other man confirmed, he couldn't help himself, with nodding and pushed-out mouth and amenities and three cameras. He was preparing for another question (How do you live over here? Is it expensive?) when Karin said: Let's go. And got up and was standing outside in the street and suddenly had lots of time that afternoon. The day was clear. They had sat outside, at a white-clothed table under a large colorful umbrella and were served by a young waiter who was giving a great deal of thought to Karin's eyes behind her black glasses and smiled with an effort every time she smiled.

After a couple of hours they arrived in the village whose name had crossed the borders to the West as a memorial or as indignation or pride, that had been crystallized into news which was sold to the highest bidder. Some of the inhabitants were active that way, walked unobtrusive through the streets, lived in houses, led a normal family life, were friendly neighbors and

colleagues. The village was strung out in hilly country, domi-
nated by the gaping slate-roof buildings of the ruined manor; to
begin with, right after the war, the new government had turned
over the land of the estate to day laborers, refugees, smallhold-
ers; citified houses with pointed gable roofs linked to stable and
interior yard stood around the ruins, durably built from massive stones, for masters who passed them on from generation to
generation, but now no more. The side streets had no pavement, only the main street that led through the village, rough
and cobbled, up to an empty square framed by ten-year-old
trees, and on it the tavern; and the newly built mayor's office.
Empty trucks were standing in the sun on the thin grass of the
village square. Nobody was in the streets. They had seen nobody working in the field. Behind the closed doors the dogs
were loose and restless. The sun stood obliquely in the sky,
made the view pleasant. Everything still smelled of life.
The graveyard lay at the edge of a small forest. On its extension
which the community had carved out of the fields only a few
years ago, there were two fresh mounds against the low wall,
one covered with wreaths and flowers, the other bare clay. The
smoothed-out, sandy edges were dry, whitish and already crumbly. The church was down in the village, new wheat was growing all around, nothing stirred on the paths through the fields.
By evening the people had told them: There had been a meeting in the village by the end of which the farmers had not agreed
to turn their property into a co-operative, whereupon a brigade
of workers in the chemical industry had arrived from the city a
couple of days later, all grouchy because they didn't like this
assignment, they found the weather too hot, they'd walk alongside a farmer wherever they'd find one and stress the community of dialect and the common benefit of collectivization. They
had come in the name of the administrator, they spoke of German reunification, they said the proposed change was an act
serving peace, they asked who of them preferred war and the
West German warmongers. Those are the facts supposedly,
that's what was told. Since the agitators obtained access to the
barricaded farms only with the help of the police, farmers who
sicked their dogs on the intruders were jailed for breaking
the peace, and since a declaration against a peace thus formu-

lated might have become a delicate matter in circumstances not easily assessed, ten of the eleven farmers in the village finally agreed to the contract, in order to get out of sight what would be weighing from their necks anyway. Finally the eleventh farmer whom the fellow workers from the city had not left alone for a number of days, whose freshly plowed furrows they had crushed and packed down with their expressly weighted trucks, had appeared at the mayor's office with them and asked for permission to join. They didn't describe him as particularly bullheaded. The seizure of the considerable acreage of the community thus seemed completed; that evening the eleventh signed under the eyes of all assembled (none of them had had a normal day for the third morning in a row) and in the meditative silence the eleventh is said to have checked the contract once more, discovered the term voluntary in assertive form, torn up the document and walked out of the room; this rash gesture had destroyed all the other signatures, it was difficult to get them a second time, since the immediate arrest of the saboteur and his subsequent transfer to the city authorities had given the others additional time to think it over. He was described as a man who liked his work, believed in certain tenets of the Lutheran Church, was known and trusted in the entire village and not even more respectable than his neighbors. The only son had been killed in the war. A slow old man of sixty who had been given the farm not by the government, but by his parents. He couldn't understand. Then the ride through the night on a truck, then the jump into a ditch, the chase across the fields, the encirclement of his farm: that's where he'd seek refuge. The police guards stood and watched, they were still standing and watching when his wife had found her husband dangling from a rope and cut him down. He was said to have been a levelheaded man. The minister behaved with taciturn dignity, showed incomprehension: a person who had committed suicide is not entitled to a Christian burial. But he had been given a regular burial, and where he lies is not the corner for suicides. Then there is supposed to have been, or not to have been, some incident about the wreaths, but they all contradicted each other, this didn't become clear. Other ministers behaved differently; other farmers ran across the border; but most of them stayed where they were, under the new contract. During those six weeks the entire agriculture of the East German partitioned State had been collectivized: how many farmers in proportion to a few no longer verifiable deaths. With this philosophy one of Karsch's friends described his impressions after he returned to his country, and he sent Karsch the newspaper, which didn't arrive. Because, among the citizens whose presence appears to us like belonging, working, and living together, some must be entrusted with jobs that only a higher administrating perspective of society can assign as essential for the prosperity of the State which tries, obviously or inscrutably, to improve the life of even the recalcitrant. Or something to that effect.

Karsch read this particular paper at a meeting of the State Union to which Karin had been permitted to bring him as a guest. They had pushed back their chairs and sat close together, away from the meeting workers who, after the third point on the agenda, were listening to the chairman's report, tired now, with greater indifference. The chairman beneath the trusting gaze of the administrator sat bent over his elbows and was elaborating on his notes about the criminal sabotage the West German government was perpetrating against the reunification, he invited the opinions of those present; he transmitted the administrator's pleasure at the final completion of the long-hoped-for collectivization, as well as the latter's regrets about certain abuses, he invited opinions. During these days, people were sitting in similar meetings all over the country in similar rooms decorated with flags, saying the same things, listening to the same things; of all the chairmen this one alone may have distinguished himself by the bloated cold that deprived him of his respiration, blurred his brain, that was autonomous and as surprising as unfair for this time of year. He concluded with a request of the official city newspaper: asking that the more prominent participants in the East German arts and sciences sign their contempt to the slanderous report of a certain West German journalist who had abused hospitality and had written an unscrupulously inflammatory report against the progress of socialism in the environs of the city, once again the chairman leaned one shoulder against the back of his chair, passed his hand over the semigray curve of his hair, vertical wrinkles quivered in his face next to the horizontal mouth movements. From time to time his unique cold made him look as though he were asleep. The long room was hot and smoked full with impatience, a cooler wind swept past the open windows and did not come in. Karsch had pushed back his chair beside Karin's, they were leafing through the heavy first-quality paper that had been lying on the table as though forgotten, they held it by its outer edges, supporting the joint in the middle with the backs of their hands and pulled-up knees. The article did not mention where the village was located, it could be any village that an approximately thirty-year-old gentleman might visit, with curiosity, without prejudice, and depict through conversations, photographs, and the vaguer impressions of moods. He described the question about wanting or not wanting peace as one that left no issue or choice, according to the villagers in all the localities he had visited, he had a neat explanation of the advantages of compulsory collectivization, his photos showed the conditions of the farms and the spring sowing. In a shorter paragraph he mentioned a fatal outcome, showed ordinary trucks on typical village squares, described the requirements for a Christian burial. He had been able to obtain a photograph from the dead man's army records; framed between swastika seals a work-worn face, low forehead, narrow eyes, firm lips set into a sturdy chin, looked vaguely and kindly at today's observer from above the uniform collar of the defeated army. At one corner of the mound one could recognize the recent tracks of Karin's shoes by the neat angular hole around which the sole had moved back and forth irresolutely. The widow was not shown; the reader might imagine her as the former inhabitant of a stolidly squatting farmhouse barricaded behind a picket fence, and they had seen the dog lie exactly as treacherous and angry on a potato sack in front of the deserted house, his eyes were black and yellow, he stopped growling only after Karin withdrew her hand from the latch on the gate. The article carefully weighed the circumstances that had led to the death and expressed doubt in the forcible arrest of the widow after she had supposedly attacked the policemen with a stanchion, when they finally entered; however Karsch would have used virtually the identical words to outline what the farmer's wife from the neighboring farm intimated with a gesture to Karin: that the helpless old woman had struck out the way a fist might strike diagonally past a cramped chin and another fist again a little lower at a breathless neck, hesitating, with increasing vigor, blindly into the void, which, however, must have been a youthfully upset policeman's face at the time, since the indictment speaks of resisting the authority of the State.

—No: said Karin. She wasn't aggressive, her hands lay relaxed on her knees, her eyes were narrowed but she looked calmly into the blinding light which, to anyone looking at her from the side, made tiny hairs stand out and tremble between rigid eyelids and taut skin above the cheekbones.

Her name did not appear in the next issue of the official city paper as a signature expressing indignation about the gangster tactics of West German journalism; however, the gap did not show, since she was the youngest prominent representative and known only to a few moviegoers as the memory of a longish dark-skinned girl's face turning at a certain angle in front of the panning camera, or as the presence of a sometimes crystalline, sometimes hoarse voice in the darkened auditorium; and in the editorial comment Mr. Fleisg asked with sincere indignation: how could anybody (who had been permitted to work for money and to live in this State) keep aloof in this way from men and women of better will. During the days that followed he printed letters from readers all over the city who had signed their full names to protests against tolerating persons who refuse to choose between the two German States, who are backing the West German powers, etc., whose talent and performances had, anyhow, been vastly overrated for quite some time. Now imagine kitchens in various states of activity and equipment, in some dinner had just been put on the table, in others dirty dishes were being stacked, in still another a couple was dancing, when Karin questioned grumpy men during supper or righteous women who sat darning socks or girls her own age who were ironing why they had sent the letters she received in the newspaper and what exactly they meant; picture Karsch waiting outside wooden or glass or iron doors for Karin to come down the stairs with her long sideway stride and an extremely closed face. She didn't give an imitation of the conversations, she didn't describe the rooms she had been in, she merely reported what they had said to her: that they hadn't meant it like that.

She remained relaxed but not always good-humored. She was refused a part in a new play at the theater, she had less money, she moved without informing Achim. When for days on end Karsch drove her to different radio stations which the rumor had not reached, where she was allowed a chair in front of a microphone and the job of transforming a written text into a young woman's casual though plausible utterance, she was often gay and told Karsch about the past eight years as though they had been good and fun to live. And Karsch would tell her about other foreign countries he had visited, they'd compare the colors of mailboxes and the variety of behavior of foreigners in arranging their private lives, this looks good as long as you are moving. She still had as many visitors as before, Karsch often met Mr. Fleisg in her house, in his shabby postwar clothes he'd sit engrossed in conversation with Karin, apart from the others, a glass in his hand, with gradually subdued gestures; after a while he would grow restless if he didn't see her, he'd look at her face from the side as though there he might find what he failed to understand. Mr. Fleisg had had a difficult time during his college years. He had two children and a sickly wife his own age who was timidly pretty, she'd sit next to her husband with eyes cast down and wouldn't join in the conversation when Karsch went over to him occasionally and invited him to have a beer and a general discussion about the way newspapers are put together in Germany, one way or the other way. He was impatient and severe with his four-year-old sons, the head-of-the-family role did not become him if anybody was looking. When he came to Karin's alone he'd wear a print shirt, swallow in his sinewy throat, rub sad eyes behind frequently removed glasses that dated from the time you couldn't buy any better ones, and was noticeably silent when Karin talked to someone else.

Sometimes she'd say, with a determination that seemed to be courage: But, agriculture on a large scale, the way they'll be able to farm now on the collectivized fields, that's really an advantage; don't you think they'll realize that, huh, Karsch, what do you think,

and turn her head impatiently, stand up with a sigh, walk

around the table to Mr. Fleisg's side, pull him back into their conversation by the scruff of the neck and pout only for occasional sideways glances in Karsch's direction. Karsch took it for a conspirational gesture. —No need to discuss it with Achim. And Achim said, later, after he'd got the newspapers and could read it all over the pages: Karsch, you tell her that she can't do that.

—What do you mean: said Karsch.

—She can't do that: said Achim, he was very quiet, moving his head back and forth, thinking behind almost closed eyes, repeating his gesture of negation. That was toward the end of the big race, before he went back home: when he could have gone to see Karin the next day. He was sitting on a bench in the early-summer park between official receptions, with the order of merit for his country already pinned to his lapel. He was tired.

He was no longer listening when Karsch told him that his friend was trustworthy and how they had accompanied him on his ride to the place where it had happened. Achim raised a deprecatory hand, waved away the regards Karsch gave him. Because the lively thirty-year-old gentleman who was so fond of traveling in foreign countries would have been interested to meet the bicycle champion who sat in a room paneled with precious woods and represented the people and held up his hand in approval of the administrator's agricultural reforms, who stood up and thanked the administrator in the name of the farmers who had hardly had a chance to get to know him since their very different profession lay at a distance from the big highways, but had, nevertheless, elected him unanimously the year before.

Perhaps worry is too strong a word. For Karsch these were merely circumstances of the making of a biography. He would certainly have mentioned them, but his subject was a bicycle champion and he thought you wouldn't want to know about all this.

Could one write anything at all under such conditions?

Karsch enjoyed interrupting comments. He made notes of a stiff-necked head-jerking gesture of indifference, because he believed in Achim's importance, therefore he retained a young mathematics student's willfully pushed-out lips, also Achim's father who watched them quarrel, leaning in the open kitchen window, head on one arm, as though it gave him pleasure (there were tiny twitchings about his mouth, as if he were chewing the inconsiderate remarks they were exchanging:)
—You'd better write about something else.
Some evenings an elderly man in cement-dusted clothes would hang his cap on a hook above the counter at which Karsch was sitting. He didn't come alone, but after a couple of beers he'd become friendlier and lean on his elbows and turn to whoever sat next to him, usually Karsch, that's why they acted as though they were acquaintances. So Karsch tried to tell him from his notes what was to be a book someday, the story of a life, he wanted it to be understandable, most of the time it sounded ambiguous. The old man would turn a rough chin and narrower eyes across the bar up to the portrait of the administrator who looked down more sternly here in this place on the heads bent in conversation or over glasses, and ask:
—Now that he's riding his bike all the time, how do the two of them get together?
—You can just use his own words.
—See? That way you don't tell a thing.
When Karsch moved in with Mrs. Liebenreuth, she folded her hands under her apron and shook her head, she was straining hard to think. She had no idea in whom Karsch was interested. He told her Achim's private name. She felt ashamed, she shrugged, she would have liked to know who he was, but she had no idea.
—Never heard of him.
Karsch often chose his table in the area served by the waitress in the garden restaurant where Achim had yielded the first bits and pieces of his life, he enjoyed her hesitating between curiosity and withdrawal, if the girl was moments ago so curious

about the famous guest with the dark glasses, then why did she have second thoughts, what made her careful? She'd lean against his table, raise her arms at an angle to readjust the stiffly pleated little cap on the first wave of her hair and say, not unfriendly:

—I didn't mean anything.

—But wouldn't you be interested in a book about his life?

—That's no life he's living.

Mr. Fleisg dangled long bent legs without being aware of it, fixed cautious eyes on Karin and said hesitantly: That's not the way to look at it; he handled words with greater care since spending his evenings with Karin and not with his family. Karsch was told that Mr. Fleisg would break away from the stream of walkers outside the printing plant in the evening and slowly stroll through small side streets in the direction of the park where Karin lived; Karin told him, she saw him arrive. (Karsch did not talk to him about that: he could use being left alone now by Mr. Fleisg.) Karsch didn't want to see Mrs. Ammann again before Achim had backed him up by saying: That's about how it was, all right. What was the way to look at it? Everybody thought of a man thirty years old, who made his living from bicycle riding, and who was famous, his astonished smile was believable, his long tough-skinned head made nobody uneasy, he conducted himself with modesty, everything he did was in the open and lauded by the administrator, who, like everybody, did not mean him, but his view of him; Karsch was unable to make those views tally, he wrote them down in his notebook, but appreciated interrupting comments.

An example. Karsch was now working on the episode with the three-speed gearshift Achim had once bought in West Berlin. Karsch hadn't asked him about it, they were in Berlin together, the presence nudged him, he remembered, he said: That's how it was when we started. My first three-speed shift, I went across the border, got me one . . . everything there looked like Sunday, me being so awkward. He looked amused, out of the corner of one eye, shook his head as though he couldn't understand it now, repeated: Today we make them ourselves, and the bikes too.

Nineteen years old, in the blue shirt, he marched next to blue shirts and blue blouses through the main streets of East Berlin. From the head of the column blasts of brass thumped backward into the intervals between steps, fluttered off, came back with renewed breath as the rhythm and melody of the song of the Communists who had fought the Spanish war on the side of the legally elected government, —Freedom: sang the last row of marchers, naked arms clasping naked arms, boys and girls marching forward, marking time, full throats hacking at the first syllable of the last word, overlapping, four wavering rising sounds, and the harsh impact of the second syllable, while up in front the next verse came out of throats and vibrating brass. Red and blue strips of cloth shouted letters down on the streets, the charred window frame of a bombed-out butcher shop carried a gigantic poster in nervous Gothic script, passers-by turned into spectators on the sidewalk, around noon it got hot. In the middle of the blue crowd empty streetcars stood waiting, nonplused and yellow; for hours cars had been standing resignedly pushed against the curbs by the endless march, columns turned corners barring their direction, flags swayed way above the heads, held up next to white cardboard posters proclaiming the home towns of the groups. Frequent halts, when the angular formation of bodies would break into jerky waves, clusters thickened, doors sucked in uniforms and devoured them, distances balanced from broad to narrow, inside wide circles couples were dancing to the clapping of hands and peasant tunes on accordions. It was a celebration for the State Youth Organization and cost a lot of money in a defeated country. The swinging skirts of the girls, the festively decorated streets, the constant human contact set off a feeling of enthusiastic agreement in Achim, head stiffly turned to the right he was floating along in ecstasy, past the extremely high and remote podium of the administrator, innocently held arms to his chest, laughed, talked effusively and turned sullen only during the long, thirsty march back to their lodgings, because of the forbidden purchase he planned to make in the other part of the city. Back home there would be normal life again. Then nothing of all this would remain, except the lack of a gearshift which his self-esteem needed when he trained with the others who had one. The marchers dispersed in a wide suburban street that appeared bare suddenly in the heat. The broken ranks: the comparatively ugly sight of individual figures running or idling away in collectively blue shirts strengthened his decision. He gathered indignation, until it became imperative that he, too, should infringe the strict interdiction, like the others. (The march back to headquarters is to proceed in closed formation.)

A boy in a white windbreaker and shorts was leaning against the door of a moving Berlin subway train, casting worried glances at the map inside the car, comparing it with the stations that entering or leaving passengers exposed to him between opening double doors, that disappeared again with the hard joining of the two sides closing; he expected to come to the thicker line on the map that shifted the means of transportation into politics. His face had not found its final shape, it looked undecided, sometimes greedy for something that remained hidden in a quickly averted glance. Every so often he'd stroke his hair, because there used to be a part where the dense blond thicket was now fashionably forced straight back, the former part would reappear, be quickly flattened down, reappear immediately. The last red-circled point before the hatched border-worm on the map became a long tiled cavern with small booths, underground lights bounced into the incoming train and with it the louder voice of the train announcer who invited all participants of the State Youth Festival to get off, serenely pronounced the name of the station, then, bent over his microphone, again warned them against continuing the ride, his eyes staring as though grieved at the floor. The boy in the white windbreaker watched the blue shirts being sucked out onto the platform, but he managed not to move. The jerk of the start pulled him along into the tunnel and shook the stiffness out of his pose.

It looked like Sunday to him. Had it been a holiday? No. Did Achim think of a residential street with spaced low houses and quiet trees and garden fences, a woman and a child taking a placid walk, the eyes of a bored old man behind a curtainless window, a car stops, nothing seems to move. Surely no one sells gearshifts in a street like that. No, for a long time he walked between extremely high houses, only once did he pass a tidy little square with old trees on grass, he remembers the rows of cars parked at the curb, dignified dogs striding beside shopping

166

bags, everything looked so neat. But that wasn't really what he was thinking about. Nine years ago some person got off the subway somewhere in West Berlin, climbed out of the shaft and emerged in the afternoon haze of an August day, crossed the moderate street traffic, looked about him, walked into a smaller street, as though he were searching for something. He was wearing a windbreaker and kept pulling it together at the collar as though trying to hide something at his throat. What gave him the impression of Sunday? The quiet in the streets away from the center? Achim hesitated. The rubble had been leveled, the houses had been repaired, everything looked dressed up for the weekend, an exceptionally large number of women were out walking in the streets, not at work, as though this were a holiday, their coats and dresses were of better materials and better sewn than the best Sunday clothes? That was not what Achim meant. A little of all of this, except the feeling that he came from a poorer country. If not the quiet, then the noise, the heavy traffic, the prosperous look of the street scene. You and your street scenes. The unworried faces of the people, their more colorful clothes, more space to live in, with more objects designed for their comfort! Achim shook his head. He had thought of something else. Outside the windows of a wooden shack stood a thin-necked boy, thumbs anchored in his back pockets, examining from a somewhat overly assured position on legs spread apart the bicycles that were hanging on hooks behind the narrow dirty pane. The walls of the shop were cracked and weather-beaten, peeling varnish scantily framed the two windows. The shack had been built on the leveled basement of what had once been an apartment house, next to it rose the impeccable wall of a new building, bulldozers were at work across the street, the shack was awaiting its turn. After three steps the boy came back, once more he read the blue-pencil inscription on a piece of cardboard attached to the first of the suspended bikes: French make, eight shifts, inquire price within. The rear-wheel axle was hidden by the wall. It seemed very dark inside the shop. Achim turned, walked past the other window with accessories and examined them almost without stopping, the door creaked as he entered. A girl in a blue smock came out from somewhere in the back and inquired about the customer's wishes, pushing a pencil behind one ear through very thick hair. Achim practically stammered. He did not use the technical term, he knew it and thought it but did not say it, clumsy and hot-cheeked he described that he needed a three-speed gearshift and that it was to be built into an ordinary bicycle, an ordinary one, you understand. The girl bent down without taking her eyes off him, found a box under the table, pushed it toward him. He understood that the gearshift was in the box. He asked a lot of questions, weighed the contraption in his hand, talked at random in order to delay the question: Do you accept East marks? he asked. He had wanted it to sound casual, in a man-of-the-world tone, he hesitated. Infraction against the inner-German currency regulations. The girl recalculated the price on the exchange rate basis, he stared at her thick chaotic hair, he was happy. He was ready to find her torpid face pretty, he felt grateful to her, he talked a great deal: it's very nice of you to accept Eastern marks (to sell me anything at all, I beg your pardon) since I'm not from here. He tried to extricate the money from his breast pocket without opening his windbreaker. In the street he suddenly felt exhausted. Exhaustion was proud of the small heavy package he was carrying, exhaustion was alone with the precious object, exhaustion asked the people in the street arrogantly for directions: I want to go to the East, which way is the East. But it took him an hour and a half, since he didn't dare take the subway from a Western station with his East money, he considered the exchange rate an actual favor on the part of the salesgirl. A wide street through a long park led him with the falling night to a square near the border where boys and girls of the State Youth Organization were doing acrobatics and singing on a stage made of planks. At the edge of the spectator crowd a boy bought an ice cream, he was wearing a white windbreaker. The top was unbuttoned, and he had just turned the collar of his blue shirt up and over the jacket collar. His hands looked very black next to the white ice cream, he remembers accordion music and the astonished face of the saleswoman, two ten-pfennig pieces, a sweaty dirty hand next to something cool, the sensation of home-coming. An impression as of Sunday. He says it felt like Sunday, he says one can't explain it. Listen here.

He wouldn't have known whom to ask. If he had lost his way, or wanted to stay over there: the policemen wore different uniforms, a different cut in a different color, crankily or cheerfully they were performing tasks of which a nineteen-year-old from a differently governed country could only have the vaguest notion. The inscriptions on administration buildings were incomprehensible to him, at the newsstands he read headlines about events he had never heard of, which he did not believe. He didn't know what the money here looked like, how it felt, he saw bank buildings soar hugely toward the sky, but also apartment buildings. Who might be running this country. Nothing invited him. The people he passed in the streets lived mysteriously for him, he couldn't guess whether they worked in factories stores offices, as he was able to by glancing at a casual pedestrian in his home town, they drove their cars, walked with inexplicable purposefulness to unimaginable places, moved their faces toward objects and situations he didn't understand: they were all there, he saw everything, he guessed nothing. Unknown persons discussed unknown things in an unknown language, next to him they lived in the balmy evening of a different country, they lived with one another secure in what he didn't know, he was as distant from them as the impression of Sunday morning from working days; there was movement all around him that left him standing still, the way Sunday stops and leaves one standing, alone and helpless in lonely rooms. In this clean remoteness, in this neat foreign country, Sundaylike alone and insecure.

—Something like that perhaps? asked Karsch.
—Might be: said Achim. —Perhaps: he said: In a way . . .
In a way (thought Karsch) was extremely precise. Perhaps in a way could be described in a way.
The navy sentinels outside the wrought-iron gate to the administrator's official residence stood stiffly at attention, holding their machine guns diagonally before them with both hands. That's not the way you hold a child in your arms. Across the street they saw the two gentlemen approach once more between the park benches. The one in the gray suit with the sunglasses who walked with such a loose stride reminded them of

someone. The other man was much shorter and talked with his hands. Caught up in animated conversation they kept pacing back and forth in the thickening evening light that was tinting the open lawn. Now they shook hands, the tall one stepped over the curb and came toward the palace. Stopped by a thought he turned his head backward and asked something.

—Why do you keep asking about that, you don't want to put that in the book, do you?

The departure of a convoy of trucks hid the princely yellow house front, singing and motor noise filled the entrance. The gate chain clinked to the pavement. An officer waved a red and white signal, the trucks started up again. Stiff and mute the honor guards saw the tall gentleman stand in the same position on the other side of the street, but he was not looking at his companion, the back of his head was turned toward him and he was shaking it with lowered face, one surmised a pensive expression. Then he approached steadily across the street, removed his sunglasses a few steps before the gate and smiled. They recognized Achim. They saluted him with a hardly perceptible jerk, stood even straighter as they let him pass.

Had Achim gone across the border, felt like Sunday in the foreign country, did he own a three-speed gearshift nine years ago? All that is long ago. Nobody remembers. What happened that year?

That year Achim took part in a rally of the State Youth Organization in the former capital now divided. The following year the country's foreign trade was able to import a few West German racing bicycles; one of which was allotted to Achim.

That could be written under these conditions. The conditions abbreviated what would have been ambiguous even in a longer version. Not to mention the interrupting comments. And not to mention the: In a way.

But it isn't true!

Achim had gone across the border, had spent money illegally. An incident that lay blurred and remote behind a ten-year thicket. In the course of a conversation about the street scene he happened to mention it to a man from West Germany, just because he happened to recall his first impression of the differences, which were what he had in mind, and not his purchase. The conversation would not endure. The book about his life was to be offered to people in a durable binding. He didn't mind having lived with a purchased accessory for the duration of an intimate conversation, he did not want to have lived with it in the book. What's not true about that?

Is the way it was the truth? True his entering the dark crowded shop, the gentle odor of metal and grease, his creaking halt on the warped floor boards that are sinking with their beams toward the lose rubble underneath; true, consequently, the pride of a nineteen-year-old who has changed a desire to tangible reality, in secret and alone, the lonely risk of offending a law, fear tearing at him in the void on the sidewalk, at street corners on the way back, the impotent rage against the multiplied price as though against fate, a fate that bears the inexorable face of a harder currency? Is all this not true, and because it was like that? As to Karsch, he wrote down what Achim's memory was fishing from the unseeable, unseen past, pieces of wreckage of a once-lived afternoon; Achim knew what Karsch could only guess at.

If we do not mention the border crossing and the infraction against Achim's State's currency regulations we omit what has happened, and incompleteness is a lie? This was one day Karsch had chosen among the three hundred and sixty-five of the entire year: but he had omitted the afternoon in the thickly overgrown ditch beside the superhighway where Achim took a swim in the ice-cold muddy water with a girl, and took her, and was shocked when she came and hid the clear sky above his wide eyes behind the swaying strands of her hair and the more and more fluid contours of her head; Karsch had omitted the festive day and hour when Achim was asked to step forth from the meeting framed by flags and slogan banners, his flushed breathing on the podium visible to all, when he was given the radiant yellow honor medal for a job well done, after the handshake with the administrator's representative he had leaped almost blindly toward the stairs at a one-hundred-eighty-degree angle and would have stumbled without the good-natured warnings from his teammates in the second row; and he had omitted another day and the hours spent working in the garden on the strawberry patch, when he made peace with his father for the rest of their lives as they knelt side by side in the sandy heat; and he had omitted the rainy morning before Christmas when Achim's brigade was ordered to take down the scaffolding after they had finished the building, which was not part of their job and the fault of fat men who sat forgetful behind desks and knew nothing of the rain during a dangerous job, all were indignant, they tossed the planks down blindly, not caring how they sailed through the air, butt first, and broke and splintered on the ground, they tore the bolts out of the clamps and let the slender poles tilt and didn't give a damn about the scratches and holes they made in the fresh stucco, and only the sight of legs slipping, followed by the sighing of rubber soles on wet beams and the collective feeling of fright that accompanied a mason's swooping down through the air toward the bristling confusion of beams and stacked bricks and finally the unanimous cry toned down their rage to cautious grips and Achim still didn't know what to look forward to in the evening: Karsch had not described any of those days, they had not fitted into his selection, or were too numerous, although they would have completed his description, and incompleteness is a lie? Karsch didn't want everything about Achim, he only wanted to pick what distinguished him (in Karsch's opinion) from other people, from other bicycle riders, for that was the purpose of his choice among the different episodes of a life, that's what he wanted of the many truths. And what do you want with the truth?

Neither to you nor to Karsch belongs what Achim was willing to yield of his life. What would finally appear on Karsch's pages and go on sale as Achim's life in words: which was to show him the way he had recently come to understand himself. To say: Here, look at me. I, Achim T., was a young man after the war who wanted to live his life just any old way. I built houses for you, in exchange you kept me clothed and fed. I did my work, and afterward I lived as you did, I had nothing against you, I cared nothing about you, we bartered money for effort. Then the State stepped into the picture with the administrator's party, and said: That's not enough. So I did a little more. And the State encouraged my hobby and made it into my profession and gave me a job to do and made me responsible for our special togetherness and gave me something to do for you and I began to care. And you, before you criticize the administrator and his State, stop and think what he is doing for you, letting a bicycle racer represent the people and talk to him. That's what the book should say. Achim didn't deny the things about himself, he didn't conceal the fainthearted purchase that particular day of the enthusiastic rally: to himself that is, he remembered it, but he remembered it with shame and called it an error. (The way he wouldn't like seeing the Achim again who had crudely ditched a girl in a hostile village almost fourteen years ago, as though he had been deaf.) He didn't want it said: Achim never went across the border, never spent money in disobedience of the second clause of the law regulating the export of currency from one Germany into the other, merely: he didn't want it to become publicly known, he didn't deny it, it remained a part of his life, Achim had a right to feel ashamed about it. But the people who shouted their enthusiasm from the borders of the highway, or advised him as to the well-being of the State, or proposed him marriage devotion emulation in innumerable letters should mean the Achim of today in a gray suit, at an honors reception organized by the powers of the State, where he smiled and bowed and shook hands like a brother, the Achim who was willing to admit that he had by necessity got to where he was now, not by sheer coincidence or persuasion. Yesterday no longer fitted the man who accepted money from the administrator, and decorations, and all kinds of daily advantages, he could not be the one who had taken money over the border as though it were worthless, who had been self-centered then and distrusted his country as though it would never be able to buy and eventually build racing bicycles for him. He didn't want to be the brutal Achim who had en-

173

joyed his membership in the disbanded former State Youth Organization, better delete that; not a boy who was afraid of the Red Army, who would have denounced his father (denounced him for an unworthy cause), whom we've had to force into the blue shirt, and he never really understood. He wanted to have lived all along the way he lived now, as a member of the administrator's party for the last five years: at last convinced and committed to the justice of a State which had shown him nothing but pleasant aspects. He was looking for indications of this tendency in his life and not for the other trends, that's what he wanted of his truths, and they were his, after all.

Although they were briefer and excluded the things Karsch might have liked to tell about a life: the boy's timid face above a brown shirt, a taut face above a blue one, the way kitchens look in the night, fear and classroom smells, etc., well you know: the things you'd call the truth, since that's how it looks to you.

But there's no substitute!

Oh. The deforested stretches could have been reforested with what Achim called My Development Toward a Political Conscience: Such footsteps in the passage of his everyday past. For instance a young mason marching as file-leader in the column to the market square each time the administrator's representatives had some information to communicate also to those who were still disinclined to buy newspapers (What makes the West German government turn down our proposals? The others, not we, started the war in Korea), he'd walk up pushing his bicycle, listen for a while, then he'd back into the ranks holding his bicycle, stand again for a while grumpy at the edge of the crowded square in the thinner sound zones of the loud-speaker, leaning against a cornice or a shopwindow, at one point he'd have his bicycle between his legs and waddle with alternating kicks past the more loosely grouped people toward a side street and race away through the deserted lanes as though driven by urgent necessity. Sometimes he'd stay a little longer, finally he once stayed to the end of the announcement, close to the platform, upper lip between his teeth as though lost in thought, straying from the yelling head to the hammering fist to the leather shoes of the speaker at eye level with the gathered people; and again he (Achim?) was displeased when they dispersed in chaotic groups and clusters to the hearty sounds of brass, instead of going back in the rank and file order in which they had come from their jobs from all over the city; they might have listened for a change. And people who knew him saw that this time he hadn't left before it was over, and according to their purposes and moods, but with the same words, they said to each other on the way home: So that's the guy he is, well, we couldn't care less. Or meetings of the construction workers' union, or quarrels about the working norm: five masons sitting on a wall in construction during lunch break, lashing out at a sixth who is trying to convince them that they must put in more effort, voluntarily, for the good of the State (who may also have been Achim, at one point?), who suddenly finds himself all alone, with no one talking to him, without casual friendliness, the center of tacit contempt or spiteful needling, he wants to get in thick with the party; that could be told taking in the view of the city spreading beneath the edges of the new building, with streets running away into the twilight and soot-black walls and shocking holes which they'll have to build up again as long as they live, or under slim sheaves of sunshine with gilded tips glowing in the September distance that could not be seen from too close. Or it could be written in dialogue:

—Come on, you could also carry a poster once in a while.

—I just carried one the last time.

—I've got my bike, will you carry it for me in the meantime?

—What's it got written on?

And then it may either have been Achim who refused, without reason or hostility, to hold the grave-looking portrait of the administrator on a stick above the marchers' heads and did not want to be seen under it as the guy who carried that sort of thing; or, on the contrary, it might have been Achim who was holding on to one swaying pole of a cloth with a slogan painted on it, stretched across a wooden frame, screaming, in the nar-

175

row corridor of the administration building while everybody was rushing past him with ostentatious business: Now grab a hold of this somebody, you lousy bunch of shirkers!

—All you can do is take take take; the State sends you to school, gives you vacations. You might do something in return for a change.

—Get off it, man. The State pays that with our deductions. Get a move on! in which case Achim could have been the one who repeats nervously, patiently what he is supposed to say: or the one he's in the way of, who reaches for the brick, calmly, not looking up, who slaps the mortar on, presses the brick into place, reaches in back of him, sticks the trowel into the basin, don't stand around here. Whom he used to understand, whom he understands now, because there was a time when he hadn't cared either, about anything, just like that guy, he too once had had that idea about deductions.

Or an Achim who gets stuck with the function of group chairman in the State Youth Organization, nobody wants it, suddenly he finds himself sitting all by himself at the head of the table and is supposed to talk about the administrator's projects in such a way that the others around the table take him back as one of them, and still believe what he hasn't thought, isn't prepared to say; a grouchy brooding face above a sheet of paper, bits of sentences resentfully spat out, forced casualness and again the sensation of being abandoned.

Or another Achim watching another guy do just that, glad not to sit in his place.

Or, with less precision, the shadows of a campfire moving about him on evenings of a harvesting detail, clumsy grunts mixed with clear girls' voices in new songs, but again at the campfire and not alone, singing with the others into the more human night. Huh?

Because, whether he did the one or was the other: they would not have teased him. He was still good at dealing a blow the way he had learned it: not in anger, but forcefully until the other guy realized that he'd end up on the floor under these calculated efficient blows. Nor did the stubbornness with which Achim spent his free time on his bicycle and his money on improving it make him ridiculous in the eyes of his colleagues (as they called each other); twice they let the air out of his tires, then never again, they'd come to know him in the meantime. He was almost considered a loner. The foremen said he was capable, because he'd push his team ahead with tenacious, almost unthinking effort, the architects noticed that he knew how to listen and how to read their blueprints; in those days, at first glance, he looked sleepy. (Whatever he had missed in trade school he sat down to study one winter, head in hand, because at that time he still thought he had to justify his bicycle riding by doing better work.) As a result the directors made him an assistant instructor and after a couple of weeks the younger ones would jealously gather around him, run after him, believe what the older boy told them, fast and low, out of the corner of his mouth, they admired him for training in the bicycle club after work and didn't even ask him what for. Then his first wins (in local races, later county races) made the headlines on the sports page and they grew shy toward him because they were proud of him, finally he became altogether distant: for two years they kept the memory of his demanding fellowship alive and worked for it as though chained together, then they were allowed to become a brigade called after him, and to this day some of them wrote him letters and asked for advice: What to do about a girl friend, she already had a child by someone else, but he couldn't give her up, and what would Achim do in his case? And Achim answered gratefully, because he hadn't had an intimate friendship like that since, and none that had been so reliable.

Yes. And when, after a few years, he had pedaled himself to as much fame as anyone could have in this country, the administrator's party offered him the first racing bicycle that had been secretly built in an East German factory. That was during training for the summer races and his team would have preferred to keep the machines that had been imported from West Germany. But Achim said:

—Let's give it a try.

—You'll just wreck yourself. Yes, if we had more time

—Let's give it a try

and persuaded the youngest in the team: come on. Because, several times, the youngest had understood without a word what

Achim might have in mind in the middle of a race, just a slight wobbling with the back and the boy had been by his side with all his untested strength just as he began to raise himself on the pedals and, furiously treading, shot away from the surprised group. He was short and stocky and rode just for the fun of it and had not wanted to give up his profession, he was a shoemaker from a small town and proudly took the sheer zest of the racing season home to his parents and his girl friends like vacation souvenirs. There was little they could talk about. For a week, with the shoemaker, he broke in the factory's new machines, making them rebuild what was necessary to bring them close to the West German ones. After that they just were a bit heavier. After twelve hundred racing miles each machine broke a frame and Achim's gearshift split, the mornings after the falls the doctors said it was up to them if they wanted to go on, they wanted to go on, they wanted to have it out. Achim finished the summer races in average positions and the little shoemaker had changed back to one of the imported machines, both, worn to the bone, posed for the press, one grinning sadly, and the other roguish under short black hair, they said resignedly:

—Well, they're not as shitty as all that.

The administrator's party remembered Achim for this. The following year they all rode East German machines, but before they did the trainer had come to Achim, dour-faced and white-haired he had asked confidentially with apparent kindness: if Achim hadn't noticed how the new doctrine had taken hold of him and developed, in events known to him from his own life? or given him, increasingly, the sense of belonging?

—I don't understand.

That was in early fall on the terrace of a rest home, the view stretched over a silence of pines and a quietly shining lake, for two weeks Achim had reclined lazily, his legs on the parapet, writing letters to the factory on possible ways to improve the machines that had taken a deeper hold on him, after that summer, than the West German models. In the course of a respectful conversation he learned on that terrace that he had contributed to the prestige of the administrator's party, and now it seemed only fair (because the mental connection trapped him and he was not unwilling to return, a changed man, after the end of his cure, to the remote everyday life, a new man you have no idea of) for him to say:

Yes, well, if that's how it is I want to join the party.

(While the other man, who never overtensed his sinews, who never had to fight nausea or fatigue by more than a contraction of his eyebrows, the man with the almost jovial look of mischief in his eyes, probably answered: If it comes to the final count, I don't want to have been the last one, because they asked him the same question, and he went across the border, because he told himself more or less: that, after living through that summer, he could live through a lot more. After bicycling enough money together in the other country, he retired into his own shoe store with adjoining repair shop and had his parents—but none of the girl friends—join him and relinquished fame: better cross him out.)

—Yes, said Karsch, which was meant to indicate up to where he was able to follow Achim's political development: And how about what you're doing to the farmers? he said.

Picture Achim straightening up with annoyance, but not because he is hardhearted, don't mistake the controlled patience of his speech for your perception of cruelty, perhaps Achim was not without pity, merely remote from unfortunate incidents, as he explained to Karsch as though for the seventh time and with a tutor's patience, the thing that mattered in the transformation of the agricultural setup was the future of the East German partitioned State, and not individual misunderstandings.

—Of course they are regrettable: said Achim, withdrew his eyes, fell silent as though he were pondering the sorrows of everyday life that buzzed around him at a muffled distance. Then he smiled, he seemed perfectly used to possible breakdowns in communication between the two of them, a wink as though they were in this together, superior, he added: But do bear in mind that I said something different before!

Karsch was willing, at this point, to replace the gaps with minute-by-minute descriptions of all the races in which Achim had ever participated. In any case, it had been the expository representation of bicycle racing that had tempted him into describing a life.

After all: a bicycle is a bicycle

Let's face it, the crudest characteristics of this two-wheel contraption are its single track and propulsion caused by circulatory treading. The beginner who has learned to keep himself upright on his four supporting points, his heels and the balls of his feet, often before he learns to speak, on the bicycle touches the ground only in two places, topples again like a child. (Comparison: as though he were walking on stilts.) Almost without knowing he tries to maintain his center of gravity (to use a term for the conceivable meeting point of his entire body weight) within the framework of the body's intereffective ground contacts, in this case merely the two contact spots of front and rear wheel, they ride away under him, the center of gravity curves with the pedaling motion of the body. Not yet familiar with the steering, the beginner must control his swaying before the moment of the fall: by steering toward where he begins to fall. At the outset, this dictates the rider's direction. Once he has learned everything about his bicycle and its possible movements and knows it as though it were part of himself (since he falls and rides with it), he'll know where to shift his weight and correct his swaying from the start, serpentining around poplars on a narrow street requires concentrated attention of the advanced beginner and makes him curious to try more. (A well-planned training might have started with exercises on a child's scooter whose single track produces the same effect with the danger cut down to a minimum, but when Achim could still have wished for one he would have preferred to be grown up and a member of the Hitler Youth.) Increased speed seems to take hold of the rider and overrule him, between toppling and redressing himself, he rides with ease, he can't trust it, he becomes accustomed to something almost uncanny (after his velocity guided him irresistibly into a poplar trunk that came racing toward him from one side without leaving him the time to think to steer to put the brake on. His shoulder smashed into the trunk, he held on by sheer pressure, the shock still growing. His father ran toward him for a very long time and didn't come any closer. Then he shook him. Did you hurt yourself! —The lamp: said Achim in a small voice, because he thought it was his fault. —Never mind: his father said gruffly, tore the splintered plastic headlight socket from the frame, hardly looked at it, threw it away, stooped to pick it up. He straightened the boy in the saddle, led him back into the bluish-black facing of the trail that the sinking sun flecked with warm shadows. —Pedal! he said, still out of breath but calmer, with hanging head Achim watched the movements of his own feet, jiggled himself into position, separated the bicycle from his sensation of shock. That was before his father's promotion, before they moved back to the city; in the evening his father sat bent over the broken pieces of the headlight, they probably didn't have the money to buy a new one). As the wheels turn faster, a gyration effect sets in, on a larger scale, increasing the rider's balance. (Experiment: One wheel held by its axle ends can be laid on its side. A rapidly spinning wheel resists being toppled, a resistance reinforced by the number of rotations and the exterior weight of the rushing felly and tire. You can't topple it without its cutting into your fingers, it is best held upright by its fixed axle.) If the beginner aims his bike in the direction of a curve, the centrifugal force takes him by surprise and throws him several times toward the outside before he understands what is happening and how he could correct it by leaning toward the inside, the heavier the rider and the narrower the curve the greater the inclination. (Experiment: Spin a stone on a string around your wrist or about your turning body. Hand or body is pulled by a force that increases the faster you spin or the heavier the stone or the shorter the string.) If the force becomes greater than the adhesive friction of the bicycle on the road, the less weighed-down front wheel slides away and throws the rider off. He should have used his brake, the one on the rear wheel which is more heavily weighed down by the saddle. After he has mastered the curve with hurts and hazards he might let go of the handle bars just for the fun of it and sit placidly above pedaling legs, his hands in his pockets or crossed over his chest, ride down the gravel road to the settlement past head-shaking adults and perplexed playmates as though it were nothing at all. But it's against the traffic regulations and why should you watch somebody perform in the arena what you can do by threading your way through the dense weave of bicycle traffic alongside the highways, twisting in and out between cars that are stopped by a red light and race on the rough rustling pavement faster and faster through the countryside? Do you pay money to watch that sort of thing when a bicycle is just a bicycle and he isn't that much better on it than you are?

Quit bragging

Maybe that's how it strikes you. Karsch didn't quite know what to call it, although it would have been almost enough for a new beginning:
How Achim became a pro.
Not on a pro machine at first. A few days after the honorable finish during the first tryout, the frame broke near the yoke, on the uneven pavement, because the bicycle that had been requisitioned on a Thuringian farm had been manufactured for ordinary use and was not mounted on socket joints; it had been just about able to carry milk cans. Terror-struck he led the softly grinding ruin with one hand along the curb from mechanic to mechanic almost through the whole town, until he came to one he'd never gone to before, whom he had no right to ask for help. Who let him stand at the door of the shop and went on preparing inner tubes for patching as though he were alone. In between he'd turn to other jobs spread out on his workbench, let a warped sprocket run through the straightening fork, rewire a couple of spokes, check to see if his tire patches had dried, without ever looking at his hands, his eyes staring at the courtyard surrounded by high houses as though he were deep in thought, observing the awkward supplicant only imperceptibly, making Achim fall silent after a few bashful words, standing there, the warped frame in his hand, only curious now and embarrassed. —Can't that be welded? The man barked at him. His face was firm but elusive. As though closed behind a frown. Achim did not like the thick blond hair above the coarse wrinkles of the forehead, but the eyes were kindly and looked as though he'd do it, while the scolding came pouring out like rain:

They've already told you in every shop throughout this whole goddamn town that pull and pressure come together in this spot, you dumb shithead, don't stand there as though you'd been peed on, can't you think for yourself! Weld at that spot! The man wasn't even beginning to be out of breath, didn't look away, held his head high for a while, in silence, thinking about something else, stretched an inner tube over the back of his hand, testing it, seemed to be smiling to himself. Achim was eighteen at the time. He didn't protest. He began to feel unhappy because of the damage. In those days the shopwindows weren't full of bicycles as now, many shops still had wooden planks in the place of glass and the money of the occupation force was not yet considered legal tender for a great many favors and acquisitions. Achim thought hard what he had to offer the man, so far he had no idea. A minute too long he stood there at the door in the twilight, between the interior of the shop and the lighter courtyard, so much at a loss, it looked like patience, when the man cast another glance at the blackened windowpanes in their iron frames and said: Can't you ask me if I haven't an old frame maybe?

—Do you happen to have an old frame around, maybe? Achim said promptly. The man slightly turned his head, repeating the malicious smile with a corner of his mouth, pointed into the shop.

For a quarter of an hour Achim looked and searched and chose, came back with a scratched-up frame that had no pedal bearings, the back yokes were barely a finger thick and ended in an unusual hook that supported the axle (maybe the wheel is hung in from the bottom, but what if I don't want to turn it around, say with the frame between my knees, but that's a racing frame, boy)! —That one: he said.

The mechanic took his hands off the glue press, saw the frame, jerked it away from Achim, angrily he carried it back to the gallowlike suspension on the rear wall.

—Too good for you. There are others for twenty-eight.

—Precisely! Because it's a racing frame! That's the one I want.

—Your pedal bearings wouldn't fit on it. And I don't have a fork for it either.

—Haven't looked for any yet.

—Shut your trap . . . go and get it then.

Achim was given two spanners (they'll have to do) and was sent outside into the yard. He knelt on the smooth stones, taking apart the bicycle that had been a gift from the Red Army. The days were longer again: every now and then a whiff of warm air and a smell of grass came drifting into the courtyard pit. Children, cats, customers stopped beside him, all baffled by the tenaciously patient boy who wouldn't look up even for the most astonished question. After closing time the mechanic came out with a low three-legged stool and sat with his back against the wall of his house like a spectator. He didn't say a word, only every so often Achim thought he could feel the man's eyes turn from the wrong to the proper spanner. Once he gave him a quick look, but merely caught a swaying head against a scratching hand. Achim realized that he had to deserve the new frame first: that it couldn't be had for money.

When he got to the pedal bearings, he leaned back, still on his knees, and said, head hanging, it was either do or die: I don't know. He felt he was doing the right thing. He noticed something like agreement winking in the mechanic's eyes, he got to his feet grunting with long-expected satisfaction. He went into the shop, came out again with a special spanner which he handed to Achim wordlessly, he settled back against the wall and started to smoke. Achim didn't dare offer him a cigarette, although that would have been the customary gesture to start bargaining. Leisurely watching out of half-closed bleary eyes, smoking, his head against the wall, the mechanic advised him what to do next. He had a couple of maxims: force doesn't come from forcing. The felly mustn't rub: although what doesn't. (Pedal and wheel sprocket are in a calculable ratio to each other:) Everything is interdependent, but too big doesn't do well with too small, nor does too high with too low. And: Learning isn't for sale. After a while he no longer leaned against the wall, squatted, bending forward with rigid neck, held back only by hands pushed against knees, finally he was right there on the ground beside Achim, they did the job together. They finished up with the acetylene torch. Their shadows bobbed, gigantic, up and down the courtyard walls when they stood up. The mechanic inspected the finished job, wiped his hands, said nothing. Actually Achim didn't like him any better now than he had at first, although he didn't seem much different from any other stocky fifty-year-old man. He was a strain, one careless answer would have ruined their conversation, their working together. Even an inadvertent mistake would have been enough.

—A gearshift, that's what we now want: he said. But you couldn't buy a gearshift in this country. How Achim managed to get a gearshift (because the next year he suddenly had one) can no longer be verified. For this was long ago.

Achim was not the first to climb on the new bicycle. The other man pulled it out from under him, dashed through the cellar passage out into the street where he began riding small circles in the thin light of the street lamps on this high gray March night, slow turns from curb to curb across the street, his head turned sideways toward the bicycle under him listening like a doctor. Then he shoved the bike toward Achim and stood on the deserted sidewalk with hanging hands, watching the boy ride.

—What do I owe you? Achim said finally. He had stopped beside the mechanic, one foot on the curb, he tried to detect an expression in the wrinkle-padded hollows of his eyes, they were dark, the head seemed not to be seeing. Hesitantly Achim climbed off and placed the bicycle between them as the object of the barter.

—If you don't come back in a week and you've varnished it! the mechanic said menacingly.

Achim wasn't used to receiving gifts, he never accepted this one. He rode home along the wide streets through the night, taking his time, from lamplit circle to shadow back to light, conscious, at each turn of the pedals, of the preciously improved riding sensation. The transmission ratio was higher, and eight hours ago he hadn't owned such curved racer's handle bars either. But he wasn't happy. And he didn't grow accustomed to the gruff cordiality that greeted him again unfailingly at his next visit, because he didn't know what to make of it. The mechanic's taciturnity struck him as devious, because it seemed to be based on hidden matters he didn't want to be dragged into. When the man was no longer allowed to take in apprentices,

Achim already was on top and had him hired as the mechanic for his team, but he still felt he owed him something. They were not on friendly terms, they grunted at each other, but Achim covered up whatever the mechanic said against the administrator and his measures. —He's an old man: he'd say. — Where would you be without him, he works well, but it's too late for him to learn our way of thinking. Leave him be! he'd say, or something to that effect, in order to keep the old man on the job. The old man didn't thank him by being more amenable and nobody saw how they made it up. Since then they'd been together for seven years, Achim gave his bikes to no one but him. If one saw them in the shop side by side, one could have thought they were inseparable, many reporters had already photographed their two heads bent, close together, over a piece of machinery, and sent them to their newspapers as the symbol of two generations working together. (Once Karsch stood beside the old man while Achim was being lifted off his bicycle and practically staggered past them, head down, toward the locker rooms. Under deep immobile forehead wrinkles the old man's harsh voice said: The idiot. Then he leaped into the crowd and yelled at the assistants who had left the bicycles lying on the grass, he picked Achim's up, holding it high with one arm he came back, checking it as he walked with rapid glances that looked concerned.) A brand-new modern racing bike, all to himself, was assigned to Achim much later, and as a reward. The first time he appeared as a racing bicyclist was as a subject of conversation among three functionaries of the bicycle league, one of whom had watched him at his first tryout. At that time he had merely noticed the boy's crude energy that could be formed: perhaps. They had him watched by the club in whose training sessions he participated. They had been told that on his first visit he had hung around riders and their machines, envious, longing, humble like a puppy, they had merely thought that someday he might possibly take a stand, feel equal to the others, become tough-mouthed like the rest, although not more demanding. Shortly after they learned to their secret delight that he acted the rebel and refused to listen to things he already knew. He usually made the best time and held out the longest when they tried to stick him with endurance exercises. They looked at one another, let's see what he can take, and turned down the application for a province-wide race he'd sent in on his own initiative. He came to see them then, was no longer humble, disdainfully he sniffed their office air, asked them what did they want from him after all. They were welcome to polish his ass with their tongues if they wanted to keep him down. He was perfectly happy to be a mason! They explained to him that he should start in gradually, be careful, too much exertion at the start would finish him prematurely. He laid his cap on the corner of their desk, sat down without another word. He realized that they'd been thinking about him. They needn't have promised to enroll him in the instruction course at this point. He was already willing. They were told that his old pedals had been replaced by regular racing pedals, the chrome hadn't worn off yet and the leather straps were also brand-new and had been bought they knew where. They heard about the gearshift and the price he had paid for it which, calculated in the country's currency, constituted a major crime, and said nothing. They sat in a narrow back room at night in a meager light and formally discussed matters of the league which separated them from their daytime occupations; they mentioned Achim's name with mockery and expectations. Someone was justifying them at last to their friends' mildly snide remarks and the threatening nagging of their wives, because they had discovered someone, in their city, in their club, who made their hobby respectable: who rode the limited obligatory races as though he were bored, who never got enough, who learned all they had to teach him, who would reach the very top and from there point to them and confirm them, not with affection but with respect. Only one of them had entered the headlines on a bicycle, twenty-five years ago, then the war had stopped him, now he had a stiff leg and other men rode in his stead. The other two, who also had their jobs in the city and were older now that the war was over, could barely have said more than that they were interested in sports, that it was beneficial for the health of the nation, etc., which did, perhaps, also include the feeling that overcame them during the uproar that surrounded the arrival of the others on their precious machines and their herolike exhaustion.

187

Well, so what?

Then the steel for a road racing machine is melted down electrically, a very expensive process, the frame must have a torque resistance of seventy pounds per square millimeter under hydraulic pressure and for all contingencies, it may weigh not thirty-six pounds like your coffee grinder, but twenty-one pounds at most. Arrive in the midst of city traffic on a thing like that, the sky is already darkening, the white-caped guys with rubber truncheons in their wide belts will stop you, ask, cool and polite: How come, buddy? You're on your way home from a swim, you've got to buy something before the stores close, you've worked overtime, it's later than you thought. That's not what they're talking about. They're talking about the headlight required by regulation, they look for the generator and for wires, what use do you have for that on a racing machine, what use is it to traffic regulations, a danger to their life and yours and to possibly approaching pedestrians, don't you know that, at your age!

—So I'll ride: he had said before, perhaps referring to the joy he derived from the speed, his satisfaction with the smoothly working machine. They cured him of that attitude during the December course: bicycle racing is a complicated variety of technical sport with an apparatus. It is cyclical like swimming running walking etc. and not meant to cover any arbitrary distance but one of considerable length in the shortest possible time. Just ride, forget about arrival.

He was susceptible to the dynamics and dimensions of the world he now entered as the youngest, the newcomer, alien but fittingly his bicycle pushed life to its right and left into a backdrop. He no longer could have explained to the bundled-up peasants who saw the racing packs of bicycles pass their log wagons again and again, always on the same pine-lined road, what he was learning to do, it was something totally different, it didn't have to be of immediate utility, was therefore something almost superior. He was responsive to the process by which the blindly instinctive ducking before an onslaught of wind changed to something concrete and thinkable: a concept. The racer who sits erect on his bike offers the wind a target of approximately one square foot, but he can diminish it one-half square foot by bending down or doubling over: and the resistance of the air of course increases by nine if the experimenter triples his speed. In the case of certain harsh governmental measures we can no longer speak of families left behind and wretched life in unheated rooms with the wind ever present like a brother: we mustn't forget that our State is using us for socialism, only this principle makes it possible for us to view the many often contradictory occurrences of daily life so that they fall into a pattern. In the beginning Achim preferred theory to training, because the things he was learning had never occurred to him that way, they seemed to him like a view from some great height that telescoped the details into a greater purpose, all the others just take life for granted and don't know a thing. He eagerly took notes, regretted every muffled word, turned and whispered to his neighbors who were sitting there, hands behind sleepy heads leaning against chair backs. Oh. From time to time he'd fall back into his previous reserve. Twenty of them had arrived in an unfamiliar house the first evening, all the others had already been there before, he had no friendships to back him up, most of the others knew each other and he did want to do the right thing if they should ask: What kind of guy are you!

They taught him that he should bend over during fast rides, not only from the shoulders but evenly all the way down, not because this was an order, but because otherwise the chest could not breathe freely and the lower organs would be compressed by abdominal breathing. Keep your arms at an angle, that way you intercept collisions and it also facilitates breathing. It all made sense, then why shouldn't the administrator's measures make sense, nothing is an order, why should the one thing be not true if the other was true, all right. Very effective for high speeds once you do not discuss their sense is the use of the round or double tread because, if you kick your legs down only vertically, you have two dead points, the highest and the lowest of the circle, and your pedal stroke affects less than half of the pedal rotation: therefore, lower your heel before the dead point at the top and push the pedal forward with the tip of your foot rather than straight down, whereas, at the low dead point, you lift your heel and press the pedal backward with your toes and

pull it back up, while the other foot . . . ; and don't turn
your knees outward, and keep pedaling but don't strain, that
way the inhibiting muscles calm down and the others stay relaxed. Notice how it works better and better? As a matter of
course sports are possible only in peacetime, and we no longer
have any capitalists sitting around who don't know what to do
with their money, so they start a war against which, as a matter
of course, we must defend ourselves, of course.

They taught him how to start: flying, from a standstill, alone
and with his team; relay and taking the lead; riding on level
stretches, up and down mountains, narrow curves, wide curves,
close to another's rear wheel; pushing ahead of the pack, throwing yourself across the finish line; jumping with the bicycle, the
feet strapped to the pedals. They watched him closely and noticed that his torso would sway when he rode a long, not too
eventful course, he had fun with the slight loops but didn't
understand them actually, he was grateful to the trainer. Who
reminded him of his first-grade teacher, for again to begin with
he counted for nothing, but instead of the anticipated contempt he was given the same attention he felt he did not deserve. Except that the other one had been older, with bleached
hair and a face emptied by life, whereas this one with his hard
chin and one-time glory wanted you to fight for his friendship.
—Can you ride freehand?

Achim nodded. Bent over he pushed his way out of the standing group, slowly, into the road, lifted himself, pedaling, out
of the saddle and rode as fast as he could toward the forest
that lay shivering, clammy and dark in the early fog, about a
hundred yards away. He turned, came back, let go of the handle bars at a considerable speed, insecure fell back down on
them, finally felt as sure as usual, straightened up, rode a beeline ahead. He knew it was wrong, but he couldn't resist fold-
ing his arms across his chest; embarrassed he toppled forward
and put the brake on when he came up to the waiting group.
Some were smiling, but the trainer had a stern face as though
he had just shaken his head. Everyone had a white cloud of
breath in the gray air.

—Do you know what makes automatic steering?

—Sure: said Achim: everybody knows that. Gyrating effect and
velocity!

—You know: said the trainer as though he were hesitating, but looking at him all the while as though he were a disturbing stranger. Now nobody smiled. Achim felt very small, although nobody had walked away: That tone . . . it doesn't go in our group.

Achim returned his gaze, brazen and silent, he shrugged, turned away. None of them had known it, they didn't avoid him throughout the day, but they talked to him with caution as though he'd had a very private accident. At supper he couldn't bear it any longer, he left the room and lay down on his bed. Alone with the three other cots, hands under his head, he stared up at the fine uneven cracks in the ceiling. The heavy cardboard lampshade swayed light into his face. When the others came in, he hid his head under the covers. He was not asleep. He was waiting to hear what they were going to say about him. But they mentioned him so casually, he felt they were doing it on purpose. He would have liked to sneak outside in the middle of the night, perhaps it's snowing: he thought. But the house rule didn't permit that. He had to lie there in the moonless light next to the three sleepers, motionless, more and more alone. The next morning he stood up and asked to have automatic steering explained to him. He spoke very softly, only toward the end did he realize that he had been taken back in, faces came turning toward him, became more precise to his clearing eyes, the teacher nodded pleasant agreement, a feeling of order comforted him, saved him in this odor of pine-wood tables and ink and chalky blackboard, allowed him to lean back in his seat, to relax the tense muscles around his mouth. Toward the end of the lesson, the teacher called him to the blackboard, draw us a frame.

The remembered impression of blueprints steered the chalk in his sweating hand, the feeling of solid transparent paper and of the general but inescapable lines guided him. He felt recognition in the collective silence. The room was warm, a smell of pine branches came seeping in from somewhere. When he came to the front yoke, he looked for confirmation in the others' eyes that this time it was part of the rest. Then he became too happy and curved the fork in its entire length.

—Think again.

Achim wiped his left hand white with chalk, tried to recall front wheel forks. They had to tell him, and now he let only the lower tip curve forward, wiped his hands on the damp rag, stepped to the side.

The crown is tilted backward, the front wheel fork curves forward at its lower end (pointed index finger at the end of an outstretched arm). If you project the center of the crown to the ground on which you ride (with the flat of the chalk Achim drew a wide track under the frame, added a straight extension of the crown in a dotted line to the imaginary roadbed, it hit at an angle), the contact point of the front wheel (projection from the end of the fork drawn to the ground) lies behind the point where the crown extension bisects the roadbed: the wheel follows the point of bisection. What happens if a bike is lifted by its front frame?

—The front wheel slams down: Achim said modestly. So many things were thinking inside him, he had trouble keeping up. And why? Because of the way the fork curves. Take notes on that: the ground pressure lifts up the weighted front wheel: in the direction of its course. If the rider leans into the curve, the front wheel turns around the contact point on the ground, due to its own weight, and moves into the direction of its incline (the turning is increased by a side effect of the gyrating effect). The bicycle does it all by itself: just don't interfere. Now you may say: sure.

—Sure: said Achim.

He would have walked back to his seat more detached and more relaxed, had he realized that he alone had understood. They asked him several times to explain it all over, during lunch heads gathered around him over a drawing he was by now able to repeat on any table with a wet finger, or on a smooth floor with the tip of his shoe (he can draw it to this day), and the baffled headshakes of the older riders at this unexpected discovery were also meant for the boy who had got it right away. Without having been told Achim stopped swaying his torso during long freehand rides, and the second evening he went to apologize. He stood before the bed of the teacher who was lying in his gym suit reading beside a pink-hazed bed lamp and listened with a frozen smile as he was told that the State demanded that one adjust to the community because the State wanted to help everyone and not only a few, toward a completely new goal. He didn't believe it, he no longer knew what he had to apologize for, he felt embarrassed and backed to the door and out, in the hall he shrugged his shoulders helplessly (they and their politics all the time), he scratched his head, continued on worried though wiser legs. But he admitted that they could demand that of him. He no longer thought that they could all polish his ass with their tongues. He admitted: they could have given me a much rougher time.

Then he returned home to the garden shed and sat sulking beside the Christmas tree his father had trimmed for him, both disappointed they shouted at each other. Achim missed the feeling of being with so many others, in the morning he woke up disgruntled because there was no early-morning run through the deserted sleeping neighboring village in the early light and no calisthenics in files outside the school building, the kitchen maids had always been lying in the windows, watching, he missed the overwhelmed astonishment at the theoretical reproduction of a familiar body movement and the salutary thoughtless exhaustion after the scientifically consuming training. When he went back to the building lot, the morning after Christmas, he was sincerely afraid that they might forget him, that they would not let him be part of the consistently magnificent life of bicycle racers, because many times in the course of detailed laborious preparation he had had the intuition that all this could not possibly lead to something ordinary, that it could never be compared to the arid never-changing day in, day out every day.

Enough of that!

Don't complain! The accuracy which you demand permits more than an additional: how long is a racing bike actually, I mean over-all length. But enough of that. And now, I'll tell you Karsch's next-to-last plans for putting some order into the scraps on which he had stored pieces of Achim's life. From childhood and adolescence only the tough times for all decent people were left over, little else: Children's games, childish pranks, forty pages cut down to one did not mean one word kept from each page, but new not yet written words. And if we compare several bicycle racers according to height, chest circumference and weight, we must realize that they were not born that way (conditioned by their childhood and adolescence), but came to be that way because of training and constant repetition. That too would make a plausible beginning, further pretexts might be found.

A) Karsch had no desire to describe each of the ten years of bicycle races in their chronological sequence, but to condense them instead into Achim's last racing season: to combine what he had seen with what he had been told. Starts, magnificently surrounded by countless spectators who were sent, cheering with the joy of a day off from work, to an impressive place in the center of cities, white kerchiefs fluttering from the overlooking windows, smiling policemen damming in the crowds, persons from the cultural side of life, often kindly referred to by the papers, would step forth, applauded and applauding, and cut the ribbon and everybody was together under swarms of pigeons that were let loose, etc., even during early-morning single starts the riders would find the stadium peopled with rows of white and blue shirts and kerchiefs of uniformed children who had been let out of school, tender voices roaring in unison, emblems and faces woven into flags wrinkled on high swaying poles, army bands marching across the grass still wet with dew, their glistening angularity shifting in the meager sun, not an empty second: however, ten years earlier, few people would stand between the hasty race on the roadway and permeable ruins of houses and shake their heads or yell timidly, the riders were full of enthusiasm but hardly strong enough for this type of exertion, during the war their inadequate machines had lain hidden in the earth or as dismantled scrap in attics, clattering vehicles accompanied them, occasionally a clumsily painted poster might greet their arrival, scheduled streets were deserted or couldn't be found, confused mayors plundered butcher shops, and stood afterward a hand to their heads, because the fat-bellied washtubs filled with bread and sausage had not been enough to feed the unshakable stragglers of the trip, and the initiators of the East German bicycle sport had to sleep on scanty straw, with half-empty stomachs, and yet were enthusiastic in the morning, although their presence was not welcome everywhere in the destroyed hungry towns.

B) Or not with flashbacks, but the past inside the present, with constant parallel comparisons: the cross-country race through the neighbor States of the Eastern military alliance that took place once a year, whose outcome incidents atmosphere are, at this point, subjects of analysis the world over, on telephones and teletypes, had had its start years ago with the idling tours of fellow believers, back and forth through their own countries. Now riders from almost every European country were eager to sign up, they voiced cautious praise of the government, mentioned the exemplary management on the course route in firmer tones and used the race as a tough workout for their races back home, for honor's or for money's sake, for the remuneration of the races here was supposedly the preparation of peace in a world which makes it, in a way, a consequence of the war. They arrived like ambassadors, their competition according to the rules symbolized the possible agreement between their nations, once upon a time, in Warsaw, each ruined house had been pointed out to the East Germans by angry fists, now the French were allowed to keep silent about the cost of their war in Algeria, cordiality or fairness: and a victory scored over there increased one's rating on the Western sports exchange. In the early days the riders had been obliged to wait in line outside miserable factory cafeterias next to the workers, left alone by them, in the meantime there were chefs who cooked every national specialty and interpreters who spoke every possible dialect, and the hosts said: See? Nobody came to the start with bags and boxes now, everybody left his luggage in the reserved hotels, because in the evening it would have followed him to the next destination of this symbolic voyage and all free for nothing. They crossed frontiers as though they didn't exist, and yet once upon a time they had stood in front of barracks and turnpikes, all in one group, no one the first, because somebody else had forgotten to telephone; since then who hasn't seen trains held up at road crossings, because passengers could wait but not the merry chase in the interest of foreign policy? Before, deserted highways had led to skimpy receptions by mayors and administrators, now school children were brought and sang, peasants dropped their tools at the announced time and waved to them from the edges of their fields standing under blossoming trees which had been all there was fourteen years ago. And on every anniversary of the German surrender the leader of the East German team stepped up to the captain of the Soviet team with a bunch of red roses and embraced him and thanked him for having liberated them from the unjust dictatorship and for having set up a just one instead and apologized as deputy of his countrymen for what the German armies had done to the Soviet Union: but did not apologize to the Belgians the French the Dutch the Danes the British the Italians who were standing by: color photos of this event are usually shot from below, one sees hands shaking above straight-standing legs and a blue sky above Warsaw East Berlin or Prague, for the German fighting forces collapsed in May. This race started Achim and made him stand out, he is invited to West Germany and wins a championship, in Rome he is pursued as the legendary strongman, in Denmark there is whispering about Achim, the ethical brain of his team, without a trace of emotion Achim says about some of the Western military alliance countries where he is not wanted: they can't get by us, they'll be begging us one of these days, you wait and see. And the East German team on the tracks of the Olympic Games, and sport makes nations understand each other, this is not a very rewarding paragraph.

C) Another possibility: to describe Achim's rise to fame as if it were comparable to a citizen's rise to the heights of power and prestige, done in flashback: Achim's chest next to the hard angular strapped bosom of a professional girl swimmer, the camera dwelling upon the administrator's insignia on their lapels, Achim also in his Sunday best, they smile, raising champagne glasses in the sweep of the camera and greet the silent spectator as the two most popular athletes of the year, he has voted for them and admires their incredible speed in water and on land. The year before that Achim had visibly given away his best victory: the newsreel shows two men in sweat shirts standing side by side on the heat-bleached concrete track, alternately they raise their arms, gesticulating as they speak, a huge close-up of a trembling ashen face appears on the screen, the unexpected winner who says ACHIM how can I EVER make up for that; the cut flashes back to a steep curving street, tiny and delicate two bicycles are climbing side by side, the smaller one is falling behind, the bigger one pushes one arm out behind him without interrupting his rapid pedaling, a stretched-out hand grabs the other man's saddle, pulls him forward, up and past Achim who rides more calmly now, behind the other's flying downward rush, after the peak, imaginatively the film jumps back to dialogue, bent over, almost menacing, Achim walks up to the receiver of the gift, for a second his singsong voice (SHUT UP! NOW it's your turn to be champ!) covers the commentator's explanation that disappears immediately under the screams of brass instruments while both winners are shown standing on the tribune, Achim on the second-highest pedestal, the camera swings from the smaller man's neck to Achim's exhausted face, he turns his head at once, and then the football news. The aggressive early-summer air seeped hot through the walls of the projection room of the State Film Archives. Karsch was making notes of the film reports in the dark on his knees; sometimes during a blinding reflection he saw Karin's face staring as a mask, images flickering light and shadow across her unmoving eyes. They were alone. Before them, rows of upholstered chairs stood fat and dignified. The projectionist was a small man in a loose-hanging blue smock who had accepted their permit with a sour face and walked off without a word. He didn't answer from the height of his projection booth when Karsch asked him to run sections over again or named another year. Once Karsch asked over his shoulder: Can you see it too? A querulous voice replied from the shadowy screen: I do as you tell me. But if . . . Abruptly the voice drowned in the fading lights of the room. Almost every citizen managed to sound equally vague. Achim as image and sound, twenty-eight years old, with the spontaneous winner's laugh, a step above him the smiling administrator, shaking Achim's clumsily grasped arm in the mud-stiff sweat shirt upward, downward. A girl in a blue blouse trying to find an empty space on Achim's lapel for still another medal, he is bowing, his hair falls forward with quivering tips. At twenty-six a famous Achim leaning against tables in assembly halls, telling silent young faces about Egypt: it's true about the pyramids, they're exactly like the pictures, but you can bet that we thought less about them than about that miserably hot stretch, all dust and sand. At the beginning of last summer he gets stuck in carefully filled-in streetcar tracks, his bike spinning like a top out from under him, motionless he lies at the gutter. A hospital bed viewed from above, obliging him to raise his head to dignified visitors, he lives through the rest of the year in street clothes, receptions, medals, he is elected representative of the people. The previous May he becomes team captain for the first time, a half-open door shows racers and managers gathered around Achim who is talking companionably to them, a close-up of Achim bent over figures calculating with narrowed eyes something that is beyond the average spectator's grasp, he chews on his pencil, looks up, answers the correct thing. This shot looked as if it had been rehearsed, but not enough. Karsch had found the figuring moving lips mentioned frequently as specially sympathetic; he asked to see it again, still couldn't make out why this should be so. The noise of streetcars and automobiles outside the windowless building let in the present day, Karsch also heard Karin talk to the projectionist in the aisle, at some moment she had shaken her head as if she didn't understand, and groped her way out. He crossed out what he had written, not even Achim would remember that. Against a staggered display of flowers he stretches his hand toward the membership book in the administrator's party. At twenty-four his name is not interchangeable, a whirl of a race through East Germany coins the sentence: has he let some other guy win today (this time)? (City councilors step discreetly up to the garden shed that must have looked good fronted by sunflowers, they make him a present of the house, he abandons the mason's trade to study sports and lives on a grant offered by the State: there are no extant pictures from that year.) He returns from the first race through allied countries with ribbons for the best single performance, modestly he turns his head in the symbolic sweat shirt, bashful, often with eyes looking elsewhere, he tells the public about the sacrificial gesture of a West German athletics club, they had invited him, why did I refuse, because I . . . Gratefully he nods to explanations proffered by the people around him, passes his hand over his hair, steps aside. The earliest photo shows him at the edge of a ceremony to honor winners, he is third, by sheer accident the camera has caught surprised parts of his face bent down to children who are tying a blue kerchief around his neck and knot it loosely under his unknown chin, he is holding still as though he were listening. He signs his first autograph in a notebook buckling in his hand, gives it back, shakes his head with a cowardly smile, the knot of the kerchief moves on his throat as he swallows (the cameraman had been concerned with what was typical in this scene). This may have been a year after the winter training course, he had already stopped smoking, he no longer took the midnight streetcar home from some dance, leaning with very slim hips and a face with absent-minded eyes, which had been thin and not bold. At that point he had wanted to get married and buy furniture and have children with the girl with whom he had bathed in the swimming hole beside the superhighway, who had lain beside him afterward in the lush grass and frightened his shoulder with the weightless clinging pressure of her fingers, and had looked at him with very wide eyes. (First you've got to find the right girl.)

D) Or the physiological approach. The body of a bicycle racer must be in working condition all year round. No irregular sleeping hours, no tobacco, no alcohol, or else he doesn't have enough strength stocked up and his nerves begin to flutter. You have to possess a doctor's permit. Already in the winter, when the streets are still cold, he must train his muscles with many kinds of exercise and learn how to be tough enduring quick and nimble. Up and down the Swedish ladder, lift push up swing the dumbbells, throw kick lift medicine balls with his legs from a horizontal position, swing around the horizontal bar, flex his knees by himself and with another on his back, run up long stairways alone and carrying a partner piggyback. Sprint, run, start from standing and crouching position, javelin and discus throwing, broad jumping, high jumping, playing ball, skating. Headstands, handstands, neck balance, wrestling, walking rapidly across the balancing beam. Also endurance training on snowy terrain, running, sometimes with skis. Then cycling with small transmission and no coasting, clear the gym, several layers of the official party paper under his pullover, who is cold has to get off and push, calisthenics of paralyzed fingers on cold handle bars, riding every day, to work, to see friends, shopping, to the workout, every mile counts, never interrupt, not even for a couple of days, or else the body forgets its acquired automatic rhythm. In the spring, prepared, it must learn to ride fast, and endurance, and repetition, the legs must know, and convey their actual speed every moment of the ride. It must be able to anticipate the approximate moment of exhaustion, the will (psychological approach) must overcome the dead center as soon as it becomes aware of it and go on riding until it would like to stop but does not have to stop, and it must know how to start right in with great effort and not diminish it for a long time, and it must know how to change speed with precision, all this it absorbs with repressed consciousness. But the individual has to cut his peculiarities to fit the interlocked structure of the team, the weakest among them must be pulled along, the strongest must hold back, because over long stretches all must ride at the same balanced speed, because the leader must not outpace the led who are taking a rest next to his rear wheel with sideways pedaling and trunk movements, but each must expect the utmost, because during the struggle against other groups his team cannot ask him at which speed he would rather ride; here the body needs (psychological approach) discipline and self-reliance to push those who are dropping behind on and forward toward the vanished, out-of-sight competition. And it must not be aware of what it is doing, invisible, unseen its brain automates its movements, lets it think anything it likes, except about its nerves. The body must learn to eat calmly right in the middle of exhausting strain, it must get used to carbohydrates, to sugar and salt, too much fat makes you tired, too much liquid is a stress for the heart, drink two quarts a day, after that just rinse your mouth. It notices how the conditioning agrees with it by the rhythm of pulse and breath, by the expansion of lungs, the increasing girth of thighs (the muscle fibers grow thicker, but don't increase); does it feel sluggish and dull, or does it love to ride, can't it get enough of it? During races it is not supposed to loll around on the days of rest, and feel tired, it has to walk in the woods or swim, because that way it recovers its strength more precisely for the next morning; the massage helps it by and by. That's natural exhaustion, don't fuss. It's worse when the cerebral cortex goes on strike: then movements are no longer computed to complete harmony, speed agility endurance disappear, a completely unfamiliar voice tells you that all this racing is a lot of horseshit, it's uncanny how you can't go to sleep, you start to lose weight, you don't feel like eating, you're deathly pale with fluttering wrists. This one shouldn't see a bicycle for a fortnight, the body should act as on vacation or on a cure, they check it, send it on walks in the woods, play tennis with it, why don't you go to the movies, it's ages since you've been to a dance, don't stay out too late though, until the nerves relax, remember their work with less and less resentment, the organism gets hold of itself again, it's already going very fast on a bicycle, slows down, speeds, pedals slowly, rushes once more through the landscape, pushes blood through the hard-working muscles, but less during the intermissions, at the beginning of the pause the heart spews great quantities of blood into the body, more oxygen is let in, breathing becomes deeper, well prepared the body throws itself into the period of greater strain, Achim wrote his examination paper about the enlarged heart of the athlete, in my case they discovered that it responds favorably to intense endurance stimuli, it rides on and on as though nothing had happened. The fall training simply maintains the level of the body's achievement, does not try to increase it, leaves the nerves in peace, sends it to the winter sports, keeps it under a doctor's observation until the new training cycle starts with the next spring, for New Year's you may stay up until midnight, but don't drink too much, March is going to be tough.

Or *as a film, what do you think?*

E) Or as a film. The thirty-year-old hero appears on the screen, irrefutable before an oblique wall of roaring spectators, exhausted he tries to bring his helpless panting to a smile, again and again the gray contours of breathlessness emerge under a softer expression, on the synchronized sound track mountains and valleys of roaring voices swaying, changing to the heavy slapping of crashing breakers (to justify the comparison, finally), the sandstone portal of the town hall makes its appearance in unexpected silence, mute among the crumbling stucco, fingers write his name with a cracked pen, the space reserved for entering the death date disappears, empty, under a wiping palm. Forcefully singing columns of brown uniforms march indisputably from left to right, from top to bottom, fuse in from the background, red flags with giant swastikas stand close together in the wind, form a barricade, bow to the sound of cannons, a long row of houses loses its eyes and becomes hollow and collapses shuddering into high clouds of rubble, his mother's passport pictures over a four-year period pop on, aligned beside the masklike strictness of the wedding photograph, with round cheeks, but narrow eyes and dropping shoulders, a bony face holding thin-lipped barrenness together, the last photo has an absent-minded smile one ear showing between dry stringy hair, the photo blends into the negative, recalls a skull, a huge still empty pit lies in whistling summer wind between uneven heaps of sand, the edges are beveled, pale crushed stalks of grass, a lump of clay crumbles off the sharp edge, rolls down onto the rough floor of the pit, bursts noisily into tiny fragments, and a spray of sand. Repetition of the picture of the wedding day, Thuringian loveliness, darkness sweeps it up, dissolves once more before the girlish tenderness that disappears immediately, as though one had seen enough of it. More documentary shots in the usual sequence, nighttime cities festively illuminated by fires, the name Stalingrad, first in Cyrillic, then in German, then in Cyrillic script, walls with bullet holes, empty nooses hanging quietly for long moments, Achim's mean-looking face above the brown leather-knotted collar of the uniform (from the family album). Another example, conditions after the war along the German border: soldiers' coats of different color and machine guns enter the autumn twilight of a forest path, the mirrored image of the moon in the nocturnal lake collapses as a human body falls doll-like into the water (and sways, unnoticed, in the reeds), running steps hammer on iron plates, glistening railroad tracks rust to dullness, disappear under a growth of barbed-wire coils, wide-spur plows advance in echelon formations industriously through the roadbed of a highway, follow their own course along birch forests, deeply planted concrete pillars stretch wire mesh to a fence, a bewildered-looking man writhes between emptied suitcases under the silent stare of uniforms that stand around him, he pulls a T-shirt over his head, he looks well fed. And pictures of so-called race events understandable even to the uninitiated: an endless onrush of bicycles mounted by colorful riders across the entire width of the street, the sound of rolling friction increases as they came nearer, decreases as they ride off into the distance, a calm voice says: We deliver the milk; the field is extending, the lead seems to jump, every now and then a sweat shirt crumbles away, a gap closes, opens, the routine voice says: The mail is leaving any minute now. A couple of guys have left for work, couple of guys are out on work, couple of guys have gone to work, —the eye travels backward, sees a stocky rider on sturdy legs standing all by himself at the shoulder of the road, he is waving to the trucks, his bike is hanging from his arm and looks broken, finally bicycles racked up like sides of beef sway forward on a platform, stop beside him, the rider looks up, in German he asks for help, in French a bicycle is lowered down to him, the mechanic jumps down and gives him a push, the rider hunches off measuring the distance between the immobile supply trucks and the field quivering in the distance, and the voice says: comrades help each other; and overlaying its last sentence, spontaneously derisive: but the most helpful mechanics are getting prizes, later that evening, on the stage, wrist watches; irritated the voice continues in the previous tenor of official statements: One day, when all nations will lend a hand—the straggler is floundering on the fringes of the tail end of the main pack, his head hangs from a sagging neck, lower than the curve of the spine, whirling legs tie themselves into knots in the spectator's perception. All such stuff. For long moments the camera rides over grooved blocks of bluish pavement, the eye no higher than the foot of rapidly fusing trees, an arrow of dust shoots out from under the narrow track of a tire that is rushing away on a sandy strip beside the lumpy asphalt road, a second track crosses the first, the hub of the rear wheel drops into the picture, a foot on a rigid pedal slips in, the movement freezes soundlessly in the fall, with other bodies thrown to the ground at sharp angles across the body that is already lying there as though they had been catapulted, the forward-moving emptiness becomes cloud-mirroring asphalt, wetness of rain, dust, snow drifts, ice holes, joints, dull concrete square in the sun, a wooden bridge thunders, the delicately curving pattern of Hanover pavement, behind a smoking steam roller men are kneeling side by side on a layer of gravel covered with sticky tar, they level the hot viscous asphalt with boards, their hands in awkward gloves, their lips tightly compressed above the acrid smoke, they don't look up; the voice says: so that we can ride. Along the roadside, the schools factories monuments prisons of Achim's country, roughly excavated slag soil around furnaces, the haze of steel fireworks on the horizon, drag-lines scraping the slanting slopes of surface coal mines, a patriarchal factory gate bearing the administrator's name in modern script, bulldozers plucking house foundations out of scanty pine forests, a pile driver hammering oversized concrete pillars into water muddy with sand, children on the warpath, creeping through the heather, fiendishly ambushing each other, three recruits reaching for a flag that is being held out to them, watching the officer's reserved lip movements, a crowd of people sitting in a cold hangar under iron rafters on waiting suitcases, old yellowed walls on top of a steep hill with small thickly grated windows, rows of chairs fanning out with a gathering of people in everyday clothes, silently contemplating a table draped in red on an elevated esplanade, blue-shirted marchers singing forcefully from down to up and from right to left and then suddenly from the foreground in one endless fusion, flags huddling in the wind, wide-open eyelids starting to quiver, walls with bullet holes. Along the road the pyramids of Giza, the Eiffel Tower, the Roman Capitol; along the streets the West German otherness, the capital's marble edifices combing the sky, endless noise-happy traffic through city streets, schools, monuments, factories, prisons, three recruits reaching for a flag that is being held out to them, watching the officer's reserved lip movements, in close files, like insects, cars are projected in spurts, shopwindows, road conditions, the statistical mean of people's expressions, walls of all kinds, and so on. Just labels, nothing but appearance. Think so? Better not.

F) Or as an anecdote. The famous bicycle champion Joachim T. was once asked the question: if he had an inner perception of the expression of absence in trance or dream that appeared on his face when he was riding at exaggerated speed? what did his consciousness know of the almost fluid interplay of his movements? whether there still existed a center that he could control? The question came up after the projection of a film whose more than five hundred exposures per second had been unable to break a somnambulistic floating end-spurt down into its separate motions. Joachim T. replied: During his years of apprenticeship he had thought bicycle racing unduly hard work, he had been all tensed up and he had thought that it ought to pay much more. His studies had taught him that the riding motions of a highly trained body are steered by the central nervous system, and any control by will and consciousness confused the automatism for quite a while. Helped by this explanation he had been able to accept the states of empty trance brought about by practice and endurance. At first he had been dismayed every time he thought about these trances, whereas now he was able to anticipate them and space them out, as soon as the calculations and strategics of the race stopped claiming his attention: when he rode alone, during certain spurts, less often in prolonged exertions. He couldn't say exactly. Consciousness wore blinders at such times, he'd hardly see the road, only the track, with the encouraging shouts floating toward him as an extremely distant homogeneous noise. It now seemed to him that, at those moments, he remembered the days of his childhood when he had first experienced his bicycle's speed, its organic intimacy with his body, because the feeling, the mood of this state had the same color as his memory of those years. And because he kept rediscovering this happy sensation (which is lost to most of us, most of us cannot return to our childhood and are forced to live with tangibles and not to expect the impossible) in his profession as a bicycle racer without harm and hindrance, therefore: he added: he was surely a happy man. This was in his thirty-first year, fifteen years after the second German war.

G) Or something else entirely. H) Or not at all. I) How many letters are there in the alphabet?

Now something else, for a change

Something else, like the letter Karsch received in the beginning of June. He didn't actually receive it, it may have been in his jacket pocket, because one morning he found it lying by the chair leg under his jacket which was lopsidedly hanging over the back of that chair. Mrs. Liebenreuth always put her notes to him on the table (to put the chain on please when Karsch came home at night, which he always forgot to do: she didn't like to tell him such things; she'd write down any complaints of this kind in such a tiny looped handwriting, it made the paper look yellow), but for the last four days she had been away because someone had died in her family, Karsch was alone in the dark sour-smelling apartment. He got up and walked from door to door, thoughtlessly. Mrs. Liebenreuth's room looked untouched. The chain was dangling, but corridor and kitchen didn't look burglarized. He yawned, walked back: the letter was still lying in the same place, one of its corners touched the rim of light the window made on the rust-brown floor boards, green summer light was warming the sooty street. The mail carrier, a woman, wouldn't get to this section of town for another hour. Karsch picked up the letter.

He ate breakfast sitting on the sill of the open window, looking down into the street or over to the parched park square that blocked it off. He saw children with their satchels on their backs skip to school across the gleaming sandy path, below him a sleepy girl went into the bakery, came back out on the sidewalk with a white bag, looked into the light from under a shading hand. In the house across the street naked arms were putting bedding in the sun. From time to time Karsch looked at the letter, turned it in his hand. The envelope was ordinary, white, and contained something hard; its empty edges had been folded over the inflexible contents, as though the letter had at one time been too large. The old-fashioned wallets that Karsch had seen would still be too small to contain it, even for the reduced dimension. The envelope was spotted as though by wet clay. Karsch's name was written on it, printed in nondescript block letters, the way German architects write. The stiffness inside was heavier than cardboard. Then he forgot about the letter, and put an old photo album of Achim's into descriptions, without great eagerness. Merely because he didn't want to forget why he wasn't going home.

At noon on his way to lunch he telephoned Karin. From a small restaurant in a suburb at the west end of the city, between two bridges, the telephone stood between flower pots on the window sill, Karsch spoke distinctly, three young carpenters were leaning against the bar, waving beer glasses in gregariously raised hands. Karsch was carrying the letter in the same pocket from which it had probably fallen if somebody had put it there before.

—What's with this letter? he said after somebody picked up Karin's phone. —What's with this letter . . . ? he said. —What letter: asked Mr. Fleisg's voice as though he were making a definitive statement.

—Yes: said Karsch enthusiastically: Or you. Can you write normal block letters?

—I beg your pardon! said Mr. Fleisg. Karsch pictured his metronome headshake. Then Karin grabbed the receiver away from him and asked what Karsch was talking about.

Karsch admitted speaking of a certain letter, he described it. He was the only guest now in the place, no one behind the bar except the flies.

—Don't open it: she said.

—Nonsense: said Karsch.

—Give me ten minutes: she said.

Karsch stood waiting at the streetcar stop, thinking about the letter just for the heck of it. His jacket was wide and loose, the side pockets had no flaps. He had been wearing it every day, he had arrived in it. The evening before, he had been sitting in his room reading in the history of bicycle sport (he wasn't doing much else these days); late that afternoon he had made the rounds of the city for three hours, looking for typing paper (because he didn't feel like going to see Mrs. Ammann, they still hadn't agreed about Achim's childhood), he remembered small private shops with embittered salesmen around the university, later he had stood in line in front of the office equipment section of a government department store, a fat woman had pulled him maternally by the arm to take her place, —I only want to buy wrapping paper for Christmas: she said. When his turn came, there was nothing left that would withstand ink, and he couldn't take that kind of paper, because all Mrs. Ammann's marginal objections were ineradicably in ink. In another department store he stood in another line next to two girl students (he thought they were students) behind a number of women for quite a long time, the women were rummaging through the postcard boxes; while the waiting people murmured in vague agreement something about a paper mill that had burned down, which accident the official city newspaper blamed for the lack of stationery. Just one mill? Karsch said in his surprise without thinking, he hadn't wanted to butt into their conversation, he just wanted to know, the two girls disappeared at once, one of them looked offended as she walked away. In the end he was sold perfectly usable light blue airmail stationery after he declared himself willing to buy the envelopes as well. The saleswoman seemed glad to get rid of this article. To stock up a little reserve he further bought a ledger, piles of which were lying about all over town, and slowly rode home under the blanching sky, through the main streets with their after-work strollers, past crowds of people each of whom might have come near his jacket, although whatever for. He put his hand to the pocket that was drooping a little and felt for the stiffness inside, whereupon a woman who sat beside him and who had been quietly snuffling in the heat pulled back a little and sighed. All right with me: thought Karsch and searched the day before. In the afternoon he had returned from Achim's training camp, because Achim left for a lecture tour through the southern parts of the country. Somewhere along the superhighway he had picked up a young man in faded mechanic's overalls who claimed to be a student, but became vaguer and vaguer in his answers, finally Karsch preferred to ask the young man what he knew about Achim. The young man had said: Aren't you a West German? This sure will cause you a lot of trouble back home. —One hears things: he added as an explanation, then he said no more. He pretended that he knew nothing about Achim, except how much he made, the figure was higher than what Karsch had been told, they discussed it. The young man lacked assurance, most of his remarks were made in a questioning tone, toward the end he hesitated as though he wanted to say something more, but didn't. He thanked Karsch almost cordially. This one asked to be dropped outside the city limits, at a bridge across the river, where no roads could be seen branching off in any direction, only a footpath next to the white flaky water that led toward the woods: improbable. In the evening he had been invited with Karin to the house of a newly married couple who had assistants' positions at the university, there had been other friends of the couple who greeted the stranger briefly and respectfully and then left him to himself; they spoke about nothing but science, kept the radio switched off and looked over to Karsch only as though to reassure themselves that he wasn't bored. They answered questions about their private life in general terms: oh we are doing nothing particular, just living like everybody else, I have never heard about that incident. Karsch felt so bored, he tried to start a quarrel about their country's jurisdiction in political matters, again they pretended ignorance, said they were not qualified to voice opinions, looked questioningly at Karin, two of them burst into a new subject and returned to their previous conversation. Stiffly, although with curiosity, they listened to him tell about Achim's life; he asked them about the years which Achim usually paraphrased with My Development Toward Political Awareness, but they couldn't remember details, it was so long ago. All Karsch had wanted to know was what the ration cards looked like. His hosts were extremely embarrassed and tried to interrupt with remarks about other things; Karin sat across from Karsch, every now and then she'd laugh soundlessly through her nose, she wasn't helping him at all.

—Wasn't there once close by a statue of the next-to-last Soviet premier, the street name has gone, what ever happened to the statue: said Karsch.

—Oh, I see. He must mean the . . . (you understand). Yes, the second before the last. Well, nobody knows for sure.

—Do you think it could be standing in a shed somewhere? said Karsch.

—But who's mentioned a shed: they said, refilled his glass, looked at him almost with annoyance.

—So this guy rides all the time: Karsch repeated dreamily: that's backbreaking, every day doctors check him inside and out, nothing he doesn't have to ask a permit for . . . do you think anybody will thank him for that someday?

They nodded their comprehension. The married couple were different in size and looking loving. Everybody was sitting around the low table in shirts and blouses, sweating alike, talking differently.

—I mean: what's your opinion?

—Yes: they said. It had never occurred to them. Although, theoretically, one couldn't deny that sport and the health of a country, of any country . . .

Nobody denied that there was a lot to be said about Achim. Karsch informed them: that, in West Germany, Achim's name was known only to the initiated.

Really? They wouldn't have thought that.

When he came back from the hall where he had left his jacket, they were discussing the radius of absolute destruction (bricks ground to powder) after the dropping of a modern atom bomb, they were reading texts to each other, they were a closed group. When he got up to leave they seemed sorry. On the way through the deserted sultry night, across gray-lighted squares, under trees, in the shadow of street lamps, past lovers and drunks, Karin told what she knew. The tall one with the shock of hair on his bony forehead, the one who always looked so absent-minded: after the Hungarian revolt he had had to make some public apology. Some article he wrote supposedly; and he never talked much, he loves a girl he never brings along. The married couple (their hosts) had not felt like talking about their life in one furnished room, because a year ago the State had promised them an apartment and they didn't want to appear ungrateful. They'd rather live in the nineteenth century, they pay no attention to the administrator because he leaves them alone. The young girl who was just watching and smoking so much, they don't quite know, she had a boy friend who suddenly went to the West, she doesn't like to talk about it, she generally refrains from statements, when she made that remark about sports as an education for the people

—She looked very innocent then: Karsch said perplexed.

—You see: said Karin.

—I'll never catch on: he said. Everybody would have cordially shaken the hand of a Mr. Fleisg, and treated him with silence. All of them lived in specific parts of the city, on streets, in houses, but not where the subway is going to be extended to someday, or around the corner from the opera, or way up north: as they had chosen to say: they merely wanted to spend the evening together and talk, they were quite satisfied with the colorful twilight of summer dresses and cigarettes in the balmy darkness, they want to go on living in peace and privacy and forever, can't you understand that, Karsch couldn't understand it: to him it seemed uncanny that the inhabitants of this country had let the government, the habits of the fat ruling houses with their telephones, into their daily life, as lines of conduct, into their jobs, even into the scented streets, into their evening conversations among friends, and made it unrecognizable, they wouldn't put something into the jacket pocket of somebody who had goofed.—It was great: laughed Karin. Karsch shrugged, ill-humored, said nothing. —But they were just testing you: she said.

Until midnight he wandered about various bars by himself, he had been hugged, pushed, at one point he had been sitting at an isolated table alone with another man who looked like an overland truck driver, who sat huddled inside his leather jacket, talking soberly but loudly about the intelligentsia that would be hanged one of these days; but he wasn't talking to anyone in

211

particular. Karsch finally realized that the silent people at the other tables had been listening for quite some time, that they were waiting. They were pleased when he left. On the stairs, outside Mrs. Liebenreuth's door, he found two sleepy gentlemen waiting for him under lopsided hats, they said they were from the police and wanted to know: where Karsch had dropped a young man disguised as a garage mechanic. Karsch couldn't remember. They advised him to try. He remembered a parking lot on the superhighway on the other side of the Elbe; for a while they stood around him, polite and yawning, making his room feel small, avidly they stared at the open drawers of his desk, left reluctantly, for Karsch to think back if he could indeed have been where he pretended to have stopped that afternoon, he thought it improbable, and now for the first time he thought: uhum, and then again: horseshit. Still, and even for the simplest everyday decisions he couldn't help worrying in retrospect: as though he should have asked some native's advice, and this among people whose language and gestures and faces he had considered as reliable environment since childhood.

He was holding the letter in his hand when Karin leaped from the streetcar, the wind made her white coat stand out like a bell around her body, she was running with long steps, her open hair flying about her head. She was not out of breath, she raked Karsch with one quick look, took his arm and lovingly strolled off with him under the wide linden trees in the vacation-bright street: so that the people left in the streetcar thought they were riding past a couple of lovers.

—You oughtn't have said that to Fleisg! she said.

—Did you open it! she said.

—I can be wrong of course! she said.

In Karsch's room she placed the letter in her lap, pressed it down with her handkerchief and carefully cut open the letter with Karsch's car key. Karsch noticed that she didn't touch the paper with her fingers, she put her hand in her hair, shaking her head at the same time. He handed her the key and said: You're acting very silly.

Bent over she continued to tear the letter open, looked at him, nodded agreement. She pushed her hair out of her face, seized the letter between thumb and index, opened it completely. —I was nervous: she said. She tilted the envelope and shook the contents into her lap. Looked over her shoulder. Karsch leaned forward.

It meant nothing to him. The object Karin was staring at between stiffly raised hands was a streaked aluminum plaque with two recently cut-off sides; on it, in the middle, the print of an ordinary snapshot had been glued. It showed a sunny street, and between the houses a column of marchers without flags, in the foreground the first row of men in white overalls, their arms locked together. Noticeable among them a young man in a white shirt and dark trousers who looked less serene than the others, his mouth was open in embarrassed laughter. The column of marchers stretched all the way to the back where it blocked off the left lane of a road fork. The outlines were clear, each face recognizable; of course Karsch saw that it was Achim walking in the first row, but it meant nothing to him.

—Now you can leave: said Karin. Carelessly she threw the plaque over onto the table.

Once more Karsch was leaning toward her, trying to understand her better. Uncomprehending, he said: yes, of course.

She sat before him, her hands against her temples, and said in a very low, very rapid voice: But don't you see that that's the uprising, the sun the first morning, don't you recognize the street corner with the gas station, they were only two hundred then, but they had already been seen for some three thousand yards, people were still joining them from the sidewalks, and then the tanks met them. And jail after that, and Achim right there in the front, don't you see it, hasn't anybody bothered to tell you about it!

Very much alone, very surprised, she stood up, smoothed out her skirt as though she were leaving and said, head down, distractedly: I didn't know it. I didn't know: she said in a small voice. It was obvious that she was helpless. For seven years she hadn't known, that's how long ago it was.

And Achim?

Karsch wrote to him, to a random address somewhere on his lecture tour. Of course.

Achim didn't take much time and sent a young woman to his house one afternoon, she was clothed in leather, she kept her hands in her pockets while she talked, she walked downstairs in front of Karsch, stiff and masculine, before the official car of the athletes' training school she bent toward the rear door with surprising softness. Achim was hunched in one of his gray suits with the insignia of the State in place of the heart; angularly he turned his head toward Karsch, immediately gave the woman driver his address. He seemed embarrassed and cut Karsch off. —Later: he said, and more loudly: I said later! While they rode through the deserted afternoon of the working city Karsch looked at the thickly braided girlish bun the woman was moving above her leather collar. In the mirror he saw her eyes envelop the scanty traffic; she didn't look awake, she didn't look tired, just indifferent. Her dark eyebrows were tightly knitted, it gave a sinister look to her pale face. At one point she casually glanced at the two men in back of her without any contact. At that moment she looked pretty. The car was hot from the heat outside, but completely closed. It seemed to be at the disposal of a number of people, scarves and newspapers lay under the rear window as though they had been forgotten there. In front of the house entrance, under the arcades that pretended age, Karsch tried to shake the driver's hand; she disregarded it as though the gesture were unknown to her. Achim had thrown back his head and was staring up at the graceful gables to the windows behind which he had an apartment; he was waiting angrily. —Have you finished, you two! he said. Karsch turned at the door, saw the woman's slanting legs slip under the wheel, straighten up at once, reach for her record sheet. For a week Achim had been on the road with a woman he didn't trust; that's an impression which Achim later denied. He had nothing against her. She ought to get a little more sun: he said.

Achim was still opening the windows of the stale hot rooms above the deserted arch of the street, saying several times: Why did Karin have to leave right away! She didn't have to do that! Without a word!

Karsch explained: they hadn't gone to the station originally. Karin had dragged Karsch through the city and shown him the scarred evidences of the uprising: on this stoop women had stood screaming across to the windows of the police prison: You'll get out! You'll get out! And the following day there had been machine guns outside the building and the hands and chins had disappeared behind the barred windows. She was raging, tenaciously, unwilling to give up her anger, it made her speak more loudly, more carelessly than the West German even, and she paid no attention to whoever was walking beside or behind her. Many people looked into her face, shocked as though they had seen a person cry, walking beside a helpless companion. Her voice had grown hard and independent: as though it had to portray a character she believed in.

—I see: said Achim. He acted as though bored by mistakes that could have been avoided, that are no more than a bother to the man of experience. He acted grumpy. —Did you two report it at least: when will you finally realize that one doesn't send that kind of picture in a letter? he nagged. They were standing, hands in their pockets, amidst motes dancing in the sun, in the front rooms, they often turned their backs to each other. Karsch examined the clipped lawn in the park behind which the crane had still been laboring over an empty hole when he had first come here. Now it was bending over the bleak structure of a narrow-windowed cube that was linking the treetops with a dotted line. He saw groups of students walk on the red sand of the paths, under the eyes of seated old men and women. A kindergarten expedition had arrived on the steepest mound of the playground, around their guardian's apron small multicolored figures were whirling slow circles. As the distant whistle of a streetcar turned the curve and leaped across the landscape, Karsch thought he heard awed children's voices cry: The crane! The crane! as children do, but older inhabitants had been equally surprised by the unusually deep foundation of this building and its coffin-shaped narrow cells, now what's that going to be for, haven't I seen that somewhere before. He hasn't said a thing, I assure you. A citizen is entitled to take a look. No, they had not reported it; they might just as well have told the police about the nurse and the old people on the park benches, name them rather than the other six hundred thousand inhabitants of the city. By the time Karsch turned his head to answer, Achim had apparently forgotten his question. He walked from one piece of furniture to the other, ran his hands along the tops, making sure that Karin had not lived here for the last six weeks. He was not in control of himself, his shoulders sagged, his feet walked by themselves. Looking about aimlessly, and bemused, he asked if there wasn't a film showing somewhere in town with Karin in it.

—She also told me how they elected the bicycle champion representative of the people: said Karsch.

—Yes: said Achim, startled, yes! he said, more and more furious, his head hunched between his shoulders he walked up to Karsch, came very close to his face as if to make sure he'd be understood, but his eyes slipped away and to something else while he recited in a low embittered voice: She told you how she arrived at the hundredth electoral district, the noon air was thin between seasons . . . (these pauses kept happening to him, he'd fall silent, nod as though to check himself, add: she says . . . , then he'd go on talking with angular movements of the head, expressionless:) school children at the steps waving newspapers, carefully clutching money in fists, the way she talks, Karsch!, excited as though they were celebrating something, a little girl with braids was waiting for me at the school door: for her, you understand, she was shaking a cardboard box to make the coins jingle inside, to make them say: that's been hard on other people already . . . she says . . . I had my hands in my pockets just then, I said thank you, I was going to vote, I wanted to . . . afterward there was a long school corridor, it's not true that all schools smell alike, I had gone to another one, there were posters on the walls THE CHOICE IS UP TO YOU, I stood reading it, as well as the one beside it and so on down the corridor, slowly, step by step, an election official, you know with a band around one arm, approached me from the side, asked me urgently: Well? Well? he asked, people stopped, looked over as though hopefully, everybody was dressed in his Sunday best, besides it was Sunday. EVERYBODY CAN KNOW THAT YOU WANT PEACE we all read together, but we didn't stay together, we were separated according to streets and districts and voting booths, and then . . . she says (Achim's head came up with a jerk, possibly he remembered this also) . . . the classroom was brighter than the long corridor, tobacco smoke, the pale sunshine, that's no help either, and underneath ten official torsos at a table hung with red, people passing in front of the table as though on rails, that was the first thing I saw . . . a woman sitting at the door like a guard, at a table stacked with lists, she is a secretary, she asks for your name, doesn't believe the name you give her, wants to see my identity card, I hand it to her. Didn't throw it on the table, not yet. My name wasn't on her list, she isn't sure if she oughtn't to beware, I say: It's a supplement. I had just come to the city, it was supposed to be for good, I had given up a few things, quite a few things . . . Yes: says the secretary, she nods, you know her hair was mussed as though she'd slept on it, she communicates a jolt toward the gentleman beside her, he hands me the ballots, one from each pile, I accept them, I'd already pulled one hand out of my pocket. The voter stands in the center of the room at equal distance from all the tables, the children had been asked to write something on the blackboard, they have made him feel so embarrassed, he has to read each ballot over, he leaves them as they are, he doesn't know what to cross out just yet. The voting booth stood in the farthest corner. There were two small blackboards at an obtuse angle, like this, you know . . . pushed one against the other on a table, one could have bent down between them, but they had put up long tables blocking the corner and were sitting behind them, the space between was just enough for one person, like a frame, with democracy put into the corner . . . no, she said that in some other way. And still another poster DECLARE YOURSELF OPENLY FOR PEACE, stopped by eyes, shunted aside, later friends tell you: that they couldn't find a pencil between the two blackboards anyway, it was all useless from the start. And to top it off, the little man who came trotting up to me, withered, retired, stalk thin, educated since he wore glasses, he takes my hand with the forms and explains to me forestalling politely:

—Well so these are the ballots, see! You must put them in over there, see. In any case, if you're for the candidates who stand for peace. In that case you won't have to make any changes, see. (She had told it differently to Karsch, more briefly. Hardly more

than a sentence: Not because of me. But because they were
doing that with everybody.)
—But if you ('cause this happens sometimes) if you should be
for the West German imperialists and the destruction of our
country, then you may want to go into the booth maybe. Go
ahead!
What's he want from me she says (What do you want from
me) I say and I'm already past the narrow entrance to the booth,
I'm at the last table and don't know how I got there. In my
ear suddenly the high-pitched voice (there you are see that's
all there is to it—, and to the next voter, helpfully reaching for
the hand with the ballots: Of course these are only suggestions
. . . naturally, of course, of course!) I see fingertips leaping
down lists, I raise my hand with the ballots, someone else's
hand is helping my limp one to force the ballots into the open
slot, adroitly, rapidly the slot closes, I put my hand into my
coat pocket. And then I saw a truck with blue shirts, everyone
shouting as though to music, later I talked somewhere until I
fell asleep. And all through the wet night I ran past street lamps
and bawled about our secret democratic ballot system that was
electing you: I don't want to see you again . . . ; she told you:
Achim said breathlessly. —She told you. Yes. That's what she
was like then.
(When Achim had met her.)
—She didn't tell me about the bawling: corrected Karsch.
—Okay, all the same: Achim said, discouraged. He shrugged as
though he didn't care either way. —In those days she'd still cry
about that kind of thing.
Toward evening the neat bareness of the front rooms had
driven them into the kitchen in the back. They sat at the window, staring out at a chaotic building lot that lay quietly in the
twilight blush that was spreading across the narrow circle of
houses, and before them cold gray shadows. All the doors stood
open as though they were expecting visitors. Achim began
many things and forgot them immediately. He tried to make
tea, sat down as though going to sleep, searched the icebox
again, wiped off soot on the outer window sill with a rigid finger.
His eyes narrow he was thinking what he could not say, what
he said was what he feared, came out as a reproach:

—She told you I made her watch her tongue. And you believed her! Because you think you know her!

Karsch didn't know about that. After she left Karsch, she finished her courses at the actors' school. It was a large, dignified house, not yet invaded by the State's blue shirts and nightly slamming doors; she had been content inside the enclosure (she rarely shopped in West Berlin, nor did she read the East German papers), she thought she'd stay in this country, but for the sake of art. Then she arrived at some small-town theater with a single suitcase, she played parts that the uncritical spectator notices only when they're clumsily played or left out; during the day the small-towners would watch the actors constantly and expected incidents which could be retold, or tips about the latest fashions. For almost two years she had dinner at the best restaurant in town, in the room reserved for the most respected patrons, and came to know the new big shots: administrators, schoolteachers, whatever shop owners had remained, newspapermen. Is that how they are. She felt maternal toward a group of high-school boys who had a crush on her and wanted to draw her into the details of the resistance against the administrator. The administrator disrupted the scarcely repaired economy, barred the frontiers, united the carefully calculating and the clumsily spontaneous resistants in the jails and did all the things her dead mother had taught her as being contrary to the achievement of eternal salvation. The uprising touched the small town only with its fingertips, Soviet tanks were already stampeding through the horse carts while the burgers were still sitting in front of their radios like the proverbial hare in its lair and recalled the last days of the war and their private feelings then. At that point she felt quite ready to move to the other country where life seemed to be treated with impartiality, where for the time being lots of people were free to start lots of things to each other's advantage rather than disadvantage: where all kinds of things happened to the surprise, and benefit, of at least some. This part of the country she considered lost. At this point school friends remembered their stubborn classmate, the one with the uncompromising eyes, and sent her a film script in which she was permitted to say: Thank you, for everything. For everything, in which she played the

219

interpreter to a Red Army officer who was leaving, without a kiss, he had loved the better Germany in her, but never did more than touch her hand, because he had a wife waiting back home: conflict. She didn't look pretty and modest enough for the part, she had trouble saying the sentence, but she learned it and acted it. She was tired of a decency that can't do or say anything but no. I'm an orphan, nobody takes care of me. Nobody to put butter on my bread, and butter is the least. For a while she lived temporarily in a larger town with one of her classmates whom she'd run into, who had been silently in love with her in school. Who now wanted to start a cabaret to bridge the gap between the administrator and his citizens, who believed and convinced her that life must go on, that it can be made better, and why not by jesting? With him she was allowed to play only parts that resembled her: she had to be impudent, ignorant, a girl who could be taught, impudent even when humiliated. Now she had people all over the country who'd help her out, be dependable, speak warmly about her to the party in power. They thought of me as their pal, consequently they treated me like a pal, for their own sake in fact. Incidentally, this cabaret was being closed down because of a song, the refrain of which had similarity with one of the administrator's quirks of speech; her friend went to the West, it was an emergency, he hadn't thought it through, she thought it was a lesson for him and for the spectators, but not for her. They had had an alliance that could be terminated by both sides. As it turned out, the government intended to forgive her for the song and gave her leading roles, making her face so well known that her absence would have been noticed. That's not much. She began collecting newspaper clippings like a security. They praised her, because she knew how to portray a variety of people and make them seem believable, she had learned to be a variety of selves. She thought she wasn't lying too much when she'd praise the good sides of the administrator's State and omitted what one wouldn't want to experience oneself. Yes. No. Maybe. (Depends, how you want to look at it.) A few cities and landscapes clung to her and acted like home. They liked me here at one time, I lived a very hot summer here once, I used to know people in this town, just say you're a friend of mine and they'll put you up for the night. She learned from Achim that a man who decides to see socialism wherever people give it that name feels at peace. I too want to survive. West Germany isn't just, East Germany isn't just: maybe we're closer to achieving justice. I'd love to hear those ridiculous remarks again that Karsch used to make. Everybody may be made happy by compulsion, I wasn't given any time to think it over either. Then I sincerely believed that I couldn't live without seeing and knowing a specific person every day. At first Achim avoided her, after she refused to shake hands with the administrator (I don't want to touch what I will be guilty of one day); until some bystanders recalled firmly witnessing that Karin, with her usual timidity, was pushed out of the receiving line by the milling crowd of congratulators and could just about save herself from falling by one quick step to the side, contrary to her intentions, all the time her host's champagne in one raised hand: they remembered with certainty and couldn't help themselves. After that Achim showed himself again with her in public. It was hard for her to acknowledge what he did not say. I don't want to harm his reputation, don't want him to harm mine. Being near him gave me a feeling of security. Perhaps his steep shorn head did matter to me after all (just the way it looked), more than dependable information conveyed with a trustworthy, no, an accomplice's voice. The next time she avoided Achim of her own accord, after she hadn't wanted to sign the statement about the fortunate peasants whom the administrator had relieved of private ownership. —Is she still in town? asked Achim. She could have reacted differently to all these incidents than what she says: She didn't have to be afraid of the steel monsters that swarmed over the placid little country town ready to shoot, she didn't have to cling so uncompromisingly to the tenets of an ineffectual religion about right and wrong among people, she didn't have to fear the State prisons that much, she was not irreducibly forced to make her home in only one of the Germanys, it is highly improbable that one places one's dependence on one person only. Be that as it may, her face had been trained by all this, like a piece of sculpture with many planes on which light and glances are imperviously refracted, soft receptive edges camouflaging the lazy glassy movement of the

221

eyes with a polite outline that muffled them; only occasionally, professionally, a unifying expression would slide across the details of her mask: the way heat lightning changes a familiar landscape to something strange and dangerous.

—But she didn't tell me about herself, just what happened, one thing after another: Karsch said. —When we were walking through the city: he tried to explain, but Achim, sitting on the edge of his brand-new kitchen chair, didn't look like a man who was still listening.

At one point he went into the dark front rooms to the telephone and excused himself for the next couple of days. —I'm sick: he said. From then on they called him incessantly. Because even when Achim went to see certain persons, arrived at or left certain places, he wasn't traveling: he was being taken. Airplane seats would be blocked off, train compartments reserved, hotel rooms waited for him, his name filled future dates in the engagement calendars of trainers, doctors, city officials, student groups, factory managers, photographers, long before he knew where he was going to be, without his taking any initiative about it. The next day he was scheduled to visit a bicycle factory, during the lunch break he was to speak on this year's races, the administrator's policy, about deficiencies in the manufacture of his bicycle; he must have been afraid that the photos showing him talking to an awkward crowd of mechanics wouldn't show a man who cares for what is being explained to him: he had to be sure that, bent over gearshifts or speaking under the administrator's portrait, he wouldn't look like somebody who believes in what he is saying. Still, again and again he left the kitchen every time the phone screamed from the other room; he seemed to be waiting for a voice that didn't call.

—What on earth did she want with that Fleisg! he said, then forgot about it.

—You should have reported those guys! he said.

—What am I going to tell my father? he said.

—One doesn't go to the West for a thing like that! The stupid girl! he said in the tenderly querulous tone in which he used to prevent Karin from doing things that seemed unwise to him. (I won't shake his hand. I'll never forgive the Russians for this. You've got to shout it to their faces.)

—He knew me well: she had said in the station, next to the waiting diesel. They had come to the station to eat at the restaurant, that's when it occurred to her that she could leave. That was in the evening, which could be seen at the end of the platform as soft dusk studded with sharp signal lights and which absorbed the color of the clumpish smoke clouds. Karin stepped aside from suitcases and travelers, kept her eyes on the clock, pulled her coat together against the wind and didn't seem conscious of what she was doing or what was noisily pushing along in the fallow light of the gigantic hall. Karsch saw her sit down in the dining car, startled by the waiter's bowing approach. She believed herself unobserved. She pushed her loose hair out of her face, holding her hands to her temples as though to fix the direction of her eyes, looking much younger suddenly and vulnerable. (—Achim knew me quite well: as had others. He couldn't tell me about the uprising, because he realized that all of us were taking it as a new way of counting time. That it served as a new way of counting time, before and after.)

Achim nodded patiently as though he'd always known it, before he started to contradict violently, jumping up and yelling. Or he'd nag, almost smiling, speaking with little explanatory sweeps of his curved hand, almost mocking: How can she know that I was one of the marchers on the photograph. I might have happened to be there by accident. They may have pulled me along, for instance? Perhaps I was trying to stop them. Perhaps it's not even me: he concluded, so tired and distracted, he seemed no longer to know what he was saying. The telephone rang and he jumped up, startled.

—Bring her back! he said. —Bring her back to me!

But she had gone to visit friends in some other town, she had not gone across the border. Achim had misunderstood. He couldn't imagine now that she would stay in the same country with him. He thought she still depended on him, because he still depended on her.

Why did Achim actually dislike West Germany?

What we can describe is an incident that occurred a certain time ago and was allotted not more than seven lines in the West German dailies and not less than seventy lines in the East German ones, and was used for the identical vileness, either of abusive or of idolatrous defamation, before Achim had time to realize what had prompted him in the minute described and made him an offense to the nation? or an exemplar for the nation? In East Germany newspapers, magazines, radio commentators and writers kept repeating what Achim had done, a similar scene was set up for a documentary on East German soil, indigenous throats singing the West German anthem, Achim stepped down from the home-manufactured concrete slab and under the eye of the camera he headed toward the crowded exit as unswervingly as on the day under a scarcely remembered sky, several times he had to climb back up on the slab with his friends—turn his head—your lips a little tighter please—to the irritating sound, nudge the others on the lower slabs with his hand and eyes, until the director of the film finally preferred to believe the imitation. The incident that attached itself to his name, his Greatest Deed for the East German Cause, like another definition of his profession: was his self-assured conduct at an international sports festival in Austria, to the surprised panic of the organizers who had been living in the belief that East Germany was occupied by the Russians who ruled the country like grand dukes, that the population didn't have enough to eat, that many people were arrested every night exactly as in Hitler's days and that it was too small an area to be considered as yet another independent State inside Germany: and on that basis offered provincial opinions to which Achim, sweating even before the start of the race and with very little patience, was supposed to oppose the truth as he knew it. —Do we look underfed? he said. —Well, you guys of course: the interrogators tried to admit. —Am I not a free agent: Achim asked them. —Well, here of course: they conceded. —Our racing bikes were built in Saxony, without any foreign aid! he'd say, and they'd answer: Well, those bikes of course—; and couldn't tie his hosts' left-handed concern down with his affirmations thrust out with both hands, proof for which he would have had to bring with him. Achim was bored with the misunderstanding curiosity that surrounded him, and with the muggy weather, he rode the race anticipating the journey back home, without thinking, through veils of dreaming he recognized two men from his team, pulled them along ruthlessly against the soft waves of dust-laden wind, until it began to burn much more sharply all of a sudden, and chew at them and stood still: perplexed they were the first three to arrive and were able to change by the time the honors celebration for the winners would no longer be disturbed by incoming stragglers. Nevertheless, the sight of the three of them waiting beside the honors podium humiliated many riders who had thought their lungs were bursting while they straddled machines that had turned to lead, but who yet were finishing the race to the bitter end, while their besters were already washed and stealing the spectators' attention in their dry gym suits. From wide sweeping rows of seats in the elliptical building spectators saw near and afar what radio announcers were perceiving from elevated glass cabins and translating into the usual words: That the loud-speakers announce solemnly the results of the individual performances. That the three valiant fighters mount the rostrum, at least they're all from German land: says the far-carrying voice. The winner in first position, a lean, sinewy man, bends forward his exhaustion notwithstanding, reaches his hand out to his teammate, pulls him up, laughing, on the platform beside him. That this symbolizes the image of comradeship, they all shake hands, the tall one brushes over his—wheat-blond—hair; applause greets them in front of all represented countries, while the organizers hang laurel wreaths around the winners' necks, they bow and smile, the winners' bicycles are already being carried in for the honor lap. That the German national anthem is ringing out, while thousands of spectators honor the heroes in silence. (Now the audience is united by the same electrical circuit with the honors platform, excited and connected as when they were watching the earlier soccer match:) That the tall one has turned his head, why does he turn his head? Toward the amplifier next to him. From which, as mentioned, came floating the first bars of the West German anthem and now, look at him,

225

more angular than the funereal wave of music the one at the top has raised his hands to the wreath, lifts it over his head, touches the other two with the ripped-off garland, they repeat his gesture in synchronicity with the music. That three tiny figures are leaving the honors slab, one sideways, a hand on the concrete, the others by a simple leap, three leaf circles, tossed in the air by three arms, are lying on the bare concrete, shimmering like fish scales in the sun, afternoon sun of course: alone above the whirling ballet, danced by startled figures near the platform, beside before behind the retreating winners across the cinder track all the way to the locker rooms, late panting riders find their path inexplicably blocked as though by fate, cannot get through to the finish line just a little farther ahead, a white double line drawn across the finely ground cinders waiting for them.

From the windowless cube inside the slanting wall the electromagnetic tape continued to transmit the acoustic symbol of the to-be-honored country down to the abandoned wreaths (one thick one and two more thriftily wound), the neat geometric pattern of spectators began to curl under the observer's eye, while the overwhelmed organizers of the race were met only by the functionaries of the East German team in the locker rooms, that is, after they had straightened up before their suitcases which, however, were still open. The hosts, who for months had been expending the State's moneys, their own free time, and the tenderest care and consideration for a harmonious unfolding of this day, were unconsolable that they supposedly had offended such outstanding athletes, for they heard only later, from the man at the gate, with what puckish salutes, a finger to their temples, the four (outraged) riders at this very moment had stalked through the wire-enclosed entranceways out of the stadium. The flustered gentlemen took it genuinely, though with self-control, to heart that the two German States did not share the same national anthem, much less could make both ends meet with one. They bowed wordlessly. But since they neither knew nor had a supply of the other German anthem, they found it difficult to make amends to the East German State, whose dignity was, in turn, forced to refuse the proffered handshake; left to themselves and their confusion

226

they attempted a conversation that was to smooth everything over and smoothed out nothing with their sincere, downcast inquiries: And how does it go, this anthem of yours? You do, indeed, have an anthem of your own?

—They actually thought they were being polite: Achim said in the tone of a traveler who has been forced to put up with little knowledge of the rest of the world in a foreign country: very different from home.

—Had you been in cahoots? asked his biographer.

—What do you mean? said Achim.

—Had you planned to ruin their celebration? added Karsch.

—But I don't know what you're talking about! said Achim. Well, was it perhaps the music that Achim didn't like, that had initially been abducted from a string quartet by the Austrian composer Joseph Haydn (1732 to 1809) to reinforce an appeal to God in favor of the Hapsburg dynasty, later, after the flight of the German emperor and empire, it was declared the national anthem of the Weimar German Republic, with different words and different rhymes, after which it was adopted by a State that intended to take at least the exhortation of the first stanza literally, to put Germany Germany above all else, from the Adige to the Great and Little Belt, that's how we fell apart; so that the subsequently proclaimed West German State, temporary as it was to be, temporarily kept the melody, although with the more modest propositions of the third stanza: Unity and right and freedom, still to the same melody which Achim disliked, perhaps, for musical or aesthetic reasons, or perhaps because of what had happened before? The champion of bicycle riding weighed the question in his head, shook it: he had nothing against the music itself. He was curious to hear the string quartet. Consequently he must have disliked something about the country that was living under this anthem.

Well then, what rubbed him the wrong way in that country and what, on the contrary, would have been to his liking? What did he choose, since he was allowed to make comparisons; what made him contemptuous toward a State that . . . —Let's not forget that! said Achim.

That had started with the reopening of the free market in freedom? When it became evident that capital had well survived

227

the war and was in a position to buy things like labor force. Some of it even came from the other side of the ocean, together they set the energy of the disadvantaged to work, manufactured, sold, invested and saved under the eyes of the victors who were at the beginning interested in order, that protected ownership and the freedom to use it against lack of ownership. What did he have against that?

—Besides, that's not how it is! said Karsch.

—May I please have my say! requested Achim who had not listened:

And in the course of a few years the merciless competition of needs built apartment houses in the holes dug by the war, because fewer factories had been destroyed, they built streets and government offices and barracks, and educated the portioned citizens until they longed for better and still better food and better and still better implements for the requirements of the more prosperous life, how can one object to the reciprocal use of people for differing but mutual benefits? Did he already see the life-enhancing fruits of the exploiting competitors waste away in the future and science of the worker's parties? Or had he no desire to live in the once again richest country of Europe, since it was founded on the changeable health of capital, and did he not like to see monopolies grow irresistibly in commerce as well as in manufacturing, since they were to have been demolished after the surrender and he felt about it as the proverbial burned child feels about fire? Skeptically he says: That too; and what else? It must be for political reasons! So the armies of the foreign conquerors had given permission to found a State and the parties for once refrained from worrying about the Soviet-occupied zone, they made the old agreements into right and law and constitution, so that everything would be as it had been, but no more war. And isn't that right? And he disliked the chancellor of the so-called Christian Party who bargained with the rulers of industry and labor unions and the lobbies and bartered with them behind the parliament's back?

—But how can you know that! said Karsch.

—I do! contradicted Achim.—Just read the papers, and I've read them for years, how can I approve of a person who,

who tied the country to its former enemies with military alli-

228

ances and yet had the constitution changed to include military service for its citizens against the army of the East German administrator? who accepted the advice and administration of an individual who had already justified the perhaps not altogether satisfactory solution of six million people to Hitler? who allowed judges to judge who had already misjudged Hitler's opponents and condemned them to death, but whose old age was more comfortably padded than that of their victims? who staffed his army with generals officers admirals who had raised their hand to salute Hitler and had served him beyond his death? who on Sundays had his ministers agitate to reconquer the Urals, and the one-time German areas in the East?

—What kind of paper is that? asked Karsch.

—But of course: said Achim: yours don't write how that man who admitted the corruptibility of his functionaries? who ordered some nobody to represent the State to the eyes of the world and allowed him to compare Bertolt Brecht to a pimp and a thug? who adulterated voters' opinions with pensions and pay-offs, the day before the elections? It was unjust of him to be annoyed: because that man kept being re-elected in protected and secret booths and once again the so-called Social Democratic Party followed him into the atomic army, and all these years the delegates of the West German Provinces hadn't found fault in him; and he refused to be pleased with so many followers and wanted to despise the citizens, on top of it, because they liked it and were footing the bill? Shouldn't he have first tried to live with them in Liberty: to buy or not to buy the things of prosperity with one's work, to praise or not to praise the chancellor, to do or not to do one's military service, to trust or not to trust the law, to harm one's neighbor or to harm him less, to act or not to act against communism, to pervert or not to pervert the truth, and all this without risking more than three weeks in jail? the good man makes good. Did he like so little there that he could dislike it all?

Achim showed embarrassment. With frequent understanding nods he set a place aside for his interrogator in the discussion grounds for the latter to live unmolested in his naïve trust in the agreements of bourgeois democracy: he leaned forward, tilted an immobile tight-lipped face on rigid neck toward the

229

other man, to make him balance the previous nagging with a new though limited appearance of patience, he might just as well have spoken half loud with averted head: For you—it may be all right; Karsch understood that Achim wanted to stop the quarrel. Although his left hand was outlining a gesture that usually stands for fatigued disapproval (do I have to go on telling you. You just can't understand. If I had your worries!) as far as it can be described; beyond its direction, toward what actually.

Yes but. Yes but perhaps it was only what he remembered of his first trip to the West German Provinces that made him climb from the platform? His first crossing of the border (when there was no border to be seen, no difference entered the reserved compartment in which they were sitting, all six of them looking for the beginning of the foreign country in the mildewed meadows, because they had seen the East German border police jump from the locomotive and fall more and more behind in the gray-colored fluid March landscape, making them feel outside and alone with a dull hollow of quivering nerves above the stomach. They saw the wooden booths of the guards on their high weathered stilts, but the dead eyes of the floodlights were nothing new to them, and they had long been familiar, from army barracks and prison camps, with a uniformed silhouette, crossed by a diagonal rifle: so far nothing had changed. They saw loose barbed-wire fences run from the incision of the embankment up to the hazy edge of the mound before the sky: that still wasn't new. They saw farmyards furrowed by sunk-in plow tracks and abandoned houses and field paths in rainy desolation: that was still not foreign. They had to make an effort, force themselves to compose the announced foreignness in their heads, out of landscapes and West German border control, an advertisement for something unknown, sooty embankment walls, a wide crowded street made of marble and glass and light, and the changed rhythm of their train, before they got to the other country, before it was the foreignness announced to them that would say: we are free, you are not. Tell them they're not free, but we are. They'll call themselves a democracy, call us a dictatorship: tell them we have more democracy than they can think of. They will claim that their State is the only legal one, that ours is illegal: tell them that we hold our warrant from the working classes, whereas they are merely the successors of a broken Germany; they'll say that they're arming because we are: tell them that we're arming because they are; they'll say that we are trying to infest them with sabotage espionage; tell them they are infesting us with sabotage espionage; they'll say that only their State is worth dying for; tell them only our free legal democracy is worth dying for, in which sports, for instance, as you can see for yourselves, explain this to them!) was rough on him. Everywhere he was groping in the void. Not a word, not a gesture, not a single smile snapped him into the cordial good-will ambiance of their visit, even the harsh spring air felt stranger on his skin than the sweat shirt he had brought from home. Since the small-town bicycle club could not afford to invite them to hotel rooms, the participants in the contest had been distributed among the families of the club members. Achim's man-of-the-world Saxon dialect coincided rarely with his hosts' North German; the feeling of otherness overpowered him. The supper table had been set in the scrubbed kitchen: expensive sausage, rare fish, real butter, beer bottles rose from the glistening traces of sponge on the oilcloth. The table looked too small for so much food in the swaying light of the ceiling lamp. And Achim had thought poverty was of the same mind in all countries. But this poverty had carried loads and raised children for some fifty years, without using up much of the tenderness that was now reaching out to meet the other which had known nothing but bicycle riding up to now. And the first one said: Dig in, boy. For once in your life eat your fill. Whereupon the other felt obliged to declare in a firm voice that it got enough to eat on its East German ration cards: while it had meant to speak of reunification. Since you're not well off either. —You're so skinny: said the woman from the edge of her chair, her hands holding on to the table to keep them from stroking the boy's face. —Yes, but over here they're preparing for war: the intimidated boy said to the old people and put his sandwich down. —Yes: that you have to go through that too! protested the old people and began to talk more eagerly of the beginnings of their bicycle club. The woman had only watched all the time. What a laugh.

231

All the children were dead. They couldn't imagine that the boy might want to defend his country. —But they're jailing so many people over there. Why don't you dig in. They had grown heavy and ponderous, their age silenced the boy. They were both leaning forward on the table wanting to watch him eat, to feast on having a guest. They were hardly aware that their visitor avoided their eyes and answered shyly: rapidly, as though under pressure. He hadn't been provided with the exact figure of those in jail at home. Two lives seemed to have saved up their well-meaning hospitality for this evening, the effort could be felt, it disturbed the boy because he didn't want to be moved. He didn't eat enough. He didn't recognize himself in the underfed Soviet-German kid whose forward remarks could be overlooked with parental benignity since he knows next to nothing of the world. His hosts had simply taken his tenderness by surprise, just when he had wanted to yell at them. He would have liked to speak in a loud irrefutable voice: to make something happen. In the moist haze between the houses he returned to the limping afternoon race under the strange banners that had praised wares rather than the administrator's justice, not even the chancellor's justice. What makes them content here, to live like that. Then he lost his way. Softly distorted lanterns swam in the canal mists, the sound of his steps rang in his ears, he wanted to go home. Endless rows of front gardens and house doors, unidentifiably many forms of vehicles and curbs and consolingly lighted windows sent him away. The streets were not laid out at right angles, the way he was used to. They were named after people he'd never heard of. He stood outside the bright door of a tavern and counted his change and didn't go in; he thought they'd notice something about him. Several times he walked through narrow streets always around the same church, he no longer looked up. He arrived at the lighted shopwindows around the market square in a blind rage: I can't afford to buy that. And that's all they want from me. Then he found the place where he was staying. They had made up a bed for him in the kitchen. As he fell asleep he succeeded in thinking of his mother. In the morning he tiptoed out of the house. He has always wanted to excuse himself, to thank them with a postcard; but then he's never found the time. When he got back home, he was ready to confess, but the youngest of the team was not asked. So, how was it? —I didn't like it much. At the next West German race he was already famous enough to rate a hotel room. He thought he had understood plenty and asked no more questions. —That clerical fascist government of yours, no rain is going to wash it off: he said. Or else one can discuss team-racing techniques: We do that differently. This is how we do it.

—But I don't mean by that what you mean! Achim said at once: It wasn't at all like that. You take it all much too literally.

—And it had nothing to do with disrupting the honors ceremony? asked his biographer. They were merely discussing it. He hadn't taken any notes, he couldn't see the connection too clearly.

—No: said Achim, —That was much earlier. I had forgotten all about it by then.

Well, then the East German melody was more to his liking perhaps, which had been lifted from a defiant film the liquidated government had made about the hard men of North American pioneer days, slightly changed it no longer regretted the great great times we had, just you and I. Although it's over now, too late too late to try—but united the singers with somewhat nobler words and turned them away from the ruins all together toward a future where the sun would shine over Germany more brightly than ever before, where no mother would have to mourn her son any more. Did these propositions come through more clearly to Achim, did they make more sense to him, and did he, therefore, prefer to listen to this brass band issuing from a loud-speaker rather than to the other? Achim admitted that the solemn march of his own anthem seemed to enter into him more comprehensibly. It's more rewarding. It's something new, after all. But if I hadn't known it all these years, it could have a different melody; all right. He must like this country that wasn't ashamed of this music. But why? Did he like everything so much there that he was willing to love the whole thing and not exchange it for something else and not compare it? What might it be that pacified him about a State, that had after all.

That had, after all, been lent to the Communists after the war, over one third of Germany, for them to prove what was meant by: socialism after this war. So Achim couldn't wish to object to the Soviet army's distributing all the large estates among poor peasants and refugees for fifteen years at most, he was glad to see schools and courthouses emptied of Hitler's henchmen and liars, and glad to see the monopolized factories and shops broken up and signed over to the name of the people, he had to understand that the conquerors were moving out whatever had been inside. Did he, too, wish to have lost the war? And did he perhaps like the slogan of human selfishness being reoriented toward work that profited all and not just the property owners? although, after fifteen years, the holes dug by the war were still not filled in again with apartment houses and streets and railroads, whereas they had been filled in with factories, barracks, government offices, prisons? although the country's inhabitants had, in the meantime, been educated to an everyday life of deficient food, clothes and mutual assistance?

—Now I have explained everything to you: said Achim, and more bitterly:—There you stand and talk.

—My version is: said the hypothetical Karsch:

Did Achim wish to disregard the economic failures, since this was a scientific problem with promises of a future under a beautified sun? It must be for political reasons! Therefore the victors let the administrator build a State in accordance with the teachings of two nineteenth-century sociologists, after the model of the Soviet Union. And so he built houses with telephones for his club all over the country, and put soldiers at the entrances; together they sent the labor force of the disadvantaged to work, manufactured with them, sold them meager surplus, invested and saved for armament against the West German chancellor's army and for their government's eternity, so that everything should not become as it had been, and no more war. Had he agreed when they asked him?

—Yes: said Achim.

—Really: said Karsch.

—Well, what do you want! said Achim.

And did he want, trustfully, the administrator to rule who secretly distributed the benefit of labor and took it out of the workers for the apprentice years of his clumsy club? Who was keeping from them what he planned with them? who beat them into accepting his laws instead of guiding them? who cheated them out of their right to vote and their say in the administration of the State, worse than a bourgeois police force State? who hunted them down for passing on truths that could help them against him? who impressed them into his army and bound them to the other conquerors? who locked them out of West Germany and refused to release them into reunification? who defiled their everyday life with his loaded theories so that reality gave birth to such miserable children as sloppy production, refugee camps, submissive fear of the selfish club? who imposed a penalty upon any doubt in his inhumanity, because he didn't want to be capable of error?

—It's shabby to speak this way of us:said Achim.

—But whom am I speaking of? inquired Karsch.

—You're always asking about the street scenes . . .

—You're speaking of someone I trust, who has become an example for me! said Achim. —A guest doesn't do that. It's not polite! —But I'm not talking about you: Karsch tried to extricate himself.

—But it's me you are insulting! yelled Achim.

To describe love for that one you need somebody who says: the people have built an economy into the State for the glory of the club. They settle for the smaller share, because they can't take their eyes off the administrator's countenance. And they elected him again and again. They keep things going, because they don't want to put the club to shame by a strike. Three million of them never crossed the dangerous border one by one, because the penalty is jail. They don't stand up against the tanks of the Soviet army, because they've learned what socialism is after the war: not to buy the things of prosperity with their wages, to praise the administrator, to do their military service, to fear the law, to distrust their neighbor, to act against capitalism, to pervert the truth, and all this risking more than three years in jail and sometimes a death sentence; consequently Achim had made it.

And why not? Or why, or why at any cost? Did he prefer to live in East Germany because he hadn't that much preference for West Germany? Did he not want to live in West Germany, be-

235

cause he happened to live in East Germany? Did he live there?
What led him to compare two countries: that there was a border between them? One can describe his expression in the documentary: Very light dry hair and a lazulite-blue sky framing
clean-cut indignation. A sensitive face, but invulnerable in its
belief in something which isn't there but seems to be known to
it. A face with which any man his age would like to appear in
his girl's dreams: young and incapable of any evil urge. It seems
unthinkable to strip the skin that shapes the expression from
the intention that plugs the brain into a national anthem. It is
not moved, but moves the spectator. And so forth. In stories,
letters to the editor, poems, this instant is expressed by words
like pure, responsible, unshakable, it makes their breath come
faster; and even eyewitnesses think that that's how they must
recall it: do recall it like that.

But then he can't have been one of the marchers!

—They want to trap me: said Achim.—Me at least: he said.
Anybody could have asked him about that on the phone or in
the dark: his face kept its grave pensive expression, unchang-
ingly, made the narrowed eyes look more hostile after a while.
He seemed to be remembering.
Karsch had been told: there hadn't been any singing though.
They'd come down over the glistening hump of the street, one
man beside the other, relaxed. On the way they passed one-
family houses among lush trees, white breakfast tables at open
windows, a child carefully stepping in moist grass, a woman
alone in an attic window, dogs lying across empty stoops in the
early-morning sun. The older section of the city began at the
top of the hump. Very high wall-to-wall houses. They, too, lived
behind such narrow windows. The channeled morning light
gathered the sooty façade ornaments into a single shimmer.
The mirrored image of the sky shattered against innumerable
gaping windows, arms were pushing bedding aside, waved
down to the long white-smocked line of marchers that was brim-

ming over the street. That squeezed oncoming cars to the curb, made islands out of streetcars, sucked the pedestrians from the sidewalks so that the color became more mottled and the faces closer together. Where Achim would have stood, the bicycle between his legs, beside the flattened curb of a driveway, he heard the drawling dialect as loud and reciprocal as on no previous day. The masons were not boisterous, almost quietly they marched forward arm in arm; they answered calls and waved back with the serene dignity of adults who are all together on their way to the market place to defend their cause. When Achim recognized the familiar faces from his old building lot (if Achim was there), he pushed his bike through the open door of an empty shoemaker's shop and ran after them on the crowded sidewalk, elbowing his way through to the marchers. The ranks opened and let him in. Or perhaps he had met the marchers head on, on his way to training, had put the brakes on, amazed by the unhoped-for parade in the deserted suburban street, and they had recognized him at once and called: Achim! Hey, Achim! as a greeting and to let him know what they were up to, but they didn't have to ask him along? (One assumes that from the photograph. Besides, a bicycle with racing devices is actually said to have been left in a shoemaker's shop, several times its sunken basement entrance was pointed out to Karsch, on the low workbenches everything had looked as though dropped in haste. Three low stools stood there, they said. Later, the bike had been leaning against the long wall under the shelf: where the customers would wait for their shoes on other days.) But it may also have been the first early-morning glimpse from a window under the eaves that waked him with the tough milling of people under the network of streetcar wires, so that he would have become aware of the noise more as a blend of milder waves. So that he did not button his shirt, shook the girl from her sleep and began talking, sitting on the edge of the bed (because all eyewitnesses think they knew right away what was spilling over the pavement) and yet couldn't wait until she was dressed and came along. And then he probably felt sorry, because he didn't want to be without his lover even when he had nothing left to wish for in the proximity of the able bodies in their cement-powdered smocks: in the fresh cool June morning:

237

in the expectation of fast movement and changed life that had waked him up hopefully once, the first morning of a vacation. That day he was far from famous. Nobody even tried to speak to him more slowly than to another or to study him first a little from the side. He hadn't been away from the building lot that long. The masons from his old work brigade had gotten up long before he had, and ridden to work through the same street in crowded streetcars, they had waited more eagerly for this morning's news, but they took him (if he was there) happily along, as they had all the workers from all the factories who had been standing in their path: they put him in line, surrounded him, relied upon him, that day.

—And it wasn't about a couple of pfennigs either: lectured Achim. His head was touching the wall, revealing the loose-skinned face of someone who is alone. He spoke like a blind man. As though he didn't know what he had once seen. As though the words didn't contain what they meant.

Karsch had been told and kept in mind that it had started over a couple of pfennigs the Berlin construction workers would have lost when norms were raised for work on buildings in honor of some Soviet premier, they didn't want that and decided to go on strike. And yet, the early news that came over the West German network a hundred and forty miles south of the strike was so unbelievable that everybody rode to the job with his working gear. But what each of the assembled confirmed to the other already applied the five sentences of the newscaster's voice. They must have lived in such a way, to that day, that they recognized it as truth. The meetings didn't last over half an hour, it was said: after that the factory gates stood open. The participants remembered the tenor, not the words of the speakers. All must have said the same: one led to the other: made it more possible, more real, feasible. Thus it was inevitable that they would meet in the center of the city where they'd usually passed through after work. They found themselves outside the arched prison gates, because they wanted to wait for their relatives to be released; they hadn't practiced the choruses before, but all agreed on the same words. The roaring crowd was shot at from upper-story windows. The embittered people kept flooding forward, they had nothing to duck behind, they looked for protection in the hall and pushed against the wrought-iron gates that glisten quietly today in front of empty stairs and guards' steps. They dropped files into the street which they wanted to burn because their names were in them. One guy was waving a black-red-and-gold flag. But they couldn't find the door to the cell block. They made fires outside other houses that administered their money, their wages, their lives, they gathered up the papers that fluttered down on their heads, into their hands, and carried them tidily into fires on the thinly asphalted wooden pavement. The streets were so crowded, you could advance only very slowly, one step at a time, and don't forget the great light of the first day, the unanimous trust, expectation, help at last. The streetcars rolled up without the administrator's posters, the club insignia on their outsides were crossed out with chalk, whoever was wearing one on his lapel was told to take it off or else he'd be picked out. At the corner of the market place they demolished the wooden barrack that had wanted to imbue them with belief in the fairness of their condition with films and loud-speakers and posters. They climbed ladders and took the lettering down from the nationalized department stores, apparently they had never believed that they belonged to them. All of this was a symbol for words like Democracy, Free Elections, Reunification that, written neatly, were held up on posters, that made the excited yelling of the speakers on top of the wooden booths around the market square comprehensible. But nothing had been planned. They fraternized: they were as boisterous as on a fairground. They knew what they didn't want, not what they wanted. They waited one for the other what he would do. (They were not prepared for this day, because it had seemed impossible.) They forgot the radio station. They forgot to speak to the army garrisons. They forgot the other cities in the country. They thought of tomorrow with joy, but vaguely. The strike committees didn't elect a council that could lead them, they didn't assume the right. They had no arms. Many people tell about it with words whose value has been effaced, they merely mention the incident: as though they felt ashamed.

—And it didn't do them any good: said Achim. Hardly ever had he stayed up until two in the morning, on a kitchen chair. His words came out blurred. —It didn't get them anywhere. Did it? Because, at the central station, the lackeys had kept control from the start. Tanks were circling the area. No trains were allowed in. Outside the entrance, the Soviet army was arresting people whom the German army clubbed into offices and baggage rooms. Already the first day at noon Achim's father saw jeeps waiting outside the Soviet armory. The second day it rained, no sun. The city was emptier, soberer. It didn't look improved. The exterior aspects of the ruling power replenished themselves with power and were not demolished again. No more marching. Policemen lying flat on red fire trucks drove through the streets and shot into the thinned-out crowds. At the corners the columns with loud-speakers found their voices again and shouted interdictions and named those criminals who had built them and who were paying for them. Between two waiting police cars something crushed was lying in the gutter, with a velvet collar, and looked old, soldiers carried it away, instead of civilians. There was shooting in the night, in the morning tank tracks were imprinted in the asphalt. Three persons were executed under court-martial law. Years later, the people's secret police were still searching for the strike leaders and arrested them in their apartments where they let themselves be found, not believing they were guilty. It didn't get them anywhere, they said it themselves but not to Achim.

Achim? Do you know the guy in the photo. That one. Maybe it's you. Where were you that day. How did your neighbors react. What do you think about it today. Do you know him. Is it that one? that they could go and pick Achim up at the training site, in the garden, at the building lot and drive him through the streets in a closed car, with handcuffs, to a house that looked like hundreds of others? Or did they club him into a cell the very first night, while he heard the guards shout at random in the inner prison yard and beat harder: Move on! Move on! Move on! or did he ride past the prisons for weeks afterward and see the guards march around the roofs with their rifles every time he happened to glance up? he mustn't necessarily have felt like a criminal before they arrested him as one. He didn't notice anybody with a camera: he says: what do you mean, I wasn't even there. Let them keep their traps shut. What kind of racing bike do witnesses say had been stored in the shoemaker's shop under old sacks until August? They spoke respectfully of the mechanical equilibrium of the bicycle, they recognized the effort that had gone into it, but they couldn't remember the looks of the guy who later came to claim it. Somebody came and said: Remember: that certain day. Was that Achim? The basement shop is two hundred yards away from the photographed place. The low door is easily overlooked, its single outer step is narrow. What did the senders want Karsch to learn from the photograph? There were other faces on it. Perhaps it had long ceased to be dangerous for them to have someone see them who could not be trusted. They didn't trust Karsch. They wanted him to see that Achim had been with them. That he had changed. Did they want him unchangeable? Had he been thrown in jail before the others? Had he hit back? Did he continue to persist after three hours of stock-still staring at such a picture as it trembled enlarged on the large-meshed projection surface: I don't know a single face among them. Aren't you satisfied to have me, I'm far from being the right guy? Who came to see him in prison? Did he want anybody to come to see him? What was he pardoned for only two months later, and by what name did he call the street that led him back to the city from the rusty glass-spiked masonry, what was he going to do there, he'd rather ride ten years for what

Mark of question, of misunderstanding, no longer of interest.

—Stop turning that over and over in your head: Achim said patiently.

—Why should I have marched with those people?

A few remembered approximately.

—They'd hardly want to tell me to my face.

No. And Karin recognized him.

—She didn't even know my name in those days.

Because the one in the front row looks as much like him as the one in the family album.

—He does look like me, the guy in the photo: said Achim.

—There were quite a few of the likes of me in those days. But seven years ago you could mistake quite different people for me than yesterday.

—Can you? said Achim.

—Can I? Karsch confirmed.

241

—That week I was away training: added Achim.
That week he'd been away training. He wasn't even near the town.
—Right: said Achim.—On some old maneuvering grounds on the beach, you know?
For instance at the seashore. Between bombed-out bunkers and batteries a preserved concrete band runs along the inlet. From the motionless air of the mixed forest (Colors of the mixed forest. White birch trunks, green dangling branches, leaden heat, suchlike) the ride heads into the thrust of the ocean wind, hunched mottled backs rushing toward the ruffled water that looks green in the morning. A stop watch held across the track by an outstretched arm simulates racing conditions. A remote country spot, empty sand paths keep it separate, the next day rain hammering on the barracks roofs, eight-bar music comes over the radio, not a soul in sight, and so on. Until a new high-pressure system makes for warmer weather, lying in the hissing grass beside the track to stretch a bit and watch planes block the sky above the coast line with vapor trails, a couple of years later they'll be able to land and start and land on the strip where young men in gym suits, Achim among them, the tall one over there see him don't you see him.
—Well? said Achim.
—I can't picture it: said Karsch.
—But you were able to picture so much: Achim reproached him, surprised. He caught him in a rapid, wide-awake glance, he asked if Karsch did perhaps not want to go on with it.
—I can't think of anything more: said Karsch. He couldn't think of anything more.

How did Achim take that?

Regretfully. He showed regret. He seemed to regret it.
(Perhaps he regretted something else. They agreed that Karsch would drive home the next morning. Achim made him promise a specific hour. But Karsch was half an hour late and conse-

242

quently the two men under their lopsided hats still found him at home and questioned him about the superhighway. They had had their sleep. A boy in mechanic's overalls must have told them in the meantime: no, that was somewhere else. At the bridge across the river, outside the city limits, I'll never forget it.

—Ah yes: said Karsch. He remembered now. He couldn't pay attention to all the customs of a country in which he was a stranger.

The two gentlemen had come to grant him that. That's why they would be happy if he made no other stop before he got to the border.

—Is that an order? asked Karsch.

—Please understand our position: they begged of him, and Karsch agreed although he didn't understand. He had had a different reason for leaving, there are more than one, and don't you imagine it would be the same one for you.)

Achim seemed to regret it. For another fifteen minutes they called each other by their first names. Each told the other it was too bad, too bad, you know the feeling

—Too bad, and

—I might have liked the book, it was really about me

and told each other a few other things that are readily forgotten on a morning along the superhighway at the control barracks saying good-by to the uniforms

and in Achim's deputizing life as well, after a few days. Because what was it that started again and again, what did he go on representing? Not victory (one yard distance between two racers on the finish line is just a difference, after a three hours' ride over a hundred miles. If you sit obliquely at the finish line, one looks parallel to the other to you, the human eye reacts without comprehension, even the umpire can only approximate, and only fifteen minutes later the photo-finish camera will prove what nobody else was able to see fifteen minutes before. Nor are the last arrivals devoid of honor, even if they ride, much later, into the honors ceremony of the winners. Why pick a specific stretch and agree upon it with the police or the stadium, nominate a manager for the event, estimate the expense, try out the track, have posters printed, order wreaths with ribbons

243

for the firmly expected winners, rent offices and locker rooms, have sweat shirts and start numbers sewn, hire rooms, baths, food, doctors, ambulances, have loud-speakers set up for just one day, requisition cars to accompany the race and prepare gas stations for them, write the text of the program, the posters are already slapped to the walls, certificates, trophies, flowers block view and work in the office, lap timers and ushers must be told what to do, slogans must be hung up, the track has to be marked, the newspapers route their telephones, straw bales hem in the regular traffic, poles with ropes are stuck into the pavement, and so much change of money and persons does not just expect the last second and the victory of a single man or a single team) but the competition of individuals or groups for whatever purpose you wish, or for whatever you're willing to substitute for. The participant investigates his opponents before the race: how have they done so far, do photos show them as tenacious, do statistics and reports indicate vulnerability, what in the newspapers stiffened their backs. He checks the route, either riding it slowly or on the map: are there holes and where, are there any gravel stretches, can I make this slope at my usual speed, must I train some more, I must be prepared for these cobblestones, I must remember that this curve is blocked, at the next corner I'll make my escape, should I change the gear ratio, are my tires too heavy, and what if it comes out some other way I haven't thought of? Health, body condition, foreknowledge of opponents, location and condition of the route, probable wind and weather prediction compose the strategy of the individual rider and his team. They start, they represent. Just a minute! Make no mistake. I act innocent, you act innocent, you will see my back still, now you're surprised, it was just a joke, now I take off and you overtake me, now you take off and I overtake you, we'll wear you down yet, you've got to make a mistake somewhere, the good man makes good, we've got our connections, trick us and we'll trick you worse, everything pleasantly and according to the rules, you're not supposed to understand our code, the beat man is easily fooled, we'll do you, we'll get you, we'll kill you, I'm really rolling great today, let the loners go it alone, his face is enough to make me sick, we're helping each other and we exploit you, everything's got to work for me, beware the man with the hammer, no offense intended, trust for trust, you didn't expect that, only the papers will tell you, spare yourself and you'll be defeated; victory isn't for the whiners, let the weak drop out and admit it, how long do you think they're going to keep this up, cut it out, will you, man, that was a mess, we never thought we'd live through it, they've got the devil on their side, that's no sane way to do it, where's that going to end up, we had it coming, if he doesn't understand, a friend must be able to take that, don't let me catch you at that again, if you only could wait, well if that's how it is, until that guy gets out of bed!, before you get that through his head, because you can't keep your trap shut, because you'll land us in the soup, I'm through with you for good. Oh my God, now I'm in the shit myself, beset I am with adversaries, they've battered my pride, it doesn't pay off, a modest life that's the idea, why are you acting the strangers, why don't you help me, just wait, I'll report that, I'll pay you back for that, you haven't seen all of me, you'll never forget me, you'll be very sorry, I do my duty, I do what I can, no one gives a damn for me, always it's the others, I'm finished, I don't care any longer, if only I could care, I'll let you down next time, if only there were some sense to this, it's pure luck that I pass you after all, let's do that again I liked that, I still got something left in me, I'm really rolling great today, you should have thought that much of me, oh yes, you can tell right away, I underestimated myself, can happen, see that's what we can do, got more in us than you any day, go shove it up your ass, we're better off than you, easier breathing up here, down there that's where you belong, we need you only for the difference, we fought and you were beaten, I'm as proud as you were, I don't kick the man who's down, that's where it got you, get down on your bellies, not even crawling any more, good for me, what a stupid thing to do.

And how was the trip?

Karsch got home with the dusk. He put his shirts into the drawers and the rest on his desk, he set the suitcase in the closet, put on the record with the Capriccio on the return from a long journey, and let it spin. He organized his mail and counted the rolls of film (they couldn't be organized), then the tea was ready, and he could sit down at his table and begin homecoming. The record was still playing. At the last sound (the famous after clap of the cembalo, which syncopated the final chord and had always seemed witty to him) he stubbed out his cigarette and got up. He walked over to the sideboard and took out his machines, pulled the lamp across the table, switched it on. The room provided book shelves, cabinets, couch, armchairs, kitchenette, the table stood in the center under the long window overlooking the wet evening street, his telephone next to his record player next to his tape recorder, the typewriter out in front on the left, the chair rolled on coasters. He typed as far as this and
the telephone
—Karsch: he said.
The connection gave him a soft murmured conversation among several people. It seemed far away from the diaphragm and the voices didn't become recognizable. The contact flickered for a second as the receiver was replaced, first casually, then precisely, and broke off. The gesture could be imagined.
Most of the letters were too old to be answered. His bank account was close to zero. An hour later the table was cleared. He looked at his watch, pulled the paper out of the typewriter
telephone
—How was it? you said.

The characters are invented. The events do not refer to similar ones but to the border: the difference: the distance
and the attempt to describe it.